Boulc

Elizabeth —
I hope you enjoy
reading this as
much as I enjoyed
writing it.
Happy reading!
[illegible]
2/12/20

Remember Me When the Moon Hangs Low

---

by CYNTHIA L. CLARK

outskirts
press

Boulder Girl, Remember Me When the Moon Hangs Low

v3.0

Outskirts Press, Inc.
http://www.outskirtspress.com

ISBN: 978-1-9772-1920-6

Cover Images by Cynthia L. Clark

PRINTED IN THE UNITED STATES OF AMERICA

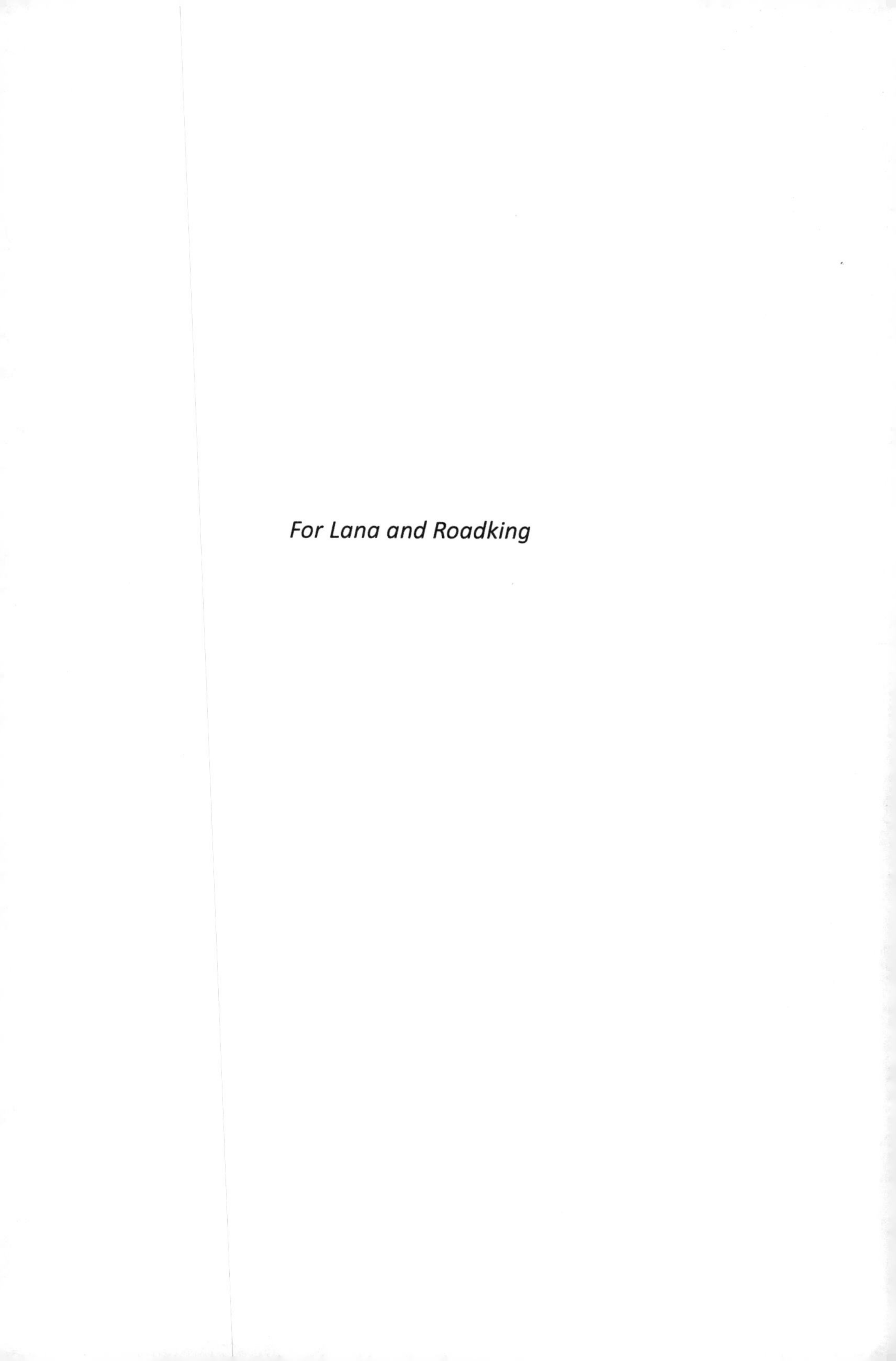

For Lana and Roadking

Remember me when the moon hangs low
In the dark southwestern sky
How we held each other that cold winter night
Never expecting to say goodbye.

Remember me when the words "I love you"
Are whispered quietly in your ear
By a soft breeze blowing from north to south
Carrying my thoughts of you in the air.

Remember me when you hear a song
Of love that was lost then found
Or a gentle melody with poetic words
Of two hearts that are eternally bound.

Remember me when you close your eyes
After a long and endless day
That I'm far away with a heart full of love
And that for you each night I pray.

Cynthia L. Clark "Remember Me"

INTRODUCTION

In Chapter 2, it is written that "in Lana's mind, her life's journey had been accompanied by an elaborate soundtrack of diverse music". Throughout the months of Lana's life that I wrote of in *Boulder Girl, Remember Me When the Moon Hangs Low*, she and other characters listened to or were reminded of specific songs which provide a musical background to the events that unfolded. At the end of this novel, I have listed the songs by the chapter in which they first appeared. I encourage you to listen to them to enhance the mood and tone of the reading and to get to know Lana and the other characters as well as I do.

CHAPTER 1

"You may be seated in here, Mrs. Chisholm." Angela, the legal administrator for the firm of Randolph and Danielson, P.C., directed Lana Ross Chisholm to the law firm's conference room. "Mr. Randolph will be with you momentarily. Would you like coffee or tea?"

"Thank you, no," replied Lana.

Lana was thirty-three, pretty, slim, leggy but average height, and lightly freckled with long, light red hair and eyes that changed from blue to green and then back again. The ambience in the law firm was still and quiet, almost as a testament to the many solemn transactions which had taken place there over time. Lana came to sign legal documents to end her ten-year marriage to Lucas Chisholm. Lana surveyed the room as she waited. The conference table was long, shiny, dark cherrywood. She smelled the scent of lemon furniture polish in the room and the earthy smell of the leather chairs. Dark colored legal treatises and tan volumes of statutes lined the oak bookshelves that covered the walls. *I wonder if anyone even looks at those anymore,* Lana pondered, knowing that the law was easily accessible online. *And why are these offices always so dark that lamps need to be turned on in the middle of the day?* she mused. She wondered why she thought about such mundane matters while she waited. A sliver of sunlight filtered through the wooden blinds. She was unaware that it had cast a shard of light on her hair and illuminated a section of it in streaks of copper and gold.

Michael Randolph, Esq. entered the conference room. He was middle-aged with dark eyes and hair and very white teeth that were slightly visible when he spoke. "Hello, Lana. Lucas and his attorney are on their way. You know it wasn't necessary to jointly sign the final papers here today. You could have done this separately anytime."

Lana nodded in agreement. "Michael, I needed for the end of the marriage to be ceremonial in nature, just like the beginning, and for it to feel just as significant. Since Lucas agreed to do it this way, I don't expect that he'll create any problems. I understand the terms of the settlement so there is no need for a confidential discussion between us."

"Hello, Michael." Richard Hunt—Lucas's attorney—and Lucas, proceeded into the conference room. Lucas noticed the beam of light in Lana's hair and for a moment he was drawn to her as he had been when he met her for the first time on Pearl Street in Boulder eleven years earlier. He blinked hard and quickly looked away. Lucas Chisholm was serious and rarely smiled and appeared to sulk. This occasion was no different. Lana noticed the scent of Lucas's cologne. It was a light, subtle spice scent but never overwhelming. She knew that her olfactory memory would always attach that scent to Lucas.

"Well, let's begin," suggested one of the attorneys. Legal papers were passed from one party to the other with little preamble. Lana received the deed to the house in Columbine Point that they had built in the months following their marriage, the Cadillac Escalade that had been a gift to her from her in-laws, and a lump-sum settlement for a share of Chisholm Cadillac, the fifty-year-old family business that Lucas had purchased from his father five years earlier. Lucas retained ownership of the business and the properties. Lana avoided looking at Lucas, but out of the corner of her eye, she saw him clench his jaw each time he was asked to sign a document.

The entire process seemed to go quickly while it wiped out ten years of their lives together with a stroke of a pen. When they exited the conference room, Lana unintentionally walked next to Lucas. As she felt the awkwardness of their silence, she said to him, "Have a happy life." Lucas looked at her blankly with his sullen blue eyes as if he didn't know her. He had a slight smirk on his face but didn't respond.

"Lana, can I speak with you for a second?" Lana's attorney took her gently by the arm as he led her back into the conference room doorway. "I want to remind you to get the locks changed in the house as soon as possible. And there is the matter of your name change. You may stop by the office next week. Angela will have the document ready to sign."

"Thank you for handling this, Michael. Have a good evening."

Lana walked out of the office into the late afternoon sun, thinking about the name change. She would no longer be Lana Ross Chisholm, but just Lana Ross, as she had been since birth. She needed to rid herself of the Chisholm identity and make a clean break with it. Her mind wandered. She always liked her name, Lana. In a generation full of Jessicas, Emilys, and Sarahs, she felt fortunate to have a first name that could only mean her when someone said the name, "Lana."

Lana Ross—that's me again, she thought.

CHAPTER 2

Lana Ross loved music. She was raised on classic rock and country music as she rode in the car with her mother singing along. One of her early memories was of riding in the car to preschool at age three, listening to "I'm No Stranger to the Rain" by Keith Whitley and then riding home to the sounds of the Eagles singing "One of These Nights." In Lana's mind, her life's journey had been accompanied by an elaborate soundtrack of diverse music. "Goodbye Time" by Blake Shelton popped into her head. She found it on her playlist and let Blake's song of heartache be her companion as she drove away from the law office. Lana wasn't sad, but mindful of the bittersweet ending of a promising life together and simultaneously excited about what the future may hold for her.

She needed to stop by the market to get a few things. As she drove, her mind bounced from thought to thought as she reminisced. Lana had met Lucas in Boulder on Pearl Street eleven years ago. She had been celebrating her graduation from the University of Colorado with a BA in English Literature that day. Coincidentally, Lucas had graduated with an MBA the same day. Boulder's bars had been hopping that night and somehow, Lana and her friends had ended up at a dance club. Lana had walked up to the bar to order a margarita. Lucas had been waiting for the bartender to deliver a beer to him. Lana had known who he was since they had both grown up in Columbine Point, but she had never met him. Their eyes had locked and he'd said, "Lana Ross, I would know that long red hair anywhere. What brings you to Boulder tonight?" She had been flattered that he'd known her. He had bought her a drink.

Lucas had short dark hair and clear blue eyes. His features were chiseled and aristocratic. His build was stocky and he was just a couple of inches taller than Lana. She had spent the rest of the night talking to him. He had seemed interested in her career plans, her childhood, her views, and her future. When she had gone home that night, she could smell the light spicy scent of his cologne on her clothes from being so close to him. Lucas had put his hand on her back and given her a long kiss. It had felt electric. She remembered that a song by John Mayer had played in the background at the bar.

As she lay in bed, she thought about the significance of that day—graduating from CU and meeting Lucas Chisholm. From that day on, they had been a couple. Lana had gotten caught up in the thrill of dating a rich, good-looking man from a prestigious family. He had never asked her to marry him. It had just been assumed. But as the months had flown by and they'd gotten closer to the wedding date, she had begun to have doubts about him. His attention to her had waned. He hadn't been as interested in the wedding plans or the honeymoon choices. She had chalked it up to the pressures of business. It wasn't until after the wedding that she had realized that he was married to his business and she was just an accessory. He had either been annoyed with her or sulking. There had been no partnership, no real intimacy, no companionship. As the years had flowed from one to another, a voice inside her head had repeated over and over, *I can't do this anymore*, until finally she'd left. And to her surprise, he had let her go. She had thought that perhaps he had made it easy to keep the gossip at a minimum so as not to affect the dealership sales. She thought that Lucas had since moved on. Lucas was building a rambling new house in a subdivision near Coal Creek, and she heard he was dating someone.

To many people, it seemed that Lana had it all and they would have been happy to have stepped into her shoes under any circumstance. She had never had to worry about money or the comforts of life that Lucas could offer. But Lana had known that she was losing herself in the charade. She had never really known what he'd expected of her, so she had given and given of herself trying to make him happy. Fortunately, there had been no children. Lana believed that there was perhaps a biological mismatch, if there was such a thing.

Lana arrived at the market parking lot and sat in her car for a moment listening to the ending of the song. "Goodbye, baby," Lana said silently. She went in and grabbed bread, cheese, eggs, and nectarines. As she exited the market, she saw an old, green service van in the parking lot. The advertising on the van said "LOCK UP 24-Hour Locksmith Leon Alvarez" with his telephone number. She had seen the van around town many times before and recalled that Michael had admonished her to have her locks changed. She quickly entered his phone number into her smartphone.

As Lana drove the white Escalade away from the market, she searched for "Freebird" by Lynyrd Skynyrd on her playlist. She suddenly felt the freedom that she gained that day as she sang along with Ronnie Van Zant all the way home.

CHAPTER 3

"Hello, I'm Lana Ross and you must be the locksmith." Leon Alvarez arrived to change the locks. He nodded and said nothing. His eyes scanned her from top to bottom. Lana felt a slight uneasiness by his almost sinister appearance. His dark hair was long and tangled. His eyes were blue but made almost iridescent due to the contrast of the iris color to the intense redness of the sclera. They seemed almost diabolical, like something she had seen once in a nightmare. His dark beard was long and scraggly with a Fu Manchu mustache that blended with it and then extended well past his chin. She quickly thought that he must be okay since he had been in business in the area for a while now. But her intuition radar was on high alert and was telling her something different.

Lana was dressed in black yoga pants and a little, white T-shirt because she thought she could work out while the locksmith was there. But after she saw him, she felt she must be aware of his presence and not be lost in music and movement. Leon was quite conscious of what she was wearing because it made the shape of her fit, little body pleasantly apparent.

"Let me show you what I need done. It will be the front door here, the back door, and side entrance to the garage." Leon still hadn't said a word, but she heard his heavy footsteps and could feel him looking at her back as he walked behind her. The layout of the house was sprawling with rooms that flowed together. Lana felt uneasy as they made their way to the back door. She heard him breathing loudly through his nose. She figured he must be a smoker since she could smell smoke on him—a combination of tobacco and marijuana. Leon finally spoke and asked her if she wanted copies of the keys. She expected a gravelly, gruff voice, but his voice was surprisingly normal. As he spoke, he strung the words together in a slow drawl.

"Lana, here is yer key and two extra. The same key will fit all of them doors. Now is there anything else I can do for ya, darlin'? What about the interior door to the house from the garage?"

Lana was taken aback when he called her "darlin'" and quietly told him, "No worries. You can only gain access to that door through the garage anyway and for that you'd need the garage door opener."

"Now ya let me know if ya need anything else done here now, darlin'." He paused for a minute and said, "Or if ya need a security system installed." Leon handed her the invoice. She paid him and walked him to the front door. She took a quick look at his dented, green van, which was missing all four wheel covers. The windshield was cracked. Rumpled and peeling stickers clung to his back bumper. Despite the condition of the van, the words, "LOCK UP" with his name and telephone number painted in black on the side were quite distinct and clear. Lana was relieved he was leaving. As he opened the van door, he turned and looked at her for several long seconds before he got in.

That was weird, she thought. Oddly, she began to feel like he seemed familiar to her for some reason. Lana changed from her workout clothes to her office garb—a little, black dress with black ballerina flats, turquoise and silver earrings, and a pearl bracelet. She was the editor of the *Boulder Essence* magazine—a monthly publication containing upbeat articles, glossy photos, and ads about the latest happenings around Boulder. The job, which she began as a feature writer, had been her salvation for ten years, and she believed that without it, she would have truly lost herself. There were some looming deadlines that she had to meet.

As Lana drove to her office, she thought about how so much had changed in just a couple of days. She listened to her playlist—Chris Stapleton singing "Either Way" with so much pain. The words penetrated her thoughts. "I'll be fine on my own," she quietly said to herself.

CHAPTER 4

Leon Marcus Alvarez had been born thirty-four years ago—the fourth of five sons born in a single decade to Joe and Bonita Alvarez. When Leon was six years old, his mother had died. She had been the last warm and loving person that Leon would ever know. Joe, overwhelmed by Bonita's death and the responsibility of working as a mailman and feeding and raising five boys, had been detached, uninterested, and cold, leaving Leon feeling abandoned and empty. As the teen years progressed, Leon had continued to regard his mother with great reverence, but his memories of her affection for him had waned. He had become forbidding, detached, and sociopathic, feeling insignificant, worthless, and angry. In high school, he had had few friends—a couple of troubled boys like him. The other kids had steered clear of him, sensing he was disturbed with his cold, lifeless stare and expressionless face. There had been rumors swirling that he'd carried a switchblade and had used it in a fight in town and that on another occasion, he had smashed the windshield of a football player's car with a chain after he had called him a "sick pit face fucker."

Despite his venomous personality, he hadn't been able to help but notice Lana Ross the first day of ninth grade. It was her long, reddish-blonde hair that had caught his eye. She'd had braces on her teeth and was still scrawny and flat chested. She had been standing talking to friends at the entrance of Sky High. And while the other girls had been animated and talked loudly trying to get the boys' attention, Lana had been quietly laughing among them. He had thought she was pretty and had liked what he'd thought of as "her quiet ways." Gradually, as the high school years had moved from season to season, Leon had noticed that Lana had been changing and becoming a beautiful girl, even though he had always believed she was pretty.

Leon had happened to be enrolled in a class with her once—English Composition. One day, as a pop quiz, the teacher, Mrs. Sorrento, had showed the students three items: an autumn maple leaf, a pine cone, and a seashell, and had asked them to choose one of the items and take fifteen minutes to write everything they could observe about it. She said, "Composition isn't only about grammar, sentence structure, and the proper tense, but it's also about the words we select to convey what we observe." The next day, Mrs. Sorrento had returned the graded pop quizzes to the students and had selected Lana's to read to the class. Lana had chosen the autumn maple leaf to write about and had not only described its physical characteristics in detail down to its color variations and texture, but she had also included a short monologue by the leaf as it reflected on its own short life from spring to fall. All of that written in fifteen minutes. Leon had thought she was brilliant. He had written three sentences about the pine cone. Despite all the reasons he'd thought of to hate school, seeing Lana each day was a reason to bother showing up, even though she was undeniably out of his league.

One day, as Leon had walked to his car in the parking lot, he'd noticed a couple of the guys in letter jackets, standing near Lana and her car, a '90s white Jeep Cherokee. She had tried to open the car door, but one of them had held the door shut. She had looked upset and he'd heard her say, "Knock it off, Jeff! Let me go!" Leon had walked over to the situation and stood a few feet back and said nothing. In a matter of seconds, the boys that had teased Lana suddenly walked away. As Lana had opened her car door, she'd looked to her right and saw that Leon had stood near the back of her car. Although she couldn't be sure, she had thought that maybe he'd scared them off and she'd smiled slightly at him, not saying a word. Leon had felt strangely good about himself for a minute. She had needed him, and he'd answered the call.

Leon had dropped out of high school at the end of his junior year. He'd begun to work for a fence company and moved out of his father's house. He rarely saw Lana anymore. Sometimes he would park near the high school parking lot, light up a joint, and wait to see if he could catch a glimpse of her walking to or from her car. Lana had become a knockout—curvy but slim with beautiful hair and eyes, even prettier than he had imagined she could be. But positively out of his league.

When Lana had graduated from Sky High and left for college, Leon knew that there was little chance that he would see her again. A few years later, he had heard that she'd married Lucas Chisholm. *Well, that little gal is set fer life,* he'd thought to himself. He had put Lana out of his mind. He'd had a couple of short-term girlfriends with no self-esteem, whom he'd treated badly and many one-night stands in the back of his van when the bars closed. He had spent a lot of time at the local bars drinking beer each night to numb his worthless existence. He had been banned from some of them for fighting and brandishing a knife.

Eventually, one of his brothers had become a locksmith apprentice for a lock company in Denver and suggested that Leon might want to give that profession a shot. The idea of having the power to legally unlock and enter any door had appealed to Leon. And thus, Leon had begun his career as a locksmith, a profession where people had to ask him for help.

Leon had all but forgotten about Lana until the day she'd called him out of the blue a few days before to ask him to change the locks in her house. *I'm one lucky bastard that she chose me,* he thought. *And that spoiled little son of a bitch, Lucas Chisholm, let her go?* When he'd met her at her house, he could see that she didn't remember him. In his eyes, Lana needed him once again, like she had once in high school on that afternoon in the parking lot. But after seeing her again, the seed for an obsession for Lana had been planted—this time with a crazed, dangerous, psychotic strength that would overshadow any adolescent crush that he had had before. Her face, her eyes, her hair, her voice, her figure, the way she moved—everything about her captivated him. She was unattached again and he wanted her and had to have her. He would make it so she would need him no matter what he had to do. "Lana, girl, yer gonna be mine. This time I'll make it happen. Yer gonna see. Yer gonna need me, darlin'," Leon whispered to himself when he lit up a joint as he drove away in a cloud of smoke after he changed the locks.

CHAPTER 5

"Okay, let's do it. I'll meet you and Olivia at the Boulder Brewhouse at eight." Lana was finally going to make a night of it with her two best friends, Olivia and Cate. It was Friday. The week had flown by and was full. On Monday, Lana's divorce had become final. The November edition of *Boulder Essence* had been sent to press and published online Thursday. She had time to think about the future now, to sort things out, to redirect her energy. She and Lucas had been separated for the last eight months but had kept it relatively quiet at his request.

Lucas had been stunned and angry when she had announced her plan to separate from him. His eyes had been bulging and his face had been crimson. "What are you thinking? You have it made. What will my mom and dad say? What will people think? You'll get nothing!" were Lucas's exact words when she had cautiously told him she wanted out of the marriage. Not "Please stay" or "I love you." Just threats. The lack of words that would encourage her to stay had confirmed her decision.

"Where were you, Lucas? Every time you told me you were too busy, I knew how insignificant I was. You don't need me, and you never have." Lana had limited her words. She hadn't wanted to say more. She had already packed a few things before she'd told him.

"What do you want from me?" Lucas had yelled. His voice had rattled in his throat.

"My freedom." It had been over. Her fear of telling him had melted into a feeling of relief. She had gotten in the car and left. The rest would be up to the attorneys. Ultimately, his attitude toward her had been the same as it always had been—alternately disinterested and annoyed but now with added contempt. She could live with that. Lana had agreed to keep the separation quiet for a few months. She had even attended some charity events with him that had been scheduled several months before. She had maintained an invisible existence—occasionally meeting her friends for dinner but staying out of the limelight. For the first couple of weeks, she had stayed in a local hotel. But soon Lucas had moved to a small house that belonged to his family in the prestigious part of Columbine Point. He had made plans to build a new house near Coal Creek and to let her keep their big house at 1974 Hill View Road. He seldom texted or called her anymore. *Now I know he's finally accepted that we're over.*

Lana left her office a little bit earlier than usual and headed home to her house in the rural area surrounding Columbine Point. It was going to be a couple of hours before she drove back to Boulder. She felt drained and realized that she hadn't eaten all day. She rolled up a flour tortilla with crunchy peanut butter and jelly in it and drank a bottle of water. She changed clothes and jumped on the treadmill for a few miles. Lana did not relax very easily and needed to stay busy. That trait was in her nature and was enhanced by Lucas's neglect of her. The treadmill was not enough. She wanted to be outside—a subconscious need to feel free. She took a walk along Hill View Road. It didn't matter how far she went. She was listening to music and breathing in fresh air and looking at the beautiful Flatirons, the majestic rock formations in the foothills of nearby Boulder. Oddly, as she returned to the long private driveway that led to her house, the locksmith, Leon Alvarez, drove past her on the road. He nodded at her. She smiled slightly and hoped he wouldn't stop. He continued. *I guess someone else out here needs locks changed or opened.* But it reminded her of that last long uncomfortable look he gave her when he left her house after he changed her locks.

Lana took a shower and got dressed to go out. This would be the first real night out on the town in eleven years. She chose bootcut jeans and a green silk shirt with an antique silver cuff bracelet and turquoise-green earrings and her red boots. She wanted to look good but not draw too much attention. She left for Boulder as the September sun was beginning to set.

Lana arrived in Boulder and parked in the public underground parking on Walnut Street and walked across the street to the Boulder Brewhouse. Olivia and Cate were already there and had found a table. "Hey, redhead!" Olivia hollered and waved to Lana as she entered.

Olivia Carelli and Lana had been friends since high school. She was a bubbly brunette with curly, medium-length dark hair, a little shorter than average, always on a diet, and full of energy. Whenever she spoke, her words were always expressed with great animation. She could be a little too noisy sometimes, but Lana was amused by her. Olivia was married for a brief time to a local TV sports broadcaster but had divorced about five years earlier. She was a wedding photographer.

Catelyn (Cate) Branson, on the other hand, was quiet and serious. She was a willowy blonde with blue eyes but quite plain-looking and refused to wear makeup even though her blonde eyelashes and eyebrows were almost invisible, which gave her a blank expression. Cate had been Lana's college roommate during her freshman year. Lana appreciated the calmness that she possessed, but it gave Cate an air of aloofness and made it difficult for her to connect with men. She had a beautiful smile but seldom used it. Cate had only had a couple of boyfriends over the years. It didn't appear to bother her. She believed that the right man would eventually appear. Cate was a paralegal at a law firm that specialized in estate planning. Lana and Olivia speculated that she was having an affair with one of the attorneys.

As Lana seated herself, the three friends were amused by the fact that there they were—a blonde, a brunette, and a redhead—out on the town. They ordered dinner and drinks and made their way ultimately into the music venue side of the restaurant. Men and women were in groups drinking, talking, laughing, and checking out the scene before the live music started. The three approached the bar and ordered drinks. When the music began, the bar appeared to become more crowded. The band was a Neil Young tribute band that called itself Harvest Moon and covered his timeless acoustic music quite close to the original version. Neil Young's music was in Lana's wheelhouse.

As the band began to play "Cinnamon Girl," Lana felt a tap on her shoulder and heard a voice that said her name. She turned to find Alex Wilson, a guy she had known since elementary school. She was surprised to see him and hugged him spontaneously. He hugged her tightly. He looked the same as he always did—average height and build, spiky brown hair, average features except for very long, thick black eyelashes that were the envy of his female high school classmates.

"I didn't expect to see someone from Sky High here tonight. How have you been?"

Alex told her that he had been living in Wisconsin and was the plant manager at an industrial equipment company. "I married a beautiful woman named Callie that I met in Wisconsin, but she passed away last year from leukemia. We had a son named Spencer, who is six now. Grandpa and Grandma are babysitting. How have you been? I heard that you married Lucas Chisholm."

Lana gave him the shortened version of the past decade. When the band took a break, she introduced him to Cate, who nodded and gave him a slight smile, then continued silently sipping chardonnay. Olivia, who knew Alex from high school, was involved in a lively conversation about the Florida Keys with two guys at the bar. Olivia seemed excited to see someone from the past as well and hugged him and exuberantly exclaimed "Alex! You look great!" They exchanged a little bit of small talk and she turned to resume her conversation with the men at the bar.

Lana ordered another margarita. Alex seemed to be glued to her side for the rest of the night. She figured that he was lonely and just wanted to talk to someone about what he had been through. She was okay with that since she wasn't quite sure what to expect being newly single out on the town. As the night progressed, she began to drink water, not wanting to be buzzed when she drove home.

Alex continued drinking and talking and eventually said, "Did you know, Lana, that I had a huge crush on you for a couple of years in high school?"

Lana was surprised by that revelation. "Well, that's news to me. I thought that you and Allison McGregor were a couple. At least that's what she told all of us."

"Yeah, we dated. She was just okay. I wasn't really into her. I liked you."

Lana thought that he must have drunk too much and tried to change the subject. Olivia and Cate approached about midnight and were ready to leave. She planned to leave when they did.

"I need to go, Alex. It was nice talking to you again. Take care."

"Could we meet for coffee or a drink next week? I'm leaving next Thursday. I'd like to see you again."

Lana gave him her cell number. "Yes, that would be okay. Lunch?"

"Okay, I'll call you." He leaned in to kiss her, but she quickly turned her head and he kissed her cheek.

"See you soon," she said. Lana had spent so much time talking to Alex that she did not meet anyone new at the bar and didn't really notice who was there, although initially she felt that they all looked younger than her. Lana, Olivia, and Cate headed for the elevator to the parking garage. Olivia was chattering on and on about someone named Jason that she met. Cate was quiet but admitted that she had fun, loved the music, and that she had met someone named Mitch but did not elaborate.

"Thanks so much for getting me out of the house, out of my routine, and out of my rut," Lana said as she waved to them. Olivia and Cate had ridden together and began walking to Cate's car. Suddenly, Lana realized that she could not remember where she had parked.

Oh no. Why didn't I make a mental note of the letter and number on the parking lot column? she mentally scolded herself. *I know that I'm on this level though. I hate to have to use the panic button on my keys to locate the car. How embarrassing!* She began to dig for her keys in her purse, feeling a little frantic alone in a parking garage after midnight. The panic button would eliminate her wandering all over for too long.

"Having some trouble there, darlin'?" Lana was startled but recognized the slow drawl of Leon Alvarez and that combination of smoke in the air. She felt a little surge of fear and admonished herself for not being aware that he was so close before he spoke.

"I'm good," she said, not wanting him to know that she felt so vulnerable. "Just looking for something in my purse. Thanks."

"I seen you twice today. On Hill View Road and here at the Boulder Brewhouse. Great band, huh?"

Lana continued to dig in her purse and began to feel her face flush.

"I think I seen your car near mine when I parked. Want me to walk with you? You never know what kind of low life is hangin' out down here."

Lana was stuck. She could say no but she still couldn't find the car, or she could take a chance and walk with him. She wanted to go home badly now. "How far is it?"

"Just around the corner.

She didn't answer but quit searching for her keys and walked in the direction in which he pointed. Leon walked next to her. She could hear him breathing again. It seemed like they walked for five minutes or more, even though it was probably less than twenty seconds.

"There you go, darlin'. There's that white Escalade."

The Cadillac fortunately had keyless entry. She tapped the door handle, and the door opened.

"Thank you, Leon. Bye." She quickly closed the door and locked it. She didn't look at him. When she looked in her rearview mirror, she saw him standing in the parking garage as he watched her drive away. Relieved to be on her way, she mused, *I seriously locked my car door with a locksmith standing there. He could get in whether it was locked or not.* She still felt like there was something familiar about him.

As Lana left Boulder, she drove in silence, not wanting to be distracted by melodies or lyrics. Her mind leaped from thought to thought about the evening's events—seeing Alex from high school, hanging out with her friends, the music and the band, the encounter with Leon. The tequila buzz wore off and she was tired and sleepy. Fortunately, home was only twenty minutes away. There was a full moon and the sky was dimly lit, which made an outline of the landscape visible. She decided to listen to the workout playlist that she created with hip hop and old disco to keep her awake. "Uptown Funk" by Bruno Mars and "Simply Irresistible" by Robert Palmer.

The house was dark when she arrived. She forgot to leave a light on inside. She surveyed the exterior as a matter of habit and pulled the car into the garage. Opening the door to the interior of the house, she flipped on the light switch. For no apparent reason, Lana felt a little uneasiness as she opened the door. She had been living alone in the house on Hill View Road for over eight months and never felt insecure. But she had keen perceptive abilities—almost like a sixth sense—that were suddenly on alert. Everything seemed to be okay as she cautiously surveyed the interior of the house and checked the doors to make sure that they were locked. There was no sign that anyone had entered.

Lana sat at the long pine kitchen table and watched her reflection in the kitchen window for a few long minutes while she ate some Ritz Crackers. Feeling that the uneasiness had subsided, she decided to go upstairs to the master bedroom and get ready for bed. She turned on the lamp on what had been Lucas's side of the bed. And there, lying on the light green comforter, was a portrait of her in a silver frame, which she kept on the tall cherry dresser in the corner of the room. Lana had given it to Lucas as a gift three years ago. It was particularly distinctive because it highlighted her hair and eyes. Lucas did not take it with him when he left. She didn't remember moving it or even touching it since the last time she dusted the bedroom furniture. The drawer in her nightstand was open too. She looked inside but couldn't tell if anything was missing or moved. It contained her jewelry and her undies. Lana was feeling a little perplexed. Perhaps when she got ready to leave, she had been on autopilot, unaware of subtle actions, and left the drawer open and the picture on the bed.

I'm being paranoid after that unexpected encounter with Leon, Lana thought, not having developed a comfort zone yet for being newly single and out on the town. She set the photo back on the dresser.

Lana undressed and caught a glimpse of herself in the cherry-wood-framed pedestal mirror in the corner of the room. As she gazed at her figure, she was pleased to see that she still had the same tight, little athletic body that she had had in high school. It excited her, which became noticeable in the long, white CU T-shirt that she wore. Maybe she still had a slight buzz from the tequila. As tired as she was, she was unable to sleep. She listened for the usual sounds in the house as it settled each night. Coyotes howled in the distance. She heard the rumble of a train a few miles away as it passed through Columbine Point. She listened to her own breath and could feel her heart beat a little faster than usual. She wanted to sleep but still felt an uneasiness like something strange had happened there while she was gone. Lana was very private and would not tell anyone since nothing had really happened, only a suspicion. She described herself as self-contained, never asked for help, and kept her thoughts and troubles to herself for her alone to solve. Finally, exhaustion gave way to sleep. But throughout the night when she tossed or turned, she looked in the direction of the tall dresser to see if the silver-framed photo was still there.

CHAPTER 6

The next day was Saturday, and Lana began to feel comfortable alone in the house again. The day went by quickly with Lana doing household chores, working out, shopping, and calling family members. Lana had grown up in Columbine Point. When she was a college freshman, her parents had divorced and moved away separately—her mother to Durango, Colorado, and her father to Steamboat Springs, Colorado. She rarely saw them. She believed that the return to Columbine Point brought back painful memories for them both and they intentionally stayed away. Her mother, Sharon, was a librarian, and her father, David, was a jewelry designer. They had met at Regis University in Denver and moved to Columbine Point when David had decided to open a jewelry shop there shortly after their wedding. He had even designed Lana's wedding ring at Lucas's request. It had been white gold with small diamonds circling the band, crowned with an exquisite, one-carat, black diamond. Sharon and David led separate lives. David was absorbed with the business of jewelry design. He was tall and blond with a slim build. Lana thought he looked like a California surfer. Sharon, who was short with dark, curly hair, worked at the library as much as possible and used her spare time to take fitness classes.

Lana was an only child. She had always had everything in the way of food, shelter, clothing, and opportunities—for which she was quietly grateful. But her parents had always seemed preoccupied and detached. Sharon seemed to harbor an underlying anger. David appeared to be numb. They had rarely talked and when they did, it had been a single sentence here and there. There had always been music playing in the house, especially classic rock, which tempered the sharpness of the silence. Instead of leaning on them, Lana had become quite self-reliant at an early age.

When she was twelve, she had learned that there had been a stillborn baby brother a couple of years before her birth. Lana speculated that perhaps the grief of that loss had caused them to protect themselves from pain by not opening their hearts to each other or to her. She often thought of the moment that she had learned of the stillborn baby. Her mother had driven her to middle school that day. An Eric Clapton CD had played softly in the background. As they'd arrived, Lana had seen the carloads of kids emerging from their families' cars and asked, "Mom, why didn't I ever have a brother or a sister?" Lana's mom had answered quickly and without emotion. "There was a baby boy a couple of years before your birth. He was stillborn. Do you know what that means? We named him Landon. Landon Alexander." Lana knew what stillborn meant but the shock of hearing those words that her mother had spoken had kept her from responding. She had said goodbye to her mom, and while she'd gotten out of the car, she had felt a chill as she'd heard Eric Clapton singing "Tears in Heaven"—his own tribute to the young son he had lost. For the rest of the day, she had felt like someone had punched her in the stomach. Landon had never been mentioned again. Over the course of the years, she had wondered if either of her parents would have told her about Landon if she had not asked that simple, innocent question. She thought about the similarity of their names—hers was Lana Alexis. She wondered about him—what he might have looked like, sounded like, been interested in. She wanted to believe that he would have been a friend and companion to her.

Lana never bothered Sharon or David with her troubles, and they never really asked how she was doing. They knew about the divorce and both made comments about the money wasted on her wedding, but they also knew that she was fully capable of taking care of herself, and for that they patted themselves on the back. She had realized after a few years into her own marriage to Lucas that he was as detached and preoccupied as her father had been. She recalled a night when she had implored Lucas to spend more time with her. He had turned to her and coldly said, "Do you really think I have time for that? How much do you think you matter anyway?" Lana wanted more than to simply exist like her parents had done. She wanted a partner in life who valued her as the unique woman she had become and made sure that she always knew it. *Is it possible that there's a man out there like that? I won't settle for less next time,* she told herself.

In the early evening, Lana checked the pantry and refrigerator for something to make herself for dinner. She had only snacked during the day and felt like she needed some real food. Salmon and rice. She headed to the market and picked up a salmon fillet, some fried rice from the deli, and sliced strawberries. *I believe I'll treat myself to some prosecco as well,* she thought as she stopped into the liquor store in the same neighborhood shopping mall. There, in the center aisle of the liquor store, she saw the back of a familiar figure perusing the red wines. It was Lucas. She ducked behind a beer display near the back of the store and waited until he paid and left. If he saw her, he didn't acknowledge it. She didn't want an awkward exchange with him. She hoped that he had accepted that the marriage was over. He had not called or texted for a couple of months.

As she left the mall parking lot and stopped at the first light, a plume of smoke wafted from a vehicle near her and washed over her windshield. In the corner of her eye, she saw the familiar, dented, green van containing Leon Alvarez in the lane next to her. He was looking straight ahead waiting for the light to change, exhaling something that was quite smoky. Lana looked straight ahead, too, not wanting to inadvertently make eye contact with him. When the light changed, she waited a few seconds so as not to drive parallel to him. He managed to turn right very soon. Lana thought to herself, *Two awkward, near encounters in a matter of minutes.*

Lana arrived home and made dinner, turned on the TV, and sat down with her plate and a glass of prosecco. The sparkling wine put her in a light, almost celebratory mood. She turned on some music and began to dance around, twirling on the hardwood floor, glass of prosecco in hand, taking in the beat of Carlos Santana's "Maria Maria." "I'm free to do this whenever I want to. No scowling from Lucas. No Lucas period. I'm so happy," she said out loud to herself. But in a moment, out of the corner of her eye, she thought that she saw a slight movement. *Am I just dizzy from the wine and the dancing?* she wondered. Then she saw it again—a slow, smooth, sliding, gliding movement between the couch and the sofa table. She turned off the music and stood silently, listening and watching, still holding the glass of wine. Then she saw it—a large snake was in the house! Her heart and mind raced simultaneously, not knowing what it was exactly, where it was now, and how to get rid of it. She ran upstairs in terror, not wanting to be near it, not knowing where it was hiding at that moment. She held her head, which was pounding with adrenaline. *What should I do? What should I do?* For a second, she thought of Lucas. He would be annoyed with her if she called him. He probably wouldn't even answer. Her mind cleared a little and she called the Sheriff's Department.

An animal control officer arrived within a few minutes. Lana pointed out the location where she had last seen the snake. It was found within minutes curled up under the couch. The officer captured it with a noose and put it in a gunny sack. It was a four-foot-long bull snake—not venomous but a genuine sinister presence. The officer planned to take it and release it in a nearby field.

Before the officer left, he said in a monotone, "You better inspect your property and the interior of your house to determine how a snake like that could end up inside."

The question of how it got there had not crossed her mind yet. She just wanted it out of the house. *What if there is more than one in here? How long had it been here?* she wondered. The light mood that she had earlier was long gone, and what remained was apprehension and confusion. She cautiously walked through the main level of the house, taking slow, purposeful steps and went upstairs to her bedroom. She would call an exterminator in the morning to check the house for snakes and their pathways into the house. Lana did not sleep much that night and when she did, she would wake with a jolt, imagining the sensation of a snake slithering across the bed.

A local exterminator arrived the next morning, even though it was Sunday. He might have waited until Monday morning if it had not been a snake and he was going to charge extra for the call, for which Lana did not care.

"I've checked the perimeter of the house, and there doesn't appear to be a breach in the foundation. That snake, though, is a native species for this prairie country. It found a way in somehow, but it may have just been a fluke. I'll do a quick walk-through of the rooms now. But, Ms. Ross, I have a feeling that this was an isolated incident and not likely to happen again," the exterminator explained.

When the inspection was finished and the exterminator had left, Lana still felt apprehensive about being in the house. It was a beautiful, bright Sunday morning. She decided to call Olivia and Cate and invite them to brunch on Pearl Street.

CHAPTER 7

"You are fucking kidding me! A snake was in your house? How did that happen? What did you do? Where did it come from?" Olivia reacted as Lana described the terror after finding a snake in the house. They met at the Santa Fe Diner on Pearl Street for brunch. Lana rarely revealed private details of her life, but this was too weird and terrifying to keep to herself.

Lana described the whole incident to Olivia while they drank mimosas and sampled the Southwestern brunch buffet. Just talking about it brought a chill to Lana once again that she hoped the mimosas would extinguish. Cate joined them after about an hour and quietly listened as Lana described the snake episode again with the dramatic assistance of Olivia. Cate was her usual stoic self and had the same questions as Olivia but calmly asked them.

"You've lived in that house for ten years surrounded by the same hay field, and that has never happened before. Do you know how it got in there? Why now?" asked Cate. Her questions were left unanswered and dangling.

The conversation turned to the usual topics—men, work, and gossip—and the discussion rambled. The trio managed to stay for a couple of hours and a few mimosas. Lana was not ready to go home yet. The snake was still slithering through her psyche.

"You know I work here near Pearl Street every day, but I never manage to just window shop and browse. Let's just tour the shops for a little while. I could use a couple of new outfits to match my new single life."

It was a beautiful, warm Indian summer day. The chiseled Flatirons were clear and sharp blue and green and gray. Lana always loved those Boulder foothills and felt like she could almost reach out and run the palm of her hand across their tops. There was a buzz of adults and children on the mall.

After a couple hours exploring clothing, jewelry, craft, and candy shops, the afternoon drifted away. Cate left the group, explaining that she was going to work for a while to finish up some estate work for a meeting first thing in the morning.

"Cate seemed unusually quiet today. That snake experience of yours seemed to put her in a somber mood," commented Olivia.

"Cate is always serious. Hmm . . . I guess I didn't notice that it was more significant than usual. I still wonder if she isn't having a secret affair or something. Her mind seemed to be preoccupied today."

"Olivia, I have some prosecco that I just opened yesterday. Why don't you just follow me to my house today and we'll finish it up? I think I have some amaretto or tequila or brandy for some shots too. It's still early." She hesitated for a second, knowing what Liv was thinking, and said, "The snake is truly gone."

Olivia agreed and followed Lana home. Lana precariously opened the front door, still unsure of what might await them inside. She turned on the TV—football, which she loved. It was the one thing that she and her father had in common. But she and Olivia hardly watched it as they chattered away. Their conversation turned to high school, and then Lana brought out the dusty leather yearbooks.

"Look at me. And I thought I was quite beautiful in this picture," Lana laughed as she looked at the high school photo of her in her sophomore year. "Braces, bad hair, and awful makeup. No wonder I didn't get asked to homecoming."

Olivias's reaction to her own photo was about the same. "Oh my God! That hair—frizz city! And those braces—what a mess!" They continued to thumb through the pages, reminiscing about their classmates and wondering what might have happened to them. They turned to the page with Alex on it.

"He hasn't changed much since high school, has he?" Lana

observed. "You know, Olivia, I think that he was wanting to get close to me. At least that's how he acted the other night—clingy and close. Maybe it was the atmosphere and the drinking. But it seemed awkward. I'm just not ready for a one-on-one relationship this soon, unless the perfect guy came along. And sad to say, it is not Alex. I hope that when I have lunch with him Tuesday, he's less flirtatious."

"I thought he seemed to be that way, too, but I was busy talking to that new guy at the bar. I knew you could handle the situation if it turned into one."

They continued to thumb through the yearbook when suddenly Lana said loudly, "That's him! That's why I felt I knew him! It's Leon Alvarez—the lock and key guy! We went to high school with him!"

Olivia looked puzzled at Lana's sudden words. "Yeah? Him who? What are you talking about?"

"I had to have the locks changed in the house last week. I called a locksmith, and it was him. He kind of gave off a bad vibe and made my skin crawl when he was here. It was the way he looked at me and his loud breathing and the long stares. Maybe he recognized me from high school and wanted me to do the same. Didn't I tell you about him? I ran into him Friday night in the parking garage after we left the bar too."

"He does look a little creepy in the yearbook. There's a sinister look in his eyes, but what about now?"

"He still does. Long, dark, scraggly hair and a long, black beard and stringy Fu Manchu past his chin that curls up at the end. He smells strongly of smoke. Drives a crappy looking van." Lana paused for a second and placed her fingers on her chin. "But you know, I am remembering now," she paused, "he helped me out one time in the high school parking lot. One of the jocks, Jeff Morton, was teasing me and wouldn't let me get into my car. He was saying things like 'Lana, I'll let you get in and leave after you spend some time in the back seat with me.' What a jerk! Leon must have appeared and was standing behind me. He didn't say a word. Jeff left suddenly and when I turned, there he was. I didn't even know he was there. Hmm . . . it seems weird that I happened to call him to change the locks."

After a short while, Olivia decided to go home but she wanted the buzz to wear off first. Lana made grilled cheese sandwiches for them. She found a classic movie on Netflix to watch—a romantic comedy with an unlikely plot. After an hour or so, Olivia went home.

Lana remained curled up on the couch with a warm, blue fleece blanket and toss pillows. She was tired from the wine, from the events of the week, from always pushing herself, from the unending work left to be done. She fell into a deep sleep.

Suddenly, there was a loud knocking at the front door. At first Lana had trouble shaking off sleep enough to determine what the noise was. The inside of the house was pitch black. Then there was a second set of knocks—knock, knock, knock—loud and hard on the solid wood door. Lana tried to gather her wits as the adrenaline surged through her veins. She was not going to answer that door. She wanted to know who was there, but she didn't want to know. Her heart was racing. She lay there motionless, barely breathing, waiting for another set of knocks. In a few minutes, she sat up slowly and looked in the direction of the door. There was no shadow of anyone. She stood up, still wrapped in the blanket, and walked toward the door. She cautiously peeked out of the sidelight and could see that no one was there. *But what if they moved to the back door? What if they were looking in the window? Why were they there?*

There was a direct view of Hill View Road about a quarter of a mile away from the house. As she looked out the living room window, she saw that a vehicle of some kind must have been parked out by the road when the headlights came on and it drove away. She watched until it was out of sight. If that was the person who knocked, they would have had to walk down the long driveway to the house to get there. It didn't seem that it could be accidental.

Perhaps someone had the wrong house, Lana tried to convince herself. But she saw a pattern of odd events that began in the previous week. The picture frame, the snake, the loud knocking. Were those events linked somehow?

Lana was asleep on the couch for only a few hours before the knocking began. It was 12:30 in the morning. She dragged the fleece blanket upstairs with her. It was still warm from having been wrapped around her while she slept. For some childlike reason, she felt secure clutching it. She shuffled into the bedroom, turned on a soft lamp on the nightstand, and began to turn back the comforter on the bed when she saw it. The silver picture frame was lying on the bed—again! She had not been in her bedroom since she came home from Boulder. *Oh, no, not again!* She held her head in both hands. Questions ran through her mind like an electric current. *When was that picture frame moved there? How?* She knew that she didn't put it there. *Had someone been in the house? Who could it be and why? What was going on?*

Her head was pounding loudly from the wine and the adrenaline. She knew that she couldn't sleep. She took some Advil. She wondered if someone was still in the house. But she couldn't bring herself to explore. She got into bed fully dressed, lay on her back so that neither ear was buried in a pillow, and listened. And she listened some more. Every sound made her jump. Soon the sky began to change from indigo to a blend of yellow, orange, and charcoal as the sun rose. It was Monday morning. The daylight began to lessen the fear that had kept Lana awake.

CHAPTER 8

Lana got up from her bed and looked in the mirror. Her eyes were puffy and red from the alcohol the day before and from the lack of sleep. She got a washcloth, soaked it in cold water, rung it out, lay on the bed, and covered her eyes with it for ten minutes. She got up and looked in the mirror again. There was only a slight improvement. She took a shower, got dressed, and tried to look her best. She wore the most comfortable dress that she could find in her closet—a fitted navy blue dress with white accents and navy blue flats. Her clothes looked good, but she looked bedraggled, tired, and sad. When she arrived at work, her outlook seemed to improve as she was carried by the momentum of the day.

Finally, the routine workday was over. When she arrived at her house, she made a cursory visual survey of the property. Everything looked fine. *Please don't let there be anything out of the ordinary in this house tonight*, she silently prayed to herself.

She made a salad of romaine, kale, tomatoes, radicchio, and rotisserie chicken with a cucumber yogurt dressing. She tried to watch TV but was not interested. *I need sleep.* She remembered that she had a lunch date with Alex from high school the next day. She felt obligated to go, even though she didn't feel entirely comfortable with the idea. *I'll deal with it tomorrow*, she thought as she undressed and went to bed.

On Tuesday morning, Lana woke up feeling rejuvenated and strong. If anything happened in the house during the night, she had slept through it. She dressed in a long, Peruvian, multicolored skirt and her Australian boots. She felt like she needed to look good but on the other hand didn't care.

Alex arranged for them to meet downtown at an elite bistro in the Boulderado Hotel. He hugged her and kissed her cheek when she arrived. They ordered lunch and began to talk about their classmates and their lives a little. After the waiter brought their plates, she noticed Alex looking longingly in her direction. He probably had been doing it the entire time, but she averted his glance by concentrating on her quiche and fruit. When she reached for her goblet of water, Alex reached over and grabbed her hand and held it. It was unexpected, but she did not pull away.

"Lana, I really would like to see more of you. I must go back to my job in Wisconsin, and my son needs to return to school. I've been here trying to regain myself after living through the lengthy illness and death of Callie. But I want to know if you'd be here for me when I come back."

Lana was afraid he would say something like that and didn't want to hurt him, but she had to be honest with him and herself. She looked directly into his long-lashed eyes. "Alex, I'm flattered that you want to see me again and that you like to be with me. But I must be honest—I just ended a ten-year marriage and I need to get to know myself again. And you probably need to do the same thing. I'm not ready to make promises yet. When you return to Columbine Point again, we can visit."

Alex held her hand for a few more seconds after she finished speaking and gazed steadily at her face as if he were trying to commit it to memory. He was fond of her, but Lana thought logic would let him know that he was just lonely.

"It's a deal," he said. "Let's keep in touch. Goodbye, Lana." He walked with her out to the sidewalk, hugged her briefly, and rapidly disappeared.

Lana felt bad, but she knew that it was best for them both. She walked back to her office, still thinking about the lunch, but was quickly swept up in the typical tasks of editing, decision-making, and design. She looked at her calendar and realized that she had an appointment at eleven the next morning with Vincent Romano, the owner of All Roads Harley-Davidson, in Louisville. She was planning to interview him for an article about exploring Colorado on two wheels for a series about travel in Colorado without a car. She researched Harley-Davidson and read some blogs about riding to prepare for some relevant questions.

Wednesday morning arrived. Nothing odd had occurred at her house since Sunday. Perhaps the strange events were random and not linked together as she had speculated. Lana knew who Vincent Romano was but had never met him. She knew he was good-looking and wanted to look good when she met him. She pulled on a fitted, gray wool dress that hugged her figure and tan Frye boots. She wore a tan leather blazer.

Lana arrived at All Roads Harley about ten minutes early. The receptionist let her know that Vincent was in a meeting but he was aware of the appointment. While she waited, she decided to browse the showroom. She had never seen so much chrome in one room. The Harleys were beautiful machines. They were sleek with an aerodynamic design and beautiful colors. The showroom smelled of leather. There were more models than she expected, and she wasn't discerning enough to know the differences among them—the Road Glide, Electra Glide, Street Glide, Softail, or Road King series.

Lana meandered over to a section of Harley clothing. She picked up a black leather riding jacket and was surprised that it was so heavy. Despite their need for functionality, the jackets were beautiful and of excellent quality. She tried on a Harley jean jacket. It felt good and looked good on her. In a moment, she heard a voice behind her say, "So are you a Harley girl?"

Lana turned and looked up at Vincent Romano. She was struck by how handsome he was and for a moment could not speak. He was several inches taller than her and had dark hair speckled with a little bit of gray. His eyes were a golden hazel color and he had beautiful white teeth. His smile was contagious. She smiled back and said, "Not yet. Maybe you can convince me to be one. I'm Lana Ross," as she reached out to shake his hand.

He held it for a long second and said, "Vincent Romano. But they call me Roadking."

Lana realized that she was still wearing the Harley jean jacket. She quickly took it off and hung it up. She grabbed her leather jacket, purse, and laptop while he watched her.

He was still smiling and said, "Shall we talk?"

As they walked to his office, she could see how great he looked in his jeans. She was still admiring his good looks as she sat down on a dark blue leather chair. He had muscular shoulders which she could see through the light blue denim Harley shirt that he wore. His skin was tan and smooth. He had a dark mustache, which framed his smile. She guessed that he was in his late thirties, maybe forty. Vincent sat behind his desk and swiveled back and forth slowly in his burgundy leather chair as he looked at her. Lana did not know it, but he had some thoughts about her too. He liked the long, reddish hair, the blue-green color of her eyes, her figure, her height, her voice, and the little blush that appeared on her cheeks when she first looked up at him.

Lana told him what her vision for the article was—seeing scenic Colorado in every season by various means other than a car, among them a train, ATV, hot air balloon, snowshoes, a hike, and even vicariously by a drone. She would be sending a photographer from the magazine in the next few days to take some photos, if he didn't mind. He nodded and smiled.

"So I'm going to record our interview because I want to be precise when I quote you or paraphrase your comments. Do you mind?" Roadking shook his head and smiled again. He enjoyed watching and listening to her. "My first question has to do with your nickname, Roadking. I saw a Road King Harley out on the showroom floor. I figured that your name and the Harley are somehow related. Why are you called Roadking?"

"The Road King Classic is a touring motorcycle that has the looks of the original touring Harley with leather saddlebags, leather seats, and original badging on the fenders and engine. It doesn't have a stereo, Bluetooth, GPS, heated seats, or grips. I like to hear the roar of the patented Harley sound on a Road King. It's a classic because it's a true ride without all the bells and whistles. Simple and classic but awesome, like me." He smiled. "The Road King Classic has always been my ride, and everyone knows it."

"So when you say 'always,' how long have you been a Harley guy?"

"Since I bought my first Harley when I was sixteen. I've been fortunate enough to make a living while living the dream at the same time." He was giving her some great material for the magazine series. She was glad that she was recording his comments. She was so distracted by her attraction to him.

"Well, tell me . . . tell me what is it like to ride a Harley?"

Roadking paused for a minute and swiveled in his chair and looked out of his office window. He searched for the words to describe the many sensations of riding a motorcycle. "Riding makes me feel free . . . with the wind in my hair and the sun on my face. The ride is effortless. The vision is so different from that of a car. The view is open and sweeping and panoramic—without the frame of a car to limit it. There are different smells while riding—in town the smell of barbecues or bacon and sausage cooking in the mornings. Riding in the country, there's the smell of the crops—corn, fresh cut alfalfa, and hay. In the mountains, there's the smell of the aspen, pine trees, smoke from a nearby chimney, the mist from a running brook. And no matter where or when I ride, the air always feels fresh and good and natural. There are many beautiful scenic rides in Colorado, but I like to travel up any of the nearby canyons just to get away for the day. Boulder, Left Hand, Coal Creek, St. Vrain, Big Thompson. I've traveled them all."

Lana watched him as he spoke. She could feel his words and knew that she wanted to experience it firsthand.

"Lana, the best way for you to find out what it's like is to take a ride. How about you and I go for a ride up the St. Vrain Canyon to Estes Park this week? How does your calendar look? Do you think that you'd like that?"

Lana couldn't believe it. That was exactly what she wanted him to say. "Vincent . . . I mean, Roadking, any time tomorrow or Thursday afternoon is open on my schedule. And I would love to."

"Okay, tomorrow—the sooner the better. Now let's look at the Harley models in the showroom, and I'll tell you a little about them and how they're different. I'll let you sit on the Road King if you'd like to."

Lana continued to record him as he talked about the Harley-Davidsons. As she walked next to him, she could smell a slight manly scent on him from shampoo or soap or shaving cream. Nothing strong, but she liked it. As he gestured, she noticed he wore a ring on the third finger of his left hand. It wasn't a traditional wedding band. It was a ring with a stone in it. She wondered if he was married, but it didn't seem appropriate to ask.

"Lana, it's almost noon. Would you care to go to lunch with me and we can continue our chat . . . off-the-record? There's a little Mexican café across the street. You have to eat lunch anyway."

Lana's heart jumped for a second, but she managed to say yes. They walked to the café and when they were seated at the booth, Roadking smiled and said, "Okay, now I have some questions. Tell me a little about yourself, Lana Ross."

Lana summarized her life growing up in Columbine Point, going to college, and marrying Lucas Chisholm, then mentioned the divorce. At first she wasn't comfortable talking about herself, given her private nature, but for some reason she felt like she could tell Roadking anything—like she had known him her entire life.

"I met Lucas Chisholm a couple of times, and he seemed serious and stiff," Roadking said.

"Yes, he was and is all business—Cadillacs. Alright, Roadking, now you do the same. Tell me about yourself—off-the-record."

He was raised in Boulder, played football, attended CU, got a BS in business management, and was lucky enough to get an opportunity to secure a Harley dealership about fifteen years ago. "And here I am now, eating lunch with you."

Lana tried to eat the burrito that she ordered but took tiny bites, feeling awkward eating in front of him. She couldn't finish it and reluctantly had to return to the office.

"Okay, Lana, I'll pick you up at your office tomorrow morning about ten. I'll bring some riding gear for you to wear. I think I can guess about what size you'll need. But wear some boots."

Lana nodded and reached out her hand to shake his, but he pulled her close and hugged her quickly—a short, friendly hug. "Hey, Lana, listen to some Bob Seger tunes on YouTube. 'Roll Me Away' is a good one. Listening to it feels like riding a Harley. Tell me what you think when I see you tomorrow."

Lana drove back to her office and listened to the song. It made her smile. It was so obvious that Roadking loved his job and his pastime. But she needed to return to the office and begin writing the article for the series while it was fresh in her mind. She would add the rest after her ride the next day. The series wouldn't be published until spring, but she and her staff still had a lot of research and writing to do. She tried to write, but when she reached up to brush her hair from her face, she could smell Vincent's scent on her hand from their very first handshake. Her mind began to wander back to meeting him just a few short hours before.

At the end of the day, Lana went home to a quiet, unmolested house again. She was a little apprehensive after the series of odd events of the past several days. She looked in her closet, picked out some tight, faded blue jeans and a navy sweater to wear on the motorcycle ride. It was the end of September. It would be chilly on the ride in the hills.

In the morning, Lana arrived at the office a little earlier than usual to take care of morning issues. She notified her staff that she would be out of the office most of the day doing some research on the Colorado travel series. Soon Roadking arrived, carrying a black leather jacket, chaps, gloves, and a black helmet. Lana's staff looked at her and smiled. She rolled her eyes to let them know that it was strictly business. Roadking followed her into her office. She slipped the leathers on. Roadking had guessed the right size. She pulled her hair back into a ponytail and fastened it at the bottom with a silver barrette with a tiny turquoise cross on it. They were ready to go.

"Before we set off on our journey to Estes Park today, I need for you to know a few basic passenger dos and don'ts. There are two ways to mount the bike. You can use the passenger peg as a step or simply throw your leg over the seat after I'm seated. The bike is balanced to accept your weight. Now when I come to a stop, keep your feet on the foot pegs. I'm a highly skilled rider and can support the bike without your help. It is important that you hold on to my waist with both hands and not hold on to my shoulders or arms, which could interfere with my control of the bike."

He went on to explain what he wanted her to do when leaning into corners. "Your body position influences steering and lean angle. It is important because what you do will affect the control of the bike. Stay neutral; do not lean either with or against the motorcycle. Look over my inside shoulder and do not shift your weight suddenly in the corner. When I brake, hold on tight and press your body against mine. When I accelerate, get a firm hold on my waist and hold on tight by gripping me with your legs. Got all of that?"

Lana nodded. Roadking had purposely brought a Road King that did not have the backrest because he wanted Lana to wrap both arms around his waist. If he braked hard or took off fast, Lana would have to hang on to him tightly. *The boob jam,* he chuckled to himself.

They began their journey up North Broadway in Boulder to US 36 en route to Estes Park. Lana began to sense the feeling of riding that Vincent had described to her the day before. But she couldn't ignore the warm feeling that she felt inside while holding on to him, smelling the scent of him, being close to him. She admonished herself that she was being ridiculous, that it was business only and nothing more.

As they waited at the intersection at the mouth of the canyon, a plume of smoke swirled around them from the vehicle next to them. Lana looked over and saw Leon Alvarez at the stoplight, looking straight ahead. *Leon again? He really gets around. You'd think he was stalking me.* Leon didn't even look their way and turned at the next stop light.

The ride began up the canyon. Lana saw the panorama that Roadking had described. The entire sky was visible as well as both sides of the canyon. The fall air was chilly and crisp, and it smelled like pine. She heard the distinct sound of the Harley engine. She felt the vibration of the motor. Through the curves and hills and valleys of the canyon, it was like the Harley was one with the road. She felt Roadking's firm torso as she hung on. She wanted to lay her head on his back and hold on forever. *Please let this moment last*, Lana silently prayed.

After about thirty minutes, they arrived in Estes Park. Roadking parked the Harley. "Let's go grab some lunch."

Lana followed him into Tony's Pizza, an old log fixture in Estes that had served pizza to tourists and residents for decades. It was dark inside, the walls were made of brick, and the floors were hardwood. Roadking ordered a veggie pizza and two beers, and they found a booth near the back. There were pinball machines and pool tables near them.

When they were seated, Lana said, "Okay, now I know. The ride was fantastic, and I think I can describe it to my readers. But most of all, I think I'd like to do it again. Thank you, Roadking, for your words, the ride, the beautiful day, and the pizza and beer too."

Roadking smiled at her and thought to himself, *She is so perfect in so many ways.* Then he noticed that there were felt tip markers on a nearby table that people used to write their names on the brick walls. He found a brick with faded writing on it from previous decades and wrote "VINCENT." He handed the marker to Lana, who wrote her name "LANA" on the brick next to his. Roadking wrote the date underneath both bricks and said, "In case you come here again, you'll remember that we were here."

Lana was not about to forget.

They talked and laughed and attempted to play pool. Lana was not very good at all. Roadking didn't care. After a couple of hours, they headed back to Boulder. The canyon ride was beautiful but in reverse. The sun was shining lower and from a different direction, and the shadows were beginning to build from the mountains. It felt chilly, but she was comfortable in the leathers. Lana held on to him again. Lana felt peaceful and comfortable with Vincent. It had been a perfect day with the perfect companion. Once again she admonished herself, *It was nothing but business.*

As they arrived in north Boulder, suddenly a vehicle pulled out in front of them. Roadking braked hard and was able to stop in time. It all happened so fast, Lana didn't see any of it. Roadking pulled into a parking lot at the next opportunity. They both got off the Harley. "Are you okay? Did you see what happened? Some asshole in a van pulled right out in front of us. It could have been serious." Roadking was clearly angry.

"I'm fine," Lana said quietly. She held on to his arm for a second. It was a beautiful day, but it was slightly marred by a near accident.

Roadking and Lana arrived back at the *Boulder Essence* office. It was four thirty. Her staff had left for the day. Roadking walked with her back to her office. He was quiet and still clearly shaken.

"Thank you so much for a beautiful day. I loved the ride and am so grateful that you offered to take me up the canyon. As I mentioned, I'll be sending a photographer to the dealership to take some photos. I'll let you decide what shots work best as we profile the Harley and your business."

Lana reached out to shake his hand again. That was the professional thing to do. Roadking took her hand and pulled her close and softly kissed her on the lips. It lasted a couple of seconds. It was affectionate but not passionate. Lana was surprised but kissed him back. Roadking noticed that she blushed slightly when he stepped back, and it made him smile. "Thank you, too, for being my companion for the day."

When he left, Lana gathered her things and went home. She would be thinking about this day for a very long time. Roadking left an impression and had taken a little piece of her heart with him.

On Thursday morning, while Lana was in an editorial meeting, a courier delivered a package. Lana asked them to put the package on her desk. A couple of hours later when the meeting was over, she opened it. Inside was the Harley jean jacket that she had tried on at All Roads with a note, "This should belong to you. Thanks. Roadking Romano." Lana was stunned by his generous gift. She thought that he shouldn't have, but he evidently wanted her to have it. It would always remind her of him. And that's what Roadking wanted.

CHAPTER 9

Lana picked up the denim jacket and, without thinking, brought it up to her chest and held it. The gift was so unexpected and thoughtful. His kiss and the feeling of her arms around him floated through her mind. But she caught herself and thought, *It was a quick kiss. That's all it was. Forget about it.* She couldn't. The melody and lyrics of the old song "Can't Get It Out of My Head" by the Electric Light Orchestra kept repeating in her head. She knew that what appeared to be a mutual attraction like that was a metaphysical power that logic and common sense could not rein in—even if he's married. But it could prevent her from acting on it. She had been divorced for less than two weeks. It was beyond belief that someone like him could come her way and be interested in her so soon. *Lana, you are a fool,* she scolded herself.

Lana folded the jacket, laid it in the box, and set it on an antique oak chair near her desk. She picked up the note from Vincent and read it again. She clasped the note between her hands as if she were praying and raised her hands and touched her index fingers to her lips. She thought about him. She realized that she was daydreaming and shook away the thoughts. There was still work to be done. Even so, she couldn't help but glance at the jacket several times. It was a great Harley jacket, but to Lana it represented something that she learned about herself—the emotional damage done by Lucas through his neglect had not destroyed her ability to feel. *I need to thank Vincent, but do I call? Do I email? Text? I don't want to bother him.* Lana recalled how Lucas was always annoyed if she interrupted him, and he would cut her off in mid-sentence if he received a phone call or walk away from her if he perceived a Cadillac buyer in the showroom. She decided to call Vincent. At least she could hear his voice one more time.

"Vincent, uh, Roadking . . . hi, it's Lana. Lana Ross."

"Hello, little redhead. And how are you?"

"I'm good. I wanted to thank you for the Harley jean jacket. It was a great surprise. But you really shouldn't have. I don't know what to say."

"Lana, when I saw how you looked wearing it, I knew it should be yours. It just seemed right. Besides, I'm the boss; I have permission to give away Harley gear if I want to." Roadking smiled as he said those words. "But I'm glad you called. I know that your photographer is coming on Monday to do some shots around here and with me, and I've been thinking—I have some photographs from some of the Harley trips I've taken around Colorado that may be useful to your story. They're not digital, so maybe you'd want to come over to All Roads and look at them. Tomorrow afternoon? What do you think?"

Lana was thrilled that there would be another opportunity to see him and, secondarily, to acquire some good material for the *Boulder Essence* magazine. "Sure, would two o'clock work for you? I'll make sure you get credit in the magazine for any shot that we use."

For the remainder of the workday, Lana was in advertising and budget meetings, which interrupted her daydreaming. She decided to go for a run after work. She grabbed the box with the Harley jacket and hurried home to change.

When she arrived at home, she changed her clothes, picked up her headphones and her phone and ran out the door. She took off on Hill View Road away from her house, heading south and listening to Bob Seger again. His music energized her and reminded her of the day in Estes Park with Roadking. She ran a couple of miles until her house was out of sight. When she turned around, she paused to stretch out a little and then jogged back.

The September sunlight was beginning to weaken to gray streaked with orange when she arrived at the front door. Lana opened the door with a little hesitancy. After all, it was only recently that a snake was writhing through the house. And then there were those episodes with the silver picture frame lying on the bed. Everything appeared to be in order as she walked in.

Lana took out her laptop before she made dinner for herself. She wanted to read the article that she had begun to write about scenic travel in Colorado on a motorcycle. But what she discovered was that she had written more about Roadking than about the Harley experience. *This will be a difficult edit.* She put her laptop aside and made herself an omelet with mushrooms, onion, spinach, and Colby cheddar cheese, as well as a slice of multigrain toast with chokecherry jam on it. She flipped the TV on and started to watch the local news, got bored, and washed the dishes. She decided to go upstairs and change out of her workout clothes.

As she turned on a lamp, she glanced at her pillow and felt the blood drain from her face and her knees weaken. There on the bed was the silver-framed photo, and lying squarely on top of the glass was the silver barrette with the turquoise cross that she had worn the day before on the motorcycle ride. Thoughts tore through her mind. *What the fuck? What is this? Has someone been here? I was gone thirty minutes. Is someone still here?* She stood there frozen and motionless. She turned slowly to look behind her. Then she scanned the room from left to right and then back again. She stopped and listened for any sounds. Nothing but her heart beating loudly. She walked over to the nightstand. The drawer was already open. She reached in and pulled out the 9 mm Glock that Lucas had given her. She had only been to a target range a few times, but she felt she had no choice but to appear to be able to defend herself. She took slow, deliberate steps as she left the bedroom and walked up the hall to the other bedrooms on the second floor. She quietly approached the closets and opened the doors. She checked the shower stalls. She got up the courage to look under the beds. And she was still listening, but there were no sounds.

She silently descended the stairs one step at a time, hoping that none of them would creak. As she stepped onto the main level of the house, she stood still for a few seconds, holding her breath with the gun pointed in front of her, almost expecting an encounter with someone. Still nothing or no one. As she cautiously tiptoed from the living room to the dining room and then from room to room, each step forward brought her a little sense of relief. She began to believe that she was alone. *But someone had been here. Someone is messing with me. But who and why?*

Lana crept over and sat down on the tan leather couch. She laid the gun on the cushion next to her. She was still listening. She toyed with the idea of calling the police, but what would she say? How foolish would she sound reiterating the events of the past couple of weeks? She had been living alone since the separation from Lucas eight months before, and she had never felt unsafe before now. She had ignored the strange events long enough—the picture frame on the bed, the snake, the knocking, the silver barrette. Her powerful sense of privacy and her stubborn inability to ask for help prevented her from calling anyone. But then she remembered that Leon Alvarez had asked her if she needed a security system. *Perhaps he's right. It's time.* She would call him in the morning.

The sun set completely, and the house was totally dark and full of gray shadows. Lana finally turned on a lamp and the television with no sound. She was still listening. She sat on the leather couch with the gun resting next to her for what seemed like hours. She finally stood up, walked through the house, and checked each door to make sure they were locked. She went to the kitchen, poured some orange juice, and added a shot of vodka to the glass. She drank a little and carried the glass of juice and the gun upstairs to her bedroom. She put the picture frame back on the dresser and put the silver barrette in the drawer with her jewelry. The box with the Harley jacket was lying on the bed where she had left it. She got undressed, but before she got into bed, she brought the jean jacket into bed with her and clung to it like a security blanket all night.

CHAPTER 10

It was Friday morning. Lana woke up a little earlier than usual. She wanted to have a little extra time to get ready for work. She was going to see Roadking in the afternoon and wanted to look good. She showered and then stood looking at her closet full of clothes. Nothing seemed special enough. She finally picked a black leather skirt and a black and gray, cropped sweater and tan Australian boots. She took her time with her makeup and made sure that mascara was perfectly applied to each lash and that the eyeliner was applied with linear perfection. She dried and brushed her hair and curled it a little. She toyed with the idea of wearing perfume but decided against it. She rarely wore perfume to the office, and she didn't want to wear a scent that reminded Roadking of anyone else he knew.

When Lana arrived at her office, she found Leon Alvarez's number in her phone. "Hello, Leon, it's Lana Ross. Remember when you were at my house changing the locks a couple of weeks ago and you asked whether I needed a security system? Is that something that you can install, or could you give me the name of someone who could?"

"Well hello there, Lana, darlin'." Lana cringed when she heard him call her "darlin'" again. "Well, I'd be glad to set up a security system fer ya, darlin'. I'd need to come over to the house first and take a look and make a list of the parts for ya and yer house. When could I come by and do a walk-through?"

Lana had made plans with Olivia and Cate for Saturday. Oktoberfest in Downtown Boulder. And he probably wouldn't want to do business on Sunday. "Monday, Leon, I can get away from the office for a couple of hours if you're only free during the day, or you can come by after work. What works for your schedule?"

"Well, let's see here, darlin'. Let me think on it fer a minute. How about after work? Five o'clock? Five thirty?"

Lana decided that she didn't want him to be in the house after dark or too late. *It seems silly that I'm leery of the man I want to install a security system for me*, she chided herself after hearing his voice. "Five o'clock. See you then. Thank you."

"You bet there, Lana, darlin'. Want ya to be safe out there in the country." Leon smiled to himself.

Lana had meetings scheduled with staff all morning. The next publication of the magazine would be the holiday issue, which would be packed with lavish print ads from Boulder area businesses. The first meeting of the day was with the advertising department. The magazine had no shortage of businesses wanting to advertise in the holiday issue, which made the advertising staff's jobs easy.

"I have to tell you, Lana . . . Lucas has withdrawn his ongoing ad for Chisholm Cadillac from the magazine. It's not going to make a significant difference to our bottom line since we've picked up so many new ads for the holiday issue. But I thought I would mention it. It's probably directed at you."

Of course it was directed at me. It would be his loss. The Chisholm Cadillac ad was classy, featuring a full-page glossy photo of a black Escalade on a black background with the text in gold lettering, and she knew that Lucas was pleased with it.

Lana then met with the art director to discuss their mutual ideas for the cover and feature article layouts for the holiday edition. The editorial deadlines were being met by the staff, and it was coming together. But even with all of her professional responsibilities, Lana was anticipating her meeting with Roadking later. She kept her eye on the clock.

Lana ate a quick lunch of salad with no dressing and drank some sparkling water. She wasn't hungry at all. About one thirty, she looked at herself in the mirror, touched up her makeup, brushed her hair, and approved of what she saw. It was time to visit the

Roadking. Despite her heart racing a little, she reminded herself that it was a professional meeting for professional reasons and nothing more.

When Lana arrived and opened the showroom door, Roadking walked out of his office to meet her. His smile was big as he walked toward her. He was wearing a denim Harley-Davidson jacket as if he had just arrived there himself. He reached out his hand to shake hers and then turned and put his hand on her back as they walked to his office. Roadking took off his jacket and hung it on a hook on the wall. He then sat down on a leather chair next to hers. His laptop was open, and on the screen were photos. There was a little stack of print photos next to it.

"So hey, Lana. How have you been?" Roadking looked directly into her eyes as he spoke, as if he were looking behind them to see what she was thinking. He was sitting a few inches away, but she could feel the warmth of his arm emanating through his shirt.

"I'm good. Been busy with the magazine, working out. What I usually do during the work week. And what about you?" She was looking directly at him as she spoke, savoring his handsome face.

"Just taking care of business. Living the dream. I took a little ride yesterday afternoon up Left Hand Canyon a ways to Buckingham Park, just testing the ride of a new Road King. It was good to get away for a couple of hours. You would have liked it too."

"Yes, I'd love to do that again. Listen, Vincent, thank you again for the Harley jacket. It fits perfectly. You are so generous."

Roadking didn't respond. "Well, I took a little time today and pulled out some of my digital photos that I thought you might like. And what I noticed as I was looking at them is that there are many parts of Colorado, not just the mountains, that are scenic or unique when seen from the wide vision of a Harley seat or any motorcycle."

Lana began to record his comments. Roadking talked about each photo, where it was taken, the roads traveled, the season, his memories. He purposely chose photos with him and the motorcycle in them to accompany the text that Lana would write. There were photos of the awe-inspiring views from the Million Dollar Highway that runs from Silverton to Ouray, of the meandering Highway 133 that follows the Crystal River from Carbondale to Marble, of the trek up Mount Evans Road—the highest paved road in North America—and back to Echo Lake to Idaho Springs, of the drive over Trail Ridge Road from Estes Park to Grand Lake in Rocky Mountain National Park and the narrow road from Independence Pass to Aspen. All the photos were enhanced by his presence in black leather.

"Those spots are so beautiful, but so are these," Lana said as Roadking brought up another screen of digital photos. Lana noticed that he wasn't wearing the ring on his left hand. The question of whether he was married or not still rested in the back of her mind.

"This is a photo of the Pawnee Buttes up in Weld County. See the white and gray streaks running through the buttes? There isn't a more panoramic site than that to be riding on the prairie and see that the horizon surrounds you completely—360 degrees. And to ride at night on the prairie . . . there are more stars than you can count."

He reached for the little pile of print photos. "These were taken in southern Colorado on the Los Caminos Antiguos Highway. One thing I want to tell you is that the scenery may be beautiful and unique as you ride, but the destinations—like the little towns or lakes or hot springs or cafés or whatever—make a ride unique too. And like I've mentioned before, there are different scents and sounds wherever you travel on a bike, and you travel with all your senses. So on the ride on Los Caminos, you'd see Colorado's oldest Catholic church, Our Lady of Guadalupe. See, here's a photo. And near the town of San Luis, there are the Stations of the Cross, bronze statues representing the crucifixion of Christ." Roadking began to talk faster as he wanted to tell her everything that he could about the photos and the rides he had taken. Lana listened and watched him and let him talk until he had shown her everything that he had chosen for her.

"These are just a few ideas for photos I had that you may want to use for the magazine. There's so much more, but we'd be here all day and you'd get tired of listening to me talk."

No chance of that, Lana thought. "So when you choose a highway or destination for the Harley trip, do you always ride the Harley to that place or do you sometimes trailer it?"

"It depends. I do sometimes trailer it if the weather isn't expected to be good on the way there or if I need a vehicle other than the Harley to travel around the area for some reason. But not usually."

"Well, I've learned so much from you. Thank you for your ideas and for taking the time to talk to me and to choose the photos. I don't know how I'll be able to choose among them. Can I take some of the print photos to my office for a few days while we convert them to digital for the magazine article? Your appointment with Tessa, my photographer, is Monday morning at eleven, so she can return them to you then. Is that okay?"

Roadking smiled at her. He was so happy to see her, have her there, and to help her.

She is so easy to be with, he thought. They had been talking for a couple of hours, and he noticed that it was four o'clock. "It must be happy hour somewhere. How about a drink?"

Lana loved the idea. She wanted to spend more time with him. Her office closed at four thirty on Fridays so there was no need for her to hurry back. "Yes. Off-the-record," she said.

Roadking smiled and when he did, his eyes crinkled.

"Well, you have that little skirt on and you probably don't want to ride the Harley."

Lana spoke up, "I'll drive. Where to?"

"Old Town Louisville. There's an old historic building that houses an old-time bar like in the coal mining days. It has a great feel. Let's go."

She grabbed her laptop and the stack of photos. They walked to the Escalade.

Lana's radio was set on a classic rock station. She sometimes listened to the new hip hop, country, or alternative rock; it depended on her mood. Today she felt retro. The Eagles "Try and Love Again" played. It wasn't one of their most popular songs, but it sounded so good on the stereo in the car.

The Coal Creek Miner's Inn was a storefront building on Main Street. Lana parked in front. As they walked in, Lana saw what Roadking meant about it having a great feel to it. She would call it rustic elegance. The coal miner's theme was apparent. The ceiling was open, cross hatched with large pinewood beams from which white milk glass pendant lamps hung. The floor was wide-planked, golden pinewood that creaked a little with each step. The tabletops were shiny, ebony marble, which looked like coal. The booth seating was rustic pinewood and covered in genuine black leather. Each booth was separated by a distressed railroad tie, which held an antique brass miner's lamp that contained a small candelabra lightbulb. Mounted on the wall at each booth were a small beveled oval mirror and an amber, vintage, carnival glass wall sconce. But the real masterpiece in the tavern was a grand, antique, walnut sideboard with a white marble top where the liquor bottles stood. It was about fifteen feet long and held a massive beveled mirror framed by delicately carved fluted columns. The bar was constructed of dark walnut with a spiral vine intricately carved on each edge in a style to match the sideboard and had ebony marble on top. There were eight small milk glass pendant lamps evenly spaced and hung over the bar. Roadking noticed that Lana was taking in the ambience of the inn and told her that the owner had shipped the massive antique sideboard from England in several pieces and had it reconstructed on-site at great expense and then hired local craftsmen to build the bar to match it.

The tall, muscular bartender looked up as they walked in and said, "Hey, Roadking, how's it going these days?"

"Good, Jack. Can't complain. Could I get a Negra Modelo? This is my friend, Lana. And you will have?" Roadking turned to Lana.

Not wanting to make the bartender fuss over a margarita, Lana said, "A glass of pinot noir or cabernet or whatever the house red wine is."

Jack said, "Cabernet it is," as Roadking and Lana walked to the back of the bar to a curved corner booth.

Lana slid into the center of the booth, and Roadking slid in next to her. Jack brought the drinks.

"So Lana, where do we begin—off-the-record."

"Tell me about you, your family, your passions, besides the Harley."

Roadking began by telling her that his Italian father, Angelo, was a custom home builder and his Latina mother, Eva, was an interior designer. They were both born and raised in Louisville with strong family ties. They often worked together on projects. But both were high-energy high achievers, and that combination created a lot of animated discussion when he was growing up. He had two sisters, Dana and Bianca, whose own drama added to the noise. "Our dinner table was definitely the stereotype that you see in movies with noisy Italian families," he told her. He had attended a Catholic parochial school in Boulder in the early years. Although he'd hated it, he came to realize how much of what he learned there was part of him. He had played football at Boulder High School.

Lana told him about her quiet upbringing as an only child with distant parents. Roadking looked at her and listened intently, although she expected he would lose interest. But he wanted to know her and everything about her. He guessed that there was something deep there that was yet to be discovered.

It turned out that they both liked classic cars, classic rock and roll, and old classic black-and-white movies. "Both of us are old souls," Roadking laughed.

Lana did not want the afternoon to end. As she sat next to him, she could feel the body heat radiate from his leg and his arm again. It was almost electric.

Finally, Roadking said, "I have to be somewhere at six, so although I hate to, I need to get back to All Roads."

The two left the bar and walked to the car. They were both silent as they drove back to the dealership. Both were lost in thought about the last couple of pleasant hours spent together and wondering what to say next.

As she pulled into the parking lot, Lana said, "Well, thank you,

Vincent, for the drink, the photos, and for the afternoon, but I guess I'll see you again when—"

Roadking interrupted her. "Lana, I'd like to take the Harley up the canyon to Nederland on Sunday, and I'd like it if you'd come along. You said you wanted to ride again; what do you think?"

Lana's heart began to race a little at the prospect of seeing him again, holding on to him, smelling his scent. But she stayed cool and said, "I'd love to. Thank you."

"I'll call or text you about the time. Should I pick you up at your house?"

"Yes, that would be good. But it's a little out of the way." Lana tried not to let her voice reveal her excitement.

Roadking responded, "Well, then your Harley ride will last longer. And it's a little more background for your article."

"Okay, see you then, Vincent."

Roadking looked at her and reached over and touched her arm and pulled her close and kissed her on the cheek. Lana reminded herself this had been a business meeting with some personal conversation. But she felt a little disappointed until Roadking pulled her as close to him as he could with the car console between them and kissed her on the lips. It was a long, soft kiss. Lana felt her body tingle and get warm, as her heart pounded in her chest and her breathing quickened. Roadking smiled as he opened the car door. She didn't know it, but he felt it too.

CHAPTER 11

When Lana left the parking lot, she was still wrapped up in the last moments that she spent with Roadking. She thought about the kisses and the jacket and the invitation to ride. She admonished herself not to overthink anything that had happened, because she tended to do that. "I'm going to let this thing with Vincent navigate itself, whatever it is or will be. No questions, no questioning, no wondering, no speculating about his past or other women. He'll tell me what he wants me to know, if anything," Lana spoke to herself out loud as she drove, only subconsciously aware that she was driving.

When she arrived at home, her eyes scanned the property as had become her habit. From the outside, everything looked the same as when she had left that morning. She pulled the car into the garage and entered the house with a little hesitation. It was only yesterday that she had found the silver frame and silver barrette on her bed. Lana walked through the house, looking in each room for anything out of place or out of the ordinary. Everything looked secure.

Lana wasn't hungry but knew she should eat something. She poured herself a glass of red wine and grabbed some hummus and pita chips. She turned on some music and sat quietly thinking until the sun went down and the room grew dim. She opened her laptop. Roadking had sent her an email with the digital photos attached that he had chosen for her. She scrolled through each photo, remembering what he told her about them and zooming in on the handsome images of him in each one. *I wonder who took all of these photos. He was with someone who shot them. Stop it.*

After Lana scrolled through the photos two or three more times, she began to work on the article, which was the reason she had met Roadking after all. She started to type on the laptop, occasionally stopping to listen to the recording of his voice that she had made on her phone while he spoke. She was inspired. Lana finished the rough draft of a section of the article and put the laptop away. It was Friday night. She didn't have to work tomorrow. She jumped on the treadmill, plugged in her music, and worked out for an hour. She ran upstairs, took a shower, put on her long CU T-shirt, and jumped into bed, falling asleep immediately. The wine, the treadmill, and the emotional excitement of the day had worn her out.

Lana woke Saturday morning and remembered that she and Olivia and Cate were planning to meet around one o'clock on Pearl Street for Oktoberfest. She threw on her workout clothes and decided to go for a walk or run for a couple of miles to burn off calories to accommodate the bratwurst she planned to eat later. As she opened the front door, she was surprised to see one long-stemmed white rose lying on the doormat. She picked it up and put it on the kitchen table. It was pretty and looked fresh, so it probably had not been lying there too long. *Interesting. But where did it come from? Who had been there? Why did they leave a rose?* She was perplexed but relieved that it was a flower and not something sinister. She thought about Leon, who was scheduled to come on Monday, and then very soon a security system would be installed.

Lana returned, showered, and got ready to meet her friends in Boulder. She wore some tight jeans, a white silk shirt, and a belt with a turquoise buckle along with her favorite red boots. She checked all the doors to see if they were locked and headed to Boulder. She knew that parking would be jammed in downtown Boulder, so she parked at the magazine lot and walked down to the mall.

Lana found Olivia at the Boulder Brewhouse, one of the many breweries participating in the Oktoberfest celebration. Olivia found a table and ordered mugs of beer for them. In about ten minutes, Cate arrived to meet them. Lana and Olivia looked at Cate and then looked at each other. Cate was wearing mascara on her white eyelashes. Cate never wore makeup.

"Cate, what the heck? You're wearing mascara. So . . . who is he? Who are you trying to impress?" Olivia teased.

Cate turned red and looked down. "Nobody. Well, somebody. But I can't say who."

"Cate, that's great. Are you happy? Does he treat you well? Why the secret? I guess I'm asking too many questions. Sorry, Cate. It's the journalist in me. Anyway, you look great. I hope you'll tell us about him when you're ready," Lana assured her. Lana gave Olivia a look that said, *Let it go.*

Cate sipped her beer quietly, still looking down. "I'll tell you about him someday."

Lana turned the conversation to herself. "You know that series I've been developing for the magazine about travel in Colorado other than by a car? Well, I interviewed Vincent Romano at All Roads Harley-Davidson for the motorcycle segment of the series. Have either of you ever seen him? He is so stunningly handsome. Well, we took a ride on his Harley to Estes on Thursday—for my article." Lana was intensely private, even with her best friends. Revealing even that much about that experience surprised them. But it had been on her mind. "Have either of you ever ridden on the back of a Harley?" asked Lana.

"Well, not a Harley, but I dated a guy who had a Vespa," Olivia said. "He wore love beads and had a 'Mother Earth' tattoo on his shoulder."

Lana laughed at Olivia's comments. "Not even close. Who was that? I don't remember you dating a guy with a Vespa." Lana was still laughing. Even Cate cracked a smile.

"He was a guy in my apartment building. His name was Weldon. He caught my attention when he ran into the trash cans behind my building with the Vespa. Next thing I knew, we were making out."

Lana was laughing so hard that tears streamed down her cheeks. Lana wiped the tears from her face. "Seriously, Olivia. That can't be true. You are so funny."

"Yeah, I'm ashamed to say it is true," Olivia somehow managed to keep a straight face as she continued, "It was short-lived relationship—only one week—until he realized that I wasn't a vegetarian, and he broke it off and completely moved away from my building."Lana continued to laugh at Olivia.

"So Lana, tell us about Vincent. I think I know who Vincent Romano is. Where does he live? How old is he? Are you going to see him again?" Cate was asking the questions now.

"I don't know where he lives or how old he is. I'm just getting to know him. He's about six inches taller than me. He has dark hair, hazel eyes, a beautiful white smile, dark mustache . . . and he smells so good. His nickname is Roadking, which is the model Harley that he rides. I'm going to see him again tomorrow as a matter of fact. He asked me to ride up to Nederland with him on his Harley tomorrow. Well, I guess the experience will make for good copy for the article."

Lana continued to talk about him but was really speaking to herself. "I met him under strictly professional circumstances. And yes, he is so good-looking, but someone who looks like that can't possibly be detached. He's just being friendly, that's all. It'll be fun though. It was nothing."

Olivia glanced at Cate with a knowing look. They knew that Lana could be protective of herself. Her words let them know that she was doing just that.

For the rest of the afternoon, the trio bounced from café to brewery, sampling the German ale and eating bratwurst, sauerkraut, and potato dumplings. They listened to the festival music and connected with friends and coworkers until late afternoon. Lana's stomach was full of the beer and food. She felt the need to work it off. "Come on, you guys, let's just walk for a little while. We can come back and hang out. Let's just get away from the festival and walk in the neighborhoods for a few blocks."

Olivia and Cate liked the spot they found in one of the breweries and didn't want to leave. Lana told them that she would be back in a half hour or so.

She began to walk a couple of blocks from the festival. She could still hear a conglomeration of music from the venues. There were so many people down on Pearl Street that cars were parked several blocks into the residential area. As she walked, Lana noticed a familiar vehicle parked on the street. It was Leon Alvarez's van. Lana was surprised that he would be at an event like Oktoberfest in Boulder. It just didn't seem to fit. She didn't see him anywhere, but there were so many people. *It must be the beer. Craft beer, though?* she thought but then promptly dismissed any further thoughts of him.

By the time Lana returned to the mall, all three were ready to call it a day. It had been a full, fun day. Lana wanted to go home, jump on the treadmill for a while, take a shower, and go to bed, which is what she did. She was looking forward to the ride with Roadking the next day.

Sunday morning arrived. Roadking messaged Lana and told her that he would arrive at her house to pick her up at ten in the morning. Lana texted him with directions to her house. Once again, she took great care to apply her makeup perfectly. She fiddled with her hair so that it looked perfect too. She knew that the helmet would flatten it during the ride but at the very least wanted Roadking's first glance of her to be one of approval.

Roadking arrived at ten with leather gear for Lana to wear. Lana pulled her hair back into the silver barrette with the turquoise cross. As she slid the chaps on over her faded blue jeans, he walked over and buckled the belt on them for her. Then he reached around her and touched her waist in the back to see if the fit was good. She slipped the leather vest on over the black, thermal, weave shirt she was wearing. He zipped it up. She put the leather jacket on. He zipped it up. All the while, Lana was watching him as he dressed her. She got that warm, liquid feeling inside as he touched her. Her knees felt weak. He walked over to the couch where he had set the helmet, picked it up, walked over to her, kissed her forehead, and then put the helmet on her head and fastened the chin strap. *Getting undressed in reverse*, was the thought that ran through her mind. He handed the gloves to her. She slipped them on. He tightened the wrist band. Then he reached around her with his right arm, pulled her close for a second, and said, "Let's go."

All dressed, they made their way to the door. Lana picked up her phone, keys, lipstick, and a comb and put them in the inner jacket pockets. Lana's heart would not stop racing. The excitement generated by his touch, the light kiss, and the anticipation of the ride became even more overwhelming when she put her arms around his strong back and pressed her chest into it as they drove away.

They were eventually on their way up Boulder Canyon as the road followed the curves of Boulder Creek all the way. Rugged mountainous walls lined the canyon. It was late September and there were still red, gold, and orange trees scattered among the pines. The winding river crashed over the rocks. Lana heard and saw it all. It was familiar but now more beautiful in its panorama. After about ten miles, Roadking slowed and stopped at Boulder Falls. They dismounted. The noise of the falls was in the background. Misty droplets of water floated in the air from the falls and peppered their faces.

"I just wanted to stop here for a minute. I'm hoping someone will take a photo of us here together."

Lana was surprised but pleased that he would want to memorialize their ride together in a photo. In a minute or two, a couple of hikers descended the nearby trail and approached them. "Would one of you mind taking a photo of us?"

"Certainly. Beautiful day for a ride," one of them said to Roadking.

Roadking handed his phone to a guy in a flannel shirt and biking shorts. Lana and Roadking stood side by side, his arm around her waist, and just as they took the photo, she turned to look at him. The hiker handed the phone back to Roadking and they looked at the photo. Lana always cringed at photos of herself. She was surprised at the expression on the profile of her face as she looked at Roadking in the photo. She was smiling, but even more than that, she was beaming. She hoped that he wouldn't think anything of it.

"Good one," he said and put the phone in his pocket.

Lana half expected him to check his email messages, voice messages, or texts while he had the phone in his hand. He did not. He was so different from Lucas. It appeared that Roadking lived in the moment when he was with her.

They mounted the Harley and headed up the winding canyon and arrived in Nederland. Roadking drove the Harley into the parking lot of the Conifer Inn. "I think they're still serving brunch here. What do you think?"

Lana agreed. They found a corner table. The brunch was an elaborate buffet served with champagne. Lana and Roadking approached the buffet. Although all of it looked fabulous, Lana was careful to pick out food that she could take small bites of with a fork. And she definitely wanted the champagne.

As the waiter poured the first glasses of champagne for them, Roadking held up his glass in a toast and said, "Here's to a beautiful day, a beautiful ride, and a beautiful companion."

Lana smiled and touched her fluted glass to his.

As they ate and drank, they talked some more off-the-record. Their conversation flowed from one topic to another—their favorite classic cars, the scar on her right hand, his days playing football, her friends, his friends, their hopes and dreams. The restaurant closed the brunch buffet at three o'clock. Lana and Roadking were still there talking. They had lost track of time.

"Well, let's head back. I wanted to take a ride up to the Caribou Ranch a couple of miles away. Maybe we'll do that another time."

They rode back down the canyon. Lana wanted the ride back to take forever so she could continue to hold on to him. But maybe there really would be another time. Less than an hour later, they arrived at Lana's house. They dismounted and removed their helmets.

As they stood face-to-face, Roadking put his arms around her neck and rested them on her shoulders, "Lana Ross, I had the best time with you today."

Lana smiled, her heart racing again. "Thank you, Vincent, for the special day." Lana wanted to invite him into the house, spend more time together, listen to some music, but then he received a text message.

He had ignored his phone all afternoon, but when he looked at it, the expression on his face changed from happy to serious. "Sorry, Lana, I need to make a phone call."

Lana went into the house to give him some privacy. He walked in the front door a few moments later. "Lana, I have to go. Some jackass threw two cinder blocks through the windows of the dealership a couple of hours ago. Right in broad daylight. My brother-in-law Will is there now with the Louisville Police. I need to see the mess and check if any of the bikes were damaged and check the security cameras. I'm sorry to cut our time short, Lana."

"Oh no, I'm sorry. If you can wait a second, it won't take me long to take the leathers off so you can have them back." Lana began to remove the gloves, the jacket, and vest.

"Keep them here for the next time. Talk soon." Roadking hurriedly hugged her, kissed her cheek, and was on his way.

Lana thought about his kisses, his hugs, him dressing her, his words—"beautiful companion" and "next time." She took off the leathers and folded them nicely in a pile, set the gloves and helmet on top, and laid them on a tan leather chair in her living room. She clicked on the TV. She didn't really watch it as thoughts of Roadking ran through her head. *I think I could be falling for this guy. I don't know what he really thinks about me, if anything. Maybe I'll never know. I'm confused. But I know I want him.*

A couple of hours later, Roadking texted Lana and told her that Monday would not be ideal for her photographer to come out to the dealership for photos and that he would be in touch to reschedule. *See*, Lana told herself, *it's just business.* But she hoped that she was wrong.

CHAPTER 12

On Monday morning, Lana told Tessa, the photographer, that the scheduled photo shoot at All Roads was being postponed because there had been some vandalism there and that Roadking would be in touch to schedule a new date and time. Monday came and went and there was no phone call from Roadking. She knew he was busy and that the photo shoot certainly was not the prime focus of his day. "Oh well," she said to herself many times during the day. She thought about him and how he knew that she was attracted to him because she did not resist the kisses or affectionate touches. *Maybe he's like that with every woman. Maybe there's nothing special about me. Maybe he thinks I'm easy,* she pondered. But then a different thought plagued her as she dreaded the idea of seeing Leon again when she got home. She could have contacted someone else in the security business for a system—maybe she should have.

Sure enough, when Lana arrived home from work, Leon Alvarez was already standing in the circle drive in front of the house, waiting for her. He had evidently been looking at the outside of the house and had written some things down on a yellow legal pad.

"Hello there, Lana, darlin'. I was just having myself a look-see at yer property to get some ideas about the kind of surveillance you want outside here. Probably some door sensors on all the exterior doors except the garage door. Maybe some wireless surveillance cameras near the exterior doors. You can use those to watch for deliveries, too, from yer phone. Can we go inside and take a look in there?"

Lana pulled the Escalade into the garage, and they entered the house through the garage entrance. She could hear him breathing heavily as he walked behind her again and could smell the smoke on him. She could feel his eyes on her backside as she moved ahead of him through the house from room to room and from access point to access point.

"You probably should have a couple of surveillance cameras mounted in a few places inside the house here, so you can monitor the inside of yer house when yer gone. I can set up some monitors that you can access from your phone to set the heat and cold in the house too. What do ya think of those ideas, darlin'?"

Lana cringed again at the word "darlin'" but told herself to ignore it, that it meant nothing. "Leon, I trust that you know what to do and where to put the monitors and cameras and sensors. I think you should limit the number of motion detectors just to the entrances of the house. There are stray cats and dogs and coyotes and skunks and wild rabbits that wander through the yard at night that I don't need to monitor. Go ahead and get the parts and let me know how soon you can install them. There have been some odd incidents in the house in the past few weeks."

Leon didn't ask her about the incidents. "I can have the parts in a couple of days, and it could take me a day to set it all up. Do ya need an estimate first?"

"No, just let me know when you'll be coming back. Do I need to be here for the installation?"

"No, darlin'. You won't be needed. After the install, I'll show ya how it all works, and you can let me know if ya need me to add more stuff."

Lana walked him to the front door.

Leon opened the door and stood on the landing for a couple of seconds giving her another long look. "See ya again soon, Lana, darlin'."

After he left, she could still faintly smell the tobacco and pot smoke scent from Leon in the house, reminding her that he had been there. Despite that, she was relieved to know that she would have some security soon.

She made herself a light supper of sautéed vegetables and rice.

She began to listen to one of her playlists. She had been listening to Bob Seger since Roadking mentioned it to her. Seger's beautiful song of deep longing, "We've Got Tonight", began to play, and the lyrics stayed with her all night.

"Oh, Vincent, why don't you stay? Someday?" she whispered quietly to herself.

On Tuesday morning, while Lana was in a meeting with the magazine art director and proofreaders, Roadking left a message. He said that he wanted to reschedule the session with the photographer for Wednesday morning at eleven, and he would like it if Lana would come along too. Lana checked Tessa's and her calendar and called Roadking to let him know that it would work.

"Lana, how have you been?"

"I'm good. What about you? What happened on Sunday?"

"Some guy walked up out of nowhere with two cinder blocks and threw them into the windows one at a time about one o'clock—in broad daylight. The surveillance cameras showed a guy dressed in a gray hooded sweatshirt, sunglasses, and gray sweatpants, carrying a cinder block in each hand. He casually walked away when he was done. There was nothing distinctly visible about him, except there was a bandana covering the bottom half of his face. By the time the police got here, he was gone. We can't tell if it was a random thing or directed at me or the dealership or what."

"Were any of the bikes damaged?"

"Fortunately no. When the glass shattered, most of it stayed in the frame of the windows. Any glass that flew out landed on some of the Harleys but with no damage. We just had to be careful to get all of it cleaned up."

"Well, it seems strange that something like that would happen on a Sunday afternoon. And during a Broncos game. I wanted to let you know that I got your message, and Tessa and I will be there tomorrow at eleven."

"Lana, I didn't feel good about leaving you like I did on Sunday. I really wanted to spend more time with you. But I know you understand. Don't you?"

"Of course. I had a great time on the ride and in Nederland. I didn't get the chance to tell you."

"We'll do it again before the winter weather sets in. Next time, how about north to Masonville? Or up the hill again to Blackhawk? Or south to Cripple Creek?"

"Any of those would be lovely. I'll let you decide. See you tomorrow."

At the end of the day when Lana got home, Leon was there waiting for her again. She thought he would call her instead of just showing up, but it didn't matter.

"Lana, darlin'. I have all the parts I need to set up yer security system. I'd like to start this week if possible, even tomorrow, if that's alright for ya. Why don't I come just before ya leave for work, so you can let me in and you'll know that I'm here."

"Okay, Leon, be here before eight thirty and you can get started. Nothing strange here has happened for a few days," She was feeling a little hesitant about him being in her house alone all day but reassured herself that he probably did it all of the time. After all, he was a locksmith.

"Well there, Lana, darlin', what's been a-going on?"

"Some things have been moved around in my house when I'm gone, a snake was somehow in the house one day, there was someone at the door in the middle of the night. And less sinister, a white rose was on the front porch the other morning. Just random stuff that's unsettling."

"Sounds like you got yerself an admirer," he snickered and then wiped the back of his hand across his mouth. "This here should put a stop to that stuff or at least you can see who is up to no good at yer house."

"Yes, that's my hope."

When Leon left, Lana went upstairs to change into her workout clothes. Once again, she stood and looked at her wardrobe to choose what she should wear when she saw Roadking again. Although everything she wore looked good on her, all of it seemed ordinary and bland. She decided on black bootcut jeans and a black shirt with tan trim, which accented her hair color. *He probably doesn't notice anyway*, she cautioned herself. She went downstairs and jumped on the treadmill for an hour.

Lana woke up Wednesday morning with her heart racing a little, remembering that she would see Roadking that day. Seeing him made her happy. But since Tessa would be there, the flirting would have to be kept to a minimum. Lana showered and dressed, applied her makeup carefully, and made sure that her long, red hair flowed perfectly down her back. But soon her sunny mood was tempered when she saw Leon arrive in his green van with the security system.

"Hi, Leon. Come on in. Call me if you have any questions about placement of the cameras, detectors, or sensors."

"Okay there, darlin'," he said as his eyes scanned her up and down and then up and down again.

Lana left him there and headed to Boulder to work. The morning seemed to move slowly even though she was busy meeting with the staff about the holiday edition, which would be published in a week. Tessa came by her office at ten thirty, and they left for All Roads together.

They arrived at the dealership a few minutes before eleven. The receptionist told them to wait a few minutes and she would let Roadking know that they were there. Lana could see him through the glass window in his office, and there he was with a pretty young brunette girl with dark eyes. He hugged her and kissed her on the head and walked with her out of the office. Lana's heart sank to the pit of her stomach. *I knew it. He was just too good to be true. I'm a fool to have let my feelings get out of control like I did*, she mentally scolded herself.

Roadking walked toward Tessa and her. "Hi, Lana. And you must be Tessa," he said as he reached out his hand to shake hers. "I'd like you to meet my daughter, Ava. She's a freshman at CSU. She came to hit up her old man for money."

"Pleased to meet you, Ava." Lana managed to force a smile. Her stomach felt queasy. He had not mentioned a daughter to her. Now there were more questions. *Was there a wife? More children? A family? Exactly what was his status?* She still didn't feel like she could pry. He had a life before he met her.

"Okay, let's take some photos of these bikes." Roadking put his arm on Lana's back as they walked toward the Harleys. Tessa began to shoot photo after photo. Lana was silent, gave no direction, and just let her do her job. Roadking suggested some angles for photographs. Tessa took a few of Roadking as well.

"You're a quiet little lady today," Roadking mentioned to Lana, who looked at the floor and gave no response. "Well, it's close to lunchtime again if either of you would like to join me."

Tessa looked to Lana for the answer. "No, I think we better get back to the office. We have a publication date coming up. Fortunately, we still have time to work on the touring Colorado articles for a spring issue. Thank you for taking time from your busy schedule again."

Roadking narrowed his eyes slightly as he looked at her, trying to figure out her icy, distant demeanor. But he attributed it to the presence of the photographer.

"Vincent, I forgot to bring the print photos back that you let me use for digitizing. I'll see to it that you get those back soon."

"No worries, Lana. I know you'll return them."

"See you, Vincent."

"Bye, Lana. Talk soon." Roadking wondered why Lana seemed cold toward him. It seemed that she was really into him before today.

Lana and Tessa drove back to Boulder. Tessa was hungry, so they stopped to grab lunch at a small café in East Boulder. Lana wasn't hungry but sat with Tessa while she ate a deluxe cheeseburger and fries.

"Lana, did you happen to notice how good-looking Vincent is?"

"Yes, of course."

"Do you feel okay? You were suddenly so quiet, and you aren't eating."

"I'm okay. So much has happened to me lately—I think it's all sinking in today." In truth, Lana was quietly beating herself up for her foolishness, becoming infatuated with Roadking, and letting it show. She let herself eat a couple of Tessa's french fries.

Lana's phone rang. It was Leon. "Hello there, darlin'. I'm all done with the install. I'd like to meet up with ya after work to set up the access codes and show you how this thing works."

"Okay, Leon. I'll be home around five. Thanks for your quick work."

"Not a problem there, Lana."

The afternoon dragged on, and Lana's mood remained unchanged. She was still stunned by seeing Ava and Roadking together. The fact that he had a daughter wasn't an issue. She was a lovely girl. But there was a mother somewhere and a past or present relationship with her. She couldn't ask. She still believed that he would tell her if he wanted her to know.

Lana arrived home to Leon. "God, I hope this is the last time I come home to him being here," she muttered to herself.

He met her in the driveway. "Okay, here's the control panel for the system. Yer monitors are here. The sensors are here. The cameras are here," he said as he pointed to the controls. "This button will disarm the security system if ya want to or if there's a false alarm. If the alarm's triggered, a signal is sent to the alarm company, who'll send police to yer house. Now to set up the system, ya need to punch in an access code. Think of a four-digit code that you'll remember."

Lana punched in 1-2-2-3.

"Now it's asking you to do it again."

Once again, she tapped in the numbers 1-2-2-3. Leon watched her as she inputted the code again.

"Now, Lana, darlin', it's set now. Whenever you have to reset it, you'll need to use that number. Now's let's have a look-see at the setup here now."

They examined the outside of the house. And the inside entrances. Everywhere that they had talked about. He gave her a drawing of each location of any security device. He showed her how to monitor the house on her phone.

"Thank you, Leon. It looks like you were thorough. So I'm all set up with the security company?"

"Yes, ya sure are there, darlin'." He handed her a bill.

She paid him and walked him to the door and disabled the alarm so he could leave.

"Thank ya for yer business, little gal." As he left, she set the alarm system for the night.

Lana was feeling moody. Olivia called, but Lana didn't answer. She just wasn't in the mood for her animated chitchat. She went upstairs to her bedroom to change into her workout clothes. She thought that a workout would elevate her mood. *Let it go*, she repeatedly told herself.

As she undressed down to a black, lacy bra and little matching lacy panties, she walked over to the window and looked at the horizon, the sky, and the landscape and stared for a long while. Her arms crossed in front of her like a hug. She started to unconsciously sway slightly back and forth, on one foot to the other, from side to side, as if she were rocking to the rhythm of a song that only she could hear, still looking out the window and thinking. In a few minutes, she shook herself from her thoughts and got dressed, walked downstairs, and jumped on the treadmill for an extra long workout. If it didn't help her mood, it would at least make her tired enough to sleep.

What she didn't know was that she was being observed as she stood there at the window, rocking back and forth in bra and panties.

"There ya go, Lana, darlin'. That's it, girl. Take yer time getting yer clothes on. Nice little ass." Leon parked up the road a distance to see if his monitor of the camera that he had secretly mounted in her bedroom under the top of the tall cherrywood chest of drawers was functioning like he'd planned. As he drove away, he lit a cigarette and smiled to himself and whispered out loud, "Let the show begin."

CHAPTER 13

Lana was on someone else's mind too. She had drifted into Roadking's thoughts throughout the day ever since he saw her standing in the showroom in the Harley jean jacket. With that first introduction, he felt as if he had always known her. There was something so comfortable and familiar and genuine about her presence. He thought about how his hand fit perfectly into the small of her back when he placed it there as they walked. He thought about her eyes—so changeable and transparent that, without her knowing it, revealed so much. *There's a lot going on in there,* he reflected. He even surprised himself that he spontaneously kissed her after their first meeting. But he knew he wanted more.

Lana didn't know it, but Roadking had seen her once before. Lana and Lucas had attended a formal charity gala ball in Boulder a few years earlier. Roadking, who was also a guest at the ball, had happened to look across the expanse of the ballroom and his eyes had caught the vision of a woman in a long, emerald-green, strapless, satin gown with long, flowing, red hair. She had worn a strand of pearls that held a diamond pendant. She was stunning and had stood out among the crowd. Throughout the evening, he had not been able to help but cast his eyes in her direction. Someone sitting at his table had commented about her dress. "That green dress was certainly an excellent choice for Lana Chisholm." Roadking had made a mental note that her name was Lana. As he'd glanced over at her, he had seen that Lucas, whom he recognized, had had his back to her and had been engaged in conversation with some other local businessmen most of the night.

For Lana, the next two days were a blur as the holiday issue was due for publication online and in print. Lana occupied her time by scrutinizing the digital copy and making minor recommendations. By Friday afternoon, she gave the go-ahead to publish. About three o'clock on Friday, the staff began to unwind, order pizza, and talk about their various weekend plans. Lana, always thinking ahead, looked at the timeline for the next *Boulder Essence* issue. She hadn't given the weekend a thought. She was happy to be so busy; it helped to keep thoughts of Roadking to a minimum. She chided herself repeatedly for being so naïve, for daydreaming, for believing. She organized her desk and made some notes on her calendar. There was a light knock on the door to her office. When she looked up, Roadking was standing there all dressed in denim with that beautiful smile. Her heart skipped a beat, and she imperceptibly gasped.

"Hey, Lana. Did I catch you at a bad time?"

"No, actually, it's good. The holiday issue is out for printing now and the pressure is off. What brings you to Boulder?"

"Well, actually, you. I didn't want to text you or message you or call you. I wanted to see you and ask if you'd have dinner with me tomorrow night. With no talk about Harleys or magazines. What do you say?" Roadking could see a little blush well up on Lana's face and he smiled.

"Well, yes . . . I think so. Like where? Uh . . . well, so I know how to dress." Lana was doing her best to be cool, but she was aware that she stumbled over her words and that her face was a little flushed.

"Dress as you want. It's not a Harley date. I actually have a couple of cars to choose from when I have to," he grinned. "There's a little European restaurant in Eldorado Springs called the Canyon Chophouse. You may have heard of it. They might even advertise in your magazine."

"I have heard of it. I'd love to. What time?"

"I'll be there about six thirty. I'll make reservations for seven thirty."

Roadking still stood in the doorway, and Lana was seated in her high-backed, black leather, and oak office chair. As he took a few steps toward her cluttered desk, Lana stood up and walked around it to stand close to him. When she was in reach, he touched her arm, pulled her a little closer, hugged her, and lightly kissed her on the left cheek.

"See you tomorrow, Lana," he said as he walked out the door.

Lana was still stunned that he had been standing there and they had a real date planned. She could still smell his light manly scent in the room. She reached up and touched her cheek where he had kissed it. She was suddenly aware that the office staff was still there. But no one had paid attention to them at all. They were lost in celebratory conversation and pizza. She walked over to the window of her second-story office to see him walking on the sidewalk below. The sun had cast little splinters of light on the few gray hairs on his head. She watched him until he turned the corner out of sight.

One never knows what surprise each day may bring, she reflected. She gathered up her laptop and purse, turned off the jeweled Tiffany desk lamp on the right corner of her desk and the brass floor lamp near the tan leather guest chairs, and closed her door. Not one to miss the significance of any moment, she pondered, *What will happen in my life before I open this door again?*

"Great job, everyone. Have a nice weekend. Head on out of here," she said as she walked among her staff to the stairs leading to the building exit.

As she drove home, she wondered what to wear for the date. She wanted to look good but not overdressed or underdressed either and wondered if she should get a manicure. It seemed like tomorrow was a month away.

Lana approached the house with the usual scan of the perimeter, even though Leon Alvarez had installed the security system. Since the installation, there were no weird occurrences inside or outside of the house. The presence of the system took the edge off her uneasiness.

After she set her laptop and purse down on the kitchen table, she went upstairs and stood and looked in her closet. Nothing seemed to her to look good enough or chic enough for her date. She moved the hangers of clothes slowly across the closet bar until she came upon a black dress that was classic and elegant in its simplicity. It was sleeveless and midcalf length with a loose fit and a handkerchief hem. *This dress will have to work. I hate shopping, especially at the last minute.*

For the rest of the evening, Lana worked out with some free weights and did two miles on the treadmill, watered her little herb garden in the kitchen window, and watched TV, not really paying attention to the content of the programs. The last couple of weeks since the divorce had been eventful, sometimes scary and confusing, but also revealing to her in a sense as the emotional numbness of her life with Lucas began to evaporate and be replaced by warmth and tenderness. Even so, she was still going to protect herself as much as she could. She was still plagued by questions about Roadking that she didn't want to ask. While she sat quietly on the leather couch with a blanket in her living room, she was unaware that she was being watched.

"Lana, girl, ya ain't been givin' me much to look at tonight. What's goin' on in that pretty little head?" Leon rasped to himself as he exhaled smoke.

Another camera had been covertly installed in the living room on the underside of her TV, which was mounted on the wall. Leon could see the entire room and the bedroom through the cameras he had mounted there. Soon he got a service call that someone had gotten locked out of their house and had to leave the monitor.

"Dang it. I'll have to watch a replay later," he grumbled to himself. But there was not much to see. Lana hurriedly undressed and jumped into bed. She was tired and wanted to sleep. Saturday couldn't come soon enough.

Lana awoke early Saturday morning. She wanted to tidy up the house a little, get a manicure later, and create a new playlist of songs to listen to with Roadking if the opportunity arose. She shuffled through her extensive list of favorite songs, cherry-picking the softer ones that weren't too mushy—those that she thought he would like best and that might remind him of her when he heard them again later. Since they both loved classic rock, she chose "Beautiful Blue" with Tom Petty, "Landslide" by Fleetwood Mac, several Eagles songs, including "Tequila Sunrise," and "Someone Like You" with Van Morrison. Then she chose some current tunes by Adele, Coldplay, and Chris Stapleton.

She decided to check the wine selections in her wine cooler. It was practically empty. Maybe he would want a beer if he stayed for a nightcap. Lana decided to go to the liquor store and pick up some pinot noir, a chardonnay, and some Negra Modelo and limes since she had seen him drink that before. She stopped at the cheese import shop and bought some brie, a Swiss cheese wheel, and some grainy crackers. She just didn't know what to expect and wanted to make sure that nothing was lacking. He might not stay long enough for music and drinks anyway.

As the afternoon began to wane, Lana began to sense the anticipation of seeing Roadking again. She showered again, picked out her best lacy underthings to wear, curled her hair, meticulously touched up her makeup, and slipped into the simple black dress. She chose some dressy tan sandals and dangly pearl earrings to finish the look. She sprayed some Chanel No. 5 into the room and walked into its mist to add a little scent but not too much. She looked at the clock. It was a quarter past six. There were butterflies in her stomach. He was coming soon.

At precisely six thirty, Roadking arrived as promised and with great fanfare. He was driving a classic, black 1966 Chevelle SS 396 with white leather interior and American Racing wheels with a two-inch lift so the huge tires wouldn't rub on the body. He and Lana had talked about their mutual fondness for classic cars, but she had no idea that he would drive up in her favorite classic model. She didn't wait for him to come to the door. She ran outside to look at it and listen to the muscle car rumble from the racing cam and the tick, tick, tick idle of its engine. Roadking could see that he had nailed it by her almost childlike excitement.

"How could you know? This is my favorite classic car. I love the sound of the engine idle, and it's so beautiful. Is it yours? I can't wait to ride in it. Oh, but do you want to come in for a drink first?"

Roadking could see that she was only interested in sitting in the passenger seat of the car and didn't want to dawdle over drinks. "No, Lana, grab your things and let's take this baby for a ride."

If Lana heard him, she didn't respond. She quickly began to walk to the house, grabbed her purse and a light gray tweed jacket, set the security system, and shut the door. Roadking stood by the passenger side with the door open. Before she could get in, he put his hand on her back, pulled her close to him, and lightly kissed her on the lips. "You look radiant tonight, Lana. Really beautiful."

"Thank you, Vincent," she said as she slid into the bucket seat. She felt awkward calling him Roadking. To her, Vincent was a more intimate and personal way to address him.

Off they went. He installed an excellent quality stereo, which happened to be playing Beach Boys music and then some Smokey Robinson. Lana was content, and for the first time in a long time, she was comfortably lost in the moment and not thinking about work schedules or deadlines or her past or her future. The drive to Eldorado Springs seemed to go too fast, even though the traffic in Boulder was heavy. They soon arrived at the Canyon Chophouse in Eldorado Springs, just southwest of Boulder.

Roadking had reserved a table in an intimate corner of the restaurant. It had a European feel with pinewood walls and booths. The tables were set with elegant, floral European china and crystal on crisp white tablecloths covered with a white lace overlay. In the background soft, classical, violin music was playing. The short white candles on the table were in tiny cobalt glass candleholders that softened the light in the room. There was a petite bouquet of white and pink flowers in a clear vase in the center of the table. Lana looked at Roadking in that soft candlelight sitting across the table from her and was awestruck by the handsome features of his face. Roadking was similarly struck by the glow on Lana's face—she was so naturally pretty, both inside and out. He knew that he had to get to know her better.

A young waiter approached the table with goblets of water and asked if they would like wine or cocktails before dinner.

"Scotch on the rocks, please," was Roadking's request.

The waiter turned to Lana, "And for the lady?"

"I would like a glass of pinot noir, please."

Roadking added, "Bring a bottle of Pellegrini 2014 Pinot Noir to the table for the lady."

The waiter brought the drinks and then menus. The menu had exquisite choices of European dishes, but Lana chose a Rocky Mountain trout baked in parchment with lemon butter and capers. Roadking chose prime rib and they shared a Caesar salad for two. They took their time eating and drinking. The conversation flowed from one topic to the next. The restaurant was getting ready to close when they finally finished and were ready to leave. Lana was happy that she would still have a little more time with him since they had a drive of about twenty miles to her house. She hoped that he would demonstrate the power of the SS 396 on the drive back, which he did as he left rubber on the street accelerating from a stoplight. For the time being, it didn't matter if he was married or not, had a family or not, or had girlfriends or not. Tonight belonged only to them and she would never forget it.

When they arrived at Lana's house, she scanned the perimeter of the house as it had become her habit. Roadking walked her to the door. Lana disabled the security system with her phone. As they walked into the entryway, Roadking stood behind her a step or two. She paused to turn on a lamp in the living room, and Roadking put his hand on her waist, turned her toward him, put both arms around her, and kissed her with a passion that Lana didn't know existed. She kissed back, her heart racing again. Her body began to feel warm and fluid and electrically charged.

When the kiss ended, Lana asked Roadking if he wanted to stay for a nightcap, listen to some music, or watch a movie. Roadking didn't answer. He could feel that she was really into the kiss before. He knew that she wouldn't stop him. He was right. He kissed her again and held her tight. Her arms were around his neck and she stood on her tiptoes. She could feel his hard body against hers and wanted more of it. His hands gradually slid down past her waist as he gently held a butt cheek in each hand. Then he slowly pulled the dress up inch by inch until his warm, sensual hands were on the bare skin of her back.

Lana had only one thought and she was ready for whatever would come next. She took hold of one of his hands and pulled him gently toward the stairs. He didn't resist. She led him to her bedroom. Lana had left a lamp on, and Roadking could see the bed where she slept and where he would lie in a minute or two.

Lana took her dress off over her head and dropped it in a heap on the floor. She kicked off her shoes. She was standing there in a black lace camisole and black lace panties. She reached over to Roadking and pulled his jacket off his shoulders and tossed it to the floor. Then she grabbed the waist of his pants and unbuckled his belt. She unbuttoned his shirt and nearly gasped at seeing his fabulous chiseled chest. She pulled him down on the bed. She straddled him as he lay on his back. She reached over and turned off the lamp. In a matter of seconds, all the clothes came off and they began a journey of lovemaking ecstasy that lasted into the night.

What neither of them knew was that those private moments that belonged only to them were being watched by a livid Leon Alvarez. "What the fuck, Lana! What are you doing with that bastard! You belong to me now. Hey, Harley-Davidson—I seen her first! I knew her first!" Once the lamp was turned off, Leon could only imagine what he couldn't see. He was enraged. His heart was beating hard and his hands were shaking. He couldn't believe what was happening. He threw the beer bottle that he had been drinking against the wall of his kitchen. That wasn't enough. He cleared the countertop cluttered with dishes and food with one sweep of his arm. He picked up a wooden kitchen chair and threw it at his flat-screen TV, shattering the screen, all the while yelling, "I seen her first! She's mine! Lana—yer mine! Ya touched her, ya bastard! You're going to pay!" He pushed his filthy dumpy couch over, revealing years of accumulated filth. He kicked a hole in the wall of his living room with the toe of his boot. The rage continued to flow through his veins until he was out of breath. He got into his beat-up van and began to drive, his heart still pounding with rage, body shaking, and breathing hard.

After several minutes, he arrived at his destination. He stopped and parked at the end of the long driveway leading to Lana's house. He could see from the monitor in his van that Lana had not reset the security system when she entered the house with that "son of a bitch." He grabbed a knife with a long, black, tarnished blade from the floor of the back seat of the van and began to walk swiftly up the driveway to the house, still muttering under his breath, "She's mine, you bastard! Ya touched her, you bastard! I knew her first! I seen her first!" He approached the black Chevelle SS 396 and viciously stabbed a tire as if he were stabbing Roadking. That wasn't enough, so he continued to slash the other three tires with the same amount of fierce force. "That bastard will know someone was here that he shouldn't fuck around with!"

Leon's adrenaline began to wane as he calmed down a little. His breathing slowed. The vandalism brought him the satisfaction he needed. What began as a night of bliss for Lana and Roadking would end up as shock in the morning light.

CHAPTER 14

Lana could not sleep with Roadking lying there next to her. She didn't want to close her eyes and miss a second of his presence in her bed by sleeping. She lay there and looked at his face, listening to his gentle and even breathing. She wanted to touch his face or his hair or his arm or his back so badly, but she didn't want to wake him. She could still feel him and where he had touched her. She was falling for him and she knew it. She was aware that she always linked emotion to sex—never one to casually sleep around.

The sun was beginning to rise and cast a pinkish yellow light into the uncovered windows of the bedroom. Roadking turned over, opened his eyes, looked at Lana, and smiled. "Good morning, Lana Ross." As they lay face-to-face, he could see the rosy glow on her face from the lovemaking that had ended just a few hours before. There was a little smudge of black mascara under her right eye, and she was still wearing the dangly pearl earrings from the night before but nothing else.

"Hello, Vincent," she whispered softly. She looked into those beautiful eyes with the dark lashes and could see a reflection of her own face, looking satisfied and affectionate.

"Well, pretty girl, what do we do next?" he asked as he pulled her close to him, her chest pressed into his, and her leg crossed over his body. He hugged her tight—a hug that she would still feel hours later. And then he kissed her forehead, her cheek, her neck, and dipped under the sheets and kissed her right breast. His mustache brushed her lightly with each kiss. Lana sighed softly and let Roadking know she wanted more of him when she pulled him on top of her. And the lovemaking from the night before was reprised.

Leon watched again. "You bastard! Yer on her again! I can't see nothin' with them sheets coverin' you!" Leon felt his blood pressure rising again and a rage building—equal to that of the night before. "Wait till ya try to go home, son of a bitch! I got ya! And I'll do it again!" Leon growled to himself but then took a breath and laughed loudly, amused with himself. He watched and waited and could see rhythmic movement within the sheets, but he saw nothing but what was in his imagination.

Eventually, Roadking and Lana lay again face-to-face, talking quietly while he stroked her hair. She held her hand to his cheek, smiling softly.

"What are ya saying to her, you slime? Making promises ya can't keep?" Leon ranted. He could barely contain himself when he saw them both naked and walking a few steps toward the bathroom. They partially closed the door and began to shower—together. Roadking took some body wash into his hands and massaged it all over Lana's back and front. He pulled her close as she pressed her chest into his. The soap on her body washed over him. She took some of the soap lather in her hands and rubbed it on his back and then playfully touched some of it on his face. They stood under the running water of the shower and kissed, tightly pressed together.

Leon was frustrated that he could not see them; it seemed that they were showering for so long. They emerged wrapped in towels and collapsed on the bed again for a few minutes. Leon was in a fury as he watched, but he couldn't make himself look away. He finally got up from the monitor. Maybe he had seen enough. He walked through his house, his boots crunching the broken glass under his feet from yesterday's tirade. He walked into the kitchen and picked up a knife from the counter, which was cluttered with dirty dishes and half-eaten food, and jammed it into the wall several times—each stab reminding him of the satisfying feeling he felt as he stabbed Roadking's tires. He walked to the hollow front door and punched a hole in it. Then he opened the door and went out to his van and kicked each door, one at a time, until he could see a dent in them all. He needed visible evidence of his rage and anger. Those boot shaped dents would be a reminder of that bastard Roadking touching Lana and how he'd made him pay. He rushed back into the house so as not to miss Roadking's reaction when he saw that all the tires on that beautiful SS 396 were flat and ruined.

"Are you hungry? I can make eggs and coffee and probably toast," Lana asked softly.

"Sure. I'm hungry. There's been a lot going on since dinner last night." He smiled tenderly at Lana, and she smiled with that little sideways grin she got sometimes when she was amused.

Roadking pulled his clothes on and Lana wrapped herself in a white, fluffy bathrobe. Leon continued to watch. "Hurry up there, Harley-Davidson! Wait till you see that high-class love machine now! I seen her first and you touched her! Yer gonna shit when you see those fancy tires all cut up," Leon snarled under his breath and grinned at the same time.

Lana and Roadking went downstairs and through the hall that led to the kitchen. Roadking sat at the long, dark pine kitchen table and checked his phone for messages while Lana made the coffee and fluffed the scrambled eggs. She set butter and chokecherry jam on the table. He was lost in the memory of his grandmother for a moment when he saw the jam. "My grandmother used to make chokecherry jam when I was a kid. I didn't know you could buy it now."

"I got it at that specialty cooking shop on the Pearl Street Mall. I liked the artwork on the label and didn't know that it would taste so good too. I'm hooked." Lana brought small glasses of orange juice and mugs of coffee to the table.

"Just black, please."

She filled two white porcelain plates with eggs and set a smaller plate with four slices of multigrain toast on the table. She handed a fork, knife, and napkin to Roadking and sat down on a chair beside him. They were both famished. After a few minutes of quietly eating, Roadking turned and looked at Lana and said, "Last night with you was so fantastic. I'm kind of at a loss for words. But just know—being with you means a lot to me. More than I expected. I want to spend more time with you."

Lana gently smiled at Roadking. She looked directly at his handsome face as she spoke. She didn't know what she could say to him that wouldn't sound desperate or mushy. But the words that he used gave her permission to be open with him. "Last night was perfect—from the SS 396 to the shower this morning. I feel so close to you now. You mean so much to me too." Lana was falling in love with Roadking and she knew it, but she was far too cautious to use the word "love."

Roadking smiled and kissed her lightly. His mustache brushed her cheek. When they finished eating, Roadking pushed the pine chair back and stood up and stretched. "I'm supposed to eat a big Italian dinner today at noon at my parents' house. It's my dad's birthday. I should head home and take care of a few things and stop by my office to write a few checks. I want to see you again soon. Dinner later in the week?"

Lana stood face-to-face with him and put her arms around his neck. "Sure, Vincent, give me a call and I'll make it work."

Roadking pushed his chair in and turned to walk into the living room. There was a wall of glass that spanned the south side of the room that faced the circle driveway. He was looking out the windows as he walked, stopped suddenly, and squinted as he looked out the windows, not believing what he saw and loudly exclaimed "What? What could have happened out there last night? Look at my car—oh my God! What the fuck? How? Who would do this?"

Lana walked behind him, looking at his back as he walked in front of her. She jumped suddenly when she heard Roadking's loud voice. All four tires on the SS 396 were flat. She was horrified when she suddenly remembered that she had not reset the security system when they arrived last night. But even so, it might not have picked up the activity in the driveway. Roadking bolted out the front door with Lana scurrying behind him. His face was flushed with anger and shock. He examined the damage to the car.

"Vincent, we should call the Boulder County Sheriff. I can't imagine something like this happening. There hasn't been vandalism this far from the main road before," she said. But the recent odd incidents in her house swiftly crossed her mind.

"What's the sheriff going to do? This happened on private property. Some jackass had to make a real effort to come back here off the road to do this. After the smashed windows at the dealership, could this be directed at me? What the fuck?" Roadking was shaken and angry and spoke loudly and harshly to Lana.

"What do you want to do? Should I call the sheriff?"

"No, Lana. I'll take care of this. I'll call Rick, one of my mechanics, and he can bring the car hauler out here and pick it up, and I'll ride back to Louisville with him." His voice clearly revealed how mad he was. He tried not to glare at Lana. It wasn't her fault.

Lana remained quiet as he surveyed the holes in each tire. She felt like she had walked into a brick wall. The day had begun so softly and gently. Now it was marred by this grim discovery.

All the while, Leon watched the discovery unfold, laughing loudly, slapping his thigh each time he shouted at the monitor as if he could be heard. "Hey, Harley-Davidson! What happened to that purdy car of yers? That will teach ya, son of a bitch! Ya touched her and ya had to pay! I ain't done with ya yet if ya keep it up with her! I seen her first! Ya better learn there, pretty boy!" He continued to snicker. He stroked one side of his black beard while he smoked a joint. The rage he had felt for hours turned into sick joy. He put an end to that little lovefest.

Roadking got on his phone. "Rick, some sick jackass sliced the tires on the SS 396. Could you bring the car hauler out by Columbine Point and pick it up and take it to the shop?" He turned to Lana. "What's the address here?"

"It's 1974 Hill View Road."

"1974 Hill View Road. It's west of Columbine Point a couple of miles. Just GPS it. Call me if you get lost. I'm not going anywhere." Roadking circled the car once again and looked at the damage. At one point he muttered to himself, "At least they didn't touch the paint."

"Let's go in and wait, Vincent. Come in with me." She was getting chilly standing there in the white robe. Roadking reluctantly followed her back in and sat on one of the leather couches for a minute. But he kept getting up to look out the front windows, to look at the car and watch for Rick to arrive.

"It will be a little while before he gets here," Lana spoke softly. Roadking didn't answer her. He continued to look out the window for a few more minutes. When he felt the silence in the room, he returned to the couch and sat next to Lana. She was silent. She knew that he was upset and didn't want to add to it with her comments. She touched his arm and slid her hand down to his and held it gently.

After several quiet minutes, he took his hand from hers and put his arm around her. "I'm angry about the car, but I'm pissed that the day began like this after the time we spent together last night. I'm sorry if I was harsh with you. I can buy new tires. It's just a car."Lana smiled at him and leaned into him and put her arm around his waist and laid her head on his chest. She could hear his heart beating rapidly. They sat there silently until Rick pulled the truck into the driveway with the car hauler.

"God damn it, Harley-Davidson! Ain't ya learned nothin' yet? Don't touch her!" Leon's blood pressure began to surge again as he watched them sitting on the couch together. But his anger was short lived when Roadking left Lana and went outside to meet Rick.

Lana stayed in the house for a few minutes while Roadking assisted with the loading of the car. She ran upstairs and quickly threw on a pair of jeans and a sweatshirt and went outside and stood with Roadking as the car was loaded with the hydraulic lift. Roadking introduced Rick to Lana. She shook his hand. She wondered for a second what he thought about Roadking being there, but it didn't matter anyway.

"Okay, Rick, let's get this baby back to Louisville." Rick got into the truck and looked out the windshield and waited for Roadking to get in.

"Thanks, Lana, for the awesome night." He smiled at her and

lightly and quickly kissed her lips. She hugged him tight around his waist. “See you soon, sweetheart,” were his final words.

Lana watched them leave and went back into the empty house. She felt the void of his absence. All the passion of the night before was no longer present but had been converted to a memory—an unforgettable memory.

CHAPTER 15

"Jesus, Roadking. What the hell happened back there?"

"Damn, Rick, I wish I knew. All four tires were punctured on the sidewalls. That was no accident."

"Who is she? Does she have an angry ex somewhere?"

"Lana Ross, recently divorced from Lucas Chisholm—you know, Chisholm Cadillac. She's never mentioned anything about him. It seems that it was a quiet divorce with no drama."

Roadking and Rick were silent for the rest of the drive back to Louisville. Roadking thought about Lana and the night before. She was so giving and sweet and made him so happy. The sex was earthmoving each time. She was one of those girls that a guy could fall in love with.

Lana went upstairs, sat on the bed, picked up the pillow that Roadking had lain on and buried her face in it, breathing in his manly scent. All she was able to do was relive those past hours with him. She closed her eyes and went over each moment in her mind. The car, the dinner, the wine, the ride, how he felt, his touch, his kisses, the weight of his body—she burned them into her memory, not knowing if there would be another night with him and never wanting to forget a single moment. Her heart was telling her that he was the perfect man and that she was due for some heart-racing passion. Her head was telling her, "Don't get your heart broken."

The discovery of the tire damage wafted through her thoughts and interrupted the afterglow that surrounded Lana for the rest of the day. She wasn't her usually productive self, not wanting to do any tasks or think about anything other than Roadking. *Just let today belong to him.* But as for the car, she had the same questions in her mind that Roadking was pondering. *Who could have somehow sneaked down the long driveway to the house to slash the tires? Was it random or directed at Roadking or Lana? When and how did it happen?* The circumstances were so strange and unexpected and had cast a dark shadow on a heavenly night.

And there were still those lingering questions about him, too, that resurfaced. *What exactly is his relationship status? A family? A wife? An ex-wife? A girlfriend?* He had spent last night with her, so he wasn't expected anywhere. She was doing it again—too much overthinking and so many questions were going to ruin the essence of passion that Lana felt was still present in the bedroom. None of that mattered last night. The night belonged only to them.

In the early afternoon, Olivia called Lana and wanted to meet her in Columbine Point at a new Thai restaurant. Time spent with Olivia always revolved around food. Lana wanted to say no and spend the day at home. But she should eat something, and she had ignored the last phone call from Olivia. She touched up her make-up, brushed her hair, and curled it a little. She was still wearing the jeans and sweatshirt she threw on when Roadking was there. She didn't really care. She pulled some boots on, set the security system, and left for town. Lana arrived almost the same time that Olivia did. As they opened the door to the restaurant, Lucas stepped into the entryway, exiting the restaurant. Seeing him there caught Lana completely off guard, and she spontaneously spoke up and said, "Oh, Lucas."

Lucas stopped and took a step backward, surprised that Lana was standing there. He reluctantly said, "Hey," looked down at the floor, and walked toward the door.

Lana watched him as he walked to the parking lot and noted that he had a new bronze Cadillac Escalade.

"Jeez, Olivia. It's been awhile since I saw him. His face looks so sour and sulking. You know, I feel absolutely nothing for him at all, except relief that I don't have to deal with his gloomy glumness anymore."

Olivia laughed. "That sounds like a perfect description of him.

Do you suppose he was meeting someone here? Maybe a woman?" They snickered as they walked to their table and began to talk about the week and weekend as they were seated. Lana was reluctant to share any of the details of her private moments with Roadking, but she mentioned that they had had dinner at the Canyon Chophouse in Eldorado Springs the night before.

"So you've been with him a couple of times recently. What gives, Lana? Any spark there?"

"Well," Lana paused, ". . . he's so good-looking and nice to be around. That's all there is to say." Lana had clasped her hands and placed her index fingers to her lips, lost in thought for a few seconds.

Olivia had seen that contemplative gesture many times and took the hint. Lana might eventually tell her something, but she knew it would never be the full story. As they were eating their pad thai, Olivia mentioned that their friend, Sara White, had had a new baby boy. "Lana, all of our friends are having babies. Do you ever think about having a baby—some children? I think about it sometimes. Don't you?"

"You know, when I married Lucas, I guess I figured there would be a couple of children, a little family. As the years went by and I didn't get pregnant, it didn't seem to matter to either one of us. And in hindsight, it worked out for the best. Lucas's babies are his Cadillacs. Yeah, I think I would like to be a mother. At thirty-three, there's still time to have kids. But I want to be in a committed relationship with someone who would love to parent with me. My own upbringing was so different than most kids, and I wonder what kind of a mother I would be, too, because of that. I want to teach them everything I can, and I want them to remember that I did. What about you, Olivia?"

"I think it would be fun. I know it's a lot of work and expense. I would be a fun mom, but I don't want to do it by myself either—unless I start to run out of time to make babies. Then I'd have one anyway. I worry that I'd gain fifty pounds and then keep it. You know how I struggle."

They each sat quietly for a minute, envisioned their futures with kids. When they finished eating pad thai and mango sticky rice for dessert, Olivia went back to Boulder and Lana headed home.

For the rest of the day and evening, Lana wandered from room to room, trying to get things done, but she could not focus. The racing heart that was created by Roadking's touch was still racing. She wondered how his day was going after the way it had begun. She started listening to the playlist that she'd created for them to listen to the night before.

Early in the evening, she heard a ping on her cell phone. There was a text from Roadking. He had not done that before.

Lana, just thinking about you and last night. Awesome.

Lana smiled and texted back.

Yes, it was.

Maybe there would be another night with him. She whispered, "Please God, let that happen."

Lana went to bed a little earlier than usual. After all, she had been up most of the night before. She undressed quickly, threw on a T-shirt, and jumped into bed. She pulled Roadking's pillow over to her side and buried her face in it again and hugged it all night. *Silly and juvenile, but who will know?*

Leon would know. He was watching, disappointed that there wouldn't be much of a show for him. He hated that son of a bitch Roadking, and he knew that Lana was thinking about him. "Lana, girl, one day you'll be thinking them same thoughts about me," Leon snickered to himself, stroking his dirty beard.

Monday morning arrived quickly. New deadlines were set for the next *Boulder Essence* postholiday winter issue. Lana scheduled several meetings with her staff to make assignments and follow up on the current progress of the next issue. Future issues of the magazine were constantly in development, and Lana was busy setting priorities for the staff. She let her mind drift to Roadking and the weekend several times during the day but managed to stay on task.

The work week moved slowly. Lana wanted to see or at least talk to Roadking again, and he had said that he wanted to have dinner during the week. As the days went by and there was no contact with Roadking, Lana began to worry that his interest in her had been wiped out by the vandalism that had occurred at her house. Despite the magic of the night with him, she was afraid that the exquisite memory would forever be linked with the shock and anger attached to the discovery of the destroyed tires of the SS 396. She went home every night, hoped he would call, kept herself busy, cleaned, organized, worked out on the treadmill, and wore herself out so she could sleep.

"Lana, darlin'. Ya ain't givin' me much to look at. I'm gettin' tired of that routine of yers. I seen a little bit of bra and panties and not much of anything else. I need to see more of those good lookin', little body parts."

Late Friday afternoon Roadking texted Lana.

Can I pick you up at your office and take you someplace special for dinner?

Lana eagerly replied.

I would love to. When should I expect you?

Roadking responded.

Soon.

She didn't ask him where they were going. He evidently had someplace in mind. Lana hurriedly pulled a mirror out of her desk, touched up the mascara, blush, and lipstick. She wasn't really dressed up for a fancy place, but the black tweed blazer, white shirt, and gray pants would have to do. She unbuttoned another button on her shirt to show a little cleavage.

About thirty minutes later, Roadking stood in the doorway of her office. He rapped lightly on the trim that surrounded her office door. Lana stood and walked around her desk and hugged him. He embraced her tightly. She was smiling at him when he looked down at her face.

Lana's staff had already left for the day, so they were alone. He held her right hand as they walked out of the building to the stairs and to the parking garage below. This time he was driving a black Range Rover. He opened the door and she slid in. As they drove, they headed east out of Boulder. In a few minutes, he turned into an upscale residential neighborhood near Louisville. He drove into the driveway of a large two-story Tuscan-style house, which was laid out in a half circle on the lot. The exterior was stone. The property was elevated somewhat so she could see the city lights of Louisville, which were beginning to sparkle as the sun set. They pulled into the three-stall garage at one end of the house. In one stall, the SS 396 was parked, looking good as new. In the other slot, there were two Road King Harley-Davidsons parked side by side. One was the classic Road King that she had ridden on with him to Estes Park and Nederland. The other was a newer model Road King.

"Vincent, is this your house? Is this the 'someplace special'?" She was happy that he was willing to share some of himself with her by allowing her to visit his home.

"Yes, baby, it is." They stepped into a long hallway that lead away from the garage. Lana's house was large, but this house was twice the size. They stepped onto travertine tile in shades of tan and brown as they entered the kitchen. The kitchen had two islands—one for food prep with copper pots and pans that hung over it and one that was surrounded by tall black barstools to eat at. The countertops were covered with glistening black granite. The cabinets were a light wood like ash—some of them with beveled glass inserts in the doors. A chef was in the kitchen, overseeing dishes that he had prepared on a large stainless steel commercial stove.

"Lana, this is Paolo Carlotti. He is a head chef at the Carlotti Bistro in Superior. He was good enough to agree to come by tonight and make us a wonderful Italian meal when I asked him to."

Paolo, a middle-aged, stocky man with a thick Italian accent, said, "I have brought my nephew, Anthony, to be your server tonight. I see, Vincenzo, she is a lovely lady that you brought here tonight."

"Nice to meet both of you," Lana smiled at them and then turned to Roadking and wrapped her arms around his waist momentarily and said, "This is a lovely surprise and I can't think of a more special place. Thank you."

As they waited for the meal to be prepared, Roadking took her into a large living area. There were two long, grayish-tan, overstuffed leather couches. Two walls of the room were completely glass with no window coverings. A large fireplace with a carved wood mantle stood opposite the windows. The fireplace facade was covered with river rock. There were two large abstract paintings on the walls painted in hues of dark green, burgundy, purple, and gold. The floor was a wide-planked pecan. Lana noticed that there weren't a lot of knickknacks in the room, which is how she preferred it. She could feel the ambience of the room that was created by the glass, the leather, the river rock, and the subdued lighting, as well as the presence of Roadking.

"Come sit by me, Lana," he said as he took her hand. Lana sat close to him on one of the leather couches. Soon Anthony stepped quietly into the room and asked them if they cared for drinks. "Macallan on the rocks. And make the lady an Italian margarita."

Anthony left the room. "I know that wine is your second choice. Here at my home, you'll get what you want." He put his arm around her and pulled her close.

Lana surveyed the room. Music was playing quietly in the background—"Wicked Game" by Chris Isaak.

"Roadking, your house is beautiful." She looked up at his face and smiled and then rested her head on his chest. The house revealed so much about him.

"I'll give you a tour of it after dinner."

Anthony brought the drinks to them. Roadking sat forward a little as he took his drink from him. "Well, did you notice that the SS 396 in the garage is as good as new?"

"Yes, it looks great. You know, I've thought about it so often this week and I just can't imagine what could have happened. It's not like you ran over something."

"I know. It's all good. I put that incident behind me. I want to concentrate on you tonight." Roadking held up his glass of scotch and said, "How about a toast to us?"

Lana touched her glass to his and took a sip of the margarita. The amaretto in the margarita made it Italian.

Anthony announced that the first course was ready to be served. Lana followed Roadking into a dining room with a long walnut dining room table that sat twelve people. The backs of the chairs were each hand carved with a different winding design. Six long, white candles stood lit in the center of the table. The ceiling was beveled with a crystal chandelier centered in the vault. Roadking pulled a chair out for her next to his seat at the end of the table. Anthony brought out melon wrapped in prosciutto on small, white china plates for each of them.

"Vincent, I can see your Italian heritage prevalent throughout the exterior and interior design of the house." Roadking had visited Italy, and the conversation had turned to the art and architecture in Italy, his visit to the Vatican, and his description of the white beaches on the Mediterranean.

The second course of polenta with mushrooms and fontina was served. Lana was happy that the courses were light thus far. She sipped all the margarita. Roadking beckoned Anthony to bring her another.

The entrée course was grilled salmon topped with crabmeat and capers and a light cream sauce served over a small portion of spinach fettuccine mingled with diced zucchini, yellow squash, and red peppers. The food that the chef prepared for them was so elegant. Roadking had put great effort into making it a special night for them.

Lana tried but could not finish the entrée. Anthony brought them small bowls of mixed berries drizzled with a balsamic glaze topped with a tiny dollop of whipped cream laced with apricot brandy. "You don't have to eat that right now. Anthony, please put these in the refrigerator for later."

"Vincent, what a special dinner. And you're right, it's a special place." They walked back into the living room, each carrying their drinks. Music was still playing softly through the room—the *Jersey Boys* soundtrack followed by Adele's love ballads.

"Well, let me give you a tour of the rest of the house." Roadking took Lana's hand as he led her through a long hallway with rooms on either side—an ornate powder room, his home office with oak paneling and lots of leather, and a guest bedroom with all white linens. As Lana surveyed the house, she couldn't detect anything in the interior design or decorating that signaled a woman's touch.

In the center of the long hallway, a massive curved staircase with a carved railing emerged. There was an open sunroom with a large bay window directly at the top of the stairs that looked to the east and to Louisville's city lights. The first bedroom down the hall contained white furniture with pink bedding and room accents. "This is Ava's room. You met Ava. She rarely spends time here now that she's in Fort Collins, but she has a place when she wants to come home."

Lana wanted to ask him about Ava, but before she could say anything, Roadking said, "Ava's mother, Shannon, and I met in college. Ava was conceived in our sophomore year. Neither of us considered anything other than having Ava and keeping her. Because we were in love, we knew that she was supposed to be ours. We never talked about marriage. In fact, we drifted apart shortly after Ava was born, but Shannon and I always took joint responsibility for her and let her know that she had been wanted."

Lana was relieved to finally know the answer to at least one of her questions. He was so sensitive and candid as he talked about Ava. Lana simply said, "She's lucky that you're her dad."

Roadking led her to his bedroom. It was large with a deck

extending out of two twelve-paned French doors. The bed was a massive, walnut four-poster. The chest of drawers and night tables matched. The comforter on the bed was stuffed and puffy and was a patchwork of burgundy, black, navy, and dark green squares. The master bedroom led into a large bathroom with a sauna, octagonal tub surrounded by marble and travertine tile, and a clear, glass walk-in shower.

Roadking, who was still holding her hand, led her to the bed and they sat down side by side. "I think that Paolo and Anthony can manage to let themselves out when they finish cleaning up." Lana smiled, and he kissed her softly, then again and again. They lay back on the bed pressed closely together. Soon Roadking took off his shirt. Lana stood up and took off her pants and shoes. Roadking stood and unbuttoned her shirt. He turned off the lamps in the room. He picked her up and laid her on the bed. They didn't bother to turn back the comforter and sheets. She unbuckled his belt and slid her hand into his pants. Roadking took them off and slipped Lana's blouse off. As he lay on top of her, Lana could feel he was ready for more. Soon their bodies were entwined, making love with breathless passion that lasted for a few hours.

Lana and Roadking fell asleep around midnight after they slid into the sheets and under the heavy comforter. But someone else was still awake, watching and waiting for Lana to come home, wondering where she was, but assuming he knew who she was with. Leon had watched the monitors of Lana's house since early evening. Looking at it every few minutes, unable to walk away from it. He had been sitting for hours, smoking cigarettes, lighting joints, drinking beer, and hurling the beer bottles against the wall. "Lana, darlin'. Yer killin' me here. Where the fuck are you? With that Harley-Davidson pretty boy? I know that yer car ain't left Boulder yet," Leon snarled to himself. He turned on the TV just for some noise and maybe a distraction. But he sat for hours and watched the monitor. His blood boiled and his temper flared as he became drunk and stoned. He finally couldn't take it anymore and got into his beat-up van and somehow drove to Boulder. He had to see for himself if her car was still at her parking garage, even though the GPS tracker that he had covertly stuck to the underside bumper of her car one day indicated that the car was still there. "Lana, girl—ya musta left with someone. Who was it? Where are ya, girl? That Harley son of a bitch touching you again? Ruining you? Yer s'posed to be mine no*w*. Fuck!" he screamed to himself when he drove in and saw the Escalade still parked in the parking garage at *Boulder Essence*.

He would wait there for her and watch for her return no matter how long it took. The night turned into the wee hours of the morning. His rage and despair continued to build. The knife that he had used to puncture Roadking's tires was lying in the back on the floor of the van. He picked up the knife and held it over his right thigh and began to carve the word "LANA" in his right leg, slicing through his jeans, not caring about the blood or the pain. He dropped the knife on the floor and looked at his bleeding leg as the blood saturated his jeans. The cut was about a quarter inch deep, and Lana's name was about four inches long. It was deep enough to leave a permanent scar. He found some paper towels and covered his throbbing, bloody leg and continued to wait as the sun began to rise that Saturday morning.

CHAPTER 16

Lana woke before sunrise. She lay next to Roadking looking at the silhouette of his profile in the darkness for several minutes. As the sun began to rise, the emerging light sharpened the image of his face. He was so good-looking, classy, smart, generous, and comfortable to be with. Lana was falling in love with him—so easily, so soon. Roadking began to stir. He turned toward her, lying on his left side. He reached for her and turned her body so that she was lying on her left side, facing away from him and then pulled her close to him, her back touching his chest—spooning. He was so affectionate and romantic. Lana had no idea how he felt about her. But the effort that he made to make the night special let her know that he cared. They lay there for several minutes. Roadking nuzzled his face in the back of her neck, kissing her lightly, and quietly said her name.

"Lana. What are you thinking about this morning, pretty girl?"

"Well, Vincent, I was thinking about the beautiful surprise dinner that you made happen and the tour of the house and the awesome time with you right here in this bed." Lana turned toward him, looking into his eyes, and said, "No one has ever made me feel so important."

"You're special. I knew it the first time I saw you." He pulled her close and hugged her tight, their bare chests pressed together. After a few minutes, he said, "As much as I hate to, I need to get you back to Boulder to your car and open the dealership at nine. You lay here, I'll shower and get dressed and go downstairs and make you some breakfast." Lana was a little disappointed. She wanted more lovemaking. She couldn't get enough of him. Roadking got up and quickly showered and dressed.

"What can I get for you? Eggs, coffee, toast, juice?"

"Just orange juice. And how about the berry dessert from last night too?"

Lana washed her face, touched up her makeup, and dressed. She would shower when she got home. She wasn't going to waste a moment showering and primping when she could be spending a few more minutes with Roadking.

She went down to the kitchen. Roadking set places for them to eat their breakfast at the island with the high stools. He poured juice and set out the bowl of berries for her. And he placed a tiny bouquet of six pink and white miniature roses in an Italian crystal vase next to her glass.

"These are for you."

Lana was overwhelmed with her feelings for him, which had grown so strong in just twenty-four hours. She could physically feel the love for him literally swell in her chest. *How is it possible for a man to be so caring, romantic, and sexy?* She felt tears well in her eyes very slightly. She blinked them away quickly, not wanting to reveal intense feelings for him just yet.

"You're so kind to think of flowers. When I take them home, they'll remind me each day of last night with you."

Roadking smiled while he finished scrambling eggs for himself. He soon sat next to her with eggs, toast, and the berries. They ate silently for a few minutes until Roadking commented, "We didn't finish the tour of the house last night after I showed you the master bedroom." He chuckled for a second. "Do you want to see the rest of the house?"

"Sure," Lana said as she finished the berries. Roadking stood and took her hand and they walked to another wing of the house. There was a large exercise room with an elliptical, a weight machine, a treadmill, free weights, a weight bench, and a large flat-screen TV. One wall of the room was completely glass with glass doors that looked out onto a large flagstone patio with a firepit, built-in outdoor barbecue, brick pizza oven, hot tub, and sauna. The patio was furnished with a glass and wrought iron table and ornate wrought iron and wood chairs. It was tastefully landscaped with blue spruce and greenery to provide privacy but not block the sun. The lawn was large and was dotted with some hardwood trees that held red, gold, and bronze autumn leaves. At a corner of the property was a manicured putting green.

"Vincent, this place is like a resort. It must be hard to leave it each day. It's so impressive."

"Thanks. I just think about coming home to it each night." They exited the exercise room and backtracked to the massive staircase. On the second floor, in addition to the sunroom and Roadking's bedroom, was another guest bedroom furnished with a hand-painted antique bed, chest, and vanity. At the end of the hallway was a long, rectangular room with a library and two walls of bookshelves filled with books and a couple of oak writing desks and chairs. At the opposite end of the room was a theater with seating for eight people and a large, retractable projector screen for movies. One wall of the room contained floor-to-ceiling windows with room-darkening shades mounted above and operated by remote control to eliminate glare in the theater.

"Well, that's the old Romano homestead."

"You must be so comfortable here. Thank you for giving me the tour." Lana realized that she didn't really know exactly where they were and that she would have to make a mental note of the address and street name when they left. His address was 33 Empire Canyon Drive. She hoped he would invite her back again.

Roadking began to drive Lana back to Boulder. She took note of the route taken from his house to her office. He reached over and placed his right hand on her leg above her left knee. His touch left her feeling electrified all over again. She placed her right hand lightly on top of his. Music was playing softly on the stereo- "Open Arms" by Journey.

Leon was lying in wait in the *Boulder Essence* parking garage for hours. He was determined to see her return and see who she was with. He could only guess what she had been doing all night. His carved right leg stung and throbbed and oozed blood through his sliced jeans. But it didn't match the pain inside that was caused by the surge of his obsession for Lana and his inability to have her for himself. He tried not to doze. He was parked between two other cars so she wouldn't see him in the garage.

After the sun had risen for an hour or more, Leon saw a black Range Rover pull into the parking garage and stop near Lana's car. There she was with that Harley-Davidson bastard! He saw that Lana and Roadking leaned into each other for a long, slow kiss in the front seat of the car. In a minute or two, Roadking got out, walked around to Lana's side of the car, and opened the door. She put her arms around his neck and gave him a full body hug and another long kiss. He put his arms around her waist—his hands slipped down to her rear end and he held her close for a moment. She reached into his car and took out a small vase of flowers and walked to her car. She turned toward Roadking, smiled, and waved to him as he drove away.

Lana got into the Escalade and began to drive home. She was on autopilot, unaware of anything but her intense thoughts. Lana already missed Roadking. The special night was over. If only time could be reversed about twelve hours, she could do it again. It was so perfect. He was so perfect. "I think I love him," she quietly said aloud, surprising herself at hearing those words. "I'm sure I do."

"I fucked up," Leon snarled quietly to himself as he watched Roadking and Lana say goodbye. "I got her all secure in that there house and now she don't need me fer nothin'. I need to go back. I need to go back there," he repeated to himself. He waited for Lana to leave the parking garage before he drove out. He was sleepy, half-stoned, and in pain.

Lana arrived at her house around nine in the morning. All appeared to be well. She turned off the security system and went in the house. She ran upstairs to take a shower and change. She was energized by happiness and jumped on the treadmill to spend some of the energy. About ten minutes into her workout, the doorbell rang. Leon Alvarez was at the front door.

"Hi, Leon. What brings you out here today?" Before he could

answer her, she noticed the bloody, sliced-up pant leg of his jeans and blurted out, "Jeez, Leon, what happened to your leg? Are you alright? Do you need bandages?"

"Aw, just a little mishap with a knife. I'm good there, darlin'."

Lana was alarmed at seeing the large blood stain on the thigh of his jeans. Her apprehension built slowly as he stood there. She could hear his heavy breathing between his words as he spoke.

"I just wanted to check to see if the system is workin' like you thought it would and if I need to make any adjustments to anything. Everything been okay out here?"

Lana studied his face as he spoke, trying to discern his honesty. In addition to the bloody pant leg, he looked more disheveled than usual, and the scent of smoke was pungent. His eyes were flaming red. She reluctantly spoke, "Well, actually, there was some vandalism here in the driveway last weekend during the night. I guess I told you that I didn't think that areas beyond the proximity of the house would need to be monitored by security cameras, but I've since changed my mind and would like one that would scan the circle driveway in front of the house and possibly one at the entrance to the driveway from Hill View Road. What do you think?"

It didn't matter to Leon. He could turn the fake system on and off at will. Nothing would keep him out.

"Why sure there, Lana, darlin'. It can't hurt to have a little extra security. I can probably get it done next week, maybe Tuesday or Wednesday. Just got to mount a couple of devices. So you say that there was some vandalism back here off the main road?" Leon feigned ignorance.

"Yes, a car belonging to a friend was parked out front and all of the tires were punctured. Nothing like that has ever happened back here before."

"Aw, it was probably some dumb-ass kids up to some mischief."

"Maybe. It was upsetting though."

Good, Leon thought. *I ruined the little love connection goin' on that time.* As he stood there, he could smell the scent of Lana's shampoo on her wet hair and the scent from her soap on her body.

He looked at her glowing face, freshly washed, rosy, and happy. *What a beauty!*

"Well, I'm glad I stopped by. Do you mind if I have a look-see out there to figure out what I need to do?"

"No, go ahead. I guess I'll see you next week. Leon, you better take care of that leg." Lana shut the front door, stood behind it, and peeked out at him in the front of the house. It was shocking to see that dried, caked blood on his pant leg. He seemed oblivious to it and unconcerned. "I hope that this is the last time I have to see him around here," she muttered to herself quietly. After about fifteen minutes of scoping out the camera locations, Leon got into his van and left.

Lana felt relieved when he finally left. He looked at her with such intensity through those red eyes. He made her skin crawl. Everything about him felt subtly threatening. But seeing him today still couldn't dissolve the afterglow of the night with Roadking.

Lana hopped back on the treadmill for a couple of miles, working with the free weights at the same time. When she was finished, she brushed out her hair that had since dried. She hadn't called her parents for a couple of weeks.

"Hi, Dad. How have you been? How's the weather in Steamboat? Got any snow yet? Seen any celebrities in the shop lately?"

"Hey, Lana. I'm good. We got a little snow. Not enough to bring in the skiing crowd yet. It's been a little warmer than usual. But you know we can end up with ten feet of snow in a day or two. Actually, a couple of rock stars were in the shop last week and bought some stuff. But I don't remember the name of the group they were with. Such weird names anymore. What's new with you? How's the job going?"

"The magazine's doing good. We just published the holiday issue. I sent you a print copy in the mail a couple of days ago. Did you get it yet?"

"No, but I'll watch for it. Seen Lucas around since your divorce?"

"Yes, I ran into him momentarily at a restaurant. He could hardly stand to look at me. Dad, there's nothing there between us anymore. I'm bound to run into him from time to time since we both live here. But I'm seriously okay without Lucas. In fact, I've had a couple of dates with a man—Vincent Romano. He owns a Harley-Davidson dealership in Louisville."

"Hmm . . . I know him. I've met him. Good-looking guy. He was up here in Steamboat a few years back. He came into the shop with a little blonde gal and they looked at some jewelry. He bought her a silver bracelet. About a week after that, he gave me a call and wanted me to design an engagement ring for him to give to her. So he and I exchanged some emails about the design and I put it together for him. He wanted me to create a wedding band that matched it, but I never heard from him again. I wondered what happened to him and that little gal. Her name was Cameron. I remember that because it was a different name for a girl and I engraved it on the inside of the ring. It was white gold with an emerald and—"

Lana interrupted him. She had already heard more than she wanted to know.

"Dad, that's okay. I don't need to know all of that. He and I haven't really talked much about our pasts. Both of us probably have some baggage. We're just getting to know each other. But he is really nice and treats me well. Dad, I've only been divorced for about a month."

Her dad continued to make small talk like always. But those words "the little blonde gal" circulated in her head, and she didn't really listen to him. Now there were new questions. *Who was she? What happened to her? To them?* Lana scolded herself. None of the answers to any of her questions had anything to do with what she and Roadking shared last night and in the morning. She and her dad talked for a couple more minutes. Lana decided not to call her mom. She knew she wouldn't hear a word she said. Maybe tomorrow.

Lana spent the rest of the day grocery shopping, cleaning up, answering emails, and paying bills. She kept herself busy, but all the while she was thinking about Roadking and his house, the dinner, the passionate lovemaking, and sleeping with and waking up next to him. She could still feel him. She felt that she could spend the rest of her days wrapped in his arms. But those thoughts were interrupted sporadically by the flashbacks of Leon standing at the front door with bloody pants and the mention of the "little blond gal" Cameron by her dad.

Early Saturday evening as Lana was surfing Netflix and Amazon for a movie to watch, Roadking sent her a text message.

Last night was incredible. Let's do it again.

Lana smiled. She wanted that too. She texted him back.

It was and let's do. Soon.

CHAPTER 17

"Where would you like me to put these?" Miranda, the receptionist, held a large bouquet of long-stemmed, white roses and calla lilies, with an assortment of fresh white flowers and sprigs of eucalyptus.

Lana looked puzzled. "Set them on the bureau over there. Thanks," Lana pointed across the room.

Lana loved white flowers. They reminded her of lace. No one knew that but Lucas. She had selected all white flowers for their wedding. Lana got up from her desk and, with dread, walked over to look at the card that was attached. Just as she thought—they were from Lucas. It read "Lana, could we meet for lunch or dinner this week? We need to talk. Enjoy the flowers. I know you love white. Lucas" Lana shook her head. She was finished with Lucas. *What was he up to? What did he have to say?* He had never sent flowers to her office before. Maybe there were some papers left to be signed. That should be communicated through the attorneys. Thinking about him was going to put a damper on the day. It was Monday morning and she had just run into him on Saturday. She decided to text him and get it over with.

Lucas, thank you for the white flowers. If there is something that wasn't addressed in the divorce proceedings, our attorneys should handle it.

His response was:

Lunch at the Boulderado tomorrow at noon?

He did not respond to her comment about the attorneys. She didn't know what to do. Contact from him was so unexpected and unnerving. He was so cold and manipulative. Lunch seemed harmless enough, but she didn't want to see him again. She decided not to respond. She remembered that just a few weeks before, a long stem white rose had been left by someone on her front porch. *Could Lucas have left it there?*

The rest of the day was filled with production staff and editorial meetings. Lana let her mind drift to her time with Roadking last Friday night when she could. That romantic feeling of being with him was hard to shake, and she had to admit, she didn't really want to. As she drove home from work, she listened to the playlist that she had created for them. Romantic, soft, lyrical songs with beautiful melodies like "Someday Soon" with Firefall.

As she approached her house, she saw that Leon's dented, green van was parked there. *Oh, jeez. Not again. I hate to see him there when I get home.* She pulled into the driveway and he walked over to her car and leaned his head into the window. She couldn't open the door with him standing there, but she didn't want to be any closer to him anyway."Hello there, Lana, darlin'. I was just checking on some other stuff for the additional monitoring you want done out here. That okay, darlin'?" The smell of smoke in her face was staggering. At least he wasn't wearing bloody jeans this time.

"Yes, I suppose so, Leon, but you can just call me and let me know that you're coming by."

"Well, them other parts will be here tomorrow fer the driveway cameras and monitors, so I'll be over here tomorrow or Wednesday. I'm telling ya now, Lana."

"Okay, see you tomorrow or Wednesday then." Lana pulled the car into the garage. Leon lingered awhile longer in front of the house and finally left.

As Lana walked into the house from the garage, she thought that she detected a light scent of that smoky smell that always emanated from Leon. She didn't expect that there should be a reason for him to be in the house yet. As she thought about it, she guessed that the pungent smell was still in her nose from talking to him for a minute.

Lana left her laptop and purse on the couch, turned on some music, walked into the kitchen, and poured herself a glass of red wine. While she took the first sip of merlot, she wondered, *what is Vincent doing right now?* She returned to the living room and sat and watched the October sun set through the west windows. Soon she heard a ping from her phone—a text from Lucas.

Tomorrow lunch?

Lana muttered to herself, "Crap. He isn't letting it go. Maybe I better get it over with."

Okay, noon at the Boulderado. I have a meeting at 1:00. It will have to be a quick lunch.

Lana finished the glass of wine and ran upstairs to change into workout clothes before she made dinner for herself. The house was wired for sound and the music followed her to the bedroom. As she got undressed, she started to feel the dance rhythm of "Can't Stop the Feeling" by Justin Timberlake. She danced around the room in her pink bra and white lace panties—twirling, swinging her hips, singing along, feeling happy—she was falling in love and ignored the negativity associated with Lucas's text.

But she didn't experience that euphoria alone. "There you go, Lana, girl. Givin' me a show in your little undies. Nice moves there, darlin'. I ain't seen much of that lately. Keep a goin'." Leon smirked as he watched Lana on his monitor and whispered to himself as he held a pair of Lana's pink panties in his hands. Lana's nose had not misled her; Leon had been in the house, in her bedroom, and in her drawer, stealing souvenirs for himself.

When the song was over, still undressed, Lana tidied up the bedroom and master bathroom, hung up clothes, and changed towels.

Leon lit a cigarette as he watched the show. "Oh, Lana, girl, that little body of yers is gonna be mine. Yer gonna beg fer me," he smiled and growled to himself as he twirled his mustache.

Lana threw on her workout clothes and went down to the kitchen to make a light supper—a turkey and Swiss cheese sandwich on multigrain bread. She ate quickly for no apparent reason and jumped on the treadmill for a couple of miles while she worked out with light weights.

For Leon, the show was over. "Until the next time, Lana, darlin'." He raised his beer can up as if he were toasting her.

Lana woke up Tuesday morning regretting that she had agreed to meet Lucas. It was that same feeling of dread that she had felt each day in the last few years of their marriage. Dread of interacting with him, dread of his criticism, dread of his cold touch. She reassured herself. *It'll be okay. You're free of him. Nothing he says or does has any significance now.*

Fortunately, the morning flew by quickly as she met continuously with her staff about the winter edition of *Boulder Essence.* At 11:55 a.m., Lana left the office and walked over to the Boulderado. She saw that Lucas had secured a table for them already. She walked slowly and suddenly felt oddly apprehensive about seeing him. He stood as she approached the table, put his hand on her back, and pulled a chair out for her. The waiter brought goblets of water and a bread basket.

"How have you been, Lana?" Lucas took a slice of bread and added butter to it.

"I'm good. Keeping busy. Working hard at the magazine." Lana was a little uncomfortable with the small talk, but she assumed that Lucas was attempting to temper the awkwardness of the meeting. "Lucas, what did you need to talk about?" Lana cut to the chase.

The waiter returned to take their lunch order. Lana ordered a house salad with balsamic vinaigrette. She wasn't going to order lunch that would take any time to prepare.

Lucas, on the other hand, ordered a burger, which would take a while. Lucas began to shift a little in his chair as he began to speak. "Lana, I've had some time to think about it—so how do you feel about giving us a shot again?"

Lana's face gave no hint of a reaction, although she was stunned by the question. She felt a twinge in her stomach. She reached for a piece of bread and looked down but felt Lucas's eyes on her. She looked at his face, and in an even tone, she said, "Lucas. Where is this coming from? We were separated for eight months. We've been divorced for almost two months. Never once did you give an indication that you wanted us to stay together—that you wanted me to stay."

Lucas stiffened into a defensive posture. "You wanted to go. I let you go. But I thought you'd change your mind when you realized that you had it made with me. It was a mistake."

"Lucas, I'm doing fine alone. I'm quite happy getting to know myself again. I have my friends, work, the house. I'm thinking about taking a ballet class and learning to play golf."

The waiter brought lunch plates to the table, and the conversation was silenced for a minute.

"So is one of your 'friends' that Romano from Louisville? Exactly how long has that been going on?" His face began to turn red while he spoke. He quickly moved from a defensive posture to an angry one. His words were measured and spoken through a clenched jaw.

Lana spoke calmly and evenly to him. "I just met Vincent Romano for the first time a couple of weeks ago on a magazine assignment. Yes, I've been out with him a couple of times. How would you know that anyway? I heard that you were dating someone too. I'm okay with it. We're both young, and it's time to set our lives on track again."

"I've been out with a couple of women. They don't mean anything. You and I looked good together. People are beginning to ask about you and it's embarrassing to tell them that we split. They look at me like I'm a loser, or they get a feel-sorry-for-you look on their faces. I don't like it. Lana, the holidays are coming up and I want you to come with me to the functions that we always attended. Can you do that much?"

"No, Lucas, it would be dishonest. Not only for appearance's sake, but to ourselves. I will not be attending any holiday functions with you. Lucas, it's over. You know that. I'm not coming back." She tried to take small bites of her salad.

Lucas had not touched his burger. He kept his eyes on her, in disbelief, tried to read her face, and refused to understand.

"You owe me. You owe me big time. You would be nothing without me." He quietly snarled through clenched teeth.

Lana spoke quietly. "Lucas, I used to believe that. You said it often enough, but now I believe in myself. It's time that you listened to me. I want you to move on as I have. There are plenty of women who would love to accompany you to the holiday balls and parties. Thank you for the lunch and the white flowers. I have a meeting in about twenty minutes that I need to prep for." She set her napkin on the table, pushed her chair back, stood, touched Lucas on the shoulder, and quietly left. He closed his eyes momentarily as she touched him.

Lana returned to her office and sat in her big chair behind her desk. She took a deep breath and sat motionless, replaying the last hour in her mind. She didn't know if she should feel sorry for Lucas or if he was manipulating her like he always did. The whole incident was so sudden and unexpected. Touching him on his shoulder as she left was a gesture of closure for her. She hoped that he would interpret it that way too. The afternoon drifted by slowly.

She left the office a little early and headed home. Her refuge. She drove home in a silent car with no music. She was confused by Lucas and didn't want to think about him anymore. The decade with him began to replay in her head. But she knew herself well. Tomorrow would be a new day, and she would put the incident away in her mind before morning.

Leon was in the driveway when she arrived at home. She was seriously not in the mood to see him, but he told her that he would work on the driveway monitor. *Shit. Why today? Oh well, I asked him to do the work.*

She rolled the car window down. "Hello, Leon. What's going on today?"

"Well hello there, Lana, darlin'. The entrance to the driveway is monitored now, and I expanded the vision of the yard monitor. Now ya told me that ya didn't want no bells and whistles going off on the system when someone drove in and breached the electronic field, but a light will go off on the instrument panel when someone turns in the driveway. Or if they park in front of the house. Okay now, I think I got this right like ya want it—no alarms unless someone tries to open a secured door, but cameras monitor all the areas we talked about that you can see on yer phone and on the home monitor. Now remember, ya got yer panic button on the system in case ya need to get help anyway. But when the system is disarmed, the monitoring continues, but the doors are no longer secured. Ya got it there, Lana? Ya just can't ferget to secure the system. It's gotta be a habit."

"Yes, I think I got it. It seems simple enough. At least I can see what's going on around here. Thanks, Leon. Do you have a bill ready for me to settle up with you?"

"Not yet there, darlin'. I need to do some figgerin'."

"Okay, drop it by or mail it to me. I want to take care of it as soon as possible. Thank you." Lana pulled into the garage and shut the door. She entered the house and went to look at the instrument panel for the system and reset the alarm. She sat on the leather couch and looked at the monitoring system on her phone She saw Leon drive out on the driveway monitor. She didn't feel energetic enough to change her clothes or work out or even make herself something to eat. She turned on the TV and flipped to Netflix. There must be a good movie or series that could distract her. She chose a romantic comedy to watch. When it finished about two hours later, she finally got up and found a bottle of brandy and poured herself a double shot. She wanted to sleep all night and start a new, fresh day. She put thoughts of Lucas out of her mind and reflected on Roadking—his voice, his gentle touch, his laugh, his enjoyment of life. Thoughts of him made her smile and put a rosy glow on the next minutes and then hours as she fell asleep on the couch.

Lana was asleep for a few hours. The house was dark except

for the glow of the TV, which was still on. For some reason, she woke suddenly, opened her eyes, and turned her head toward the TV. But her vision of it was blocked by someone sitting on a chair a few inches away from her face, looking at her! She sat up with a start, her heart raced, adrenaline surged to the top of her head, and when she finally focused, she saw who it was.

"Lucas! What—what are you doing? How did you get in here? Lucas!" she gasped, gulping for air.

CHAPTER 18

"Come on there, Lana, girl, wake up. I ain't seen my little peep show yet. I know yer gonna change out of them fancy work clothes." Leon was stationed at his usual spot, monitoring Lana's moves while he watched reruns of *Dukes of Hazzard* on his iPad. He got up and walked to the kitchen to get himself a beer. He stepped on and crunched broken glass from his tirade days before. "I guess I oughtta clean that up one of these times," he muttered. He decided to make himself a bologna sandwich, pushing aside bottles and half-eaten food in his refrigerator to find what he needed.

He returned to the living room to check the monitor. But while he was absent, a man had appeared in the living room with Lana. He had pulled up a chair and sat with his face close to hers as she slept.

"What the fuck! This don't look right. Who the fuck is that son of a bitch? She doesn't even know he's there." Leon's blood pressure surged to the top of his head as anger gripped him. He ran out the front door and jumped into his van. He laid rubber as he left his house. He repeated to himself over and over, "I gotta get there! I gotta get there! She's mine!" He continued to monitor Lana's living room with the phone app as he drove, trying to watch what unfolded, trying to drive, swerving to get around pedestrians and vehicles turning, and refusing to stop at stop signs.

"Hi, honey. I'm home!" Lucas's laugh was diabolical as he spewed those words.

"Lucas, you're drunk! You stink! Get out of here now!" Lana scooted across the couch to the opposite end from where her head had been lying. She curled her knees up in front of her. Lucas reeked of bourbon.

Lucas still sat on the chair near the couch. He turned to Lana and spoke through gritted teeth. His face was red and his eyes were bulging. "I'm not done with you! You can't walk out on me and believe that you can get away with it, bitch! You made me look bad! You took my money! I gave you so much! Look at this house—you'd be living in a chicken coop without me!"

"Lucas, get out of here! I'm warning you! I'll trip the panic button. You will not get away with it! GO NOW!" Lana roared at him.

Lucas sneered and wiped the back of his hand across his face. "Oh yeah, Lana, you're always so damn smug and smart. But you forgot one thing. I still have the garage door opener. You forgot to change it out or take mine from me. You dumb bitch! Now here I am. Getting in here was a piece of cake."

Lana slowly started to lean forward to get up. She needed to run across the room to the entryway and trip the panic button. Lucas lunged for her and knocked her back into the arm of the couch. She was trapped in the corner. She began to kick and scream. "Get out now! Get out, you bastard! Now!"

Lucas grabbed one of her ankles and pulled her toward him as she kicked. Lana continued to kick and squirm. She grabbed the remote next to her and pounded him on his head with it. He was unfazed. The light from the TV screen flickered like a strobe light as the scuffle continued.

A few minutes passed, and Leon glanced at his phone again and saw that Lana had woken up and was fighting hard. It was difficult to see what was happening with only the flickering light of the TV. He was still three miles away and was driving eighty to ninety miles an hour.

"Let those cop bastards chase me—I'll lead them right where they need to be." He looked at the phone again. Now Lana was pinned down by the intruder. Lana's face was wrapped in terror, and the man's face was contorted with hate.

"Lana, hang on!" Leon hollered.

Lucas grabbed the waist of her pants and pulled Lana toward him. At the same time, he slipped his right hand inside her pants and sat on her leg. With his left hand, he grabbed the front of her blouse and tore the buttons open and off. The front of her blouse was in tatters. She kicked at him with the other leg. She landed a swift kick to his chin, knocking his head backward momentarily, but he still hung on to the waist of her pants. He pulled at them, trying to yank them off.

Lana squirmed and screamed, "No, Lucas!"

He finally broke the zipper and pulled them down a few inches. "Now let's see what you got here, little bitch!" He lunged at her and fell on top of her.

She could smell the musky rank odor of whiskey as he breathed into her neck. Lana's thoughts were flashing like a strobe light. She could only think of her survival at that moment. The blood in her head pounded. *He's going to rape and kill me, isn't he? My life can't end like this.* Words shot through her mind like an electric shock.

She was able to grab the remote again and hit him sharply in his temple. This time he reacted. Still lying on top of her, he took his hands and put them around her neck and began to squeeze. She couldn't breathe or talk or move. He looked directly into her eyes with a fury she had never seen before as he pressed on her neck. She didn't know the monster that he had become.

Oh God, please hear me now! Please help me now! Please, God! Lana's thoughts screamed for her survival. Her options were running out. He was too strong. *Oh God! Oh God! Oh God!* She chanted in her mind like a mantra. Her head began to feel like it was swelling and the white light in the room began to dim and change to a hazy yellow color.

In a matter of seconds, the security alarm was tripped and shrilly screamed through the house. One of the doors must have been breached somehow. Lana heard swift footsteps on the hardwood floor and then the loud pop of a gunshot. Lucas lurched and groaned and reached for his right shoulder. He turned in the direction of the shot and stood up. Blood gushed from a bullet wound.

Lana wiggled away from the corner of the couch, took some big gulps of air, stood unsteadily, and backed away from the scene but kept her eyes on Lucas. Then she turned and saw who had fired the shot—it was Leon! *Leon shot Lucas!*

Lucas lunged toward Leon, shouting "Who the fuck are you?" but fell on the floor facedown, drunk, and bleeding. He lay there and didn't move while Leon kept the gun pointed at him.

"Lana! Call the police! Now! This piece of shit ain't going anywhere."

Lucas started to drag himself up, but Leon kicked him in the ribs, not once but twice. Each time Lucas flinched and groaned in pain. He couldn't and wouldn't get up, but he managed to growl, "You're gonna pay. I'm Lucas Chisholm."

Leon laughed loudly. "You're scum." And kicked him again.

It was over. Lana shook uncontrollably. The adrenaline continued to pound through her body, and she felt like she might faint. Leon saw that she was wobbly, and she tried to regain control of her breathing. Despite the thrill of seeing her half-dressed, he could see that she was fragile. Lana clutched at her clothes and tried to hold them together. She wanted to change out of them immediately, but she couldn't move.

Lana found her phone and dialed 911. "Please send someone to 1974 Hill View Road! I was attacked by my ex-husband and he's been shot! We need an ambulance. Please hurry! Now!"

Leon calmly said, "Go sit down over there, Lana, darlin'. Go on now. The sheriff will be here in a few minutes." He walked over and turned the screaming alarm off.

Lana slowly moved to a chair near the window to watch for the authorities to arrive. She saw Lucas's Escalade parked in the driveway but away from the house. Then she saw Leon's van parked up by the house on the lawn and in her flower bed, headlights still shining.

Leon was watching her, and before she could ask, he said, "When I drove up, I seen what looked like some trouble through the window. I grabbed my Glock and jumped out. I guess I fergot to put it in gear." Lana looked blankly at him.

In a matter of minutes, but what seemed like hours, Boulder County sheriff's officers and an ambulance arrived. Lucas was loaded up and taken to the hospital, where he would be under police guard. They would question him later.

But as Lana began to calm herself, questions began to emerge in her mind. She was silent, still stunned by the attack and unable to formulate the questions into words yet. She replayed the events of the past hour in her head in slow-motion, dissected them, and examined them for answers.

Soon a woman from the Victim Advocate's Office arrived to assist Lana if she needed it. Lana, never one to request help, took her business card and said she would be in touch if necessary.

The woman smiled and, sensing Lana's stubborn self-reliance, said, "My name is Mary. Lana, I can at least sit with you here for a while. Do you need to see a doctor? Hon, you can't stay here tonight. They'll be investigating the crime scene for several hours. There's blood on your floor. Can you stay with someone?"

"No doctor. Maybe I'll have some bruises." Lana spoke almost in a whisper. She thought for a minute. *Who should I call? Olivia or Cate? Vincent? No, I don't want to involve him in this mess. It would scare him away.* "I have to think. Maybe just a hotel room tonight. I know I can't stay here. It's getting late and I don't want to bother my friends."

Lana could hear Leon talk to the police as they questioned him. "Yeah, I was just driving over here to give Lana a bill. I been doin' some security monitoring work for her and she wanted to pay me. And when I drove up, I seen what looked like a scuffle of some kind through the window. Not knowing what was goin' on, I grabbed by 9 mm Glock from my van. Looks like I fergot to put it in gear and it rolled forward out there. I was in a hurry. It looked like she was in danger. I kicked the front door and it wouldn't open, but since I'm a locksmith, I used a passkey I have on this ring on my belt and opened the door. That bastard was strangling that little gal. She was squirming and trying to get away, but she couldn't. I shot the son of a bitch in the shoulder right where I aimed to."

"What is your relationship to Ms. Ross or the perpetrator?"

"Well, none. I done work fer her and I don't know that sorry bastard."

"We'd like you to come to the Sheriff's Office to make a statement within the next twenty-four hours. We may have more questions for you."

"Sure thing there, Sheriff." Leon had nothing to hide except for his phony security system, which he didn't believe would be part of the investigation.

Lana was still sitting in a chair near the window and could see that a couple of local press vans had ascended on the house. She didn't think about it before, but the events that had just transpired would be the source of news for days to come. She was so private."Oh no. Go away. I don't want this kind of attention," she whispered to herself. Mary patted her on her hand.

"Ms. Ross, could I ask you to tell me what happened here?" Lana turned toward a sheriff's officer and quietly began to tell him what she had experienced, what was said, who Lucas was, and her last conversation with him at lunch that day.

When she was finished, he said, "We'd like you to come to the office within twenty-four hours to make a formal statement. We need photographs of the crime scene and, unfortunately, of you as you are right now."

Lana stood as he photographed her from all angles—clothes in tatters, hair in tangles, deep scratches on her neck and chest, her face smeared with mascara.

Within minutes, her phone began ringing and pinging with text messages. She couldn't make herself talk to anyone. They would have to wait. News of the attack and shooting must have broken on local news stations.

Mary gently spoke, "Lana, you need to go to your room and pack a small suitcase so you can leave for tonight or a few days. This will be a crime scene for several hours and there's blood on the floor and couch. I'll make arrangements for you to stay tonight at a local hotel. Do you want to stay in Columbine Point or Boulder?"

"Columbine Point. I'm not up to driving any distance at the moment." She could still feel the pressure of Lucas's hands on her neck.

Lana went upstairs. As she walked into her bedroom and turned on a lamp, she glanced at the bed—the bed where she and Lucas had slept together for ten years. "I didn't know you at all," she whispered. Then all of it descended on her and she sat on the edge of the bed, sobbing, holding her face in her hands. Tears trickled through her hands and down her arms and onto the torn clothes. After several minutes, she was all cried out. She stood up, washed her face, and began to take off the clothes she wore. She threw on her workout clothes and went to her closet and took out a small suitcase.

When she began to walk downstairs, she heard a familiar male voice talking to the sheriff's officers about what had happened. It was Vincent—the Roadking. He turned toward her as she descended the stairs. When she reached the last step, he walked over and hugged her and held her for a long time, her head resting on his chest, not saying a word, as tears welled up in her eyes.

"Lana, Rick saw something on the news about a shooting here and I had to know you were all right. I had to see that you were all right." He looked at her sad face as she tried to muster a smile for him. She didn't want him to see her like this. But she had never felt safer. She was so relieved to see him. Pointing to Mary, the victim's assistance advocate, he said, "She tells me that you're staying in a hotel in Columbine Point tonight. You're staying with me. Come now. If you guys don't need anything more from her tonight, she is coming with me." The sheriff's officers shook their heads no.

Out of the corner of her eye, Lana saw Leon standing there watching them—staring at them. She needed to thank him. He saved her from being strangled at the hands of Lucas. "Just a minute, Vincent." She walked over to Leon and instinctively hugged him around his smoky neck for a quick second. "Thank you, Leon. I'm so thankful that you showed up here so unexpectedly. I owe you so much. And the bill? Where is it? The bill you brought by for me tonight?"

"Yer welcome there, darlin'. Uh, it must have flown out of the van when I drove up and saw what was going on in here. I'll bring you another one."

She returned to Roadking's side and he turned to Leon and said, "Thanks a lot, man, for all you did for her tonight. I'm grateful too." He took her hand as they walked out the door to his Range Rover.

Lana couldn't see it, but underneath Leon seethed with anger. *That son of a bitch comes waltzing in here and takes her away from me after I saved her again. Maybe she would have come and stayed with me if I'd asked her first. That pretty boy's gonna know he shouldn't have come between her and me.* His burning hate for Roadking was only tempered slightly by the thought of the little hug from Lana.

"Are you guys about done with me?" Leon asked the officers. He wanted to leave. He wanted to leave now that Lana had left with Roadking. The officers told him he could leave but reminded him about the formal statement he needed to make at the station the next day.

He backed the van off the lawn and saw that he didn't damage too much of the landscaping and made his way through the mass of emergency and press vehicles. "I ain't done with you yet, Harley-Davidson. Yer gonna end up in worse shape than that son of a bitch I just shot. She's mine," he growled to himself.

Roadking was silent as he drove. Lana leaned her head against his arm, even though the console was between them. She closed her eyes. He rested his right hand on her left leg. Music played softly on the radio. Don Henley sang "Taking You Home." Roadking had so many questions for her. He knew she would talk about it when she was ready, but he would never pressure her, especially not tonight. His only thought was to calm her and let her know that she was safe and loved. He was beginning to realize that he was in love with her. He would never let anyone hurt her again.

CHAPTER 19

"I hate that Harley-Davidson asshole. She just melts all over him. Pretty boy, I ain't done with you. But tonight that fuckin' coward Lucas Chisholm is gonna pay. Mr. Cadillac. He hurt her. She's mine. I could have killed the son of a bitch if I'd wanted to," Leon grumbled to himself through clenched teeth. The wheels were turning in that stoned head of his. He was hatching a plan to let Lucas Chisholm know that he had gone too far. As he reached the end of Lana's driveway, he did not head toward his house but instead in the direction of Chisholm Cadillac on the south end of Columbine Point.

He drove by the Cadillac dealership slowly, scoped out the security cameras, and looked for the best spot to create some mayhem. He parked a couple of blocks away, reached in the back of his van for his gray sweatshirt, and pulled it on over his head. He tied a navy handkerchief around his face and pulled the hood up over his head. He reached into the back seat and picked up a heavy length of chain about thirty-six inches long and attached a heavy padlock to the end of it. He walked around to the back of the van, opened the doors, and searched through the trash in the back for what he needed—beer bottles, rags, and gasoline. He slowly poured some gas into each of two beer bottles, careful not to spill any on his hands. He tore the rags so that they fit in the neck of the bottles. Already done—Molotov cocktails—so easy.

He threw the chain over his shoulder and carried a cocktail in each hand. He was unnoticed as he walked up the street. It was late on a Tuesday night. No one was out driving in the industrial neighborhood near Chisholm Cadillac. He would have to act fast since alarms would be triggered. There were two Cadillacs parked near the dealership building, not directly under the bright security lights in the parking lot. He took the chain, wrapped a small length of it around his hand, and swung the chain with the padlock end against the windshield of the brand-new silver Escalade with all his strength. Crack! The windshield cracked, but it did not break. He swung the chain even harder a second time. The windshield shattered and fell inside the car. *Perfect,* he thought as he lit one of the Molotov cocktails and threw it inside. Within seconds, the car was engulfed with orange flames surging through it. The car alarm had gone off when the windshield had shattered. Leon hopped around, laughing out loud from the thrill of the arson. The reflection of the fire was dancing in his reddened eyes. "I believe I'm gonna do it again." He walked over to a new, white ATS Coupe parked ten feet away and smashed the windshield on the first try, lit the second cocktail, and threw it in the car and watched it ignite. *Whoosh!* The alarms in both burning cars screamed. "Well, that's my signal to get the fuck outta here." He walked away quickly, turning back a couple of times to look at the cars in flames. His eyes reflected the flames and flickered with exhilaration. Within a minute or two, police and fire trucks arrived. But it was too late for the Cadillacs and too late for Leon to be caught at the scene. Leon had sent a message to Lucas Chisholm, but Lucas would not know who the sender was. Leon got into his van, took off the handkerchief, and pulled down the hood, then drove away slowly. "Well, I don't remember when I had this much fun in one night—shooting one son of a bitch and then burning two cars." His devilish, red eyes gleamed as he snickered to himself.

"Lana, wake up," Roadking whispered and gently shook Lana's left leg with his hand. "We're here." Roadking pulled into his garage. It was about eleven o'clock at night.

"I wasn't asleep. I just had my eyes closed. I just didn't want to look at the world for a while."

As they walked into the house, Roadking asked, "Are you hungry? Thirsty? What can I get you?"

"Nothing really. I just want to sit down here for a little while. Then can I take a shower? I need to wash Lucas off me."

"Of course. Whatever you need."

"I know it's late, but I think I should at least text my friends, my parents, and my staff to let them know that I'm okay. They may have already heard about it." She saw multiple missed calls and texts on her phone. She paused for a moment, "And to tell them not to make statements to the press."

Roadking sat quietly and watched her while she sent texts. He turned on some soft music. Lana wrote, "You may have heard that there was an incident at my home tonight. I'm okay and will be in touch with all of you tomorrow. You'll see things on the TV and in newspapers. Please do not make statements to the press."

"Okay, Vincent, I'm done. Can I shower now?"

Roadking carried her bag and walked her upstairs to his bedroom. She looked so vulnerable and small. He hated what Lucas had done to her. He watched her remove some things from her bag. "Lana, I see that you packed some clothes for work. You can't go to work tomorrow. That's only a few hours from now."

"I'll know better in the morning," Lana said with a sigh.

Roadking didn't want to argue with her. He was aware of her refusal to ask for help and her fear to appear needy. He would have to convince her to stay there in a way that would make her think it was her decision.

Lana went into the master bathroom to shower. She stood and let the water rain down on her head with her eyes closed for several long minutes. She was wrapped in a big, fluffy, white towel when she came out, with her hair tangled and dripping. "Do you have a T-shirt I could borrow for tonight? I forgot to bring something to sleep in."

"Of course." When he looked at her, he saw long scratch marks on her chest where Lucas had clutched at her as he'd torn her shirt open and bruises at the base of her neck where he had squeezed. "Lana, come here. Did you see what he did to you? Let's get some Neosporin for those scratches. You might need something to help you sleep too." He pulled her close to sit on his lap for a few minutes. She was still quiet. He slid her onto the bed and went to his dresser and pulled out a black Harley T-shirt for her to wear.

She unwrapped the towel and pulled the T-shirt on over her head while he stood there. She didn't care that he watched her. Then she picked up the towel and began to towel-dry her hair. He walked into the bathroom and returned with Neosporin and a sleeping tablet for her.

"I'm not quite ready for sleep yet, but I don't want to keep you awake. I know it's late. Should I go to one of the guest rooms and sleep?" Lana almost whispered as Roadking gently applied the ointment to her chest. He handed her a glass of water and the sleeping tablet.

"No, Lana. You're staying with me tonight and that means in my bed. I don't care how long it takes for you to sleep or if we're up all night. I'm not leaving you alone tonight."

Lana managed to smile at him and snuggled against his chest for a moment. He smelled so good. He was so caring and kind to her. There was still something decent about the horrible day. It was him. And at that moment, the numbness that had enveloped and protected her for the past several hours evaporated. She couldn't help but let the feeling of the love she felt for Roadking take its place.

Roadking undressed and they both got into the big bed. Lana lay on her back with her hands folded across her chest. Her eyes darted around the room and at the ceiling. She was sorting things out in her mind. Roadking would let her determine what would happen next. *Do I want to talk or make love or simply sleep?* In a few minutes, she moved close to him, snuggled her body next to his, and rested her arm across his chest. She just wanted to be close to him, to feel safe. He laid his hand on her arm and let her rest there until she fell asleep. It was past midnight. Roadking lay awake a little longer, thinking about that cowardly bastard Lucas Chisholm and how the locksmith happened to be there to save Lana and how important Lana was to him.

Lana was awake when the sun came up. She had slept for a few hours but had woken suddenly several times during the night, feeling like she couldn't breathe. Soon Roadking stirred from his sleep. He pulled her close to his side. "Are you hungry, baby?"

"Yes, I think so. I'm sure I could whip up something for us."

He witnessed firsthand the ability that she had to be resilient, which would allow her to push as much of the past twenty-four hours aside, at least on the surface.

"No, you're a guest in my house. What could you eat this morning? An omelet, toast, fruit, bacon? What sounds good?"

"I guess an omelet and maybe a slice or two of bacon. And orange juice. I normally don't eat any breakfast, but I'm a little bit hungry this morning."

While Roadking showered, Lana looked at the messages on her phone. So many texts and emails expressing concern. The story of the attack must have exploded on the local news. She noticed oddly that Cate had not texted or emailed. *Maybe she doesn't know about it yet. Olivia would have filled her in about it by now. Oh well, I'll connect with everyone later in the day.*

When Roadking came out of the shower to dress, he heard Lana on her phone, talking to someone at her office. "I want a full staff meeting tomorrow morning at nine o'clock in the conference room. So could you let them all know? And tell them to make no statements to the press. They'll be coming around looking for me. I'm not coming into the office today. Please call me or email me if something urgent comes up. No, I'm really alright. No, I'm not at my house; it's still a crime scene. Okay, see you tomorrow. Get bagels for the staff."

Roadking was relieved that Lana had decided on her own to take the day off. "But is one day off going to be enough time for you?"

"Yes, there's business that needs to be taken care of. First the mess in the house needs to be cleaned up when the sheriff is done. Oh, that reminds me, I'll call them and ask if they're done. I want to buy a new couch—well, two of them so they match. Even if the blood is cleaned off the couch, I don't want it in the house. I'm going to hire someone to put a locked security gate out by the road and replace the garage door opener. Then there's the magazine—"

Roadking interrupted her. "Hold on there—does all of that need to be done immediately?"

Lana paused before she quietly answered, "No, probably not. I need to keep myself busy. I know myself—I need to."

"Okay, sweetness. I'll help you with anything you need. I want you to ask if you need help. I expect that you'll stay here today. Okay?"

"I want to stay here today. It feels good to be here, Vincent. Thank you so much for coming to my house and for bringing me here. You're so good to me."

Roadking smiled, his eyes crinkling. Lana loved that smile and that face. "Well, for now, I'm going to make breakfast for us."

Lana followed him down the stairs to the kitchen, still wearing the long black Harley T-shirt and a pair of white socks.

"Make yourself at home today when I leave. Use the equipment or the movie theater or the library if you want to. Pamper yourself. I'll bring you some lunch later if you want." He wanted to warn her not to watch the local news, but he knew she would anyway. Her curious mind would want to know what was reported about the incident.

Roadking thought about Lana as he left his house for work. She had been through hell and was still standing, ready to face the world, at least on the surface. He suspected that inside Lana there was a scared little girl who she would keep hidden from view. He had witnessed and learned so much about her since the attack. His respect for her grew, and his feelings for her were even stronger.

Lana showered again and got dressed. She wandered through the house, slowly looked at each painting, examined the decor of each room, and appreciated his exquisite sense of style. She eventually settled in the living room and turned on the TV. The local news had just begun.

"Breaking news. Live on the scene in rural Columbine Point

where local *Boulder Essence* magazine editor, Lana Ross, was attacked by an intruder last night in her home. The intruder is alleged to be her ex-husband, Lucas Chisholm, the owner of Chisholm Cadillac. We have word that he was shot during the attack by a local locksmith who happened to be in the home. Details are still emerging. But it appears that Chisholm's injuries are not life threatening. Ross's injuries appeared to be minor. We will provide more details as they become available. But in a seemingly unrelated incident, two Cadillacs at the Chisholm dealership were torched last night sometime before midnight. Investigators are on the scene, but early reports indicate that windshields were smashed on the two vehicles, and the vehicles were then torched with an incendiary device. Security cameras caught a glimpse of an unidentified man."

Lana was stunned and felt sickened by those words. She could see that reporters were still on her property. She could hide in Roadking's house for a day or two, but reality was out there, standing on her front lawn. Lana called the Sheriff's Office to speak to one of the investigators who had been on the scene. She inquired, "When will my home no longer be a crime scene? When will you be done with your investigation there? Is there a way to move the press off my property?"

Deputy Scott Everly responded that they would be done collecting evidence at the crime scene in a matter of hours. He would let her know when it was clear. And he would move the press and anyone not involved in the investigation off the property.

It was time to make some phone calls. She wanted to keep them short and not have to rehash the events that had occurred over and over with each call. She would call her parents first.

"Dad, I don't know if you heard about the attack at my house last night," Lana said and paused. "You did hear? Okay, well, to keep a long story short, Lucas was drunk and broke into my house last night and attacked me. A guy who'd been doing some security alarm work here at the house happened to come by, saw the attack going on through the window, had a gun, got in the house, and shot Lucas in the shoulder and stopped the attack. I'm fine."

The conversation with her mother was much of the same. She repeated the same phone conversation with Olivia. Everyone wanted more details, but she just didn't feel strong enough to relive the event repeatedly.

When she called Cate, she was oddly cold and disinterested. "Cate, did you hear about the attack already? I just wanted to let you know that I'm okay and safe."

"Lana," she said tersely, "you caused this yourself. It's your fault that Lucas got drunk and broke in. If you hadn't have met him for lunch yesterday, he might have pouted about it all day but forgot about it in the end. After he saw you, he fell off the deep end. He told me what happened. Now look—Lucas is shot, going to jail, and his business will suffer. All for what? For you?"

Lana was stunned by her words. She felt like she had been punched in the stomach. "Cate, you can't seriously blame me for the attack. We're divorced. We were separated for eight months. We've moved on. Cate, why?"

"Lucas and I have been seeing each other since the divorce. He and I were a couple. He cared about me, even though I knew he wasn't over you entirely. He asked about you all the time. Perfect Princess Lana—always so cool, so together, so smart. But I know that he wants to be with me."

Lana remembered that Cate had recently told her that she was dating someone but wouldn't say who it was. *It was Lucas. He used her to get information about me.* Cate and Lana had been friends since college. Lana felt so betrayed and shocked and hurt. It was hard for her to express it in words, so she kept them at a minimum. She felt numb by the shock of Cate's reaction.

"Cate, I'm so sorry that you feel that way. I value our friendship. Lucas has caused so much damage. Goodbye."

When Roadking came home with some lunch for Lana, he found her sitting quietly on the patio. Her mood was considerably more serious than when he had left earlier in the day.

"I saw the local news and made the phone calls that I needed to make. It turns out my friend Cate had been seeing Lucas and inadvertently provided him with information about me. He used her, and she hates me. She thought that they had a future together. All of those years of friendship down the drain for Lucas."

Roadking was silent and just let her talk. He bent down and lightly kissed her on the top of her head.

"Vincent, I remembered that I have to go the Sheriff's Office today and give them a statement. I don't have my car. Could you give me a ride to Boulder or take me home so I can get my car?"

"You call them now. Find out when you can come in. I'll take you there and stay with you. I'm not taking you home just yet."

Roadking sat with her on the patio as they ate minestrone silently. He didn't want to believe it, but he was afraid that this incident with Lucas would interfere with their connection for a while. He loved her and he would help her through it and in the end still be there for her.

CHAPTER 20

"Lucas broke in and attacked me," Lana blurted out as she and Roadking drove to the Sheriff's Office in the late afternoon. Lana was going over the horrible events of the previous night in her mind. She finally felt that she was able to tell Roadking about the attack, but she was hesitant to burden him with her problems. Roadking quietly listened to her.

"He kept texting me, wanting to have lunch, wanting to talk about something. I finally gave in and met him yesterday at noon at the Boulderado. He wanted us to get back together and was angry that I said no. I came home and later I fell asleep on the couch. When I woke up, he was sitting on a chair with his face just inches from mine. He was drunk and rambled about how I made him look bad. We began to struggle and he was pulling at my clothes. I kicked and hit and slapped. He finally got the best of me, pinned me down, and tried to strangle me. He only stopped because the locksmith Leon Alvarez shot him in the shoulder. He got in somehow, thankfully, I think with a master key or something when he saw Lucas hurting me. He just happened to be there at the right time." She spoke in a monotone, emotionless, and appeared to be looking off in the distance through the windshield of the car, as if she were watching it happen all over again. She said all that she needed to say about it to him.

Roadking held her left hand with his right as she spoke. He had questions but would never press her. He knew that the best thing he could do for her would be to listen, to help her to move forward, and to be strong.

"It's over, baby. You're safe with me."

They arrived at the Sheriff's Office. Lana was taken into a brightly illuminated room where she gave a statement to the deputies. Roadking waited in a reception area, where he thumbed through *Sports Illustrated* magazines, not really reading anything. When she was finished about twenty minutes later, he noticed how pale she looked as she walked toward him. Reliving the attack in detail less than twenty-four hours after it had happened had taken a lot out of her.

"Let's go home now." He put his arm around her as they walked out.

"They asked questions about Leon Alvarez, about whether we had some relationship or a connection. Seriously? I guess they had to discount a lover's triangle. I'm confused by that. It's probably something Lucas made up."

Leon had not kept his eyes off the monitors of Lana's house the entire day. Although he had jobs to attend to, he compulsively looked at the monitor on his phone every few minutes. There was no movement in that house. She was not there. He saw her leave with Roadking the night before. The GPS tracking device he secretly placed on her car told him that it was still parked in her garage. Leon ranted out loud to himself, running his fingers through his dirty, dark, long hair. "Where the fuck are ya? That Mr. Pretty Boy prick has probably been puttin' his hands all over ya again. I saved ya, darlin'. When are you gonna realize that yer only safe with me? When are ya comin' back home?"

He tried to figure out where Roadking lived. He checked Boulder County records online for an address listed under Vincent Romano. There were dozens of entries with that name. He paced back and forth in the room, obsessively looked at the monitor each time he walked by it, and compulsively smoked, alternating joints with cigarettes until the room was a haze of smoke. He was only able to sit quietly and look away from the monitor when the local news came on that carried the story of Lucas, Lana, and him.

Leon had given his statement to the police just hours before. He had caught on that their questions were pointing in the direction of a lover's triangle. If only he could give them the surveillance tape from the monitor of the living room, then they would see exactly what he had seen as Lucas attacked her. But he couldn't do that without revealing the secret camera mounted on the flat-screen TV. The police had the surveillance tape of the entrance to the driveway, which showed both his and Lucas's vehicles, and a tape of Leon breaking in but little else.

Leon put his hand on his thigh where he had carved Lana's name with a knife. It felt warm and throbbed when his jeans rubbed against it. But each time it stung and burned, it reminded him of his sick obsession with Lana and his hatred for Roadking and fueled his need for revenge. He would have to wait impatiently for her to come home to get another look at her tight, little body. He quietly growled to himself, "He's gotta bring ya home, Lana, darlin'. I ain't seen ya parading around in them there little underthings for a while."

Roadking and Lana drove back to Louisville in silence. When they arrived at his house, he ordered her favorite veggie pizza for delivery and poured each of them a beer.

"I'm not really hungry now," Lana mumbled.

"Come on, follow me." Roadking grabbed the box of pizza, some napkins, and the beer. She followed him upstairs to the theater room. He proceeded to sort through movies on Netflix and Amazon, searching for just the right one. "Here you go." He chose a romantic comedy with ridiculous circumstances to lighten Lana's mood.

They settled into the cushy theater seating. He pulled out a few more beers from the compact refrigerator that he kept upstairs. He could feel her beginning to relax a little and enjoy herself. She finally ate a piece of pizza. She pulled a throw blanket with a Southwestern design up on her legs. She laid her head on Roadking's shoulder. She felt so good to him. He wanted the Lana that he was falling in love with to return.

When the movie was over, Roadking turned on some music. Some ballads. "I Can't Tell You Why" by the Eagles. He slid out of his seat, stood, held out his right hand, and pulled Lana toward him and they began to dance—swaying slowly, holding each other tightly, her arms around his neck, his arms around her waist. Lana was lost in those moments with Roadking. When the song ended, he took her hand and led her to the bedroom. It was time for bed. Roadking would not pressure her after the attack and near rape at the hands of Lucas. But she needed to sleep and put another day between her and the events of the day before.

Lana walked into the bedroom, turned down the sheets of the bed, undressed, and picked up the T-shirt that she had slept in the night before but then laid it down again. She slid under the sheets wearing nothing. Roadking slid into bed next to her, turned toward her, looked directly into her eyes, and said, "Are you sure?"

Lana said, "Yes, I am. It's what I want tonight." To Lana, making love was the ultimate expression of trust. She needed to reassure herself that her ability to trust was not broken by Lucas. And as the next minutes and hours progressed, Roadking demonstrated to her that her trust belonged with him.

Lana woke again before sunrise. She glanced over at the handsome man lying next to her asleep. At that moment, she realized that all the questions she'd had about his relationship status before had disappeared. It didn't matter anymore. Whatever there had been, it had nothing to do with them. He had chosen to be with her and constantly for the past couple of days. She reached for the T-shirt and slipped it on quickly over her head.

Roadking turned over and smiled at her. "And how are you this morning, beautiful?"

"I'm good. I'm happy and I'm with you." Lana literally sparkled as she said those words. Roadking was relieved to see the return of a bubbly mood. He knew that every day would not be perfect, as issues with Lucas's situation evolved. He would take one day at a time with her and make her happy if he could.

"Vincent, I'm going to shower. I want to go to my office today. I want to work. Can you drive me to Boulder? Or should I take an Uber this morning?"

"I'll drive you. While you're getting dressed, I'll shower."

"Can I make you something this morning? Coffee at least?"

"Yes, make some coffee please. There won't be time for breakfast today. I'll grab something on the way back to Louisville."

Lana showered and then looked at the clothes she had packed for her office the night of the attack. She had not hung up the blue cotton shirt or the gray and white pinstripe slacks but had left them in the suitcase, and they were a little wrinkled. She could not bother Roadking for an iron. She smoothed them the best she could. She dried her hair, curled it, and put on her makeup in a matter of minutes, and then ran downstairs to start the coffee. She turned on the TV that was in the kitchen without thinking and heard the lead news story of the morning.

"In the news, Lucas Chisholm is due in court this morning, where he is expected to be charged with attempted first-degree murder, attempted felony sexual assault, assault, battery, and trespassing as the result of an alleged attack on Tuesday night at the home of his former wife Lana Ross, editor in chief of the *Boulder Essence* magazine. Lucas Chisholm is the owner of Chisholm Cadillac in Columbine Point. Bond is expected to be set at one million dollars due to the nature of the charges. Chisholm's initial court appearance was delayed one day while he underwent surgery to remove a bullet from his right shoulder. He was allegedly shot by Leon Alvarez, who was on the scene at the time of the attack. We are covering this story as it unfolds and will have an update at noon today."As Lana listened to the news story and saw photos of Lucas, Leon, and herself splashed on the screen, her stomach began to churn and tears spontaneously rolled down her face. She couldn't escape it even if she tried. Her world was rocked by Lucas and the attack. Tears continued to flow as she placed a coffee cup on the counter for Roadking. Within minutes, she heard him coming down the stairs. She hurried into the powder room near the kitchen to wipe the tears away before he saw her. She would not burden him with a roller coaster of emotions.

Roadking was sitting on the edge of a barstool near one of the kitchen islands drinking coffee when Lana emerged from the powder room. The TV was still on, carrying the local news. But the story of the attack was over. When he looked up at her, he studied her face and could see that she was a little flushed and her eyes were a little red, but she managed to muster a smile. He suspected that she had seen something on the news about Lucas.

The October morning was crisp and new. The Flatirons reflected the morning sun in shades of gray and silver with dark patches of green as they drove into Boulder from the east. "Vincent, you've been so wrapped up with me and my problems that I haven't heard what's new with you. Tell me what's been going on."

"Well, some Harley executives have been visiting for the last couple of days in the area, so I've had some marketing strategy meetings with them at the dealership. They wanted to meet last night for dinner in Boulder, but I told them that I had an important engagement." Roadking reached over and took Lana's hand in his. He continued. "Demo models of the new Road King, Softail, and Sportster Series are arriving at All Roads in a couple of weeks. I'll be hosting an open house for our new and old customers. You know, those bikes pretty much sell themselves anyway. But I'd like you to be there with me. What do you think?"

"I'd love to. Thank you for asking. Just let me know the date and time." Lana paused for a minute and said, "Vincent, I need to go home today after work. Could you give me a ride? I need to get my car and I need to deal with the house and the security issues and I think I'm ready. I've imposed on you long enough."

"I'll take you home tonight, but no, you have not imposed on me. You can stay with me as long as you need to." He squeezed her hand. He liked to be with her. Even with recent events, she was a breath of fresh air. The way she talked, the way she moved, the expressions on her face, the way she loved—all of that made each day with her special.

Roadking dropped Lana off at the entrance to her office building. She kissed him quickly on the lips and hurried inside. A couple of news vans were parked nearby, and she assumed that they were watching for her. She hustled up the stairs and into the reception area of the office.

Miranda greeted her. "Lana, reporters have been here, but we've shooed them away as best we can. I just want you to be on the lookout for them."

Lana walked into her office and set her purse and jacket down on her desk. There on the oak bureau was the giant bouquet of white flowers that Lucas had sent her. She took the card that was attached and put it in her top desk drawer. It may be needed later in court for some reason. "Miranda, please get rid of these as soon as possible. I don't even want them in the building."

Miranda gathered them up and took them to the dumpster in the alley behind the building. She saw a couple of reporters talking at the end of the alley. She hustled back to the office.

At promptly nine o'clock, Lana met with all the members of her staff in the magazine conference room. The staff gave her their full attention as they ate bagels and drank coffee and juice. Lana confidently began, "I know that you've seen the news or have heard that Lucas, my ex-husband, attacked me in my home on Tuesday night. Lucas was stopped when he was shot by the locksmith who had been doing some security work for me. I won't go into any detail about the attack, but suffice to say, I survived it and I'm fine. The less you know about it, the better—that way the press can't squeeze information out of you. So please don't let these events surrounding me interrupt your work, your creativity, or your daily routine. I don't intend to let it affect my work here either. But I will need to take a little time off now and then as the legal process unfolds. Having said that, I'll be taking a half day off tomorrow morning to deal with issues in my house. I'm trying to get back to normal as soon as possible. That will be all that I have to say at this time. Now since I have the full staff here, and you all have been fed, I would like full reports from each of the department heads. Thank you, everyone."

Lana realized that getting back into the routine of work would be good therapy for her and help her not to dwell on the attack and to move forward. After all, there was always a future issue of the magazine in the works.

The morning passed quickly. Lana looked out of her window during her lunch hour. The press vans were still out there. She suspected that they were going to want her comment about Lucas's court hearing that day. Although she knew that there were dozens of voice-mail messages on her office phone and hordes of emails to answer, she used her lunch hour to call a fence company to get estimates to install a security gate on her driveway and a restoration company to clean the blood from her floor and couch and any spatters on the wall. Then she called a charitable organization and offered to donate the two leather couches in her living room. She surfed the web to look at leather couches to replace them. After about a half hour, she began to get a little hungry. She had not eaten all day. *Maybe I could sneak past the press and run across the street to grab a sandwich*, she speculated.

Lana walked to the entrance of the building, opened the door, and looked in both directions. The coast was clear. She walked swiftly across the street and appeared to be unnoticed. But when she opened the door to the café, she was immediately approached by a local television news reporter who fired questions at her. "Lana. Lana Ross. Just a couple of questions. What do you think of the one-million-dollar bond set by the judge today for your ex-husband? Do you think he'll make the bond? Are you concerned about your safety if he bonds out?"

Lana took a deep breath. "I have not been informed of the court proceedings today involving my ex-husband. And I cannot comment."

Another reporter shouted from a nearby table, "Can you elaborate on your relationship with the locksmith Leon Alvarez?"

Lana instinctively knew that the outlandish question was intended to evoke a response from her that could be used as a sound bite. She did not respond. She grabbed her tuna sandwich and returned to her office, eluding a reporter who continued to bark questions and follow her out the door.

She sat down at her desk, took a deep breath, and went to the Boulder newspaper website to see if there was a news story about Lucas. She had already made a conscious decision only to read about the events surrounding Lucas and not to watch them on the local news, not wanting a repeat of her earlier reaction. And there it was. Breaking news. A photo of Lucas in an orange jumpsuit, shackled and handcuffed, even with his right arm in a sling, standing with his attorney in the courtroom and being advised of the charges against him. He had the same cold, terse expression that he always wore on his face. But there in the background, the photo showed Cate seated behind the defendant's table, devotedly looking up at Lucas. Cate and Lucas. It was shocking and unexpected. Cate, one of her best friends since college, would give up their friendship for Lucas, who probably cared very little about her. Lana thought about their days in college—the all-nighters, the parties, the angst over grades and the boys they'd dated, spring break trips, and skiing weekends as they had gradually matured into young adults. She finally ate a little of the sandwich.

Within minutes, Lana received a telephone call from the Boulder County sheriff's office. The deputy wanted her to know that Lucas bonded out of jail. There was a restraining order preventing him from having any contact with her. He wore an ankle monitor to restrict his movement.

Despite her earlier reassurance that the attack would not interfere with her work at the magazine, she spent the rest of the afternoon swiveling in her office chair while she reflected about her relationship with Lucas, her friendship with Cate, and her new relationship with Roadking. As she meditated about these things, it occurred to her that perhaps the recent odd happenings at her house with the picture frame, the snake, and the loud late-night knock on the door were the work of Lucas. Perhaps he wanted to scare her into thinking she needed him again.

Roadking arrived a little before five o'clock to pick her up. He decided to come into her office and walk her out of the building. He had heard that Lucas was released on bond and wanted to be cautious. They hustled to the underground parking garage and headed toward Columbine Point.

When they got closer to Lana's house, Roadking noticed that Lana visibly stiffened and became reserved, probably from apprehension. She was completely transparent to him, although she tried to hide behind a stoic demeanor. The last time she was home, she had been attacked and nearly killed. Lana deactivated the security system that she had activated when she was notified that the sheriff's investigation was complete. They walked into the entryway and Lana paused to survey the living room. She took a couple of steps through the French doors and into the room and saw the puddle of blood on the oak floor and spatters on the couch and wall. A restoration company was scheduled to arrive in the morning to clean it up. But until then, she wasn't going to set foot in that room. She took a few steps back into the entryway. Roadking watched and waited for her reaction.

"I can't go in there just yet. This place is my refuge and it's been violated. It'll be awhile before it feels comfortable again. But I will get over it. I will. Let's go into the dining room." They turned and entered the foyer that led through the French doors to the dining room. Lana turned on some music—something a little raucous but at a mellow volume. Bruce Springsteen's "Dancing in the Dark."

Roadking gently asked her, "Lana, do you need for me to stay with you tonight?" Lana thought for a brief second. It had not occurred to her to ask him to stay, although she was uptight about spending the first night there alone.

"I don't want to impose on you. You've been so good to me through all of this. But yes, will you stay tonight? I think if I get through this first night, I'll be fine alone from here on out. Could you?"

"Of course or I wouldn't have offered to."

Lana smiled at him and hugged him around his waist. "Thank you. Just for tonight. Okay?"

"Deal."

Lana made them a light supper of salmon, steamed asparagus,

and wild rice and brought it to the formal dining room. She opened a bottle of chardonnay.

Roadking thought about a surprise getaway for them for the coming weekend. “Lana, what are your plans for the weekend?”

“I guess I’ll set things in order around here and catch up with Olivia and my parents. Regain a routine if I can. Steer clear of reporters. Nothing specific. And you?”

“I plan to spend some time with you if you’ll let me.” Roadking smiled with those crinkly eyes that had conquered Lana’s heart so quickly.

“I will let you.”

Roadking held up his glass of wine to make a toast. “To the weekend,” he said.

They each took a sip and then touched wine glasses.

CHAPTER 21

"There's that little gal." Leon watched the monitor as the Range Rover pulled into the driveway. "Don't take too long there now, Lana gal. I ain't seen my peep show for a couple of days." Leon smiled as he twirled the end of his beard. "Goddamn it . . . he's going in with her!"

After Roadking and Lana entered the house, Leon could not see them since they didn't enter a room with a hidden camera. "I'll just keep a watchin'. She has to go to her bedroom tonight," he continued to mumble to himself. He opened another beer from the six-pack he perpetually kept by his side.

Roadking and Lana finished the supper and the bottle of wine. As they continued to sit at the dining room table and talk, Lana began to relax some. But she still couldn't enter the living room. She cleared away the dishes and opened another bottle of wine. She was feeling a little buzzed and playful. "Vincent, this might sound lame, but how about a board game? Scrabble? Monopoly? We could watch TV in my bedroom, but it's too early for bed. Or we could play poker? Strip poker?" Lana laughed as she spoke.

"Okay, Lana, I challenge you to a game of Scrabble. The loser has to wash the dishes. And the winner gets a body massage. How about it?"

"Well, I like that proposal. But remember I'm an English Lit major and an editor. I can spell anything."

"Yes, but only if you choose the right letters," Roadking teased.

Lana got out the Scrabble board and they began to play. He was right. The letters he chose were placed on the best squares. It wasn't long before the game was over. Roadking won with the high point letters *q*, *x*, and *z*.

"Okay, Vincent. How about the best of two out of three games? I was just getting warmed up."

Roadking laughed. She either wanted the full body massage or her competitive nature wouldn't let her lose. "Okay, but this is it. No more negotiating."

They played a second game. Lana won round two. The third game went to Roadking. Lana smiled at him, put the game away, and walked into the kitchen to wash the dishes but then hesitated.

"You know, these dishes can wait until tomorrow. I guess it's time for me to pay up on the wager. Come with me."

They walked upstairs to Lana's bedroom. Roadking took off his shirt and lay on his stomach on the bed. Lana straddled his back and began to rub his shoulders and his upper back and then his lower back down. Lana felt an electrical charge run through her body as she massaged his incredible chiseled and hard physique.

Lana leaned forward and whispered in his ear, "Now off with the pants. I need to work on the rest of you."

Roadking slid out of his jeans, lay on his stomach, and Lana began to work on his thighs, the calves, the ankles, and feet. Roadking loved every second of it, but it wasn't long before he rolled over and couldn't resist pulling her on top of him as he held her tightly and kissed her. One kiss led to another, each more passionate than the one before. The massage of one body evolved into their two bodies entwined as one—hot, breathless, and satisfied.

Leon watched the passionate love scene as it unfolded. He couldn't move his eyes from the monitor, even though he tried to look away in disgust. And yet there was something titillating about the sexy activity—if only she were not wrapped around Roadking. He was livid and helpless to put a stop to it. He had waited to see Lana undressing for a couple of days, but Roadking had spoiled the anticipation. He was breathing hard with rage as he growled under his breath, "I want to kill you, son of a bitch. I saved her. That means she's mine. You ain't done nothing fer her. Only keep doin' shit to her, you bare-assed bastard." Thoughts of evil acts of revenge swirled in Leon's head like a tornado. He finally got up, paced across the room back and forth, and smoked a joint, unable to calm down until the lovemaking was over. He continued to stare at the monitor but tried to look away. There was nothing left to see. As he cooled down, he came to a firm decision in his head. "I'm going to have to take him out."

"Well, Lana, I've played board games many times before but never won a prize like the one you just gave me." Roadking's eyes crinkled and he smiled and kissed Lana lightly on her forehead as she curled her body around him.

"It was the grand prize," Lana whispered in his ear. They lay together, cuddling until they cooled down. They slid under the sheets and comforter on the bed. Lana found the remote for the TV and turned it on, flipping through channels until Roadking asked her to stop at *Thursday Night NFL Football*. They propped up pillows and leaned against the headboard and watched the game. Lana rested her hand next to her on the bed and Roadking laid his hand on top of it. Lana's playful mood began to disappear as the buzz wore off from the wine. Roadking could see that serious thoughts were spinning through her mind again. He knew that she was thinking about the attack again and he wondered what she might face in the coming days. She glanced over at him and smiled, hoping that she could mask her growing somber mood. She was unaware of how well he could read her.

When the game was over, they turned out the lights and went to sleep. Even though Lana felt safe with Roadking lying next to her, she woke up with a jolt when she thought that she heard a loud knock at the door and a few hours later when she believed that she heard someone in the bedroom. Each time she woke up, she turned toward Roadking, who slept peacefully next to her, and touched him on the arm to make sure that he was real.

The sky at sunrise was rosy and peach-colored, and it cast a glow in the bedroom. Roadking saw the color reflected on Lana's face as she stretched and turned toward him. He pulled her close and hugged her tight. He had helped her through the night this time, but it crossed his mind that he would be happy to wake up next to her every day. Lana stayed in bed for a few minutes while Roadking showered. She wrapped herself in her robe and went downstairs to make coffee and multigrain toast, remembering not to turn on the TV in the kitchen to watch the morning news. Roadking walked into the kitchen, grabbed a cup of coffee, took a piece of toast, spread chokecherry jam on it, and headed toward the front door, careful not to walk through the living room. Lana followed him to the door.

"Thank you, Vincent. You're so good to me. You put your life on hold to help me through this. Now it's time to get back to work and sell some Harley-Davidsons."

"I didn't think twice about being with you. The Harleys having been selling themselves all week. But yeah, I'm the boss man. I can't let those renegades that work for me think they're in charge."

"Bye, Vincent." Lana put her arms around his neck, stood on her tiptoes, and kissed him. She laid her head on his chest for a minute, and Roadking held her there for a long moment, wanting to stay.

"Hey, I'll be in touch later today with details about the surprise weekend I have planned for us. Can you clear your schedule late tomorrow morning into Sunday?"

"Yes, I can't wait."

As he stood there looking at her, he could still see the long scratches on her chest and the large bruises on the base of her neck from the attack. He wouldn't say anything to make her feel self-conscious. She already knew they were there.

Roadking drove away and Lana was alone in the house for the first time. Her home was eerily quiet, and every little incidental noise seemed to reverberate and have significance. Lana ran upstairs and took a quick shower, feeling leery about being in a situation where she couldn't hear or see what was going on around her. She threw on some yoga pants and a sweatshirt. The restoration service was coming at eight thirty to clean up the bloody mess in the living room. Lana was well aware that she could have cleaned it up herself, but she wasn't able to bring herself to do that.

That blood was symbolic of unthinkable evil and hate to which she couldn't expose herself again.

Two men from the restoration service arrived on time. The scene was cleaned up within a few hours. Even though Lana knew that moving furniture wasn't their job, she bravely asked the men if they could move the two couches into the open garage stall to be picked up by the charity later. They agreed, and she tipped them fifty dollars. When she let herself walk into the living room, she felt relief that it felt empty. She looked at the wall. The paint showed a light stain from the blood spatters. It would need to be repainted.

The gate company arrived as scheduled. Lana walked down to the driveway entrance. They would install a security gate powered by a solar battery that could be opened with a four-digit code on her phone or with the same code on a keypad. She gave them the numbers—1-9-7-5—to use as they programmed the code. The gate would be a deterrent to entry by strangers on the property, and the security system installed by Leon would act in conjunction with it. They scheduled the installation for Tuesday the next week.

"You need to get with your security company to adjust the security camera here to show access through the gate."

"Yes, good idea." Lana had thought to call Leon anyway to have him inspect the security system that he had installed to make sure that all the components were calibrated and that everything was safe since Lucas had broken in.

"Hi, Leon. This is Lana Ross," Lana said and paused. "Yes, I'm doing well, but I was wondering if I could set up an appointment with you next week to come and calibrate the security system if it needs it and to adjust the monitor of the driveway entrance, because I have a security gate being installed out there too. How does your schedule look? The security gate will be installed next Tuesday, so how about Wednesday or Thursday? I'm anxious to get all of this in place."

Leon grinned as he watched her from the covert camera mounted on her flat-screen TV while she stood in her living room talking to him. "Yeah, I can come on Wednesday late afternoon about the time yer a comin' from yer work. I'll come there about an hour before so I can check it out before ya get home."

"Leon, the gate has a keypad, which you'll have to use to enter the property now. The code will be 1-9-7-5." Lana didn't think twice about giving him the code. After all, he had saved her life and he was in the lock and key business and was given access information by his customers. He was licensed and bonded. He must be okay.

Noon approached. She planned to work in the afternoon. It was a productive morning, and she was pleased with the progress that she'd made in a few short hours. She ran upstairs to change her clothes for work. She chose a midcalf black skirt with a handkerchief hem and a cranberry and gold shirt with black flecks in it and black suede boots. As she pulled out of her garage, she was reminded that her garage door opener needed to be reprogrammed since Lucas was able to get in through the garage. While she drove to her office in Boulder, she used her phone to dictate a list of things that still needed to be done.

In midafternoon, Roadking texted Lana and asked her if she could leave about ten in the morning. She texted back.

Yes, what do I pack?

He texted.

We're heading south. Jeans and cowboy boots.

Work at the magazine had been routine for a Friday afternoon with no major issues. The publication date for the next issue was a couple of weeks away. When she left the office, she walked to Rite Aid near the Pearl Street Mall to pick up some travel-size bottles of shampoo, moisturizer, and toothpaste. As she walked down the aisle of the store, she noticed someone familiar in the aisle next to her. It was Cate. Lana wondered for a moment if she should approach her or not after their contentious conversation after the attack. She decided to take a chance. After all, she and Cate had been close friends for ten years.

Lana turned and walked up to Cate and gently touched her arm. "Hey, Cate."

Cate turned and looked at her with a harsh, cold stare. Lana immediately noticed that it was the first time she had seen Cate without that blank, hollow look.

"I have nothing to say to you. You threw him away and then pulled him back in and away from me. Look what you did! Can't you see through those 'Perfect Princess' blinders you wear?"

"Cate, I assure you—I didn't, I mean, I don't want Lucas back. I don't ever want to see him again. He tried to kill me," Lana emphatically but quietly explained to Cate, not wanting to make a scene.

"You're a selfish bitch! Get the fuck out of my face!" Cate loudly exclaimed. She raised her right hand and swiftly and accurately slapped Lana across the left cheek of her face, hard enough to produce a pronounced smack.

Lana reached up to touch her cheek. It stung and felt hot as she looked at Cate. She was a stranger now. Some customers in the adjoining aisle had witnessed the whole incident. Lana heard one whisper to the other, "I think it's that editor of that Boulder magazine whose ex-husband tried to kill her the other day."

"Which one?"

"The redhead."

Lana said nothing to Cate. She left the items that she had planned to purchase on the shelf in front of her and walked out of the store. When she got to the sidewalk, she felt tears well to her eyes from shock and the loss of her friend. Her face was crimson from embarrassment and the sting of the slap.

While she drove home, her mind was full as she reviewed all the events of the past week. She put her hand on her left cheek again. It was still hot. She was thankful to be leaving for the weekend with Roadking. When she pulled into her garage, she didn't immediately close the door but left it open until she walked through the house in case she needed to leave in a hurry. She gingerly stepped into the house and moved from room to room until she was convinced that she was secure.

Lana went upstairs to her bedroom and looked at her face in the mirror. It was red but not as bad as she thought it would be. She rinsed her face in cold water. She began to pack a small suitcase for her weekend with Roadking. When she was finished, she came downstairs and forced herself to sit in the living room on one of the leather chairs and turned on the TV. She kept the volume low and listened for any unusual sounds. Eventually, she walked into the kitchen to make herself something to eat and saw that she needed to wash the dishes from the dinner with Roadking the night before. When she finished the dishes, she ate a leftover piece of salmon, then she worked out on the treadmill and did light weights for an hour. She made sure that all the doors were locked and double-checked that the security system was activated. She took a shower and got in bed to watch TV. It was still early, about eight thirty, when she fell asleep. It was her first night alone in the house. Once again, she woke several times in the night, adrenaline pumping, believing that she had heard something or someone. "I wonder if I'll ever get over this," she said softy to herself.

CHAPTER 22

Lana was relieved to see the sun rise and a new day begin. She would be leaving for a weekend with Roadking in a few hours. Nothing could be better than that. The air was crisp and beginning to warm in the October sun. She finished packing, showered, and dressed in bootcut blue jeans, a black corduroy shirt with turquoise stitching on the yoke and cuffs, a brown and black tooled belt with a turquoise buckle, a silver and turquoise necklace, and matching earrings. She hoped that the shirt would not reveal any of the scratches on her chest and that the bruises on her neck would just look like a shadow. She pulled on her brown suede cowboy boots and grabbed one of her leather jackets—the gold colored suede one with the beads and fringe. She stood by the window and waited for Roadking.

Lana was excited to see that Roadking soon arrived in the black SS 396 Chevy to pick her up for the weekend road trip. She opened the front door before he was even on the front porch. Roadking was amused to see her bright mood and childlike eagerness to go. He grabbed her suitcase and put it in the back seat. She remembered to set the security alarm.

"Okay, Vincent, where are we going? Tell me the surprise."

"Not yet. Just enjoy the ride. The anticipation is good for you." He laughed as she rolled her eyes at him. They drove to I-25 and headed south. The Beach Boys and Motown music from his playlist floated through the car. So perfect for the 1966 SS 396. They talked about everything and anything as they drove; one subject randomly led one to another. Laughing sometimes and other times being quiet and just enjoying the sound of the SS 396 engine and their time together.

"Come on, Vincent, where could we be going? We've already passed through Pueblo. Please, please, tell me."

"Okay, we're going to Walsenburg for a chili cook-off. There's all kinds of chili to try, different booths, live music—and I know you'll like that. And we can pick up some Hatch chiles to bring home to make some authentic Mexican cuisine ourselves. We're staying in a historic bed-and-breakfast tonight in Trinidad, south of Walsenburg. I was lucky to find a room since so many people will be pouring into Walsenburg for the cook-off."

"This'll be fun. I've never been to Walsenburg or a chili cook-off. Thank you so much for the surprise. I couldn't begin to guess what you had in mind."

"I'm full of surprises. We'll be there shortly."

They arrived in Walsenburg around one o'clock. A painted wooden sign outside of town said, "Walsenburg. A great place to be. Welcome." And it appeared to be true. There was a small-town feeling about it with apparent Southwestern and historic coal mining influences and large and small Victorian houses. The parking lot at the cook-off was packed, but Roadking managed to find a good parking spot for the SS 396. The smell of the chili and the sound of live music hung in the air as they approached the entrance. Everything was so colorful. Orange and red and purple and bright yellow and green.

"The contestants have made green and red chili. There might even be some white chili. But all of them must include Hatch chiles as an ingredient. The chili is cooked here on-site. The contestants started cooking about seven this morning. Now you can get a sample of anything that looks appealing to you using these tickets here. You can vote for a sample that you like best, too, for a People's Choice Award, if you want to." He handed her some tickets. "Come on, let's get started."

Lana followed Roadking as they moved from booth to booth. Each booth was decorated with brightly colored flags and scarves, and some were playing mariachi music in the background. Roadking stopped to try a sample of red chili made with elk. Lana tried a green chili made with chicken. They both tried a vegetarian, fifteen-bean chili."Vincent, let's do a quick walk-through and scope out all of the booths first and then make a return loop to choose other chilis to sample. I can't possibly try them all."

"Good plan."

They walked through the crowd of people and sometimes waited in line for a sample of chili. They both placed their votes for the People's Choice Award. Roadking chose the red chili made with brisket. Lana chose a green chili made with chorizo sausage. Fortunately, there was a margarita booth among the chili booths. Eating all that chili and the festive atmosphere of the cook-off put Lana in the mood for a margarita. There were dozens of flavors to try at the margarita booth, but both Lana and Roadking ordered traditional ones. There was a little kick to them.

They continued to make their way to each booth. They were both too full to eat any of the other Mexican delicacies: bizcochitos, chicharróns (fried pork belly or rind), tamales, piñons, or atoles. But Roadking bought some of each of them to try later. As they made their way past the booths, they got closer and closer to the stage that was set up for the live, local bands scheduled to perform—Los Lobos, Johnny Hurricane, the Rifters, and the Sanchez Band. All the seating was full. Roadking and Lana stood near the stage while Los Lobos performed "La Bamba."

When it was around five o'clock, Roadking said, "We've got to head to Trinidad so we can check in to the bed-and-breakfast. There's more fun to be had when we get there."

Roadking bought some roasted Hatch chiles to take home. In a little less than an hour, they arrived in Trinidad at a Victorian bed-and-breakfast on the main street of the town. Roadking glanced at Lana. She smiled at him. Her cheeks were so rosy from eating the chili and the sun. Just what he wanted—she was happy and living in the moment.

The Victorian Inn was painted in monochromatic shades of mauve with white and gray trim. A wide, curved, oak staircase expanded from the entrance to the parlor on the second floor. Carved wainscoting, chair rails, and crown molding of golden oak enhanced the ambience of the inn. The floors were original, white, wide-planked pinewood that creaked slightly with each step. There was a common dining room painted celery green with a wallpaper border of white and pink cabbage roses where a complimentary breakfast would be served in the morning. The windows were adorned in white lace draperies that touched the floor. A long walnut table in the center of the dining room, which seated twelve, was covered with a similar lace-patterned, white tablecloth and adorned with two bouquets of purple hyacinths. In their room on the second floor was a white claw-footed tub in the bathroom with a circular shower curtain for a shower and a pedestal sink. The overstuffed queen-size bed was covered with a tiny patchwork quilt of blues and greens. The windows were covered with a light green lace curtain that cascaded below a scalloped, deep oak valance.

Roadking brought the food they had bought at the cook-off into the room and put it in the refrigerator. Neither of them was hungry. Roadking made a quick phone call to All Roads to check in. From his conversation, it seemed that everything had gone smoothly. Lana lay back on the bed. Roadking came over and lay next to her.

"Let's just lay here for a while. We're going to a cowboy Western bar tonight. Are you up for that?"

"Yes, for sure. I love country music. Let's not waste a moment of these couple of days that we have to ourselves."

Roadking leaned over and kissed her. They turned the TV on to watch a couple of *Friends* reruns before they headed to the Legends Country Western Bar. Lana got up and washed her face and reapplied her makeup and brushed her hair. When she saw her reflection in the mirror, she could see the bruises on her neck and some of the scratches peeking up through the opening in her shirt. She wanted to ask Roadking if they were noticeable, but instead she decided just to button up another button to hide as much of it as she could.

About eight o'clock, they walked up the street to the bar. It was dark inside except for recessed lighting positioned over each table and some strategically placed sconces on the walls. The bar area was well lit and mirrored, accented by blue and purple neon lights. The stage was illuminated with pink, purple, and blue spotlights. It became clear why the bar was named Legends. There were framed, autographed posters of the most preeminent country singers covered in glass and hung prominently throughout the bar—Waylon Jennings, Willie Nelson, Johnny Cash, Merle Haggard, Kris Kristofferson, Buck Owens, Garth Brooks, Alan Jackson, Reba McEntire, Tim McGraw, and Faith Hill, to name a few. But on one wall, a signed poster of George Jones as The Crown Prince of Country Music hung prominently by itself, lit up by a single, white spotlight. Lana knew all of the singers from the music played in her home as a child.

She sat at a high-top table with Roadking, and they ordered king-size margaritas. A live band was playing some country rock classics when they arrived—the stuff that Roadking and Lana liked. There was a break before the headliner band would begin to play.

A couple of the waitresses came out on the dance floor and asked, "Who wants to learn to line dance?"

"Come on, let's do it. Will you?" Lana asked eagerly.

"Aw, Lana. You go ahead. I'll hold our seats here." Roadking wanted to indulge her but couldn't bring himself to make a fool of himself learning to line dance.

"Okay, watch and learn."

She was laughing, a little buzzed already. She worked at it, watched, tripped over own feet, turned the wrong way, and tried to figure out the pattern of the dance steps. After about fifteen minutes, the lesson was over and she caught on. Roadking laughed as he watched the amazing woman that he was with while she learned to line dance.

Lana returned to the table, laughing at herself. "Did you see me? What a klutz!"

The headlining band began to play at nine o'clock. Great music—rock, country, and some with Spanish lyrics. When they played the country ballad by Brett Young, "In Case You Didn't Know," Roadking asked Lana to dance with him. She was so in love with him and had already had a couple of margaritas and was so tempted to tell him that. But she didn't. She didn't know it, but Roadking felt the same way as they stood there close, arms around each other, swaying slowly. The band finished playing at eleven.

"Stick around. It's world-class karaoke tonight! Who wants to be the first to sign up?" The bartender announced on stage as the band packed up their gear.

"Can we stay a little longer, Vincent? I want to hear it."

"I'm up for that."

Lana excused herself to go to the restroom. When she returned, a parade of karaoke singers began. Some were so awful that it was funny. There was a terrible rendition of "Born to Be Wild" but a well-sung version of "You Were Always on My Mind." Soon Roadking's name was announced, and he got up and walked to the karaoke microphone. Lana was stunned. *What is he doing?*

Roadking began to sing. It was the classic Elvis Presley song "Can't Help Falling in Love". He was so good-looking. People in the bar watched him as he sang the song to her, and they smiled in her direction. What an incredible moment! He sounded so good. Lana wondered whether he sang those lyrics to her or just picked a beautiful Elvis song. When he was finished, the room erupted into applause. "More, more! Encore!" they shouted.

Roadking just laughed and returned to their table. "Well, what did you think?"

"You continue to surprise me. You were great. It was so beautiful." Lana beamed. Roadking hoped she would guess that the lyrics of that song were for her.

"Well, are you going to give it a shot?"

"No chance. Not after the fool I made of myself learning to line dance," Lana laughed.

"Then are you about ready to call it a night?"

"Yes, let's do. It's been a full day."

Roadking took her hand as they walked the few short blocks back to the inn. Lana leaned her buzzed head against him. When they entered their room, Lana kicked off her boots and flopped down on the bed.

Roadking picked up the TV remote and turned it on. “Want to watch a little TV to unwind? Lana?”

Lana had immediately fallen asleep, still in her clothes, sprawled out, lying on her back on top of the quilt. Roadking gently took the sheets and patchwork quilt from underneath her and covered her. He kissed her gently on the cheek. “Good night, sweet thing.” He turned off the TV and the white milk glass lamp on the nightstand. He undressed and lay down beside her. Thoughts about the day, Lana, his work, and his family bounced around in his mind until he finally fell asleep in the wee hours of the morning.

CHAPTER 23

White daylight slowly began to filter through the tiny openings in the lace curtains. Roadking awoke, looked around the room, and then glanced toward Lana. She was still asleep, but she was no longer wearing her clothes. She must have awakened in the night and undressed, since he saw a black bra strap on her bare shoulder. She turned over on her side and continued to sleep. Roadking got up, pulled the curtain aside, and looked out the window. It was going to be a clear autumn day. Lana stirred in her sleep and slowly opened her eyes and saw the silhouette of Roadking near the window.

"Hello, sleepyhead. So how are you feeling this morning?"

"Oh, I think okay. But I think I should take some aspirin or Advil to be on the safe side. Hand me my purse please, Vincent. And could you get me a glass of water?" Lana's head hurt a little, and if she didn't get a grip on it early on, it might hurt worse later.

"How about some breakfast downstairs? I can smell it up here."

"Go ahead if you're hungry. I need about a half hour for the aspirin to kick in. I'm sorry. I guess I had a little bit too much fun last night." She held her hand on her forehead as she spoke.

"No, I'll wait for you. There's no rush." Roadking walked into the bathroom to take a shower.

When he came out, Lana was still in bed, looking at the ceiling and thinking. But when she saw him, she sat up, got out of bed, and began to look in her suitcase for a change of clothes. Her mood had clearly brightened.

"I'm feeling pretty good right now. Let me shower and let's grab some breakfast."

Lana soon emerged from the bathroom wrapped in a towel and proceeded to get dressed without hesitation within full view of Roadking. He smiled to himself and quietly watched her sweet, little body.

"Are you in a hurry to get home today?" he finally spoke.

"No, not at all. Are you? I'm enjoying myself so much."

"No. Well, there's a highway that leads west out of Trinidad and makes a loop through the hills and then north to Walsenburg. It's called the Highway of Legends Scenic Byway. It's supposed to wind through beautiful country—certainly better than the interstate. How about it? Maybe it would be a good trip for us to take on the Road King someday too. But it will add a couple of hours to our return home today."

"Sounds great. It'll be fun. So many new experiences in one weekend. The chili cook-off, the bed-and-breakfast, the music, the Legends Bar, you singing karaoke, and I can't forget my line dancing lesson—ha!"

They left their room and went downstairs to the dining room of the bed-and-breakfast. What a spread—there were sausages and bacon, scrambled eggs, mini jalapeño quiches, mini breakfast burritos with chorizo, Belgian waffles, hash browns, homemade flour tortillas, and fruit crowded carefully on the marble top of a quartersawn, oak china buffet. White and blue china place settings were placed at each chair in the dining room with white linen napkins and light blue water goblets. Roadking picked up a plate and began to fill it with some of everything. Lana was hungry but careful not to overindulge and chose bacon, a mini quiche, and fruit. It was a lot more than she would usually eat, but it was a long drive home and they probably wouldn't stop again for a meal. The host of the B&B approached them at the table and asked if they cared for a mimosa.

"Sure, why not? What do you think, Lana?"

"For sure." Then she whispered to Roadking. "The hair of the dog . . ."

The host poured each of them a mimosa in a fluted goblet with a gold rim.

After a minute or two, Lana suddenly said, "Oh no, Vincent! There have been so many opportunities for me to take photos during this trip, but I've been so wrapped up in the fun that I've forgotten all about my phone. And last night when I could have videoed you singing the Elvis song, my phone was in the room being charged. For the rest of the trip home, there will be plenty of photos, beginning now."

Lana beckoned the B&B host. "Here, if I give you my phone, could you take a photo of us here?"

"Why, of course. You two make a lovely couple." He smiled at them as he took a couple of snapshots.

When they finished breakfast, Roadking and Lana returned to their room and began to pack up their things. Lana took a couple of photos of the room and of the view from the B&B windows. Lana insisted on taking a photo of Roadking standing next to the SS 396 before they left. They hopped in the car and made a stop at a gas station for gas and to pick up bottles of water, ice, and a cooler for the food from the chili cook-off that they were taking home.

"Could you get me a Coke, please, for the drive home?"

"Still working on that headache?"

"No, but the Coke partners up with the aspirin and it'll hopefully keep it from coming back."

Roadking put the Hatch chiles and the other food in the cooler, and they began the journey home headed west out of Trinidad. The distinctive piquant but pleasant scent of the roasted chiles drifted through the car. The scent of the chiles would always remind her of the Walsenburg weekend with Roadking.

Leon was unhinged. Lana had been gone since Saturday morning. He paced, he smoked, he broke bottles, he pulled his hair, he twisted his mustache, he tossed a switchblade at his wall dozens of times and watched the monitor of her house. She was with *him*. He hated him with a fire hot vengeance. When he could think of anything other than Lana, he plotted revenge against Roadking. *That pretty boy. Rich. Smooth. Refined. Classy.* Everything Leon was not.

But no matter—Lana was his prize for saving her from certain death at the hands of her ex-husband. He did not forget about that son of a bitch ex-husband. *What he did to her! That cowardly bastard! He deserves some ass kickin' too. One bullet won't be enough.*

On Saturday night when his lunacy no longer allowed him to remain confined to his house, Leon got into his van and drove. There was no relief from his frenzy for him by smoking pot or breaking beer bottles or trashing his house and van. He hopped into his van and drove, just to be moving, but he continued to anxiously eyeball the monitor of Lana's house on his smartphone. She wasn't coming home yet. As he steered the van through random streets, he thought about Lana. How did she weave her way into his psyche? What was it about her that fueled his obsession? Why couldn't he get her out of his head? She was under his skin and there was no rational explanation for himself. Snippets of memories of her flickered through his mind.

He drove to Sky High and sat in the parking lot, momentarily remembering the first time he had seen her there and the time he had saved her from some high school taunting. He drove around the perimeter of the high school a couple of times for no apparent reason until he found a reason. An equipment shed to store athletic equipment was built near the high school stadium. It was a small structure made of logs with a dark green metal roof. Leon parked on the avenue near the stadium. He went around to the back of his van and gathered the components he needed to concoct some mischief. Gasoline and matches. He skulked into the athletic yard and made his way to the shed, carrying a gas can. He poured gasoline along the entire perimeter of the little building and lit a match. Within seconds, the little building was consumed by flames. Leon scurried back to the van, drove away slowly, and watched the flames grow higher and the smoke become thicker.

"All right!" he bellowed. Leon felt exhilaration setting another fire and subconsciously believed it would extinguish his thoughts of her, but nothing could alleviate the intensity of his demented fantasy of Lana.

The black SS 396 headed west out of Trinidad on Highway 12, and the road began to wind parallel to the Purgatoire River. The hum of the engine accompanied Roadking and Lana as they surveyed the new scenery and talked. Through the windshield ahead of them, they could see the Culebra Range rising in the distance. A few minutes out of Trinidad, they drove through the tiny town of Cokedale. Lana googled each site along the way. From the highway, they could see the remnants of eight hundred coke ovens used to smelt coal in the distant past, which resembled the ruins of Roman architecture. She asked Roadking to stop so she could get photos of them. She thought that perhaps these photos would be useful for a future magazine article down the road too.

Soon they came upon tiny Segundo and then Weston, while the view of the picturesque blue mountains moved ever closer as they drove by the lush river valley ranches. At Stonewall, at the foot of the Sangre de Cristo Mountains, they made a turn north and the SS 396 began the climb up Cucharas Pass. From there they could see the volcanic formations on Spanish Peaks in the distance. When they reached the summit of the pass, Lana and Roadking stopped and got out of the car and took more photos of the mountain scenery and of each other. The air was crisp and cool and perfumed with the fresh scent of piñon. There were traces of snow on the ground from previous snowfall.

"I wish we could bottle up this air and take some home. It would remind us of this weekend and of this fresh mountain air. It's so beautiful, Vincent."

"It's getting chilly up here. Should I grab our jackets or are you ready to head down the pass?"

"Oh, just give me a couple of minutes. Stand over there, Vincent, with the Spanish Peaks at your back so I can snap a photo of you." He was so handsome that the beautiful Spanish Peaks were hardly noticeable in the photo that she took. Lana began to shiver, but she insisted on a couple of selfies of them.

When they reached the little town of La Veta on the other side of the pass, Lana saw that there were a few art galleries and boutiques on Main Street and asked Roadking if they could stop and have a look. Each gallery and boutique carried authentic Navajo rugs and pottery, ceramics by local potters, handmade custom silver jewelry, and oil and pastel paintings of the Spanish Peaks, wildflowers, and wildlife. Roadking patiently let her browse, admitting to himself how much he liked to accompany her as she shopped.

Lana found a small Navajo Two Gray Hills weaving that she thought would look good hanging on a narrow diagonal wall in her home. Even though she liked the ceramics on display, she was never one to display knickknacks in her house. She began to look at the jewelry and found a single strand, silver, serpentine necklace with a delicate pattern of aspen leaves etched in the silver that she purchased for herself. After she paid for it, she handed it to Roadking and asked him to put it on her.

Before they left La Veta, they grabbed a couple of the bottles of water and some bizcochitos out of the cooler to snack on. They followed the Cucharas River back to Walsenburg and began the trek north on the interstate home.

They continued to talk and laugh and listen to music and enjoy their time together. Roadking often put his hand on her left knee as he drove. Sometimes he held her hand. And sometimes Lana leaned her head on his right shoulder. He had been so wonderful to her the entire week since the attack, so understanding of her need to get away, so patient with her silence, and so comfortable to be around. Lana was more grateful than she could ever express and more in love than she would ever say.

When they neared Denver, Lana mentioned to Roadking, "I think I want to get rid of the Escalade. It was a gift from Lucas's parents, and it reminds me of him and his Cadillacs and the attack and . . ." Her words drifted off. "Do you have any recommendations?"

"Well, since you're used to driving a luxury SUV, you could look at a Mercedes or Porsche SUV. Or a Lincoln Navigator. And they make midsize SUVs that are just as luxurious as the full-size ones."

"Thanks, I might start looking at some of those models. I don't know what's in store for me this week with Lucas and the investigation. I'm having a security gate set at the entrance to the driveway, which might be a better deterrent than the security system I already have. And I'm getting rid of the leather couches that I had and getting some painting done too. I'll get it all done. Vincent, thank you for spending a beautiful weekend with me. I loved every minute of it. You're so generous and kind to me. I don't know how to thank you."

"No thanks necessary. I had a great time, too, with you. I think I . . ." He started to speak but didn't finish the sentence.

When they exited off I-25 to US 36, Roadking took the ramp onto Sheridan Boulevard, pulled into a parking lot, and said, "Okay, can you drive a stick shift?"

"Yes, of course. My dad made me learn how to. In fact, I kind of prefer it."

"Okay, little lady. Your turn to drive the SS 396." He got out of the car and Lana slid over the console and into the white leather bucket seat.

When she touched the steering wheel, she could feel the vibration of the muscle machine engine in her hands. And she could feel it in the gas pedal and clutch. *What a powerful feeling!* As she released the clutch, there was a little jolt as Lana was not used to the timing of the clutch release and simultaneous shift of the gears. Roadking chuckled.

"Lana, you look good driving this thing. Redhead in an SS 396. It doesn't get any better than that."

She laughed. "This is so much fun. I've never driven a muscle car. I love this thing."

While Lana and Roadking were having a fantastic weekend, Leon was not. By Sunday afternoon, he had gotten tired of sitting in his house watching the monitor for her return. He got into his van and drove out by Lana's house and parked on the side of Hill View Road to watch for her to come back. She would come back. She had to come back. But when he got tired of waiting in one spot, he drove to a different spot along Hill View Road. He looked at himself in the rearview mirror. He saw a madman with violent red eyes, skin that was a grayish yellow from smoke, hair tangled and greasy, and mustache twisted and stringy. "Look what that little gal has done to me," Leon remarked to himself, seemingly unaware that he always looked like that. He started the van again and drove a little farther up the road, turned around, and parked again. He repeated this pattern a dozen times.

"Where the fuck did he take that little gal?" he grunted to himself. Disturbing thoughts ran through his disturbed mind. *What if that Harley bastard killed her and buried her somewhere or what if he kidnapped her and locked her in a shack in the hills and is torturing her or—worst of all—what if they eloped?*

Late in the afternoon, the SS 396 arrived at Lana's house. Lana pulled in front of the house, disabled the alarm system, quickly eyeballed the exterior of the house, and unlocked the door. Roadking reached into the back seat and grabbed her bag and carried it to the front door.

"Lana, let me bring the cooler in and we can split up the food that we bought in Walsenburg."

"No, just bring in the tamales. I'll heat them up quickly and we can eat some before you head back to Louisville. Keep the rest and we can have ourselves a Mexican buffet someday soon." Suddenly, Lana wished that she hadn't said that. She was afraid that it made it sound like she owned him and was inviting herself to his house. She never wanted to be pushy with him.

"I think tamales tonight and a Mexican feast another day both sound great." He walked out to the car and brought the tamales in.

Lana was relieved that he'd responded as he did. She turned on some music and headed to the kitchen. "There's only a couple of chairs in the living room since the couches were moved out. So why don't you come in the kitchen with me? Wine or beer?"

"I'll take a beer to go with the tamales."

Lana wrapped the tamales in foil and set them in the oven to warm. She made some guacamole and poured a jar of salsa from a gourmet shop into a bowl. Then she took a couple of flour tortillas and created a cheese, black olive, avocado, tomato quesadilla and set it in the oven to crisp. She set a couple of colorful plates at the kitchen table and poured a beer for Roadking. She saw him look at a message on his phone.

"I need to text my mom. She always wants me to stop by on Sunday to see the family. I guess I'll swing by on the way home. She's gonna load me up with lasagna or rigatoni or gnocchi."

Soon the delicious tamales were done. She cut the quesadilla into wedges. She set the food out for them. They sat quietly and ate for a while and listened to the music.

"Well," Lana finally spoke, "I kind of told you what I have going on this week. How about you?"

Roadking thought for a moment, "Aw, just living the good life. Each day brings something new. I never know if someone will walk through that door to interview me and make my day special." He smiled with his crinkly eyes at her.

Lana smiled back at him.

"I have to stop by and see the family. Come here, baby, walk me to the door."

She stood, and he put his arm around her and pulled her close to him as they walked with his hand resting on her hip. She put her arm around his waist. As they stood in the entryway, he reached into his denim jacket pocket and pulled out some folded, pink tissue paper and handed it to Lana. She carefully unfolded it. Inside was a single strand, silver, serpentine bracelet that matched the necklace she had bought in La Veta. He took the bracelet from her hand and asked her to hold out her left arm and fastened it on her wrist. Lana put both of her arms around his neck and kissed him. And then they kissed again and again. Each time deeper and deeper.

"Lana, I just might have to stay . . ." he chuckled.

"Oh, Vincent, the bracelet is so beautiful! It is so perfect! I didn't even see a bracelet that matched at the shop. Thank you so much." She hugged him tightly around his waist. He was thrilled to see her reaction.

"You're welcome. You loved the necklace so much. When I saw the bracelet, I wanted you to have it too."

One more hug and kiss and Lana reluctantly let him go. The weekend with him had been heavenly. She sat down on a chair near the window and watched him leave, purposely going over every detail of the weekend in her mind and committing all of it to memory.

Someone else watched as Roadking left Lana's house. Leon had been parked on Hill View Road in various spots for several hours, bored and angry. His van had filled with smoke as he'd chain-smoked, alternating between pot and Marlboros. When the SS 396 drove past him, Leon started his van, slowly pulled out, and began to follow Roadking, keeping a distance between them.

"I'm a gonna find out where you live, son of a bitch, if it takes me all night. Yer gonna lead me right to your door and you don't even know it," Leon snarled under his breath as they both headed toward Louisville.

CHAPTER 24

Angelo and Eva Romano lived a mile east of Louisville on a country road called Empire on a one-acre property that was the homestead of an immigrant Slovenian coal miner and his large family. When the Romanos purchased the property over forty years ago, they demolished the little two-bedroom farmhouse and built a two-story contemporary home where Roadking and his sisters had been raised. Louisville seemed to move closer to them as the community grew, but they were still on the outskirts of town right where they wanted to be. Even though Eva was an interior designer and Angelo was a builder, the house remained largely unchanged over the decades except for some cosmetic upgrades, attesting to the comfort that was built into its original design. Eva's passions were her family and feeding them, and she looked forward to her children and grandchildren, assorted nieces and nephews, cousins, brothers, and sisters gathering at their home for dinner every Sunday afternoon. Dinner was sometimes Italian, sometimes Mexican, and sometimes a combination of both, like her Mexican lasagna with chorizo, Hatch chiles, and jalapeños. Occasionally, one or more of the family members was missing from the table, and on this Sunday, it was Vincent.

Roadking was consumed with thoughts of Lana as he drove home to Louisville. She was so alive, so pretty, so unique, so happy, so comfortable to be with. He truly hated to leave her and missed her already. He wanted her to be with him. She had divorced just several weeks before they met and had then been attacked by her ex-husband. She had been through so much in such a brief period. He wouldn't pressure her to commit to him—not yet. He surprised himself that thoughts of commitment trickled into his mind. They barely knew each other, but it all felt familiar in some cosmic way.

As Roadking cruised along 95th Street headed toward Louisville, he was totally unaware that he was being followed by a beat-up green van with a driver with ill intentions. The sun set and the sky darkened to navy blue. He was looking forward to arriving in time for round two of the Sunday feast, even though he had just consumed two tamales and half a quesadilla with Lana. He pulled into the half circle, paved driveway in front of the house. As he expected when he entered, there was the usual loud discussion among the members of the family seated at the large dining room table, as well as vigorous conversation from others in the living room who were watching football. About a half dozen children of all ages were playing and bickering. His mother jumped up when she saw him and immediately began to fill a plate for him with enchiladas and homemade pork green chili.

"Go easy, Mom. I just had some tamales."

"Where were you off to this weekend?"

"I went to Walsenburg for a chili cook-off, stayed in Trinidad, and then took the Highway of Legends route home. It's a pretty route through mountains and a river valley near the Sangre de Cristo Mountains. I just got back about an hour ago."

"So who did you go with?"

"I met a woman a few weeks ago and she went with me." Roadking let it go at that. Even though he was almost forty years old, he knew that his mother would want more information about the girl, but she would have to wait. He wanted his parents to meet Lana eventually but not until he asked Lana about it first—in good time. They could easily overwhelm her.

Eva handed Roadking a heaping plate of enchiladas and opened a bottle of Corona for him. He carried them into the living room and sat near his uncle Santino.

"So Vincenzo, what's up?" Santino spoke to him, still looking straight ahead at the TV.

"Nothing, Santino. Just took a little road trip this weekend down to Walsenburg and Trinidad. And I've been selling and trading Harleys. How you been doing?"

"Oh, okay, I guess, Vincenzo—except for those son of a bitch politicians in Washington screwing everything up in this country. They're gonna break us." It was the answer Roadking had expected. It was the same every time he asked.

"So what's the score?"

"Broncos by three points. They just punted to the Chiefs."

Roadking continued to watch the game in silence. He carried his half-finished plate of food into the kitchen, where he found his dad making spumoni ice-cream cones for all the kids, who were gathered around him as if he were Santa Claus.

"Hey, Pops."

"Want a cone, son?"

"No, I'm already going to have to add extra workout time to my routine from eating mom's enchiladas."

Suddenly, muffled sounds of pop-pop-pop could be heard over the noise in the house.

"What the hell could that be?" Angelo, Roadking, and some of the others walked to the front door and opened it to look outside.

"You guys, get away from the front door! You don't know what's going on out there! You're like a target! *Madon*!" shouted Eva at the group of men gathered at the door to see.

"Eva! Calm yourself! It's probably just some kids shooting some firecrackers down by the creek or a car backfiring," Eva's brother Antonio yelled at her.

"Antonio, stop shouting! You'll scare the kids."

The children were silent for a minute during the exchange between Eva and her brother but resumed eating their ice-cream cones and playing in short order.

Roadking opened the front storm door, looked up and down the road, and saw the taillights of a vehicle headed east on Empire Road and away from the house. Whatever had happened, it was quiet and still now. Then he happened to see a glitter in the driveway, reflecting light from the house. He stepped out the door and walked a few steps toward the SS 396 and saw that the back windshield and driver's side window had been shattered. The pop-pop-pop that they'd heard were gunshots with the SS 396 as the target.

"Jesus, Vincenzo. Look at the beautiful car! What kind of a bastard would shoot out windows in a car like that?!" Santino stood next to him and shook his head. "Lousy bastards. Dumb-ass kids."

Roadking ran his hand through his hair and then rested his hand on his chin, surveying the scene and the damage to the glass. He was silent and then took a deep breath. He began to put some pieces together of what had been a puzzle in his mind. *The broken windows at the dealership, the slashed tires at Lana's house, and the windows just shot out of the SS 396—I'm a target. Lana's ex-husband is out of jail on bond. Could it be him? Does it have something to do with Lana? Or is it some random stalker? Or is all of it coincidental?*

Roadking decided to call the Louisville Police as he had done with the broken windows at All Roads. Maybe their investigation could turn up the culprit or at least pinpoint the link between these events, if any. He might as well tell them about the slashed tires, too, even though that incident had not occurred in their jurisdiction.

Leon's heart raced and his eyes danced with excitement as he drove away from the Romano house and began his drive back to Columbine Point. Shooting at that fancy car was a thrill—so much so that he had forgotten to watch the monitor of Lana's house for at least an hour. The remoteness of the house made his mission easy. He was pumped up and listened to his Metallica CDs at full volume as he drove and pounded his fist on the dashboard and laughed. "I found out where you live, pretty boy. And I just got started with ya."

Leon finally settled down as he drove into Columbine Point and got closer to his house. He began to watch the monitor of Lana's house again. He saw her unpack her suitcase in her bedroom. Boring. It was still early in the evening. She wouldn't be getting ready to go to bed for a little while. He decided that he needed to install more hidden cameras in her house. Too often she was out of his view and he didn't like that. He would add several more hidden cameras when he was scheduled to check out the security system on Wednesday.

Two police officers arrived on the scene and took a report and had no immediate ideas about a culprit, but they were interested in Roadking's theory about a link among the events. He mentioned Lucas Chisholm's name to them, but they told him that they knew he had an ankle monitor, but they said they'd investigate whether he was complicit. They couldn't speculate about the damage to the windows of the car and the shattered dealership windows, although they would reach out to the Boulder County Sheriff about a possible connection among these events. But the police noticed a bullet in the back seat of the car and recognized that it was a 9 mm bullet like the ones they used in their police-issued Glocks.

Roadking swept the glass off the driver's seat of the SS 396 and then swept up the glass in his parents' driveway after the police left. Then he went back into the Romano house to tell everyone goodbye.

"Thanks, Mom. Great enchiladas. Go Broncos! See you next weekend?"

"Vince, what happened out there? Did the police have any ideas?" Angelo questioned his son.

"No, they're looking into it. It seems a long shot that they could find the guy. Forget about it. Continue to enjoy the evening."

The children swarmed around him to tell him goodbye as he walked toward the door. He tousled the hair on the heads of a couple of the kids and picked up the smallest little boy and hugged and kissed him goodbye.

Thoughts weighed heavily on Roadking's mind as he drove the few miles to his home in west Louisville. This was another unpleasant incident that had occurred after he'd had such a wonderful day or night or weekend with Lana. *Could any of this be connected to Lana somehow?* The simple solution would be to find the culprit responsible and get him off the streets. He would not give Lana up or let any act of vandalism keep him away, if any of it was related to her. He pulled the SS 396 into the garage. He would make an appointment to get the glass replaced tomorrow. That car had been through hell lately.

Lana unpacked her bag from the weekend trip, started some laundry, and washed the dishes from the tamale dinner. Feeling sluggish, she jumped on the treadmill for an hour and worked out with the light weights. About eight o'clock, she received a text from Roadking.

You are an awesome travel companion. I had a wonderful time with you. Thanks.

Lana smiled as she read the message and returned a text with a happy bunny sticker and sent him a couple photos that she had taken on the trip—one of him standing by the SS 396, one of him with the Spanish Peaks in the background, and a selfie of them both.

She called Olivia and asked her to meet her for lunch on Monday at noon. There was so much to talk about. So much had happened in the previous week. She needed to catch up with her. "Olivia, did you know Cate had been seeing Lucas?"

"No way! I haven't talked to her all week. Strange, now that I think about it, that she didn't call after you were attacked. Maybe that explains it. Are you sure that Lucas was her mystery man?"

"Yes, she told me. I'll tell you all about it tomorrow. I hope an hour for lunch will be long enough."

Lana turned on the TV and sat on one of the tan, leather occasional chairs and looked at the half-empty living room and thought about what had happened there less than a week before. Although she would relive the attack many times, she told herself that those moments in time were gone, never to return except in her memory. *Put those upsetting thoughts away in that little place in your head where you keep them*, she told herself and fully intended to do just that.

She walked upstairs to her bedroom to take a shower. She turned on the TV in the bedroom just for the noise, stripped completely nude, turned back the sheets, grabbed the T-shirt that she slept in, and walked into the master bathroom.

Leon was captivated by what he saw. "I been a waitin' fer that little naked body fer a while there, Lana, darlin'. I can't wait until yer mine and I can get a feel of all that you got there." He smoked and drank beer and waited for her to finish the shower.

She came out of the bathroom wearing the T-shirt, turned off the lamp and TV, and got into bed. She lay on her back, thought, and looked around at the dark shapes in the room. She missed sleeping with Roadking. She lay on the pillow he had used when he'd stayed there on Thursday night. His scent was still there.

"Good night, Vincent," she whispered to the dark.

"Well, Lana, darlin', the show's over fer the night." Leon looked away from the monitor and made himself a bologna sandwich. "Been a pretty good weekend all in all," he sneered. "Burned a shed, shot out some windows, and seen that little gal naked." Excitement surged through Leon's veins. He was still on a high from his most recent antics. He felt like he had to move, like he had to go somewhere. He got in his van and headed for Red's Bar, a little dive in downtown Columbine Point.

CHAPTER 25

"Hey, Leon. What's happenin' there, bro?" the bartender greeted Leon when he opened the door.

"Pour me a brew there, Calvin. Nothin' happenin' tonight." Leon scanned the dingy, nondescript, dark bar. He spotted a couple of his friends playing pool in the back under a dim, dusty, rectangular ceiling light.

"Hey, assholes," he greeted them. "Let me in on the action."

"Goddamn, Leon, how the hell ya been? Ain't seen ya for a couple of months," mumbled a guy named Jerry, who was covered in thick, white drywall dust.

"Well, been workin' on a job securing a house for a little gal."

"Been getting any off her?" Jerry chuckled, amused with himself.

"Naw, it ain't like that, not yet anyway," Leon laughed loudly. Leon glanced around at the dark corners of the room and spotted a woman sitting in a booth in the dark, nursing a Long Island iced tea.

"Hey, Carla, darlin'. How about let's hookup tonight?" he hollered across the room. "Get on over here, gal, so I can get a good look at ya."

Carla stepped clumsily out of the shadows. She was middle-aged, a little older than Leon. Tall, big-boned, chesty, and top-heavy with a very noticeable muffin top that hung over the waist of her jeans. She wore a men's plaid shirt like a jacket to cover her bulging waist. Her hair, piled on top of her head in a messy bun, was an artificial dull black color that didn't match her complexion. She wore hot pink, plastic earrings that looked like bubble gum dangling from her earlobes. Her facial features were large, unappealing, and almost masculine. Her looks didn't matter to Leon.

There was no doubt what he wanted her for, and he was going to get it. The voyeurism of watching Lana and the frustration of her dalliance with Roadking had caused an intense sexual tension in him.

When Carla spoke, her voice was hoarse and raspy from decades of smoking. "What do ya mean by hookup, Leon?" she smirked as she spoke. She knew perfectly well what he meant.

"How 'bout you and me head outside to my van? I can make a little spot fer us out there. How about it? You and me, darlin'?"

There was a long silence as Carla looked into his bloodshot eyes for several seconds, tried to determine if he was really interested in her or just teasing her, and then tried to decide whether to say yes or no. But she could see that the prospects of a sexual encounter were pretty slim for both of them this Sunday night. Carla gulped the rest of her Long Island iced tea down. "Let's hit it, Leon."

Leon walked out to the beat-up van, opened the doors in the back, scooted his tools over to the side, and laid down a tarp. As Carla climbed in, he gave her a little push from behind and laughed. They tried to get comfortable on the hard metal floor in the back of the van. Leon wouldn't look at her face. He closed his eyes and imagined he was with someone else. Within minutes, Leon got the release that he needed. Carla lay there, feeling a little nauseous from the potent drink and the disgust of Leon lying on top of her and her sudden shame. She had let herself be used like so many times before. She pulled her clothes back on, slid out the back of the van, walked toward a dumpster parked on the side of the bar, and vomited. Leon walked past her and snickered.

"Carla, was I too much fer ya, gal?"

"Fuck you, Leon."

"I think you already did, Carla." He roared with laughter at his clever response.

Leon walked back into the bar, gave his buddies Jerry and Doug a high five, and then played a couple of games of pool. Carla staggered back in, resumed her place in the back of the bar, and ordered another Long Island iced tea. Around midnight, Leon went home, made another bologna sandwich, and smoked a joint, feeling quite satisfied.

On Monday at noon, Lana met Olivia for lunch. "Lana, tell me everything! About Lucas! About Cate!" Olivia was impatient to know the full stories about the recent unexpected turn of events as she and Lana ordered chicken salad lunches at a brewery on the Pearl Street Mall. Lana narrated the events of the near rape and strangulation by Lucas. Olivia's eyes were big, but she didn't interrupt with questions like she usually did.

"Why didn't you call me? I would have come. You could have stayed with me." Her eyes were still wide and her voice animated.

"I called you, but I only got voice mail. I couldn't relay what happened to me in a message. I stayed with Vincent Romano for a couple of days."

Olivia's eyes grew even wider as she leaned back in her chair.

"What's going on there?"

"There's not much to say except that he gave me a place to stay when I couldn't bear to be in the house alone for a while. Blood needed to be cleaned up and I had to get rid of the two leather couches. I'm taking care of all of that. He's nice. I like him." It was a distinct understatement.

"So how does Cate fit into this picture?"

"I called Cate to let her know that I was okay, since I assumed that she'd probably heard that Lucas had broken in and attacked me. She was oddly cold and short with me. And then she blurted out that she had been seeing Lucas and that the attack was my fault for having lunch with him that day. She's convinced that he wants to be with her and that he cares about her. Fine with me. But she thinks that I was interfering with that relationship. He was using her. Lucas doesn't care about her or me. Then I ran into her last Friday at Rite Aid. I tried to talk to her. She made a big scene and slapped me. I was so embarrassed. Have you talked to her at all? Did she ever give you a hint that Lucas was the mystery man?"

Olivia was uncharacteristically silent for a few minutes with her mouth open and eyes wide as she listened intently and then recalled her recent conversations with Cate. There had been nothing unusual that she could remember.

"I can't believe that all of this happened last week. I saw that Lucas was released on a one-million-dollar bond. Jeez, I wonder if he's selling any Cadillacs now with all this negative press."

"I don't know and it doesn't matter to me. I deserve better than Lucas—I think I always have. I'm not going to contact Cate for a while—and maybe never. Our friendship is broken. It would take a lot of healing to mend it. She's like someone I never knew after falling under Lucas's spell."

The chicken salads were brought to the table.

"So Lana, how is it that the lock and key guy happened to be there to stop Lucas? Isn't he that guy from high school? Remember we saw his photo in one of the yearbooks?"

"Yep, it's the same guy. He's been installing a security system at the house for the past couple of weeks. You know there have been unusual events happening there recently—the snake for example. So he'd added some additional devices that day and he came by to deliver the bill for the work when he saw Lucas trying to strangle me from the front window. Thankfully he was there and got in somehow since he's a lock and key guy, and he had a gun and shot him in the shoulder. It could have been worse."

Lana continued. "I'm steering clear of the media and I'm not watching local TV news. It's too upsetting and a constant reminder of what happened. Lucas will be arraigned on Friday. I can see a news reporter from a local station sitting right over there watching us." Lana motioned to the corner of the room.

"They've been hounding me. Now that he sees me talking to you, he may approach you for information. They're bloodthirsty for any snippet of info they can broadcast. But I'm done talking about my stuff. What's been going on with you?"

Olivia went on to narrate the recent events in her life in her usual dramatic fashion, even though they couldn't compare to the events that Lana had just related to her. Their former high school classmate Alex, who Lana had gone out with a few weeks before, was in contact with Olivia and was planning to return to Boulder to visit her in a few days. Lana was relieved that he was no longer interested in her.

They sat silently for a few minutes while they ate. "Lana, you know, I was talking to one of the brides that I'll be photographing in the spring, and she told me that they're honeymooning at Pink Sands Beach in the Bahamas. It's on an island, I think it was called Harbour Island . . . not sure, but the sand on the beach is literally pink. What do you think about taking a trip—you and me—and visiting the Pink Sands Beach when we can both get away? We haven't done anything like that since before Lucas. And after everything that's happened, it'd be good to plan a trip. I guess we should google it and find out a little more about it, but it seems like a perfect place for two hot chicks like us to visit, and it's pink too! We'd have to buy a couple of sexy bikinis that don't clash with the pink sand," Olivia mused.

Lana thought for a moment. It was a big idea but not an unusual one for Olivia. "Well, I need to get a passport and we should research it a little more. But I think we could." Despite saying that, in the back of her mind was the thought that she would be away from Roadking for a week or so, and she didn't want that. But she thought that he would want her to go and experience it. The more she thought about it, the better it sounded. After all, she and Roadking were close but not attached.

Lana and Olivia finished their conversations and lunch. Olivia had a meeting with a future bride and her mother about a wedding booking. Lana had a meeting with the art director. The building of the January edition was underway. Progress was being made building the February and March editions that would carry the series about touring Colorado without a car—the topic that had led Lana to her first meeting with Roadking. She had finished writing the segment about motorcycle touring, and the photos from All Roads had been inserted into the edit. The snowshoe, hot air balloon, and ATV segments were still in progress.

Later in the afternoon, the gate installer called to let her know that the security gate at the entrance to the long driveway to her house was installed and secured with the gate code that she had provided them—1-9-7-5—and to let her know to program her phone with the app and code that she needed to operate the gate.

As Lana gathered her things to leave the office, she received a text from Roadking.

I'll be in Boulder tomorrow morning. Want to meet for coffee and a donut?

Of course—where and when?

Broadway Coffee Shop on Broadway and Balsam. 10:00 okay?

Yes, sounds good. See you soon.

The security gate worked perfectly as she arrived at home and used the access code via her phone. When she pulled through the gate and it closed behind her, she felt safer than she had felt in weeks . With the alarms at the doors and the security monitors at the entrance to the driveway and the front of the house, the chances seemed slim that a person could enter the property undetected.

Lana went in the house and laid down her laptop and purse. She ran upstairs to change quickly and began to work out with the hard, driving rhythms of her workout play list. She was so happy that she would see Roadking the next day. When her workout was through, she went upstairs to her closet to pick out clothes to wear the next day. There wouldn't be time for a manicure, but maybe he wouldn't notice the chipped nail polish. She made herself a grilled cheese sandwich and sliced a Gala apple for dinner. She listened to an old Linda Ronstadt album that her mother had played over and over while she was growing up. For some reason, the memory of that music popped into her head and she listened to it again. "Silver Blue," "Faithless Love," "Long, Long Time." Soft and tender, the music accompanied the loving thoughts about Roadking that flowed through her head. Sometimes she liked melancholy softness. It was a nice change from the fast music she listened to during her workout.

On Tuesday morning, Lana awoke excited to see Roadking in a few hours. She dressed in black leather skinny pants and a white, soft cashmere sweater that framed her face with fluff and rested at her waist. The weather was chilly in the mornings in October. She arrived at work a little early, knowing that she would be gone for an hour or so later and wanted to make sure everyone was on task for the morning.

A little before ten o'clock, Lana drove to the Broadway Coffee Shop. As she walked to the door, Roadking approached from a different direction. She smiled and waited for him. When he got close, he kissed her lightly on the lips.

"Hello, baby."

"Hi, Vincent. This looks like a cute little shop. How do you happen to know about this place?"

"When I was in high school, I worked here for a couple of years. The people that I worked for sold it awhile back, but it has the same kind of homey atmosphere. I bussed tables, washed dishes, and did a little bit of cooking. I come here occasionally when I'm in Boulder early in the day. They only serve breakfast and lunch."

There were about fifteen tables and booths in the little café. There was a little bar where four or five people could be seated as well. The windows were framed by white tie-back curtains topped by a matching white valance. The tables were covered with red linen tablecloths. The floor was a black-and-white checkerboard tile. There were oil and pastel paintings on the wall created by local artists.

"Hello, Roadking. And how are you both today?" The waitress seated them in a booth.

"We're good, Connie. This is Lana. Could you bring us a couple of menus?"

"Sure, Roadking. The specials today are a frittata with spinach, mushrooms, artichokes, and ham, and gingerbread pancakes topped with cinnamon, whipped cream, and toasted hazelnuts."

Connie brought the menus. Lana ate light in the morning, but everything on the menu and the specials sounded great.

"What do you think, Lana? I usually get a basic breakfast of two eggs, bacon, hash browns, and toast."

"I think I'll have the pumpkin chocolate chip muffin and to feel less guilty about that, I'll have some fruit too."

Connie came and took the orders. Lana could tell that something was on Roadking's mind, as he sat quietly for a few minutes before he spoke.

"Lana, when I went to my parents' house in Louisville after I left you on Sunday, someone shot out the windshield and driver's side window of the SS 396 while I was inside the house. I called the police this time and they found a 9 mm bullet from a Glock lying in the back seat. With the broken windows at the dealership, the slashed tires at your house, and now the windows shot out of the SS 396, I'm not certain if I'm being stalked or if these are random events. I don't know if your ex-husband could have something to do with it, or if it has anything to do with you and me at all. But I want you to know about it because I want you to be aware of your surroundings—when you go to the parking garage, when you walk down the street, when you get groceries, anytime. Pay attention to see if anyone is following you. I don't want anything to happen to you because of me."

Lana sat quietly and took it all in. Connie brought the breakfasts to the table.

Before Lana took a bite, she said, "There were some odd happenings at my house before I met you. That's why I had the security system installed, for what it's worth. I mean, one day when I came home, a bull snake was slithering through the house. On other occasions, things had been moved around in my bedroom. I guess Lucas could be up to something, but he's already in so much trouble. His arraignment is Friday. I had a security gate installed yesterday. By the way, I want you to know that the code is 1-9-7-5 for the gate to open."

"Okay, enough said about that. Well, on a brighter note, the open house at the dealership is this weekend on Saturday. And remember? I invited you. It'll run from noon to six. I'm inviting current and former customers and friends. I do this annually and it's a fun time—and often profitable too." Roadking smiled with his crinkly eyes.

Out of the corner of Lana's eye, she saw a woman quickly approach their booth. She was short—maybe five feet, two inches tall-cute, and heavily made-up with very short, blonde hair and an off-white wool coat with a heavy, white, fur collar—not really appropriate for the fall weather.

"Well hello, V.," the woman said with a sarcastic, high-pitched, nasal voice. She rested her left hand on Roadking's shoulder as she talked. Her perfume was heavy. Roadking leaned back and visibly stiffened when he heard her voice and before he turned to look at her and then quickly looked straight ahead.

"Jeez, Cameron, what are you doing here? I didn't expect to run into you here." Roadking spontaneously responded with no expression on his face. But his jaw was tight.

"Well, V., I was in town. You know I work for the Marriott Hotels now in Bethesda, and I just went to the Boulder Marriott this morning and had time to kill before I head to Denver, and I remembered this little place that you introduced me to once, and so I stopped by to get a coffee and one of those homemade cinnamon rolls. Hi, I'm Cameron, by the way. V. and I go back a ways, don't we, V.?" She reached out her right hand to Lana.

Roadking bristled as she spoke and responded before Lana could speak. "This is Lana Ross."

Lana watched his unmistakable body language. He was so clearly uncomfortable and annoyed that she was there. So this must be the Cameron for whom her dad had said he had designed an engagement ring.

"So how's your family doing, V.? Everybody doing good?"

"Yes, Cameron, all are happy and healthy."

"Well, good to see you, V. I'll be on my way. Nice to meet you, uh, what was your name again?"

"Lana Ross." Roadking responded in a monotone.

"Yeah, right. Bye-bye." Cameron breezed out of the café as quickly as she had entered. But her perfume remained.

Lana looked at Roadking and thought that he looked flushed. She would not prod him with questions. He was still leaning back in his chair. He put his hand to his face and held his fingers on his mouth for a minute. In a few seconds, he leaned forward and continued to eat his breakfast. Lana nibbled on her muffin and took a couple of sips of orange juice.

Then he spoke. "Cameron and I were engaged a few years ago. It turned out to be a big mistake. We were on opposite ends of the spectrum on everything. We had major conflicts about values, faith, family. Fortunately, we didn't marry. When I see her now, I don't know what I saw in her that made me want to share a life with her. She's so selfish and shallow. And I hate that freakin' perfume that she wears, and I never liked being called V."

As Roadking spoke, he looked past Lana and not at her. When he finished speaking, he looked at her face to assess her reaction. She smiled at him and reached over and touched his hand. She wanted to let him know that nothing that had transpired there meant anything to her. She wanted him to relax. She hated to see him so unhappy. When he saw her smile, he was relieved and knew that she would not pummel him with questions. But the comparison was clear in his mind. Cameron and Lana—night and day. Cameron and Lana—wrong and right.

CHAPTER 26

Roadking and Lana finished their coffee and orange juice. Roadking remained pensive and quiet. Lana tried to make small talk about the open house on Saturday. To ease the awkward silence, she asked if there was anything she could do to help.

"No, I just want you to be there with me. That's all I need." Roadking and Lana walked toward the front of the café. Roadking paid the check. He walked her to her car and quickly kissed her on the lips before she got in. He managed to give her half a smile. She watched him walk toward his car on the other side of the parking lot. Both of his hands were in the pockets of his jean jacket, shoulders slightly hunched, and he looked down at the pavement as he walked. She could see that Cameron had caused a certain firestorm in his mind and had brought back some memories to fuel it. Something heavy must have happened between them. Maybe he would tell her about it someday. Maybe never. But the questions that had plagued her early on about his relationship status were answered in the past few weeks without her asking. And to her relief, she felt sure that he was unattached.

Roadking was visibly rattled by seeing Cameron. Memories of harsh words, tough decisions, and a volatile goodbye roared back into his mind like a flood. He viewed her departure as a blessing, and he never wanted to see her again. He felt like he should apologize to Lana for being such bad company during breakfast. Talking about the vandalism to the SS 396 and then the misfortune of running into Cameron were bad news. He chose not to think about Cameron anymore, but in the back of his mind, just the thought of the disruption she could cause in his life left him feeling unsettled and churning inside. If the relationship with Lana happened to grow stronger, he would have to be honest with her about the circumstances with Cameron someday. But not yet.

The tasks that Leon was scheduled to work on at Lana's house would only take a couple of hours, but he arrived soon after Lana had left for work. He used the security code to open the gate and then disabled the alarm system and entered the house. Even if Lana noticed that the alarm was disabled by checking the app on her phone, he could give her a reasonable explanation, although she wouldn't expect that he would have arrived so early in the day. He immediately entered the house and walked through each of the rooms to determine where the next clandestine cameras should be mounted. She spent a lot of time in the kitchen, so maybe one on the top of a cabinet door. And in the dining room on the top of the oak trim of one of the French doors. An additional one in Lana's bedroom mounted on the top of the headboard of her bed. Another one mounted on the flat-screen TV. He didn't want to miss a thing that occurred in Lana's bedroom. Another one near the floor. "In case they do it on the floor," he snickered to himself.

After he mounted the additional cameras, he checked the system to see if they all worked. They did. He then checked the fake control panel in the entryway to make sure that it appeared to be functional. The monitors and cameras that Lana were aware of operated, but the data was never transmitted to an alarm company—only to him. Lana was clueless. Secret cameras monitored her activities for him, and visible cameras monitored the premises for her. Only the security gate at the entrance to the driveway served any actual security purpose.

Leon walked back upstairs to Lana's bedroom, opened her dresser drawers, and pawed through her clothes—her cashmere and wool sweaters, her cotton T-shirts and turtlenecks—and her jewelry, rich with pearls and turquoise. He soon paused in the lingerie drawer. He had been in that drawer before, but he couldn't stop himself from touching each bra and each pair of panties—holding them up to his face to feel their soft silkiness against his coarse and smoky skin. He rifled through them a second time and decided to take a souvenir. He took a pair of leopard print panties and put them in his pocket. He closed the drawer and walked out of the bedroom, took about five steps, and turned around and came back. There was a lacy pair of teal colored panties that he could not leave behind. He put those in his pocket too. She probably wouldn't notice. He was finished for the time being but planned to come back when Lana came home at the end of the day. He enabled the alarm and went to McDonald's for a quick lunch. There were some legitimate appointments for lock and key work. He had been in business for so long that many people used his services and expertise despite his demonic appearance.

Lana returned to work and immersed herself in activity. She thought about Roadking. He had wanted to share that little coffee shop with her, and it was spoiled by the appearance of self-absorbed Cameron. She figured that she probably wouldn't see him until the open house, and she hoped that he would move past it by then. Her thoughts turned to Cameron. Maybe it was unfair to judge her, but Lana didn't like her the minute she'd opened her mouth. But she didn't have to.

In the afternoon, she received an invitation to the opening of an art gallery in Boulder in a few weeks. It was a black-tie affair and she could bring a guest. Lana loved to dress like a princess and would accept the invitation, but would Roadking accompany her? She could only imagine what he would look like in a tuxedo. She would ask him on Saturday at the All Roads open house. It crossed her mind that the new gallery opening would be a good subject for the magazine too.

Later in the afternoon when Lana returned home, Leon was there waiting on her driveway for her. She thought nothing of him being there. She had given him the gate code so he could set one of the monitors at the gate.

"Hey, Lana, darlin'. I fixed up the monitor by the gate out there. We can check it out when you go inside."

"Hi, Leon. Thanks for taking care of that. I trust that all of this security stuff is done now."

She pulled the car into the garage and they entered the house through the interior access door. Leon walked behind her as usual, wanting to reach out and touch her little behind, but he restrained himself. Lana watched as Leon completed a check of the monitors at the control panel. Then she did a quick run-through of the monitors on her phone app. Everything appeared to be functional.

"Ya know, Leon, a person just can't assume that they're safe in their own house anywhere. Look what happened to me. And a friend of mine was visiting his parents in Louisville the other night, and someone shot out the windows of his car. Fortunately, none of the bullets hit the house or anyone inside."

Leon was stunned by her comment. He stood motionless, unable to respond for a minute. *Fuck! That's not where that bastard lives! Of course she's talking about him!* shouted a voice in Leon's head. *Yeah, but I still shot up that fancy ass car of his. But goddamn it!*

"Well there, Lana, darlin', yer place is safe and that's what counts. I took care of it there fer ya, darlin'," he said when he regained his thoughts.

"Thank you, Leon. Yes, you have made me feel safe."

Leon walked toward the front door and stood in the entryway for a minute, giving Lana that familiar long stare up and down. In his mind, he responded to her, *Yep, little gal, yer right, just what I wanted. You need me. Only I can keep ya safe.* "Okay, see ya around, darlin'. Let me know if ya have any problems."

Leon left the house and Lana enabled the security system. There were a couple of things that she needed to work on. She still needed to purchase a couple of couches for her living room and she wanted to trade the Cadillac for a different luxury SUV. And she wanted a new dress for the art gallery opening. She took out her laptop and began searching the web. A couple of hours passed quickly in front of the laptop. She was hungry and needed to work out. She made herself a whole wheat pita filled with veggies and cheese and drank some sparking water. She propped her iPad on the treadmill and began to work out but continued to research the cars, couches, and gowns as she moved. An hour passed on the treadmill before she knew it. But she had made some decisions. It was getting late. She ran upstairs to shower and jumped into bed.

Although she was tired, she could not sleep. She lay on her back, her eyes scanned the darkened room, and her mind drifted to Roadking and Cameron. She was bothered by Cameron. She tried to picture in her mind what they must have looked like together, how they interacted, how they became engaged. *What was it about her that captured his attention and his heart? How would I compare to Cameron in his eyes?* She concluded that he probably didn't think that deeply about all of it anyway and that she was overthinking like she often did. Despite it, her mind slid back to them again and again until she drifted off to sleep sometime after midnight.

On Thursday morning, Lana read the newspaper. She had managed to avoid it for a few days. And there was an article about Lucas's arraignment scheduled for Friday and, of course, a condensed version of the events that had led to his arrest and another photo of him in the orange jumpsuit at the bond hearing. Surprisingly, his brother had made a statement to the press. "We believe that Lucas is innocent of these charges and that a sleep medication that he was taking may have played a part in the events leading to his arrest."

Interesting. Lana thought. *He says Lucas is innocent and, in the same breath, provides a defense for his 'innocent' actions. Oh well, his brother's opinion means nothing. A judge or jury will decide his fate.*

She really needed to talk to Roadking and hear his voice. If she heard his voice, she could tell if he had moved past the surprise encounter with Cameron that had affected him so much. Although she had planned to invite him to the gallery opening with her when she saw him on Saturday, she decided that she might not have his full attention at the open house. She called him when she arrived at her office.

Roadking answered the phone. "Hello, sweetness."

"Hey, how are you?"

"Good. What a nice surprise!"

"Well, I wanted to say hi and invite you to join me at an art gallery opening in Boulder in a few weeks. It's a black-tie affair so you'd have to wear a tuxedo. Does that sound like something you'd care to go to with me?"

"Well, sure. With you on my arm, we'll knock 'em dead."

"Really? I need to RSVP in a couple of days. So now I have my answer and I got to hear your voice today too. Thanks. I'll fill you in on the details when I see you Saturday."

"Yep, it's a date. See you Saturday. You know the open house runs from one to six. I'd like to introduce you to a few people."

"Yes, I'll be there. I'm going to look at a couple of new cars Saturday morning before I come."

"Okay, baby. Goodbye for now."

"Goodbye, sweetheart. Until Saturday." Lana was so glad that she'd made the decision to call him and had heard his voice, which didn't sound troubled or stressed or distracted like he had been the last time she had seen him after the Cameron encounter.

On Friday afternoon, Lana let herself look at the newspaper website for the latest news on the arraignment of Lucas. The list of charges had been read to him and he had entered a plea of not guilty. The judge had ordered that the ankle monitor was to remain since the prosecutor had insisted that he was a flight risk. The order restraining him from being within one hundred feet of Lana had been continued. The judge had not increased the bond. One million dollars seemed to be sufficient. Lucas had waived his right to a speedy trial, and the judge had set a trial date in April. As she had expected, there was a photo of Lucas entering a plea of not guilty to each charge before the judge. And a second photo of him as he'd left the courtroom with Cate clumsily following behind him and a string of reporters surrounding them.

Lana leaned back in her big oak office chair and slowly swiveled back and forth, twirling a strand of hair in her right hand and looking at the clouds through the window. She thought about the Lucas she had married and the Lucas he had become and the fate that he deserved. She thought about Cate and how gullible she was. The scratches on her neck and chest were almost healed but were visible reminders of what had happened to her. One yellowish-brown bruise remained at the base of her neck. The physical healing was underway, but the emotional damage was still in the process of mending. Lana was strong and confident, but there was a little, vulnerable voice in her head that reminded her at unexpected times that life was fragile and that hers had nearly been taken away.

On Saturday morning, Lana got up, ran a mile on the treadmill, and ate half of a grapefruit and a piece of whole grain toast dusted with cinnamon sugar. She showered and looked in her closet for the jeans that fit her the best, and then picked out a black-and-white plaid flannel shirt, the belt with the turquoise buckle, and her black-and-white cowboy boots. She thought about wearing the black leather jacket that Roadking had loaned her for the Harley rides, but it seemed like it was too heavy. She decided to wear it anyway. She took extra time with her hair and makeup since she would be with him.

She went to her appointment with the Mercedes dealership in Boulder to test-drive a GLE 350 midsize SUV at nine o'clock. It was so luxurious. There was an obsidian black metallic model on the lot that she really liked. She loved it—the feel, the smell, and its charisma. Her Cadillac Escalade was almost ten years old, and there were so many functional and sound system improvements that had been made in luxury SUVs since then. It would be the right decision to rid herself of the Escalade and the baggage that was associated with it. The dealer talked with her about trading the Escalade in and gave her a quote.

Her next stop was at the Lincoln dealership in Boulder to test-drive a Lincoln Navigator. It felt familiar, like the Escalade, and was so elegant. Fit for a princess. There was a black velvet model on the lot with black Venetian leather upholstery with twelve-spoke aluminum wheels. She let them know that she was interested in trading in the Escalade and waited for the price quote. The sales manager was taking his time, as they always do. It was already noon and she needed to head to Louisville to All Roads soon.

"I need to leave. But could you give me a call as soon as you can come up with a price for me to consider?"

They agreed. She hoped they could complete a deal in the next week, but she didn't want to seem too eager.

Lana arrived at All Roads about one o'clock. Roadking had gone all-out to make the open house a fantastic affair. There were at least sixty people there with several children running through the crowd laughing and playing. There was a live Bruce Springsteen tribute band playing "Born in the USA" in the parking lot near the front door. On the other side of the lot was a line of men and a couple of women waiting to test-drive the latest model Softail. Inside there was a Harley fall fashion show underway with All Roads employees modeling Harley jackets and shirts and jeans. All the chairs surrounding the elevated platform were occupied by several women. Slips of paper lay on a table nearby to enter a drawing for Harley earrings and Harley gloves. There was a booth in one corner of the showroom with the latest ideas for customizing a Harley with sound equipment and fairing, which was manned by a guy from the service department. In the other corner of the showroom was a kid's area with coloring sheets and orange and black helium balloons carrying the Harley logo. One of the sales staff was serving ice-cream cones to the kids with a wide assortment of toppings. Pulled pork sandwiches, coleslaw, and chips were served near the side entrance to the show room. Kegs of beer and cans of soda in coolers sat outside the door. In the center of the room, the new Road King, Softail, Sportster, Electra Glide, Low Rider, and Roadster models were the stars of the show with the classic shiny chrome and the Harley colors of reds, blues, and blacks. A great ride that was beautiful too.

Roadking stood near the center of the room talking to a couple of men about one of the new models. When he saw Lana, he nodded his head in her direction and held his index finger up to indicate that he would be with her in a second. As she browsed the area, a woman on the staff approached her and asked if she needed any help.

"No, I'm just here to see Vincent," Lana smiled at her as she spoke.

Oddly, the woman's posture stiffened when Lana replied and then she said, "So . . . how do you know Roadking?"

"We're friends and he invited me to come by today."

"Oh, okay." She replied stiffly and then scanned Lana up and down. "Well, he's over there." She was about forty years old and had short brown hair and glasses and an average build. For the most part, she had a nondescript appearance except for long, manicured fingernails of orange with black tips.

"I know. He saw me." Lana smiled at her again. *Ooh, I guess she doesn't like me.*

Roadking smiled as he approached her. "Hello, baby." He touched her arm and kissed her lightly on the lips.

Lana noticed that the woman with the orange and black fingernails was staring at them and looked away when Lana made eye contact. She wanted to ask Roadking about her but let it go. "Vincent, this is a fantastic event. You did a great job organizing it, and it looks like everybody is having a great time."

"Yeah, people started to arrive even before the open house began. We do this a couple of times a year—in the spring and the fall. It gets people revved up to buy a Harley. Are you hungry? Come with me. I haven't eaten anything yet, and it smells great."

As Lana and Roadking made their way to the food table, Lana's phone vibrated in her back pocket. It was a text message from Olivia.

Call me when you get this.

Lana ignored it and decided to call her later. She and Roadking filled their plates, grabbed some beer, and headed toward Roadking's office to eat lunch.

"If I don't stow away in here for a few minutes, I won't get to eat any lunch or spend time with you. I'll let the sales staff handle things out there for a few minutes. That's what I pay them to do. We've sold about a half dozen Harleys already though. It's only one thirty. Hey, I love it that you wore the leather Harley jacket today. You look awesome."

"Thanks for inviting me. This is so much fun. The band is great too. Wow—you really know how to throw a party."

When they were done eating, Roadking leaned back in his chair and stretched his long legs out and said, "What are your plans for tonight? What do you think about coming home with me when we're done here?"

"No plans. I'd love to come home with you. Can I help with anything here?"

"Yeah, you should be the one up there modeling clothes," he laughed as he nodded toward the fashion show.

A few minutes later, her phone vibrated again. Same message from Olivia. Lana still chose not to respond. Roadking began to mingle with the customers. Lana stayed near him. Occasionally, he would introduce her to someone. Sometimes she just listened quietly as he talked. Sometimes she walked around and picked up used plates and cups and threw them away. She stood outside and listened to the band. Soon her phone vibrated again—this time with a phone message from Olivia. Lana excused herself and stood by the clothing racks and finally listened to the voice message. "Listen, Lana, I need you to call me. I can't message you with this kind of news. I'm serious. It's serious."

Lana rejoined Roadking. The open house was winding down about five thirty, but there were still a couple of dozen people there. The All Roads staff who weren't involved with customers or friends began to clean up their areas. Roadking introduced her to one of his oldest friends, Tom Hernandez.

"Tom and I went to Catholic school together and then to Boulder High. We've known each other since we were three or four. Our mothers are friends. Tom, this is Lana Ross. She's the editor of the *Boulder Essence* magazine."

Tom reached out his hand to shake hers. "Nice to meet you, Lana. Are you here doing a story?"

"No, I'm here by invitation," she said and smiled at Roadking as she shook Tom's hand. "But you know, come to think of it, this is good material for a story."

Her phone vibrated again. Lana was getting annoyed. She was going to have to call Olivia and it would have to be now.

"Excuse me, Vincent. I need to make a call." Tom grinned at Roadking when he heard her call him Vincent.

Lana went into Roadking's office and closed the door. "Olivia, what is it?"

"Lana, I have some bad news and I didn't want you to be blind-sided by a news story, assuming it's made the news already. I don't know how to say this any other way, but—Lucas is dead. I'm sorry to tell you this." Lana felt the blood rush from her face and then her head and felt her hands get numb from shock. She couldn't speak or move. She was as pale as a ghost.

"Lana, are you there? Are you okay?"

Lana gave her head a little shake in order to focus. "I'm here. What is this that you're telling me? Lucas is dead? What? How?"

"Last night Lucas was driving on I-25 and he crashed into a bridge abutment at high speed near the US 36 overpass. He was killed. Cate was with him, but she survived. She's hurt, but I'm not sure what her condition is or what's happened. Cate's sister, Pam, called me. Lana, I don't know what to say. I'm sorry to break the news. I'm sorry for your loss—I don't know what to say. Do you need me to come over?"

"I don't know what to say either. I'm so shocked to hear this." Her throat felt tight and it hurt to talk. "I'm with Vincent right now. I don't know when I'll be home. I'm okay. Thank you, Olivia. I'm glad it was you who told me. Bye for now."

Lana didn't want to talk anymore. She saw her life with Lucas flash through her mind at high speed—the night she met him, the wedding, his obsession with his business, his gradual dislike of her, his sulking. She saw his contorted face as he'd tried to strangle her. *It's over, it's over*, repeated in her mind a dozen times. She stood in Roadking's office, trying to regain her composure. Out of the corner of his eye, Roadking caught a glimpse of her standing in his office and knew something was wrong. She leaned against the doorway, looked down, and rubbed her forehead. He needed to see what had happened with her.

"Lana, is everything alright?" He spoke softly as he peeked in the doorway.

Lana looked up at him. The color was gone from her face. "Vincent, Lucas is dead. He was killed in a car accident last night. But I'm alright. The news is just so shocking."

Vincent pulled her close to his chest and put both of his arms around her and held her tight. "Let's go home. My people can close up and we can clean up on Monday. Grab your things. Yes, let's go now."

CHAPTER 27

Lana left her car at All Roads. She and Roadking rode in silence the short distance from All Roads to his house. Lana was numbed by the news of Lucas's death, but she was consciously aware that Roadking was there to pick up the pieces again—just like when Lucas had attacked her. She thought that he would get tired of having to look after her, and she felt guilty for dampening his good mood and his fun day. The truth is that she wanted his warmth and affection, but she wouldn't let herself appear to be needy.

"Lana," Roadking said softly. "I'm here with you, and if you need to sort things out, I'll listen. But I'm not going to pressure you with questions. I'm leaving it up to you." Roadking knew that she kept things to herself.

"Vincent, I feel conflicted. That's all." Lana finally spoke. "On the one hand, I'm sorry that an accident like that had to be his fate. I didn't want to be with him, but I didn't want him to die. But now, I can put that attack episode behind me and not have to relive it over and over with the trial. Even though this closes a chapter in my life, I feel like it's still unfinished, and it'll take me a little while to let it all go. I'm so sorry that the day ended like this."

"No worries. There's nothing for you to be sorry about. Let's just go home and chill." He knew that Lucas would remain on her mind; the news about him was so fresh. He would not only be patient with her, but he would also keep her occupied. But it crossed his mind that so much had happened to both of them since he'd met her. It was like a dark cloud followed them. Maybe the dark cloud was gone now with the death of Lucas. Maybe all of it was coincidental. Maybe they would know in time.

They walked into Roadking's house about six o'clock. Lana asked if they could watch the local news for information about the accident. Sure enough, there was a news story about Lucas.

"A spectacular car accident last night has claimed the life of local car dealer Lucas Chisholm. Chisholm was the owner of Chisholm Cadillac and was recently in the news when he was arrested for allegedly attacking his ex-wife, Lana Ross, in her home. Ross is the editor of the *Boulder Essence* magazine. Chisholm, in fact, had appeared in Boulder District Court just yesterday to enter a plea of not guilty to numerous counts, including attempted murder in the alleged assault. Police reports indicate that the SUV he was driving was traveling at an excessive speed and veered into a concrete abutment on I-25 near the US 36 overpass. It is not known if alcohol or drugs were a factor. An unnamed female passenger was seriously injured. A spokesperson for the family said that funeral arrangements are pending."

Lana took a deep breath and exhaled as the news story concluded. She touched the first two fingers of her right hand to her bottom lip as she often did when she was processing her thoughts. Roadking watched her as the news report aired. She was still pale and a little shaky.

"I've seen enough," she mumbled.

"Would you like some wine or a drink?"

"Yes, red wine if you have an open bottle. Or a scotch or brandy straight up on the rocks."

"Well, I have both. Scotch on the rocks? Will that do?"

"Yes, please."

Roadking was surprised that she had asked for scotch, but given the circumstances, it made sense. He just didn't want her to mix it with other drinks tonight. It would have to be scotch for the rest of the night. He poured himself a scotch too.

They took their drinks and sat on the oversize leather couch in the living room. Roadking turned on the fireplace and some music—a Keith Urban album with "Break on Me." He sat down close to Lana and put his arm around her.

"I didn't get a chance to tell you that you looked fantastic today. My friend Tom was impressed and gave me a thumbs-up. I should have taken some photos of you sitting on the new Softail. We can do that when we pick up your car tomorrow if you want. I assume you're staying here tonight."

"Thanks. I want to stay tonight unless you have other plans."

"My plans are to spend the evening and all night with you, Lana." She was still quiet, but the scotch was loosening her up a little. He could see the wheels turning."Vincent, do you think it's possible that Lucas intentionally crashed? That he killed himself?"

"I don't know. I don't know him at all, and it's hard to say. I guess, given the circumstances, it's possible. He seemed like a big ego kind of guy. That's probably an angle that the investigators will look at. I don't know if that makes a difference or not. Lana, you won't be able to figure this out tonight. How about hitting the hot tub?" He stroked her long hair as he spoke.

"I don't have a swimsuit or anything to wear. I didn't bring anything with me."

"Who says you must wear anything at all? In fact, I prefer it that way." His crinkly eyes twinkled as he spoke.

"I think you're right. Let's do it." She felt a little buzz from the scotch. She held up her glass. "Pour me another."

"Go easy, Lana. This stuff is potent." He poured her another and they walked out to the hot tub area. They both stripped their clothes off. There were white, fluffy, terry cloth robes hanging near the tub area. Lana wrapped herself in a robe while Roadking got the hot tub ready. "Let's go. Hop in."

Lana dropped the robe and stepped into the hot tub and quickly sat down next to Roadking. The water covered all her bareness and made her feel less self-conscious that she was completely nude. The water bubbled around them and felt good on her muscles that were tightened from stress. Roadking handed the drink to her and put his arm around her. They sipped them quietly for a while until Roadking took the glass from her, set it down, and pulled her over onto his lap where she sat face-to-face with him, straddling his waist with her arms around his neck. He set his drink down and began to kiss her while he held his hands on her little backside and pulled her closer to him. Lana was clearly turned on, and he heard her breathing deepen. Roadking's hands slid up to her breasts and he held one in each hand, then kissed each hard nipple. As she straddled his lap, she could feel his readiness. Roadking could wait no longer. He leaned forward, slid her off him, stood up, and pulled her out of the hot tub with him. They quickly wrapped themselves in the white robes and headed upstairs for the bedroom. Roadking laid her on the bed, untied the robe belt, opened the robe, and immediately lay on top of her, their bodies still wet from the hot tub. Neither was willing to wait any longer. The lovemaking was hot and intense and deep and passionate, unlike any either had ever experienced before. Could it have been the Macallan or Lana's emotional state or her subconscious liberation from Lucas or their deep affection for each other? Whatever it was, it was fantastic and they each wanted it to last as long as it could until the explosive finale. As they lay next to each other and caught their breath, Roadking could see that Lana's skin was no longer pale but flushed with a rosy glow.

They lay there on their sides facing each other for a long time, just studying each other's face until Lana wrinkled her nose at him and smiled. Roadking smiled with his crinkly eyes and said, "You are amazing."

Lana smiled at him, kissed him on the cheek, and laid her head on his shoulder.

"Well, I don't know about you, but I've worked up a big appetite. How about I whip something up for us? Italian and Mexican are my specialties or a combination of both. What do you think?"

"Mexican tonight. Surprise me with your cooking skills."

"We have the green chiles from Walsenburg. Let's give them a try."

They lay there a few minutes longer as they clung to the afterglow. Soon they sat up, wrapped themselves in the white robes, and headed downstairs to the kitchen. Unfortunately, the lights of the kitchen seemed to illuminate the events of the day and slightly dampened Lana's elevated mood. Lana walked out to the hot tub, retrieved their glasses of Macallan, and finished hers as she walked in to the kitchen. She sat on one of the barstools at the prep island.

"Chile rellenos?"

"Sounds good, chef. What can I do to help?"

"I'll make the rellenos. Could you make a salad? There's stuff in the refrigerator. Check it out."

"I make a good homemade vinaigrette. Could you go for that?"

"Yep. Just check the pantry over there and the cabinets for anything you need."

To Lana, preparing a meal with Roadking seemed like an intimate pastime, even though it was so routine. Cooking together in white, terry cloth robes. Lucas would have scoffed at the suggestion. But Roadking impressed her at every turn. She liked to watch him in action. He knew exactly what to do. He took four of the roasted green chiles from the freezer and set them aside while he prepared the cheese filling of cheddar and queso fresco, flour, and egg batter. When the chiles were slightly thawed, he removed the seeds and stuffed them with the cheese mixture. He heated oil in a frying pan, dipped the chiles in the batter, and fried them until they were brown. He took some green chile salsa from the freezer that his mother had given him and dumped it in a sauce pan to reheat. All the while, Lana prepared a salad of Romaine lettuce, radicchio, and tomatoes sprinkled with piñon and tossed with a homemade vinaigrette of red wine vinegar, vegetable oil, sugar, salt, and pepper. She found plates, flatware, and water goblets and set them at the dining room table.

Roadking and Lana brought the food to the table. He refilled their glasses of scotch, even though tequila would seem more appropriate, and filled goblets with ice water and lit some candles.

"Vincent, these rellenos are so good. You're an amazing cook. I hope to learn from you. You know, my background isn't as strongly ethnic like yours, so I only have a few traditional things that I can make. I'm kind of a mongrel. Teach me."

"Of course. We'll do this many times. We still have a ton of roasted green chiles in the freezer. How would you like to learn to make flour tortillas? I'll give you a tortilla lesson sometime."

"I'm always eager to learn. That would be fun."

Lana thought to herself, *I could do this every day for the rest of my life. He makes me so happy.* But thoughts of Lucas began to drift in and out of her mind. Roadking had been great to help her through the rest of the day. Questions were plaguing her. Questions that may eventually be answered—many whys and hows. Lana took another sip of the scotch. The alcohol helped her remain in the moment and stop overthinking. There would be plenty of time to ponder these things—but not tonight with this magnificent man.

They talked about the open house as they ate the Mexican meal. Roadking had sold ten Harleys, and dozens of people had test-driven the Softail. Everyone had seemed to enjoy themselves, and he was already planning the spring open house in his mind. Lana did not have the chance to tell him what a wonderful time she'd had before the news about Lucas had interfered.

"Next time I want you to model some of the clothes. And in the meantime, I want some photos of you sitting on the Harleys—maybe make a poster or two of shots of you."

"The scotch must be getting to you. No one would want a poster of me."

"I do."

Lana smiled. "Thank you for the fabulous meal tonight."

"I owe it to my mom. She made me and my sisters learn to cook the traditional family dishes. To her, it was important to pass those recipes on. I'm not sure if Ava has picked up any of it from me yet. We shall see. So I'll pass some of it on to you too." Roadking smiled. He stood and began to clear the table with Lana's help. Lana offered to wash dishes, but Roadking wanted to watch a movie. "We can do the dishes in the morning after breakfast."

They walked upstairs to the movie theater with their glasses of scotch. Roadking was not going to fill another glass for Lana. She had had enough. He found a movie called "The Ugly Truth," a romantic comedy that would not require deep thought. They snuggled together in the stadium seating, covered with the alpaca throw. She felt so secure there with him and she struggled not to nod off.

When the movie was over, they went to bed. She fell asleep immediately, but dreams of Lucas taunted her all night. She woke up about three in the morning and began to think. It was her way of processing what had happened to her in recent months, and she needed to work it out to move successfully past it and put it away in that little place in her head.

In the meantime, Leon had been watching for Lana all day. The monitors showed that she wasn't home, the GPS showed that her car was in Louisville, and he knew exactly where. If Lana was in Louisville, he knew that she was with Roadking. "Ain't gonna see that little gal today. I'll get ya, pretty boy. Your turn is coming. That little darlin' is mine," he snarled as he watched for her return. He had heard the news about Lucas. "That bastard got what he deserved. At least I got my shot at him. Hurtin' that little gal," he said aloud to himself. When it was midnight, he figured that she wouldn't be back. He headed to the bar for a couple of hours for some beers, a game of pool, and maybe some tail.

When Roadking woke up Sunday morning, Lana was already awake, lying there quietly while she waited for him to wake up. When he turned over to look at her, he thought, *There she goes again. That pretty, little head thinking hard.*

"Good morning, sleepyhead." Lana smiled at him as she spoke.

"Wow, I slept a little later than I normally do. Did you sleep well?" Roadking stretched his arms. It was eight o'clock.

"For the first part of the night. Then I was restless."

"It's going to be that way for a while I'd guess. And it's okay. You can't ignore what's happened."

"I know. I'll be okay. I just hope that some of the recent drama in my life is over."

"Agreed. Let's head downstairs for some coffee."

"Just orange juice for me." Lana replied.

They headed downstairs for breakfast. Lana began to tidy up from the meal the night before while Roadking loaded the dishwasher. Don Henley played quietly in the background. When it was all cleaned up, Lana went upstairs to take a shower and get dressed. Putting on her clothes reminded her that the weekend with Roadking would end soon and she would have to go home.

After Roadking showered, they drove back to All Roads so Lana could pick up her car. When they got there, Lana said, "Let's go inside so I can help you clean up from yesterday."

"Are you sure? You don't need to. I'd like to check on the sales orders, though, while I'm here."

"I'd love to." Lana just needed to keep busy and wanted to stay with him as long as possible. She knew that being alone meant that she would overthink things. She began to fill trash bags and take them to the dumpster. She rehung jackets and shirts on the clothing rack. She swept the floor, cleaned the bathroom, and wiped off tables and countertops.

"Jeez, Lana, save some stuff for the staff to do tomorrow." Roadking was surprised at her effort.

"This is good therapy for me. And I enjoy being with you no matter what I'm doing."

About three o'clock, Lana went home. She wanted to stay but didn't want Roadking to feel obligated to be with her for the rest of the day.

"Bye for now, baby. I had a good time with you yesterday and a fantastic time with you last night." As she thought about the night before, she felt a warm rush inside and smiled at him.

"My pleasure, little lady. And yes, last night was indescribable." Roadking kissed her on the lips and then put his arms around her and held her there close to his chest for a couple of minutes.

Lana didn't want him to let go. The strength of his arms wrapped around her made her feel like she was his. As she drove away, she said softly to herself, "I love you, Vincent Romano. Someday you'll know."

When she walked into her house, she surveyed each room and

viewed each with a new perspective. She remembered when Lucas had purchased the painting in the living room of the Maroon Bells in Aspen. She saw the pewter candlesticks on the china buffet that he had given her on their first anniversary. Everywhere she looked, she saw remnants of Lucas. But she wasn't sad. The sadness and disappointment had vanished years ago.

After a couple of hours of sitting quietly in her living room lost in deep thought and introspection, she jumped on the treadmill and worked out with the light weights. She needed to wear herself out so she could sleep. She ate some halibut and sautéed kale. She noticed on her phone that there were text messages with price quotes from both car dealers that she had visited the day before. She would deal with those tomorrow. She peered into her closet, picked out a gray wool dress to wear the next day, showered quickly, and went to bed. Just as the night before, Lucas appeared in her dreams in various random scenarios.

Soon it was Monday morning, and she knew she must face the ramifications of Lucas's death. Questions from coworkers and friends. She needed to call her parents and let them know about it too. The press would no longer hound her with questions about the attack. She wanted to know about the funeral. She knew that she wouldn't attend, but she wanted to donate money to a charity.

In the late morning, the mail was delivered by the receptionist to Lana in her office. Lana was busy editing an article about Caribou Ranch for the postholiday issue of *Boulder Essence*. She began to flip through the mail when she saw it—an envelope addressed to her with Lucas's handwriting on it. A chill ran through her veins as she held it in her hand. Her hand shook as she opened the note.

Lana,

I know I'm not supposed to contact you, and you can do what you want with this note, but it won't matter anyway. I wanted to apologize to you for anything and everything that I may have done to hurt you. I didn't deserve you, and my hope is that you find someone who is worthy of your love. I don't expect that you'll ever forgive me, but I am truly sorry.

Yours, Lucas

Lana leaned back in her big leather office chair and read the note twice more. It was so unlike Lucas to apologize. And what did he mean by "it won't matter anyway"? The envelope had been sent on Friday. Lucas had been killed on Saturday. "Perhaps Lucas was looking for redemption," Lana whispered quietly.

"Rest in peace, Lucas Chisholm," she whispered and put the note in her purse.

CHAPTER 28

"So are you going to the funeral? I plan to. You know it's on Wednesday," Olivia asked Lana when they talked later in the afternoon.

"No, it wouldn't be appropriate for me to be there. I think my presence would interfere with the family's need to respectfully say goodbye to Lucas. I don't need to cause drama, and I don't feel the need to honor him at all. His parents were always kind of lukewarm toward me anyway. His father asked me once when I was going to get a real job that made money instead of my 'fluffy' job. They might blame me for his death. The obituary said that donations could be made to a charity of choice. I'll do that, I guess." Lana had decided to donate to the March of Dimes in the name of her stillborn brother, Landon.

"I went to see Cate in the hospital. Her right leg is in traction. It was broken in two places. Her face is swollen and her eyes are black. Her cheek is bandaged. I guess she has a gash on her face from some metal or glass. She had a tough time talking because of the swelling and the bandages. I didn't ask her any questions about the accident, but from what she could say, she doesn't remember anything about it. All she said was that she thought they were going to Westminster to a restaurant. She kept repeating that. She knows Lucas is dead, and she's pretty torn up about it. I don't know if she'll even be able to attend his funeral."

"I don't know what to do. She's so angry with me. If I don't go see her, she'll think I don't care, but if I do see her, it'll upset her. And I think I need to give her some space. Did you see her sister? Does anyone know why he crashed?"

"I did see Pam and the only thing she knew was that witnesses said that Lucas was driving way too fast and suddenly, for no apparent reason, swerved to the left and hit the concrete abutment square on the driver's side. The passenger side was wrecked but not crushed, and that's how Cate survived."

Questions about the accident circulated in Lana's mind, but she kept them to herself. Other than the note Lucas had sent her with the cryptic phrase "it won't matter anyway," there was nothing to indicate that it was anything other than an accident. She guessed his parents would step in and run Chisholm Cadillac and try to restore the business. But she couldn't dwell on that. It didn't matter to her.

"Olivia, tell me about the funeral afterward. I need to close the Lucas chapter in my life."

It was late in the afternoon. It had been a productive day for the magazine. Lana had called the Mercedes dealer before she'd left her office. She'd made the decision to purchase the GLE 350 and asked him to begin the paperwork for her to trade in the Escalade. He had told her that everything would be ready the next day for her to pick up the new car. It seemed symbolic to get rid of the Cadillac Escalade the same week as Lucas's funeral.

While she drove home that Monday afternoon, Roadking was on her mind. She didn't want Lucas to interfere with her thoughts of him. The weekend with him had been magical. She could still feel his arms around her before she had left All Roads. Roadking was her future, at least that's what she wanted to believe. She didn't know how she fit into the picture from his perspective, if at all. But she knew that Lucas was the past and she must push him away and all the baggage associated with him.

Even though there was a security gate on her driveway, she still routinely scanned the perimeter of the house whenever she drove up. She disarmed the security system and went in. All appeared to be secure. She pulled into the garage and went into the house. As she opened the door, she heard men's voices speaking quietly upstairs. Their voices were so quiet that she couldn't understand the words they were saying. She stopped and listened and then tip-toed toward the stairs. Her heart thumped loudly in her chest, but surprisingly she was more curious than afraid. After all, the house was secure, the gate was shut, and there were no strange vehicles on or near the property. She stepped on the first step of the stairs, cocked her head, trying to listen, and squinted her eyes, as if that would help make the voices clearer. The voices came from her bedroom. As she approached the room, she chuckled to herself. The TV was on. The voices were coming from the TV. She didn't remember turning it on in the morning. Perhaps she had bumped the remote on the nightstand before she'd left the room that morning.

For his viewing pleasure, Leon was happy that it was Monday. He knew Lana's routine during the week, and he knew that he was going to get a glimpse of that fine body again. He saw her open the gate and watched closely, knowing that she would come in and change her clothes in a matter of minutes. He was right. He saw her walk into the bedroom and turn off the TV. She opened her drawer and took out her black yoga pants and a sports bra. She pulled her dress off over her head and hung it up in her closet. She took off her bra and pulled the sports bra over her head. She was standing a foot or two away from front of the TV for a few seconds—where Leon had recently installed a hidden camera—nude from the waist up. He felt like he could reach out and touch that fine chest while it was bare. She pulled on her yoga pants and left the room.

"Little gal, I don't know how much longer I can wait fer ya to come my way." Leon was licking his lips and stroking his mustache. He lit another cigarette from the flame of the one he had just finished smoking.

Lana went into the garage and found a little cardboard box. She began to remove things from the glove box and console of her car to get ready for the trade-in the next day. Maps, receipts, car registration, gloves, window scraper, and CDs with the music of Adele, Nick Jonas, Eagles, Keith Urban, and Alan Jackson, a mini flashlight, a small tool kit that Lucas had given her, and an umbrella. She found one lost credit card, a five-dollar bill, assorted change, and Tums between the seats. There was a ticket stub from a movie she and Lucas had seen a couple of years before and a ticket from a Carrie Underwood concert. As she held the tickets, she thought about Lucas and how he had never seemed to enjoy himself or being with her. *Oh well.* In a matter of minutes, the car was ready to trade.

She went into the house and made herself a veggie and cheese quesadilla and a little bowl of blackberries. She turned the TV on. The local news once again mentioned Lucas and the accident.

"Investigators are still trying to determine the cause of the accident that took the life of local businessman Lucas Chisholm last Friday night. An autopsy revealed that he was not under the influence of alcohol or drugs at the time of the crash. There is speculation that he may have committed suicide due to the pending legal case against him involving an assault and attempted murder of his ex-wife in her home, but investigators have found no evidence to that effect. A funeral service is planned for him Wednesday morning at ten o'clock at the First Christian Church in Columbine Point. Burial will be at the Rocky Mountain Cemetery in Boulder."

The words that Lucas had used in the final note to her gave Lana cause to wonder about his intentions. But she chalked it up to her usual overthinking. Lucas spoke plainly, unambiguously, and never with a hidden meaning. She would never know, and she would have to let it go. She sat for a while after she finished the light supper, thinking about how she was in a rut. She needed to shake up her routine a little during the week. The weekends were taken up with Roadking lately. Maybe she should take a spin class or Zumba class or a barre class or a gourmet cooking class or learn Italian to impress Roadking. She wondered if he spoke Italian. She would ask him.

Lana confirmed in an email to a furniture gallery in Cherry Creek that she wanted to purchase two chestnut, Italian Berkshire leather sofas. She scheduled them to be delivered on Friday afternoon. In the morning, the painter was coming to paint the living room a soft grayish-tan putty color. When these tasks were completed, along with the trade of the Cadillac, Lucas and the attack would feel less tangible.

As she sat with her laptop, Roadking called her. "Hello, baby. What's up?"

"Hey. I was just completing an order for two new leather sofas for my house. How was your day?"

"Good. We got everything cleaned up and put back in its place from the open house, thanks to your able assistance yesterday. Actually sold eleven Harleys."

"That's great. I didn't mind cleaning up. It allowed me to stay with you longer."

Roadking could hear in her voice that she was smiling. "Well, I was thinking—Saturday's Halloween. I was wondering if you wanted to come over and hand out treats with me? And if you wanted, you could stay?"

"That would be fun. Now that the security gate is in place in my driveway, no one will come back here to trick-or-treat. And yes, I'll stay. I was thinking, too—do you like to hike? The weather is supposed to be nice on Sunday, and we could hike a few miles up at Chautauqua if you wanted to. I love it up there. But we have to go fairly early in the day because the parking is atrocious up there."

"Sure, I'd like that. Let's take the Harley since the weather will be nice. Parking will be less of a problem."

"It's a date then. I decided to trade the Cadillac for a Mercedes GLE 350 today. I'm picking it up tomorrow. It's exciting to get a new car."

"Can't wait to see it."

The conversation paused for a moment and then Lana said, "Vincent, this morning I got a note from Lucas in the mail. He mailed it on Friday. I'm not going to mention it to anyone but you. He apologized to me for everything and wished me well. It's another step toward putting all of it behind me. But it was so unlike him to do that."

"Well, I think that's a good thing for closure for you. Fortunate timing."

Lana suddenly felt like she might have imposed on Roadking with her personal stuff. She changed the subject quickly. "The article that I wrote about motorcycling through Colorado for the magazine is finished. I'll send you a draft of it if you want to see it."

"Yes, I'd like to see what you learned from me." He laughed.

"Well, not everything that I've learned from you could be put in that article." Lana laughed too.

"See you Saturday at my house around five. I won't be home from All Roads until around then."

The rest of the evening proceeded with her usual routine: workout, shower, bedtime. Leon was frustrated that he'd received a service call for a lockout at her usual bedtime. He was going to miss seeing that little body one more time. But he had figured out how to take a screenshot of her bare chest while he'd monitored her when she had changed earlier. He had already looked at it a dozen times.

In the morning, Lana dressed for work in a long, Peruvian, patterned skirt, a long, brown shirt with a belt, and boots. It was a classy outfit to wear on a day when she would pick up a Mercedes. She disarmed the alarm system when the painter arrived to paint the living room. She could still monitor what was happening in the house while she was at work, even if the alarm system was off.

When she arrived at her office, she called the Mercedes dealer, who told her that the trade could be made at noon. She held a staff meeting. The magazine had just completed the holiday edition of *Boulder Essence*. But Lana decided to create a smaller winter edition of the magazine to be published between the holiday edition and the early winter edition. It was to be a winter fitness edition timed to target readers who had been bingeing from Thanksgiving to New Year's Day. Since Boulder was a fitness haven, she assigned her staff to visit all the fitness studios in Boulder County and take a class and write about it. She assigned herself to a barre studio, a kickboxing class, and a Zumba class held at a karate studio. The target date for publishing was in two weeks.

"Jeez, Lana. That's ambitious," one of her staff writers commented.

"Yes, it is. I have high expectations of all of you, and as you can see, I've made an assignment for myself. We'll meet on Monday morning, and I want a report from each of you of your experiences, and then we'll organize the format of the edition."

"I think this stuff with her ex-husband is getting to her," whispered one of the writers to the others. Lana overheard the comment but quickly decided that to respond to it would confirm its truth.

At noon, Lana drove the Escalade to the Mercedes dealer. The new car was parked right out in front. The paperwork was done. Lana had warned them ahead of time them that she would not wait for hours for them to complete the documents.

"Come on in, Ms. Ross, and sign the papers and you can be on your way."

Lana signed the papers and listened to the salesperson rattle off all the new features that she would need to be aware of. He handed her two key fobs and a silver key chain in the shape of the Mercedes logo.

"I see that you cleaned out the car, but if we find anything significant when we detail it, we'll let you know. Thanks for doing business with us. And we'll see you at your first service appointment in a few months."

Lana drove away in the new Mercedes. The smell of the leather seats was heavenly. It felt like it was driving itself. The sound system was the first thing that she played with, but there were so many other digital buttons and nobs to learn about. She felt like she deserved a new car. She could afford it. And it was another step away from Lucas.

Lana headed back to the magazine parking garage and ran upstairs to her office. She scheduled her first assignment, the barre class, for five o'clock. She drafted a list of questions to be answered by the writers after their assigned classes and emailed it to them. The structure created by the questions would help them format the articles that would enable the reader to make comparisons of the programs.

In midafternoon, the Mercedes dealer called Lana and gently

told her that a GPS device had been found under her back right bumper and asked her if she wanted it and then added, "Did you know it was there?"

Lana was shocked. *That damn Lucas—he was tracking me!* she thought as the blood rushed to her face in anger. "No, please destroy it. Throw it away. Smash it. Please." After the attack, Lana believed that Lucas had been to blame for the weird incidents in her house, and she wondered if he had been involved with the vandalism incidents to Roadking's car and business.

She finished the rest of the workday and went to the barre class. She loved it—the stretching and the core workout—and decided that she would sign up for one or two classes when she got a chance. The class helped to ease her anger at the discovery of the GPS device on the Escalade. She arrived home in the new black Mercedes. The living room had been painted the putty color she had selected and it was perfect. Another remnant of Lucas disappeared.

Leon was out on a service call when Lana arrived at home. He had not seen from the driveway monitor that she had bought a new car, and he was confused. The GPS that he had hidden to track her had quit functioning, and yet he saw her moving through her house. But he became distracted watching her and waiting for a strip show and forgot about it for the rest of the night.

The next days until the weekend were routine and moved at the usual, predictable pace. Lucas's funeral was on Wednesday and Lana did not attend. That day was no different than the rest, except that Lucas was on her mind a little more. Olivia called her Wednesday evening to tell her about it.

"The funeral was nice. The eulogy was short. The service was very standard. Obviously, nothing was mentioned about the criminal proceedings against him. There were more people there than I would have imaged given what's happened in recent weeks. Cate was there in a wheelchair because of her leg, sitting near the family. They didn't seem to pay much attention to her. She had to wheel herself around; no one pushed her. His father looked angry and his mother looked forlorn and small. The casket was closed and covered with yellow flowers. There was a funeral procession to the gravesite in Boulder. And then afterward, there was a buffet at the Boulder Country Club, but I didn't go. I did see Cate for a second and waved to her. She tried to smile, but her face is still bandaged on one side, and it almost looks like that side is paralyzed. I couldn't tell."

"Thanks for letting me know about it. His parents never cared much for me, but I feel sympathy toward them. And Cate—I don't know what to think or do. Poor Cate. I think I'll, at the very least, send her some flowers." Lana waited a minute or two and then said, "Now to change the subject, I'm going to Denver Saturday to pick out a formal dress for a black-tie affair that I'm going to with Vincent next weekend. Want to help me pick something out? I can't wait to see him in a tuxedo."

"I think I'd like to see that too. Sure, that would be fun. Lunch at the Brown Palace too?"

"Sure, why not? I'll pick you up in my new Mercedes about ten."

"Fancy. I'll be ready."

Saturday morning arrived and Lana headed to Boulder to pick up Olivia. Leon had finally figured out that Lana had bought a new car and he was going to have to find an opportunity to attach a new GPS. He had seen that the parking garage at *Boulder Essence* was monitored with security cameras, so he couldn't do it there. He couldn't follow her whereabouts without it and couldn't physically follow without her seeing him. He would have to figure out a way to get to that new car.

On the way to Denver, Olivia tried to get Lana to talk about her relationship with Roadking. She knew that Lana was intensely private, but she might hint at something.

"So Lana, you've been seeing Roadking a lot, haven't you? Tell me all about him." She knew that question would not be answered fully, but it was worth a shot.

"I really like him. He treats me so well." A short answer just like Olivia had expected.

Lana's workout playlist was on the stereo system, and she cranked it up to test the speakers. "Want to Want Me" by Jason Derulo. The loud music would end discussion of that topic.

Lana's plans were to go to a few shops in downtown Denver. The first couple yielded nothing that Lana liked or that looked good on her. At the third shop, she saw a dress she liked the minute she walked in the door and hoped it was in her size. It was long and black and shiny and sleek and floor length. It was covered in shimmering, black sequins with contrasting vertical stripes of copper sequins, which weaved over the bust and back and crisscrossed along the hips and then straight to the floor. The back was a racerback with a zipper. Lana was in luck; she tried a size four and a six since it would hug her figure. The size four fit perfectly. She walked out of the dressing room to show Olivia.

"Oh my God, Lana! That dress is exquisite. You look like a model. That dress is definitely you. And the copper with your red hair—oh my God!" Even the sales associate gasped when she saw her.

"I'll take it. Do you have any copper and black earrings that would go with it?"

The store carried a pair of dangly, copper medallions with a black, lacy detail on the inside. They were perfect.

"Okay, off to the Brown Palace for lunch."

It was close to two o'clock. Lana ordered poached salmon on greens and a glass of chardonnay. She would be meeting Roadking later and didn't want garlic on her breath. Lana asked Olivia about Alex, the former high school classmate she was dating.

"He's nice but a little clingy. I think he's trying to relive his high school days—a simpler, happier time in his life. But he's lonely. His wife just died. He's trying to reinvent his life the best way he knows how for him and his son. I plan to keep seeing him though."

"I got the same impression of him."

They talked for a couple of hours and slowly finished their lunch. About four o'clock, they left Denver. That would give Lana enough time to get Olivia back to Boulder and meet up with Roadking in Louisville around five o'clock.

Lana dropped Olivia off about four thirty and drove toward Louisville. She arrived a little early so she drove through downtown Louisville on Main Street and Front Street and looked at all the shops and old buildings and the old grain elevator. There was a lot of history there. She decided that she should do an article about the history behind some of the select buildings. The Louisville Historical Museum was still open. She ran inside to introduce herself and to let the museum director know that she was interested in possibly doing that story. Her mind was swirling with so many topic ideas about the small town. She handed her business card to the director.

When Lana was finished at the museum, she drove to Roadking's house. He had just arrived. He kissed her when she came inside. There was a little basket of mini Kit Kat bars and mini Twix that he had set by the front door for the kids.

"Come see my new car."

Roadking walked outside with her and checked it out. "Nice choice. I bet you look good driving it too."

She reached into the back seat and grabbed a little bag she had brought with her since she was spending the night. "I'll let you drive it some too."

Trick-or-treaters came and went, and they took turns answering the door. For dinner, Lana and Roadking decided to make homemade pizzas. Each would make their own versions of a gourmet pizza. Both Lana and Roadking used their own dough recipes, although they were similar. They dug into the refrigerator and pantry and picked out their own special ingredients. Lana used marinara sauce, artichokes, asparagus, mushrooms, pineapple, fresh basil, and pepper jack cheese. Roadking used marinara sauce, crumbled Italian sausage, peppers, Hatch green chiles, fresh tomatoes, and cilantro. Roadking lit up the pizza oven on the patio, and they slid their pizzas inside. While they baked, Roadking poured some Merlot for each of them. It was the beginning of the perfect night that he had planned for them.

"Okay, little lady, the moment of truth." He removed the pizzas from the oven, sliced them up, and each chose a slice of the other's original pizza.

"Vincent, this is amazing. The crust is so thin—it almost crunches, and those amazing green chiles gave yours a little Mexican flair. I love it."

"Well, I have to say the same for yours. The pineapple and the pepper jack cheese make a surprising combination. Let's go into the pizza business together." They laughed.

Around eight o'clock, the last of the trick-or-treaters had come and gone. Roadking and Lana sat in the living room on the leather couch while the fireplace burned and Blake Shelton played on the sound system. Against her better judgement, Lana mentioned to Roadking that the Mercedes dealer had found a GPS tracking device on her car when they'd detailed it. She tried to keep talk about Lucas to a minimum.

"I guess it belonged to Lucas."

"I was just thinking—ever since I met you, there has been a string of bad incidents or bad luck or something for us. The windows, the tires, the gunshots, the attack." Roadking casually remarked.

Lana felt the blood rush to her face and then to the top of her head. She was stunned by that statement. A similar thought had crossed her mind before, but she never would have said it to him or would want him to think that. For a few seconds, she just stared at him. He continued to sip his wine, completely unaware of what was about to happen.

"Do you really believe that? Do you really feel that way? Do you really believe that me being with you is 'bad luck'? I thought we had something together." Lana's eyes were wide. Her voice was shaking but not loud. To her, the offhand, casual comment that he'd made was his way of telling her that she was a curse or bad luck or that she was the cause of the recent misfortunes experienced by both of them. She said it again, "I'm bad luck?" Tears rushed to her eyes, but she was not going to let them fall. Her throat tightened as she spoke. She was so hurt.

"Lana, I was just talking about the timing of those things. Not so much that they were about you. I guess I shouldn't have said that or said it differently. I really didn't mean anything by it."

Lana grabbed the bag that she had brought for the overnight stay that was on the dining room table. "I think I should head home. It's been a long day after all." She walked out the door, got in her car, and left.

Roadking was left in shock—first at seeing a flash of temper from her and second that she was so upset that she'd left. He was still sitting on the couch, holding his glass of Merlot. He thought to himself that if she was that upset, it was probably good that she had left before words were said that couldn't be taken back.

As Lana drove away, she thought the same thing. She was already sorry for the flash of anger and was shocked at her own reaction. She wanted to spend the night with him. She couldn't turn around and go back. Her pride would never let her. And yet tears flowed all the way home, spilling onto her lap. She screwed up a budding relationship. And broke her own heart.

When she got home, she carried the beautiful, black gown into the house and hung it from the top of the closet door so it wouldn't drag on the floor and lamented as tears still flowed. *I guess I'll be going to the gallery opening by myself.* She sat down on the bed and cried like she would never stop, repeating to herself, "I'm sorry. I'm sorry." She lay back on the bed, eventually falling asleep still in her clothes, tears trickling from her eyes and into her hair.

Around two in the morning, she woke up, took her clothes off, slid on the T-shirt that she wore at night, and climbed under the covers. Alone—no Roadking. She had cried herself out. No tears were left, but her body ached like it did when she was sad. She got up and wet a washcloth with cold water and placed it on her swollen eyes. She fell asleep again.

She woke at sunrise. Still shaken by her behavior the night before, but with a little flash of resilience, she decided to head to Chautauqua anyway for the hike that she had planned with Roadking.

CHAPTER 29

As Lana drove to Chautauqua Park, her mind was on the dreadful incident at Roadking's house the night before. She was embarrassed by her behavior, shocked by her flash of anger, and mortified that she could speak to Roadking in any other way but soft and loving. "I Was Wrong" by Chris Stapleton played on the car stereo, its lyrics taunting her. She believed that she would never see Roadking again. After all, he had implied that being with her was the source of his and her recent misfortunes. What was worse—the same thought had already filtered through her mind, but she would never believe that it was true. She was in love with him, and now she'd ruined it.

Lana found a parking spot close to the Chautauqua Dining Hall, which lay at the foot of the Flatirons. It was a little after nine o'clock, and the parking lot was crowded but manageable. The bag that she had taken to Roadking's house for the sleepover was still in her car. She reached into the back seat, pulled the bag into the front seat, and found her hiking shoes. The morning air was chilly since it was November 1, but the sunshine was bright and golden. There was a light fragrance of pine in the mist. The cool, moist air felt good in her lungs. She took a couple of deep breaths. Her legs would be walking, but her mind and heart would be in Louisville. She decided to take the Mesa Trail—a moderate, well-worn, gravel path with a slight climb that stretched for over six miles. She planned to hike up halfway and then turn around for a total of six miles. She began to walk to the trailhead and stopped to set the pedometer on her phone and plug in earbuds. She began to take a few steps slowly, as she was still choosing music when someone touched her arm. She turned around to see Roadking standing there, smiling at her.

"A sweet thing like you will get eaten up by bears if you walk alone."

Lana took a step toward him and spontaneously put her arms around his waist and held him close before she said a word.

"Vincent, I'm so sorry I snapped at you and walked out like I did last night. I don't know what came over me. You could never know how happy I am to see you. What are you doing here?"

Roadking was pleasantly surprised at her reaction when she saw him. He had expected that he would get the cold shoulder and some passive-aggressiveness. But clearly Lana wasn't like that, and she had no intention of punishing him.

"It's all good, baby. We had a date to hike today, and I hoped you'd be here. If not, I would have hiked by myself to clear my head. You've been through so much lately. I guess I should have expected that your coolness would crack at some point. Forget about last night. Forget that comment. None of it matters. Okay?"

Lana looked up at his face as he spoke. He looked down at hers. There was an unspoken understanding between them, and they could move on. He kissed her lightly on her lips before she answered.

"Okay. I'm so happy you're here. But I was so worried that I'd messed things up."

"Remember what I said. It doesn't matter. So let's get going. If we work up an appetite, I'll take you to brunch at the Dining Hall."

He held her hand sometimes as they walked. He told her about a backpacking trip he had taken in the Basque Country in northern Spain with a college friend Ben Torres and how picturesque it was, even though they probably didn't appreciate it so much at the time. He told her about the Gringo Trail in Peru where he and Shannon, Ava's mom, had hiked to Machu Picchu, the historic, picturesque Inca estate that sits above the Urubamba River between two mountains.

"Are you fluent in Spanish?"

Roadking laughed. "Well, fluent is not the word. I was able to stumble through it enough to have made my way through Spain and Peru. You know, my mom is Mexican and my dad is Italian, so I grew up hearing words from both languages from them and the rest of the family, sometimes not knowing which language I was hearing. So in my mind, I have kind of a hybrid vocabulary of words. Roadking's Spanish-Italian. But you know, Spanish and Italian words are similar. For example, Spanish for 'good morning' is *buenos días*, and in Italian, it's *buongiorno*. And if I wanted to say to you, 'you are beautiful' in Italian, it's *sei bella*, and in Spanish, it's *eres bonita*. I know that '*tesora*' is Italian for sweetheart and '*bella*' means beautiful. Both words would describe you. "

Lana smiled. "And both languages are so beautiful—the way the words flow together, almost like a melody."

The Mesa Trail was pretty in the fall because the meadows were still green. The pine trees cast their tall, straight shadows in patterns on the trail. The sun was rising in the sky and it warmed them as they walked. Lana pulled her sweatshirt off over her head, pulling her shirt up with it. Roadking caught a glimpse of her lacy pink bra. She tied the sweatshirt around her waist.

"What about you? Where have you traveled?"

"Never out of the country. I did some spring break trips with Olivia and Cate when I was in college. To Yosemite once—we'd planned to hike there but got distracted by some boys we met. Lucas would never travel, because it took him away from his business. So most of my traveling has been short trips in surrounding states, like Wyoming, Utah, New Mexico, and a couple of trips to Las Vegas. There are some places I'd like to see in this country, though, like Vermont in the fall and the Atlantic beaches of North Carolina and the vineyards in northern California. And I'd like to go to Italy to see the art and architecture, the Tuscan vineyards, and the Mediterranean. Maybe Greece for the same reasons and Iceland too. I've always been fascinated with that country. And of course, a warm beach anywhere."

"Well, I think you should make those trips a priority."

"You're probably right. Because my magazine is so focused on the Boulder area, I rarely think of what I'm missing. Olivia mentioned that we should take a trip to the Pink Sands Beach in the Bahamas."

When they reached the three-mile, halfway point on the trail, they sat down on a large granite rock to drink water and take in the scenery.

"So what were your plans for the rest of the day, baby?"

"I have no idea. I just knew that when I woke up, I wanted to hike up here like we'd planned."

"Let's hit the Chautauqua Dining Hall for brunch, bella, and then you can follow me to my house and we can watch the Broncos-Raiders game."

"Okay, I'd like that." She leaned her head on his arm for a few seconds as they sat.

Leon was beside himself. When Lana had bought the new Mercedes, he'd lost the ability to track her whereabouts with the GPS he had attached to the Escalade. She had been moving around so quickly, coming and going. There had been no opportunity for him to attach a GPS device to her new car. He had tried to follow her a couple of times in the past few days but had been detained by traffic, and he couldn't let her see him. He couldn't go to the *Boulder Essence* parking garage and attach it, since he would be spotted by security cameras. He had watched her on the monitor on his iPad as she left Sunday morning. He had seen her crying the night before. As each moment passed while she was gone, he was getting more agitated.

"I wanna know where ya are, Lana, darlin'. I wanna know who yer with and where! I wanna know what he did to ya! I wanna know, goddamn it!" As he heard the words that he spoke out loud to himself, he became even more enraged and finally took his iPad and hurled it at the wall, leaving a dent in the drywall and a cracked screen on the iPad. When he saw what he'd done, he threw the iPad on the floor and stomped on it. "You piece of shit—yer not showing me what I want to know! Where is she, goddamn it?" He demolished the iPad.

After the burst of anger, he smoked a joint and calmed himself enough to think. *Of course there's a way to attach the GPS, but there's a chance I'll get caught. It's worth a shot.*

While Lana and Roadking made their way back to the Mesa Trailhead, they talked about the rock concerts they had seen. Both had seen Tom Petty a couple of times at Red Rocks Amphitheatre. In fact, they had both attended the same concert once. He had seen Eric Clapton in New York. They had both seen the Rolling Stones, and Lana had seen the band Chicago.

When they reached the trailhead, they walked toward the Chautauqua Dining Hall. Built in 1898, it was a large, two-story building with hardwood floors, painted white interior wood trim, and furnished with a variety of antique oak tables and chairs. The exterior perimeter was surrounded by a wraparound porch contained by a white railing. Two white cupolas reached out from the roof. It was almost noon, but brunch was still being served. Lana was so hungry that she felt a little shaky after all the walking and drinking only water. Lana ordered a cranberry sangria and a ham, spinach, and tomato omelet. Even though she was hungry, she knew she would not be able to finish it. Roadking ordered a breakfast burrito and a ginger cooler. They sat at a small table on the flagstone porch in the sun. It became a warm first Sunday of November. The sun reflected the copper of Lana's hair and the silver strands in Roadking's hair.

"So what do you do with your family on Thanksgiving? My mother always cooks for all the relatives, big and small, old and young, within a fifty-mile radius. Not unlike the gatherings at their house every Sunday."

"I don't know yet. My parents never come down to Columbine Point. Dad stays in Steamboat Springs and Mom in Durango. I may go to one of their houses if they invite me. Otherwise, I'll cook a turkey and invite any of my staff that can't be with family to my house. Thanksgiving is my favorite holiday."

"I've been thinking I'd like you to meet my parents someday soon. Maybe go out to dinner with them without the commotion of the family. Are you ready for that?"

Lana was surprised and flattered that he wanted her to meet his family already. "Yes, I'd like that." She didn't mention to him that she knew he had met her father before when he designed Cameron's engagement ring. And it didn't appear that it had occurred to him that her father and the jeweler in Steamboat Springs were one and the same. The mention of Cameron would change his sunny mood, and after what happened the night before, she would not risk that happening.

About two o'clock, they walked to her car and to his Harley and drove to Roadking's house to watch the football game. They arrived at kickoff time and situated themselves on the big, soft leather sofa. Lana leaned against Roadking's arm and he rested his hand on her leg. Pretty soon he lay on his back and rested his head on the arm of the big sofa with Lana tucked between him and the back of the couch. As the second quarter began, Roadking and Lana kissed—a long, slow, passionate, deep kiss. Roadking's hand slowly moved up under her shirt and began to move under her bra. Lana reached in back and unhooked the bra to make it easier for him. Then she unbuckled his belt and unzipped his pants. Roadking rolled her over on top of him, and they continued to kiss longer and deeper each time. They could hear the game announcer but didn't care about the game anymore. She knew in a matter of minutes what would happen when his kisses became even more intense. Suddenly, they heard the front door unlock and open.

"Dad, you here?"

Lana rolled off Roadking, sat up, and pulled her shirt down, hoping the unhooked and hanging bra would not show through her shirt. Roadking sat up and laid a toss pillow on his lap. Their faces were flushed, and they made an attempt to look expressionless.

"In here, Ava. I didn't know you were coming home today."

"I didn't tell you. I came down for a Halloween party at Gabriel's house. I stayed with mom last night. I thought I'd just stop by and grab a few things." Ava studied the scene, and it occurred to her that she had interrupted something. She was amused. *Jeez, Dad, you horndog*, she thought.

"Do you remember Lana? I introduced you to her at All Roads when she came by with a photographer to do some shots of me for her magazine, the *Boulder Essence*."

"Yes, I do. Nice to see you again. Guys, don't pay any attention to me. I'm just going to run upstairs and grab a couple of things. What's the score?" Ava watched them as they both turned toward the TV to see what the score was. They clearly had no idea. She smiled to herself.

"Okay, Ava. Do you want to stay and hang with us?"

"No, I want to get back up to Fort Collins by seven. I'm supposed to meet a couple of other kids in a study group and then hang out with this guy, Peter, who lives in my dorm." She walked toward the stairs.

When she was out of sight, Lana and Roadking looked at each other and began to laugh quietly. "Jeez, babe, if she'd walked in about five minutes later than she did, imagine what she would have seen!" They continued to laugh. The passionate mood was replaced with silly laughter.

While Ava was upstairs, they quickly fixed their clothes. Lana asked Roadking to hook her bra for her. They turned their attention to the game again, both wishing that their plans for halftime had not been interrupted. After about fifteen minutes, Ava emerged from the staircase with a few pieces of clothing draped over her arm, a little jewelry box, and a PlayStation.

"Are you headed back already?"

"Yeah, sorry I can't stay. I'll be home the week of Thanksgiving though. Wouldn't miss Grandma Romano's Thanksgiving dinner for anything. Love you, Dad," she said as she kissed him lightly on the cheek. "Good to see you again, Lana. Enjoy the game."

"You too. Be careful."

After she left, Roadking walked to the kitchen and poured a pinot noir for Lana and a Shock Top harvest beer for himself and brought out a bag of pretzels. They watched the second half of the football game snuggled together. The Broncos beat the Raiders in the last seconds of the game.

It was dusk when the game was over. The sky changed to subdued shades of blue and gray, and there was a light breeze from the southwest. Roadking suggested that they go out on the patio to sit near the firepit. Music softly played from a patio speaker.

"Well, next Saturday is the fancy art gallery opening. And we haven't talked about it much. What time should I pick you up?" Roadking asked.

"I can just meet you there. There's a cocktail hour and silent auction from seven to eight before the official opening and tour of the gallery. That's mainly for photo ops. I'll be taking some shots for future reference if I do, indeed, include an article about the gallery in a future magazine issue."

"No, I want us to arrive together. I want them to know that you're with me."

Lana smiled at him when he said that. "Okay, pick me up about six thirty."

"Are you hungry? I can warm up some of the leftover pizza from our pizza competition last night."

"Yes, that would be good. I'm not super hungry."

Roadking went back into the kitchen to heat up some slices of pizza in the microwave oven. Lana continued to sit in front of the firepit and drank her wine. The sky was dark and there was no moon, but hundreds of stars were visible and shining down on them. In a few minutes, Roadking emerged with plates of pizza and her sweatshirt. He could see she was getting chilly.

"More wine?"

"Yes, please."

"Can you stay tonight?"

"Well, I don't have a change of clothes except for some jeans and a shirt in my bag in the car. Not my usual office stuff. But I could leave early and go home and get ready for work."

"I think you could probably make the jeans and shirt look great anyway. I don't want you to have to head home early in the morning and then return to Boulder."

"Well, you talked me into it. I want to stay tonight—to make up for last night."

"Remember what I said about last night."

"Okay, it's forgotten." They sat and watched the flicker of the firepit, warmed by its glow, and ate homemade pizza. "Vincent, it's Sunday, don't you have to visit your parents today?"

"I stopped by early this morning before I came to see you at Chautauqua. Some of the family was already arriving to attend mass with them at St. Louis Church. My mom was already cooking, but she stopped to make me some blue corn and piñon pancakes. My grandmother's recipe. Let's go inside and catch a movie."

Lana went to her car and retrieved the bag with the change of clothes and makeup and tossed it on Roadking's bed. Roadking was already upstairs in the theater. He picked out an old movie with Kate Hudson, "Almost Famous," about a high school boy who gets to write about and tour with an upcoming rock and roll band for the Rolling Stone Magazine. It happened to be one of Lana's favorites. Even so, she fell asleep a few times on Roadking's shoulder. When it was over, they went to Roadking's bedroom.

When Lana walked into the bedroom, she was surprised and touched to see that on his dresser he had placed a small, framed photo of the two of them that had been taken in front of the SS 396 in Trinidad. She pulled out the T-shirt from her bag and began to undress.

Roadking took her hand and said, "Let's finish what we started before we were interrupted today."

Lana said nothing, laid the T-shirt down, climbed under the covers, and snuggled against that magnificent, generous man. It was a matter of a few minutes until they resumed the passion that had begun on the big, soft leather sofa just hours before.

Leon was seething. He had watched for her to return to her house the entire day. He had looked at the monitor on his phone a hundred times, glancing at it every few minutes, trying to stop himself, but he couldn't. He was obsessed. He had compulsively alternated between smoking a joint and a cigarette all day, knowing that she would be home eventually, and he had developed a deep cough. The little antenna TV that he had was set to the home shopping network, and it blared creating a cacophony as he simultaneously switched from station to station on the radio. When the evening approached midnight, he knew that she wasn't coming home.

"I got a plan. I'll catch ya tomorrow." Leon grabbed a beer from his refrigerator and made himself a microwave burrito. Even though he had given up on the idea that she would be home, he still watched the monitor. Still listened to the noise.

"Little gal, ya can't escape me fer long and, pretty boy, yer days are numbered." A Taylor Swift song lyric that he heard was stuck in his head, "Look What You Made Me Do."

"Lana, gal, Lana, darlin', look what yer gonna make me do."

CHAPTER 30

About five in the morning, Lana woke with a start. Since Lucas's death, he had floated into her dreams most nights, kind of hanging around in the background. Just being there. But in this early morning dream, she had heard his cynical, monotone voice say to her, "It was a mistake. Surprise—I didn't die. I'm still here."

She lay there for a while, hoping to go back to sleep, but her mind had already started racing—planning for the day, thinking about Roadking, thinking about shoes to go with the dress for the gallery opening, thinking about Lucas, thinking about Thanksgiving. She sat up, put on the long, white T-shirt she slept in, reached into her bag, and pulled out a pair of black-and-white socks. Roadking was sleeping and still. She touched him lightly on his back and then slid quietly out of bed and went downstairs to the exercise room. Her workout shoes were still in her car, but she jumped on the treadmill anyway in stocking feet and began to walk. Even though she and Roadking had hiked six miles the day before, she felt like she had been eating too much lately and not exercising enough. She listened to music from her phone on a headset that she'd found in the room and was lost in thought.

Nearly an hour had passed when she saw Roadking standing in the doorway of the room in black boxer shorts and a gray T-shirt. "Well, aren't you a vision—in a T shirt and socks on the treadmill. How long have you been up?"

"Hi. I woke up about an hour ago and couldn't go back to sleep. I hope you don't mind that I used your equipment."

"Of course not. Get on over here."

Roadking hugged her, slid his hand under the back of her T-shirt, and rested his hands on her little rear end, squeezing it lightly, giving Lana a surge of excitement. He lifted Lana up, and she hugged him around his neck and wrapped her legs around his waist. He carried her to the big, soft leather sofa in the living room, laid her down, and covered them with the alpaca throw, and they made gentle but passionate morning love as the sun began to rise and cast a rosy orange glow on them through the window.

Roadking whispered, "I can't get enough of you."

There were so many things Lana wanted to express to him at that moment, but she only said, "Me too."

Roadking went upstairs to take a shower. Lana followed and looked through her bag for clothes to wear to work and gathered up the clothes strewn about the floor from the night before. Soon Roadking emerged wrapped in a big, fluffy towel. "Your turn now—unless you're up for round two this morning." As he laughed, he flashed those beautiful, white teeth and his eyes crinkled.

Lana patted his butt as she walked by him to the master bathroom. She showered and dressed in jeans, boots, and a pink shirt that was a little bit crumpled from the bag—not the professional look that she required of herself, but generic enough to work. She dried her hair, put on her makeup, and met Roadking downstairs in the kitchen where he was whipping up something to eat.

"I'm so impressed with your culinary abilities, Vincent."

"Culinary abilities. That sounds impressive. I just take care of myself—and you when you're here." He scrambled some eggs and topped them with cheese, green peppers, and chopped tomatoes, and then diced up some tiny red potatoes for home-fried hash browns, poured orange juice and coffee for each of them, and sat down next to Lana on one of the kitchen islands. He was definitely a breakfast eater. Lana was not so much, but she ate everything he gave her. Maybe she would skip lunch. Lana helped him clean up the dishes as it was approaching eight o'clock and both needed to get to work.

"Thank you for another fantastic, memorable weekend, Vincent, except for . . ." She stopped herself.

"Just one of many to come." He gave her a long kiss goodbye. "Remember me today," he said to her as she walked out the door.

She blew him a kiss.

Lana remembered while she drove to work that she had made assignments to each staff member, and to herself, to visit specific fitness centers over the weekend and to report to her Monday. She had only visited one herself and would fit one in during the lunch hour and have a meeting with her staff in the afternoon. It took her awhile to acclimate to work, as her mind rambled back to memories of the weekend. She sifted through mail and collaborated with the art and advertising director about the fitness issue. And at noon, she went to a Zumba class—in her jeans, but at least she had brought her workout shoes. She discovered that she liked Zumba—not so much the style of music, but the workout was fun. She hoped that she didn't return to work too sweaty. She scheduled an afternoon meeting with the staff for informal reports of their experiences at the fitness centers. She wanted a mock-up of the issue by Friday.

Late in the afternoon, she texted Roadking, "I'm remembering you today."

It was a busy Monday and Lana was ready to go home at five. When she arrived at home, everything looked as she had left it. What was missing, though, was the deep sadness that she had carried out the door with her Sunday morning. Roadking had not given up on her after her outburst after all, and her mood was happy.

Leon was out on a service call when Lana arrived at home. It was a couple of hours before he saw her move around in her house. He was relieved that she was home again and regretted destroying the iPad before. He missed her changing out of her work clothes, but he would spy on her later. He hatched a plan to get to her car to attach the GPS tracking device and was eager for her to go to bed.

Lana wanted a pair of shoes to go with the black and copper dress for the gallery opening. She wanted something strappy in black and copper and got online and began shopping. If she found nothing, she had some plain, black heels that would work. She found copper shoes, but they looked orange. She found black and silver, black and gold, and black and red, and she had nearly given up when she saw them. Black shoes with a three-inch copper heel. She ordered them express delivery and hoped they would arrive by Saturday. She planned to dazzle Roadking if she could. She knew that he would look exquisite in a tuxedo and couldn't wait to see him.

She tended to her window herb garden, paid some bills, unpacked her weekend bag, and started some laundry. She jumped on the treadmill, but after about twenty minutes, she began to feel light-headed. So she made herself a peanut butter sandwich and then worked out with the light weights. About eight o'clock, she turned on the TV and fell asleep for about an hour. She awoke when her phone pinged.

There was a message from Roadking.

Good night, Lana. Dream about me.

Lana smiled to herself. She began to undress to get ready for bed. She stripped down to bra and panties when she remembered that she needed to throw some laundry into the dryer. And she had not checked the alarm system to see if she had remembered to reset it when she got home.

Leon watched her scurry about the house half-dressed. "There's my gal," he said, not taking his eyes from the screen. He missed seeing her much of the weekend because she had been with that "pretty boy Harley bastard." She stood, looking in her closet for something to wear the next day. "That's it, little gal. Take yer time." Since he'd figured out how to take screenshots with his phone, he snapped a dozen of her, front and back, side to side, bending over. Soon she stripped off her underclothes and quickly walked into the bathroom to take a shower. She emerged ten minutes later, wearing the sleep T-shirt. She hopped into bed, turned off the lamp on the nightstand, and turned the TV on. It was at a low volume and she soon fell asleep.

Leon continued to watch and wait. He would wait until about midnight to make sure she was asleep. While he waited, he smoked, drank, and planned his covert scheme. The monitor on his phone showed that she had not moved for over an hour. He got into the beat-up green van and drove to Hill View Road and parked on the side of the road about a quarter mile north of Lana's driveway entrance. He put the GPS device in his pocket, disabled the alarm systems, climbed the fence to avoid the security gate, which he could not disable, and walked up the driveway to her house. He crept his way toward the house, walking slowly and taking deliberate steps, as if someone would hear his footsteps. He made his way to the door on the side of the house that led directly into the garage. He used his passkey and went inside. He looked at his phone to monitor Lana's movements. Still asleep and motionless.

He took the GPS out of his pocket and walked over to the Mercedes and looked for a place to attach it. He reached on the underside and attached to it the front of the frame. Mission accomplished. He would always know where she was now in that car.

"That was too easy." He looked at the door that entered the house from the garage. He looked at the monitor. She was asleep. *Do I dare go into the house? What if she catches me?* But to be in the bedroom with her, helpless and vulnerable—the temptation was too great.

He opened the door but didn't pull it shut. He was inside the house. It was so dark he was afraid he would run into something, so he used the flashlight on his phone until he reached the stairs.

What if they creak and crack? As much as he wanted to go to her bedroom, he didn't want to get caught. He gingerly took each step, putting his weight on each foot slowly. There were fifteen stairsteps. He was suddenly conscious of his heavy breathing and tried to hold his breath. In a matter of seconds, he was in the hall that led to the master bedroom. He could see the flicker of the light from the TV and could hear its muffled sounds. His adrenaline rushed as he approached her bedroom. He stood in the doorway. He could see the outline of her little figure as she lay on her side. Strands of her hair splashed over her face and across the pillow. He could see the slight rise and fall of her breathing. He wanted to get closer. He wanted to touch her—because she was untouchable. To him, she was so beautiful like that—still and quiet and small. Almost angelic. He could smell the faint scent of the cucumber shower gel she had used earlier. For once in his life, he wrestled with his impulses. He wanted her so much. But not that way.

He whispered, "Lana, gal. Sleep peacefully tonight cuz I'm comin' back fer ya one day." He stood there for several minutes. She didn't stir. He needed to leave before he was unable to stop himself from what he wanted to do. He took each step down the stairs as slowly and cautiously as he had come up. He tiptoed out the door and quietly pulled it shut. As he walked away from the house and up the driveway and then over the fence to his van, he stopped a few times and turned to look and contemplated whether to go back.

"I'll get my chance later—look how easy this was," he muttered to himself. He reset the alarm system and climbed into the van.

At the moment that Leon had closed the garage door, Lana woke suddenly from her sound sleep. She saw that the TV was still on and reached for the remote next to her on the bed and turned it off. As the fog of sleep evaporated, and because of her keen sense of smell, she noticed a faint scent of smoke in the room. It seemed familiar. She lay still for a few seconds, trying to discern where the smell was coming from and what it could be. She sat up suddenly, her heart pounded, she turned on the light, and without considering if someone was in the house, ran downstairs to check the alarm system. It was fully functional and operating. The smell of the smoke was strongest in the bedroom, and it wafted through the hall and staircase. She returned to her bed—wide awake—and watched, on alert in case something happened. She grabbed her phone and earbuds and listened to her music at a soft volume. Despite her constant focus on the doorway to her bedroom, she eventually fell into a restless sleep.

A crescent moon was rising in the eastern sky as Leon returned to his house. The Taylor Swift song "Look What You Made Me Do" played on his stereo system. That song became his own personal anthem. All the things that he had done—the broken windows, the slashed tires, the burned cars and shed, the shots fired at the SS 396—were because of his twisted feelings for Lana.

When he drove up to his house, a familiar car was parked in front. It was Carla's dumpy, brown Buick sedan. Carla got out of the car when she saw him. She wore the same clothes she had worn the last time he had seen her at the bar. The smell of whiskey and smoke were strong on her breath.

Leon was clearly annoyed when he saw Carla. She had interrupted the vision of Lana that had been replaying in his head. Lana and Carla—like Beauty and the Beast. "What the fuck are you doing here, Carla?"

"Jesus, Leon. Is that any way to say hello?" Carla responded with her raspy voice.

"Hey, I didn't invite ya. What do ya want anyway?"

"Well, I didn't see you around for a while at the bar and I just wanted . . . I don't know . . . I guess . . . to see you."

Leon walked to his front door. Carla followed behind him. They stepped inside and she surveyed the house. Broken glass was strewn across the floor, and there were beer stains on the walls, a broken iPad on the couch, and a cabinet door hanging in the kitchen.

"What the hell happened in here, Leon? This place is a mess. Looks like a tornado . . ."

Leon interrupted her and with a nasty snarl said, "Hey, I didn't invite ya here. Who do you think ya are? The queen? Get the fuck out if it ain't good enough fer ya here."

"Want me to help you clean up this stuff?" She was careful not to call it a mess again.

"What do ya really want, Carla? This?" He grabbed her by the neck, pulled her face to his, and kissed her hard and rough, making her lip bleed.

She pulled away, sucked on her lip for a second, and then leaned in for more. Leon pushed her on the couch and told her to take off her pants, which she willingly and hurriedly did. He jumped on top of her and pushed hard into her. Carla got what she came for. Despite the abuse, she liked it. Leon rolled off and left her on the couch. She pulled her clothes together. Without saying a word, Leon went to his bedroom and got into his filthy bed. In a few minutes, Carla came thumping in.

"Can I stay the night, Leon? Can I stay in here with you?" she hoarsely whispered.

"Ya can stay the night—on the couch. I don't want ya in my bed, Carla. Now get out of here. Be gone when I wake up in the morning."

Carla staggered back to the couch and covered herself with her jacket and tried to sleep. About five in the morning, she tiptoed out of the house. She needed to arrive to work at the dry cleaners in a half hour.

Lana woke up around the same time. She had not dreamed of Lucas for the first time since his death. She shoved aside her worries about what had occurred in her house during the night, and with her usual bright demeanor, she began her day and messaged Roadking.

Good morning, Vincent. Have an excellent day. Looking forward to this weekend.

Roadking smiled when he saw the message and wished that Lana was there with him. He was beginning to feel her absence whenever she wasn't there, and he wasn't sure what that meant. He messaged back.

Me too.

CHAPTER 31

For the next few days, Lana was absorbed with work. She had set an ambitious deadline for the mock-up of the fitness issue. The staff had written their articles about their experiences with the various fitness centers. They had acquired or taken photographs at each location, and Lana busily formatted the issue. In addition, the advertising staff had its hands full gathering additional ad commitments from its advertisers. She worked on it at home, too, and chastised herself for the urgency she had created.

She had not spoken to Roadking since Sunday or messaged him since Tuesday morning. She missed him and hoped he hadn't forgotten about her and their plans for Saturday. He was busy too. With the holiday season approaching, interest in the Harleys and Harley products to be given as Christmas gifts increased. And there was a holiday party at All Roads each year, for which he began making preparations with his staff.

On Friday afternoon, a package and a certified letter arrived for Lana at her office. The package contained the black and copper heels she had ordered to go with her new dress for the gallery opening. They fit perfectly, which was a relief since ordering shoes online could be chancy. Since it was the first weekend in November, though, there was always the chance of snow, which would spoil the opportunity to wear them and dazzle Roadking with the full effect of the dress.

She signed for the certified letter. It was addressed to her, but she recognized the return address as an insurance company that Lucas had used. It was probably a cancellation notice or something, although it was odd that it was addressed to her. The content of the letter enclosed was:

Dear Ms. Ross,

Enclosed please find a check for the life insurance proceeds from life insurance policy number 10850 for Lucas Chisholm. You are named as the beneficiary to receive its benefits upon the death of the owner of the policy, Lucas Chisholm, who was deceased on October 23rd. A check for $250,000 is enclosed. Please deposit or cash the check within ninety days. If you have any questions, please don't hesitate to contact us. You have our sympathy at the loss of your loved one.

Sincerely,
Brad Skelton
Chief Benefits Officer
Hudson Harbor Life Insurance Company

Lana was stunned. *Did Lucas forget to remove me as the beneficiary of the insurance policy when the divorce was final? Or did he intentionally leave my name on the policy?* And running through her mind were the lingering question about his death and whether it was an accident or suicide. *Evidently, it was determined to be an accident or the insurance company wouldn't have paid its proceeds.*

She sat at her cluttered desk holding the letter and the check—reading and rereading the letter and looking at the check. Lucas had only been dead two weeks. *What would I do with the money?* She didn't really need it. Her house was paid for and she earned a lavish salary at the magazine. She would have to think. Maybe donate some of it, maybe just hold on to it for now. No matter—she would keep the news of the windfall to herself. Surprise and disbelief over the receipt of the letter and its contents made it difficult for Lana to focus for the rest of the afternoon. She would take it to the bank on Monday. She locked the check and the letter in the top drawer of her desk.

When she left her office, she got an appointment to get a French manicure. On the way home, she picked up a bottle of prosecco and a couple of bottles of pinot noir, her favorite red wine, for home. Maybe she and Roadking could drink a little prosecco before they left for the gallery. She stopped at a deli to pick up some cheeses, gourmet crackers, Greek olives, and prosciutto for a charcuterie tray. She stopped at the market and got some blackberries, blueberries, and raspberries to add to it.

When she arrived at home, she sampled some of the deli items and opened one of the bottles of wine. She planned to relax for a change and not push herself to be busy. She began to watch a new series on Netflix while she ate and drank wine. Roadking called her to discuss the arrangements for Saturday. He told her that he would be there at six o'clock and that would give them plenty of time to get to the gallery at seven for cocktails.

"I know it may sound juvenile, but I can't wait," Lana confessed.

"It'll be fun. Different from the usual motorcycle events I get involved with." Roadking smiled.

"Hey, those are lots of fun. Less fanfare. But there's room for elegance once in a while."

"See you tomorrow, baby. *Buenos noches.*"

"Goodbye until tomorrow."

The night couldn't pass quickly enough. Lana was excited to wear that beautiful dress and shoes. She drank another glass of wine while watching TV. Soon her eyes and head got heavy. She checked the security system and went upstairs to bed. She slept soundly the entire night and woke up happy and refreshed—no puffy eyes from crying or lack of sleep. But then she looked out the window to see that it had snowed a couple of inches during the night. It was November, so it could melt soon if it stopped.

It figures it would snow and be sloppy and cold when I'll be wearing a beautiful dress and shoes. I'll figure out how to make it work anyway. She turned on the fireplace and some music, made herself some hot chocolate with marshmallows and cinnamon, and snuggled with a blanket in the corner of one of the new leather couches she had bought. She thought about the insurance check.

What should I do with that money? I don't have to do anything,

I guess. Lucas hated me. I don't think he intended to leave it to me. But then she thought about the apology letter from him that she had received after the accident. She knew that insurance benefits were a matter of contract and were managed outside of probate of the estate, if Lucas had even made a will. They had never talked about one. So there would be no protracted fight with his family. They probably didn't even know about the insurance policy. *I need to put it out of my mind.* She got up and was cold. She went upstairs and changed into workout clothes. Forty minutes on the treadmill would warm her up.

When Lana finished the workout, she decided to call her mom and dad. She had only talked to them a few times since the attack and Lucas's death. They had both reacted to all of it with their usual, passive manner. She knew they cared. They just didn't care to show it. Thanksgiving was in a couple of weeks and she wanted to make plans.

"Hi, Dad. What's new?"

"Nothin', Lana. How have you been?"

"I'm good. I'm going to a fancy art gallery opening tonight."

"For a story?"

"No, but a story might come out of it. Dad, I was thinking about Thanksgiving and I didn't know if you made plans and if I should come to Steamboat—"

He interrupted her before she could finish the sentence. "Well, I've been seeing somebody up here in Steamboat and she asked me to join her family for Thanksgiving. She has a couple of kids and a couple of grandkids in Walden. Her name is Sherry. She's in real estate. A nice gal. Sorry, Lana. I didn't mean to wreck your plans."

"You didn't. I hadn't made any yet. Well, we'll probably talk before Thanksgiving, but if not, have a great Thanksgiving Day with her."

She called her mom. "Mom, do you have plans for Thanksgiving? Do you want to come to Columbine Point or should I come to Durango?"

"Well, you could come if you want, but I have plans to spend

Thanksgiving with some of the ladies around here who are single. It might be kind of dull for you hanging out with us older ladies."

"Mom, you're still in your fifties. Not an old lady. Okay, I think I'll invite some of my coworkers who are in Boulder without family to my house. You did teach me how to cook a turkey. I just didn't know if you had made plans. I hope you have a good time with your friends."

"I will. Now you have yourself a fine time with your friends too."

Lana hung up the phone. Speaking to her parents had dampened her mood a little. It seemed that they always tried to push her away with their half-hearted exchange—maybe not intentionally, but that was the obvious tone. She had dealt with it for thirty-three years and it wouldn't change. Her thoughts returned to the big night with Roadking.

Around noon, it finally stopped snowing and the sun made a feeble attempt to shine. The ice and snow on the road melted to a slushy slop. She imagined the sidewalks in Boulder would be a mess. She would have to wear snow boots with that beautiful dress, at least until she was inside the gallery. It would be awhile before she would begin to get ready. So she dusted the living room and vacuumed, made the charcuterie tray, folded laundry, sat at her laptop and wrote some text for work, and began a brief list of things she needed to get and do for Thanksgiving. The day was moving so slowly.

About three o'clock, she took a shower, washed her hair, and shaved her legs twice. She tweezed her eyebrows and moisturized her skin. She began to work on her hair. She curled the ends and sprayed them lightly with hair spray and fluffed it a little. She took her time applying her makeup, wanting no smears or smudges. Then she touched a little perfume to her cleavage and in the hollow of her neck and on her wrists. She put the copper and black earrings on. She was still wearing the silver bracelet that Roadking had given her and would not take it off, even if it didn't match the other jewelry or the dress. She would put the dress on last.

Leon watched Lana get ready. He didn't like it. He knew that if she was working that hard to look good, then she must have plans with that "pretty boy son of a bitch." He couldn't help but be in awe of how pretty she was though—all the time.

"One day she'll be mine. All of her will be mine and she'll fix herself up for me," Leon mumbled to himself. He had watched her come and go all week since the GPS tracking device was now attached to the new Mercedes. The covert cameras in the house gave him a full view of everything that she did and every time she undressed. He printed some of the screenshots that he had saved of her and taped them inside his closet door and inside a kitchen cabinet so he could look at her whenever he felt the need. Sneaking into her house while she had slept had made him feel more impatient about waiting for her to realize that she needed him to be safe and waiting for her to turn to him.

Lana finally slipped the dress on. She could not zip it up all the way. Roadking would have to finish zipping it for her. She put on the black and copper shoes and stood in front of a full-length mirror. The dress was so beautiful—it was made for her figure, and the black and copper complimented her red hair. There was still a half hour left before Roadking was to arrive. So she poured herself some wine, turned on some music, and gingerly stretched out on the leather couch, not wanting to crease the dress. Getting ready so early made her feel a little silly and juvenile and reminded her of her high school days when she did the same thing before a big date night.

At 5:55 p.m., Lana saw Roadking pull up to the gate at the end of the driveway in his Range Rover. Her heart jumped a little. Even though she couldn't wait to see him in a tuxedo, she didn't watch him get out of the car. In less than a minute, he knocked at the door, and when she opened the door and saw him, she quietly gasped. In her life, she had never seen anyone so handsome. He stood there, smiling with those crinkly eyes and those white teeth, wearing black tuxedo pants, a jacket, and bow tie with a white shirt. When Roadking saw Lana, his eyes widened and so did his smile. He had never seen anyone look so beautiful.

"Lana—that dress. It was made for you. You look stunning."

"Thank you, but—oh, Vincent! You look so handsome in that tuxedo. But you always do. I couldn't zip my dress up all the way. Could you give me a hand?"

"Sure."

She turned around and lifted her hair, and Roadking kissed the back of her neck before he zipped the dress, giving Lana that warm, melty, liquid feeling. She turned around and kissed him on the lips, which was followed by a few more passionate, long, deep kisses. Lana knew that if the kisses lasted a little longer, the fancy clothes would be coming off and they would not make it to the gallery on time. She took a step back.

"I made a charcuterie tray and I have some prosecco. How about some?"

"Yes, let me see what that charcuterie looks like."

Lana went to the kitchen and brought out the prosecco and two glasses and returned to get the appetizer.

"Fancy, Lana." He took some cheese, prosciutto, and a couple of crackers. He held the wine glass up and said, "To tonight."

Lana clicked her glass to his and said, "Yes, a magical one."

Roadking smiled at her. They talked and drank and ate a little. Roadking played with the silver bracelet on her wrist. In about a half hour, they got ready to leave. Lana put her snow boots on with the beautiful dress. She put her shoes in a tote bag and brought a little, black purse for her phone and makeup for a touch-up later.

She put on a long, black wool coat. She pulled her dress up above her ankles as she walked in the slush to the car. Roadking opened the door for her and made sure her dress didn't get closed in the door. She reset the house security system with her phone, and they were on their way. Andrea Bocelli sang in Italian softly on the stereo and set the mood for an elegant night.

The gallery was in a two-story building in downtown Boulder, a block north of the Pearl Street Mall on Spruce Street. Roadking told Lana that he would let her out in front of the gallery and he would go and park. "You wait inside the door for me. I don't want to let you out of my sight in that dress."

Lana tiptoed through the slush in the snow boots, carrying her bag of shoes. When she got inside, she sat down on a bench in the entryway and put the copper and black heels on. She hung her bag and coat on a hanger and waited near the door for Roadking. She was immediately approached by a businessman who advertised with *Boulder Essence*.

"Hello, Lana. Good to see you here. Have you been inside yet?" It was Mike Steele, a local ski shop owner. He was in his forties, about Lana's height. He was balding, but he let the sides and back of his hair grow long and pulled it into a ponytail. He always seemed to stand too close to her face when he talked to her.

Lana backed herself into a large window to keep him at a distance. In a couple of seconds, Roadking walked in the door. He took his coat off and hung it near Lana's and walked over to rescue her.

"Vincent, this is Mike Steele. He owns a ski shop here in Boulder. This is Vincent Romano of All Roads Harley-Davidson." They nodded at each other and shook hands.

"Hey, I've been meaning to try out a Harley. I'm a Triumph guy myself. But I might come check them out one of these days." Mike spoke as he backed away from Lana. "See you inside, Lana."

Roadking smiled at Lana. Mike had clearly been coming on to her. And she had tried so hard to be cool. But she was so beautiful in that dress, he knew that she would turn some heads.

"Where did you have to park?"

"Well, I made reservations for us at the Boulderado for tonight. I didn't know what the weather would be like tonight and why not? So I checked in and parked underground. We have to walk about a block to return there tonight. Will that be okay for you?"

"Yes, I can manage. I have my boots. What a lovely surprise! I've lived here my whole life and never stayed at the Boulderado. It'll be fun. Thank you."

"Yes, it will be fun, lovely lady." As gorgeous as she looked in that dress, Roadking's thoughts were of her out of the dress later and flashed on her naked, little body.

They walked into the foyer area where a silent auction of oil, pastel, watercolor, and pen and ink paintings created by local artists were on display. The silent auction was to benefit the Native American Rights Fund. They were approached by a server with glasses of sparkling wine. They each took one. Lana bid on a pen and ink and watercolor combination image of the cottages at Chautauqua with the Flatirons in the background for her office. A second server approached them with canapés. Lana asked him if he would take a photo of Roadking and her. She handed him her phone and he took a couple of shots. Lana and Roadking each took a puff pastry with cream cheese, smoked salmon, and chives on it. Lana looked at the photos on her phone. In her eyes, there was never a better-looking couple.

"Look at us, baby. Just look at these," she said when she showed him the photos. He put his arm around her and squeezed her. There was nothing to say. They looked like they belonged together.

Soon the ribbon that stretched across the doorway entrance to the gallery was cut, and after a short speech by the gallery director, the party migrated to the main gallery where a traveling exhibit of paintings by the Italian artist and sculptor Amedeo Modigliani were on display. Lana had taken art history classes in college and was familiar with the art and tragic life of Modigliani. Vincent knew of him from his travels in Italy. Many of the paintings in the exhibit were of his trademark nudes and portraits with long faces. Lana was fascinated and took many photos for a definite future article in the *Boulder Essence*.

Each of them ran into people they knew and they each in turn introduced the other. The gallery became a little crowded after a while. As Lana and Roadking turned to move to another exhibit, Lana spotted Lucas's parents enter the gallery. She immediately decided to avoid them, if possible. But if she happened to encounter them, she would be gracious and classy. She didn't mention that she had seen them to Roadking.

They continued to peruse and drink sparkling wine. Roadking saw an old friend from college Dante Fox and they began to talk CU and Broncos football. Lana stood nearby looking at one of the portraits, studying Modigliani's paint strokes when she felt a light tap on her shoulder. She turned to see Lucas's mother standing there.

Grace softly spoke, "Hello, Lana. How have you been?"

She was so gentle in her approach, Lana didn't know what to think. She had expected an attack, accusations, blame, finger-pointing, a scene. "I'm fine, Grace. How are you doing?"

"Oh, we're getting along, dear."

Lana thought of many things to say to her since Grace had given her an opening with her kind demeanor, but she kept them to herself. It was so odd. Lucas's mother had never warmed up to her. Maybe Lucas's death had softened the hard edges. "I'm glad to know that. It's a lovely exhibit, don't you think?"

But before Grace could answer, Lucas's father approached, glared coldly at Lana, and pulled Grace away. "I think it's time to leave, Grace."

Lucas's mother looked at her apologetically.

Roadking had witnessed the whole exchange. He didn't say a word. He just watched Lana. She looked down for a minute, sighed deeply, looked up at Roadking, and took his hand. Lucas was the past. Vincent was the present.

"Are you ready to head to the Boulderado with me?"

Lana felt a little buzz from the sparkling wine and felt affectionate.

"I'm ready to go anywhere with you, baby."

Roadking held her hand as they walked through the slush to the Boulderado. Lana held her dress up so that it wouldn't drag. Roadking carried the bag with the shoes. Roadking had reserved the historic presidential suite for them. He unlocked the door and they walked inside. Before Lana took a look at the period furnishings and design of the room, Roadking unzipped her dress and it fell to the floor in a heap. She picked it up and laid it across a chair, and Roadking carried her to the bed.

CHAPTER 32

While Roadking untied his tie and unbuttoned his shirt, his crinkly eyes were locked on Lana's green eyes. She gave him a gentle smile. With one big sweeping motion, he removed his tuxedo jacket, shirt, and tie and tossed them on the end of the bed. He slipped Lana's shoes off her feet. He could wait no longer to be intimate with her. He lay gently on top of her and held her tight. In a matter of seconds, he removed his pants and her bra and then he noticed that there was a gap in the blinds in the window. Even though they were on one of the upper floors, he stood and adjusted the blinds and then they turned back the comforter and climbed under the sheets. The sheets were smooth and cool and silky, and they slid about as they made love in various positions—chest to chest, front to back, side to side—with an occasional bump of the head on the ornate headboard. It was intense and exciting and passionate and deep.

Lana closed her eyes and wished it would never end. They held each other tightly as they finished with Roadking lying on top of her. His face was buried in her neck, and she felt his mustache tickle when he whispered quietly in Lana's ear, "I love you."

Lana paused for an instant as she wondered if she should risk being vulnerable to him by letting him know how she felt. Then she just let his words resonate and honesty prevailed. "I love you, Vincent," she whispered back.

Somehow he already knew that. His face was an inch or two from hers and she saw him smile and his eyes crinkle. "Then we agree," he teased.

He rolled over onto his back and pulled Lana on top of him.

Strands of her long, red hair streaked across his face. His hands were on her rear end. She rested her chin on his shoulder. He felt her breathing on his neck and could smell the light perfume that she wore. They lay there silently for a few minutes. She rolled over onto her back, and then they both turned to face each other. Lana was living in the moment. There were so many things she could have said to him, but the strength of those three words would have been diluted by other words. He touched her chin and kissed her lightly. She touched his cheek.

When they both began to get up, they each ended up kneeling on the bed somehow—face-to-face, chest to chest. They leaned into each other for a long embrace that lasted a few minutes, each of them rocking together ever so slightly. Neither of them had ever felt more loved than at that moment. Lana felt it surge through her blood. Roadking felt it in his chest.

The magical silence was broken when Roadking said, "I'm hungry, baby. Are you? Those little cocktail snacks weren't much of a dinner." He smiled as he added, "And we just finished a fantastic workout."

Lana crinkled her nose and smiled. "You know, I am hungry, now that I think of it. Can we order room service? Otherwise, we have to put on our dress-up clothes again to go out into the snow." Lana walked over to the closet nude and removed two fluffy, white, terry cloth bathrobes and tossed one to Roadking.

Roadking studied her little, naked shape as she moved across the room. "Yes, let's do."

When Lana approached him, he noticed that she was wearing only one of her lacy black and copper earrings.

"Lana, one of your earrings is missing. It must be in the bed or on the floor." They looked under the sheets and blankets and pillows and behind the bed and on the floor. It was not to be found.

Lana stopped running her hand through the bedding. "We can look later. Maybe I lost it while walking here. Here's the room service menu."

It was ten o'clock. Roadking ordered calamari, Lana chose blue crab cakes, and they ordered one Caesar salad and a bottle of Resplendent Pinot Noir to share. While they waited for room service to deliver their food, Roadking turned the TV on and began to surf the channels for something to watch. They settled on an old classic movie, *To Kill a Mockingbird*, in black-and-white. Room service arrived shortly with their food.

"Here, have some," Roadking pointed to the calamari.

"No, I think I'll pass," Lana shook her head and took a sip of the wine. "I'm just not sure about those things, even though they smell good."

"Okay, but I'll eventually get you to eat one."

"If you insist. That'll give you a reason to order them again." Lana teased.

They ate in silence and became engrossed with the movie as they sat on the bed. Shortly after they finished eating and drinking, Lana nodded off to sleep on Roadking's shoulder, who had already dozed off himself while leaning against the headboard. He woke and whispered quietly to her, "Okay, I guess that's enough for tonight."

And he laid her sleeping head down on the pillow next to his, brought the sheets and comforter up, turned out the antique lamp, and lay down next to her to sleep. A beam of light from a streetlamp was peeking through the blinds and had settled on the top of Lana's head. She looked like a sleeping angel with her eyelashes lying against her cheek and the glow around her face. He had made mistakes with love before, but he felt deep down that this time, it was right. It had happened without any effort—so fast that it seemed to be destined somehow. Roadking closed his eyes and thought about the lovemaking that had occurred in that room just a couple of hours before, and he thought of her words, and with that, he drifted off to sleep.

Leon had watched Lana get ready to go somewhere fancy. "Lana, darlin', yer the purdiest thing I ever laid eyes on," he hoarsely whispered to himself as he twirled the end of his mustache. *Ya can wear that purdy dress when I take ya out someday.* His deluded thoughts made him smile. He knew that she must be going somewhere with that "pretty boy Harley-Davidson prick."

But before he could watch her leave, he had received two separate service calls from two mothers with several children locked out of their minivans in two separate, snowy parking lots. "Damn, I gotta go. I'll see ya later, my little darlin'," he said as he blew a kiss at the computer monitor.

By the time Leon returned home, Lana was gone. Not seeing her leave left him feeling frantic. She had slipped out of his sight so often lately. His possessiveness of her was becoming more powerful, overtaking his conscious thoughts.

He ran his right hand through his greasy hair. "Where did ya go, little darlin'?" He paced back and forth, and slushy snow dripped off his boots and left puddles all around the room, which was still strewn with broken glass. He became so agitated that he kicked a hole in the wall. The drywall crumbled on the toe of his boot. His rational self told him that he must wait, that she would be visible to him again, and that he must be patient. But his distraught self wanted to destroy something or hurt something or someone, even if it was himself. He thought about the word "LANA" that he had carved on his own right leg, and he touched his thigh and closed his eyes for a minute.

There was a light tap, tap, tap on Leon's front door. Leon opened the door, and Carla stood there in a fake, red, fur coat and, despite the weather, a pink tank top.

"What the hell? Ya think ya can just stop here any time? Ya think it's Grand Central Station or something? I'm busy."

"Whatcha doin', Leon? It's a cold, snowy night and I thought ya could use some warmin' up," Carla's attempt to be flirtatious was tempered by the sound of her low, husky, smoky voice. "How about it, hot stuff? Not too busy for this," she said as she touched her hand on his shoulder and moved in to kiss him.

Leon jerked her hand off him and pushed her away. "Get off me, Carla. Jesus. Yer a piece of work. Yer a piece alright. Good for nothin' but that. Ain't there nobody else that wants ya? Yer disgusting."

Carla's loneliness allowed her to withstand his abuse in exchange for a little bit of intimacy with anyone, even Leon, even if it was only for a few minutes. Carla was a lost and damaged soul with no pride, no self-respect, and no purpose. All of it was drained away by a painful life of struggle and abuse.

Carla tried to be funny. "Let's be disgusting together. You want it and you know it, Leon Alvarez. I'm saving you the time of looking for me."

"Yeah, I never know which rock yer gonna crawl out from under." The truth was that Leon's soul was as lost and damaged as Carla's. But he had a purpose—to make Lana his. He looked at Carla. *I deserve better than this,* he thought. *But for tonight, she'll have to do.*

He grabbed Carla's hand, jerked her onto the broken-down couch and gave her what she wanted—closeness, a little attention, the touch of another human, animal sex. She lay there when he got up and wiped the back of his hand across his mouth. He barked, "Now leave! Yer barstool is gettin' cold."

"Can I stay tonight? I won't bother you. I'll stay out here." Carla still wore the fake fur coat as she pulled the rest of her clothes on.

"What the fuck, Carla? Ya homeless or somethin'?"

Carla had a place to live—a forlorn, little apartment that was once a single car garage behind someone's house. It was a cold and lonely place.

"No, you know where I live, Leon. I just didn't want to go back out in the cold after being here all warm with you."

"Stay then—but stay the hell away from me." Leon went into his grimy bedroom, took off his filthy, greasy clothes, and went to bed.

It seemed early to Carla. It was only ten o'clock. She looked around the room at the mess that Leon had made in his tirades during the previous weeks. She looked in a couple of the closets and found a broom to clean up the glass and other debris on the floor. She couldn't find a dustpan, so she used a magazine as a dustpan to gather up the dirt. His trash cans were over flowing. She found a plastic grocery bag and dumped the debris in the bag. The kitchen was a mess. Dishes were piled everywhere with dried and decaying food on them. There were empty cans and half-used containers of food intertwined with the dishes on the cluttered counter. Carla quietly removed the dishes from the sink so she could fill the sink with water to begin the tedious task of washing them all and putting them away. She found the dish soap and began to wash and dry them with the only clean towel she could find. She tried not to wake Leon. She wanted to surprise him with a clean house when he woke up. She made a stack of clean plates and lined up clean glasses. She opened cupboards to see where they belonged and began to put them away. But when she opened one of the doors, she saw photos of Lana taped on the inside of the door—dressed, half-dressed, topless. She gasped to herself, "What is this? Some porno?"

"Hey, bitch, what they hell are ya doin?"

Carla was startled when she heard Leon's loud and angry voice from the doorway of the kitchen and quickly closed the cupboard door with the photos of Lana taped inside. "I was just . . . just cleanin' up for you."

"No, ya wasn't. Ya was doin' some snoopin'. I don't take kindly to that. Now get out! I said now!"

Carla couldn't let it go. "Who is she? What are you doin' with those pitchures of her?"

Leon was livid. He stepped quickly across the room and grabbed Carla by the throat with one hand and pushed her head back into the cupboard door.

"It's none of yer fuckin' business! It's nobody! Just some pitchures I come across! But if ya mention what ya saw to anyone, I'll kill ya!" He squeezed her neck even harder to make his point.

Carla gasped when he moved his hand away and looked at him with bulging eyes, stunned at his reaction to her seeing the photos. She looked at him standing in his boxer shorts as he backed away and detected on the thigh of his right leg a fresh pink scar in the shape of what looked like letters. She couldn't make them out.

Leon caught her glance at his leg where he had carved Lana's name and stepped behind the wall that adjoined the door to hide it. "Go! Now!"

Carla hurriedly pulled her fake fur coat on and left the house. She was stunned and confused. *What did I see? Why was he so protective of it? What was that scar on his leg?*

Leon was beyond angry. Carla had come across a little part of his big secret. He hoped he'd made his point and that she would keep her mouth shut. It was his private world and she had entered it without permission. "The bitch! I'll kill her!"

Lana woke first and finally had a chance to look around the presidential suite where they were staying. She opened the blinds a little, but not so much as to wake Roadking. As she peeked out the window, she saw that the room faced the Flatirons, which were covered with snow. The windows were covered with heavy, dark brocade curtains and a valance. The woodwork was painted white. The pieces of furniture were charming, dark, antique oak. The lamp was made of amber glass. A bouquet of fresh, white flowers in a white vase was placed on a high dresser. The ornate headboard was made of white and gold antique wrought iron twisted into a heart in the center. She looked into an oval mirror perched above one of the dressers and saw her messy, tousled hair and smears of mascara under each eye. She went into the bathroom to attempt to smooth her hair and remove the mascara smears under each eye. She splashed water on her face. She had only brought a little touch-up makeup, not knowing that she would spend the night with Roadking at the Boulderado Hotel. When she came out of the bathroom, Roadking was awake. He reached out his arm and beckoned her to come back to bed, which she did. They still had not spoken. They didn't need to. There was an unspoken closeness that didn't need any more than each other's physical presence to communicate. After a while, Roadking asked Lana if she had slept well. She had. After all, she was so happy sleeping with the wonderful man who had told her that he loved her.

"Well, should we order room service for breakfast or go

downstairs in a tux and a formal gown for breakfast?" he asked and grinned.

"I think we should stay alone in this room as long as possible." She laid her head on his chest and listened to his gentle heartbeat as he ran his hand up and down her arm.

Checkout time was eleven o'clock, and it was only eight thirty. They still had some time together there, so they ordered breakfast from room service. Roadking, as usual, ordered a big breakfast of a waffles, sausage, eggs, and hash browns. Lana ordered whole wheat toast and orange juice.

When they finished eating, Roadking went into the bathroom to shower. While he was in the shower, Lana received a text message that she had won the bid on the pen and ink and watercolor painting of the Chautauqua cottages at the silent auction and to pick it up on Monday. Lana jumped into the shower after Roadking was finished. She attempted to do something with her wet hair without a curling iron and applied the makeup that she had brought with her.

When she came out, there he was in the tuxedo again without the tie. After all, that was the only thing he had to wear. He was an awesome sight. She grabbed her phone and took a picture of him standing there near the window with that beautiful smile of white teeth and dark mustache. She was so in love with him. She put the beautiful black and copper dress and shoes on again. Roadking pulled her close and put his arms around her and hugged her tight. It had been a magical night in every way—for them both.

While they drove to Lana's house, soft music of Bonnie Raitt played. Roadking held her left hand as they drove. They talked about the Modigliani exhibit and some of the people that they had met and seen at the gallery opening. He wanted to ask her about her encounter with Lucas's parents, but he didn't want to change her mood with the mention of Lucas. They arrived at Lana's house around noon. He walked her to the door and kissed her goodbye.

"Goodbye until next time," Lana whispered.

Roadking turned and took a couple of steps to leave and then turned around, walked back, and kissed her again and squeezed her tight. Lana held on tight. In her mind were the words, *Let this moment last forever with this wonderful man.* A silent prayer. Roadking left to visit his parents and whatever extended family happened to visit this Sunday. They would wonder why he was wearing a tuxedo.

For the rest of the day, Lana wandered from room to room, from one task to another, accomplishing nothing. Roadking was still with her in her thoughts, and she just couldn't let the past twenty-four hours leave her yet. She would face the real world later, which would come soon enough Monday morning.

As the evening approached, she messaged Roadking.

I keep thinking about you and the exceptional night we spent together. Thank you for making it happen.

Roadking messaged back.

Love you, Lana Ross.

CHAPTER 33

'I'm in love!' was the song Lana and Tom Petty sang together on Monday morning as she drove to work in her car. It seemed that nothing could dampen her mood. The weekend with Roadking had been heavenly. Her feelings for him were so strong that they made her tingle all over. She knew she was being adolescent, but she told herself, *This is a feeling that deserves celebration—even if it's just singing in a car on the way to work.*

Mondays were always busy with status meetings with the staff and assistant editors. The fitness edition would be published on Thursday. She congratulated and thanked each of them for their effort in pushing the extra edition through. While all of them were assembled, she mentioned that she wanted to invite any of them who would be away from family for Thanksgiving or any who just wanted to come anyway to her house for dinner. Although Lana was essentially the boss at the magazine, her staff regarded her highly and respected her as a trusted friend. She asked them to let her know by Friday if they were coming.

"There will be great food, football, board games, and lots of wine. And if the wine kicks in, we can get some karaoke going too."

Lana worked through lunch and intended to go to the gallery at one o'clock to pick up the pen and ink piece that she had purchased at the silent auction. The snow on the sidewalks had melted since the storm on Saturday. Lana decided to walk to the gallery, which was only a couple of blocks from her office. Since the Boulderado Hotel was on the way to the gallery, Lana stopped in and asked the hotel clerk if by chance someone had found a black and copper earring in the presidential suite after her stay on Saturday night. He checked the lost and found box and, lo and behold, it was there. It was a memento that marked the significance of the night with Roadking there. Another reason for a happy day for Lana.

She paid for and picked up the artwork from the gallery. It was not a large or heavy piece—about thirteen by seventeen inches—so she could just carry it herself back to her office. As she made her way on the busy Pearl Street Mall with its noon visitors, her eyes trained on what appeared to be a familiar silhouette who stood talking with someone on the sidewalk near the door of one of the local pubs in the distance. When she got closer, she could see that it was Roadking. He was talking to a woman in her late thirties with brown, spiky, layered hair that went down to her chin. She couldn't make out her face, but she was tall with a nice figure and was dressed in a business suit. She couldn't decide whether she should keep walking and interrupt his conversation or mind her own business. But when she was about a hundred feet away from them, she saw Roadking lean down and kiss the woman on the cheek and give her a swift hug. The woman turned and walked in Lana's direction.

As she walked past Lana, she could see only part of her face since she was wearing sunglasses. She wore bright red lipstick and a heavy, gold-chained necklace. Lana stopped in her tracks and looked in the direction where Roadking had been standing, but she could no longer see him. He had either walked away or was inside the pub. Lana looked down at the concrete as she walked quickly back to her office. The extraordinary mood with which she had begun her day was suddenly replaced with uncertainty and confusion and questions. *What was that? Who was the woman? Obviously, someone he cares about since he kissed and hugged her. Maybe it was nothing. Maybe it was none of my business.* Her curiosity began to shift to self-doubt. Perhaps she had been a fool to tell him how she felt about him. She was so careful with that word—"love"—and yet she had exposed herself to being vulnerable by saying it. Maybe Roadking did love her on Saturday night, but when the night was over, his feelings for her were lessened to something else. Jealousy—that rare feeling for her that twisted her guts into knots, that feeling that she knew intellectually was useless, counterproductive, negative, and a waste of energy and emotion, and that was fueled by fear—began to torment her.

Questions and more questions penetrated her thoughts for the rest of the afternoon and made it difficult to focus on even the simplest tasks. Lana chided herself as the thoughts ran through her mind. *What a joke I am, what a fool! I should have known that he was just too good to be true. But we're not committed to each other in any way. We aren't in high school. He's free to do as he pleases and so am I.*

Unexpectedly around three o'clock, Roadking stood in her doorway, smiling with those white teeth and crinkly eyes. "Hey, Boulder Girl. I had business here today and thought I'd swing by and say hi. I see that you picked up the pen and ink today."

Lana had leaned it against the antique oak bureau to hang later on a narrow wall near the door. "Hi, Vincent. Yes, I did." Lana forced a smile. Her heart leaped a little. But then he always affected her that way. "And I checked at the Boulderado today and they found the earring that I lost on Saturday night." She wanted to blurt out that she saw him with a woman whom he kissed and hugged. She wanted an explanation. But she said nothing. She did not want distrust to factor into their relationship ever—whatever that was or would be.

"Nice. How is your day going?" He was so cheerful and happy to see her. He had no idea that his meeting with a woman earlier in the day had been witnessed and was tormenting her.

"Good. I got a lot done this morning. So what brings you to Boulder?" This was the opening that she needed to find out what he had been doing without mentioning a woman.

"I had an appointment with my insurance guy to go over the coverage on all of my policies. And I met Shannon, Ava's mom, at the Sunrise Café for lunch. Ava wants to go to Europe for a summer study abroad program in Italy, and I gave her mom a check for half of the tuition. And since Shannon works in Boulder, I caught up with her after my insurance appointment."

Lana looked at him as he spoke, then looked down, turned the silver bracelet on her left wrist, then looked out the window for a few seconds and then looked into Roadking's eyes again, but she said nothing. Roadking watched her. Although she didn't know it, she was completely transparent, and he could read that something bothered her by that series of gestures. There was no way that she would tell him she had seen him with a woman and that it worried her. That would be accusatory, petty, and jealous, and it appeared that he didn't deserve that. But now a question about his feelings for Shannon began to surface; after all, they had made a child together.

"Then you made good use of your time in Boulder today." Lana seemed stiff as she spoke and looked at her desktop.

"Yes, and I wanted to come by and see you too." He smiled and stood closer to her as she sat in her office chair.

Lana looked toward the window again. But this time when she turned back, Roadking leaned over and kissed her lightly on the lips. There was no way to resist him. She could not punish him with passive-aggressiveness.

As he leaned over, he looked straight into Lana's eyes and said, "Lana, Shannon and I remain in touch because of Ava. She has been a great mom to her. I won't say that we're friends because that can mean many things. She's married and I'm with you."

Bingo! He had figured it out and Lana got the answer she needed to hear. She reached up and touched her hands to his face and kissed him. He saw that she visibly relaxed. He pulled her up out of her chair and hugged her with both arms around her waist.

"Okay," was all that Lana said. There was no further need to discuss it. He had cleared the air. And that was that. The topic was closed.

"This weekend is supposed to be fairly warm weather for November, and I think I want to take the Road King out for a short ride. Would you come with me? On Sunday?"

"Yes, I hope the weather's good. It's been awhile and I love riding with you. Thanks for the invitation."

"Who else would I ask?" He smiled again with those crinkly eyes.

Lana walked him down to the front door of the *Boulder Essence* office and hugged him and kissed him goodbye. He took a few steps to walk away from her and then he turned and took a few steps backward and said, "Dinner one night this week? I want to see you before Sunday."

"Yes. Of course. Call me." She didn't want to sound too eager, but she couldn't wait until Sunday either.

He raised his hand and waved goodbye. Lana stood and watched him walk away until he turned and was out of sight. As she turned to enter the building, she noticed the sign on her bank about a half block away and remembered that she needed to deposit the $250,000 check from the proceeds of Lucas's life insurance policy. When she went back to her office, she unlocked the center drawer, took the check out, and left for the bank. The fog of romance from the weekend and then the appearance of Roadking with another woman had caused her to forget about the check in the drawer.

While Lana was at work, there was a visitor to her home. Leon was more frenetic than usual whenever she was not visible to him on the monitor. He had seen her in the house the night before in her usual Sunday night routine, but the need to be with her became increasingly more urgent. He couldn't think of a reason or a way to be near her. As he left his house, the dented, green van seemed to be on autopilot as Leon drove directly to Lana's house. It was early afternoon. He parked his van outside of the gated driveway again. He waited until no one was driving on Hill View Road, maneuvered his way over the wire fence to avoid the gate detector, and walked up the driveway. He disabled the house alarm and entered through the garage door again and came inside. He needed to be in her house. He needed to be where she spent her time. He needed to walk where her footsteps had been. He needed to be in the places that he had watched on the monitor. He needed more—to be with her, to be her man, to make her his own. But he knew that it was going to take time for him to hatch that plan. He walked up the stairs to her bedroom. He stood in the doorway again and looked at her bed. There was an almost imperceptible indentation in the mattress where her little body had slept at night. He walked over to the bed and picked up her pillow and held it to his face. The scent of her shampoo, her soap, her lotion, her perfume, and her essence resided in that pillow. He took a deep breath—deeper than he had breathed in years—taking in as much of her as he could. He laid the pillow back down. He walked over to her dresser and picked up a bottle of her perfume and held it to his nose. He opened the bottle and dabbed a little bit of one of the perfumes on the back of his left hand and held it up to his nose. Now he could carry the scent of her perfume with him for a while. Soon his phone rang. There was a service call in Columbine Point to install new locks on a house. He swiftly left Lana's house, enabled the alarm system, walked up the driveway, scaled the fence, and jumped in his van, apparently undetected.

Carla got off work around three thirty. Red's Bar was always her next destination. She was a regular every day of the week. "Hey, Carla. Your usual?" She was greeted by the bartender as she walked right over to her usual seat in the darkest corner of the bar.

"Yep, Long Island," Carla grunted.

There were a few grizzled, bearded patrons with baseball hats sitting at the bar, nursing tall draft beers and watching the TV behind the bar. Local news came on at four o'clock and Carla glanced at it. She looked at her phone, checked her email and Facebook, and looked up at the TV occasionally, when suddenly she couldn't believe her eyes. A short segment about the opening of the art gallery in Boulder with the Modigliani exhibit was on the news. And there she was—the woman in the photos taped on Leon's kitchen cabinet! A reporter asked her what her thoughts were about the exhibit. The words "Lana Ross, editor of *Boulder Essence*" ran across the screen. "I think the people of Boulder and surrounding communities are fortunate to have the opportunity to see the outstanding, unique works of Modigliani in such a great setting. I'm very impressed with the gallery opening tonight."

Carla's mind began to race. She couldn't wait for the opportunity to taunt Leon with her discovery. That woman, Lana Ross, would never pose for photos for Leon. She was way out of his league. He must be sneaking them somehow. She sat in the dark corner, smiling to herself and hoping that Leon would visit the bar tonight.

Carla's wish came true when Leon walked into Red's Bar around seven o'clock. Carla was already on her third Long Island iced tea and she felt it in her head. Leon walked up to the bar and ordered a draft beer.

Bart Patterson, one of the regulars sitting at the bar, said loudly, "Jeez, Alvarez, you shure smell purdy. Who is she?"

"Shut up, Patterson."

Carla heard the exchange and came drifting out of her dingy corner. "Yeah, Leon, who is she? Is it that magazine gal?"

Leon felt his blood pressure rise to the top of his head. *How the hell did Carla make that connection?* "You shut up, too, bitch." Leon's eyes were wide and red and bulging with anger. He had already warned her once what would happen if she snooped.

"What magazine gal? Ya pickin' up some of them gals selling magazines on the street or something, Alvarez?" Patterson laughed heartily.

"Hey, Carla, let's you and me have a talk." Leon grabbed her by her fleshy upper arm and dragged her back to her corner table and sat down next to her. He put his face an inch or two from hers and gritted his teeth as he said, "What the fuck are you gabbin' about?"

Carla smiled, amused with herself and with her discovery, and in a snarky voice said, "I saw her on the news. The woman in the photos on your cupboard door. I saw her. They interviewed her at some gallery. Her name is Lana Ross and she's an editor of a magazine. I know it's her. Whatcha doin' with photos of a class act like that? Do you think yer her kind?" She laughed hoarsely out loud, which caused her to cough violently.

Leon was in her face, still tightly squeezing her upper arm.

"Listen to me. I already told ya what would happen to ya if ya ever mentioned them pitchures to anybody and now yer gabbing on like you know all about it. What I said, I meant. Do ya remember my words, dumb bitch?"

Carla was unfazed. He wouldn't do anything in the bar. If he did, she would holler out everything she knew about the woman and the photos so that everybody could hear. "Yeah, sure, lover boy," she said, still laughing to herself. The third Long Island iced tea had diminished any good judgement that she should have had.

"Let's go out to my van, Carla." He was still squeezing her arm.

"No way. You know what you could do though? My car needs a new muffler and I could use a couple hundred dollars to get it fixed. What do you think? A couple hundred bucks and I'm silent about your little magazine gal secret, or I start talking to them guys over there." Carla impressed herself with her sudden ingenious idea and courage to blackmail Leon.

Leon scratched his head. He didn't have time to think about how to handle this new dilemma. He reached into his wallet and pulled out two one-hundred-dollar bills and stuffed them into the breast pocket of the plaid, men's shirt she was wearing.

"Don't ya ever pull that again. This will happen only once. If ya ever threaten me again, I'll kill ya. Now get out of here." Leon had to make her leave in case she changed her mind and started to blab.

Carla was still smiling. For once, she had the upper hand with Leon. "Thanks, Leon, for the bucks."

She ran her hand across his chin and tried to kiss him on the cheek. He shoved her face away. She staggered out the door and got into her beat-up Buick. The last thing she should have been doing was driving in the condition she was in. But that's how she left the bar every night.

Leon walked back over to the pool table. "So which of you bastards wanna play?"

A couple of the guys jumped off their barstools and came over to shoot pool. They forgot all about the exchange between Carla and Leon, and it wasn't mentioned again. But it was fresh and seething in Leon's mind, and he felt it in his stomach. Something had to be done about Carla. *But what should I do? What would it take to keep that dumb-ass bitch quiet? How far do I have to go?*

After a couple of hours, about ten o'clock, Leon decided to head home. It was getting close to Lana's usual bedtime, and he wanted to see shots of her undressing and going to bed. When Leon walked to his van, he noticed that Carla's beat-up Buick was still parked in the parking lot. She had left three hours before. He approached her car, and there she was—passed out drunk, leaning forward on her steering wheel. Leon opened the car door. She didn't come to. He reached into her shirt pocket and retrieved the blackmail money he'd paid her just hours before and put it in his pocket.

"Dumb bitch." He slammed the car door. She still didn't flinch. He walked to his van and drove away. He blasted the Taylor Swift song "Look What You Made Me Do" on his stereo while he laughed out loud about Carla and the money. Soon he looked at his haggard self in the rearview mirror and growled, "Carla, ya shouldn't have done what ya did. I'm coming for ya soon. Look what yer gonna make me do."

CHAPTER 34

Carla woke from passing out in her car with a start. It was 1:40 a.m. Her mind was foggy, and her neck was stiff from resting her head on the steering wheel. She looked at herself in the rearview mirror and could see her face in the dim light of the streetlamps. Her eyes were puffy and baggy from alcohol, and her cheek was creased and indented from the steering wheel. She sat up straight. She felt nauseous and wanted to throw up, but she straightened herself up, lit a cigarette, started the car, and began the short drive to the garage apartment where she lived. As she drove, she vaguely remembered that Leon had given her money. She reached into her shirt pocket and there was no money. Her memory of the evening gradually returned—*There was the magazine gal on TV, Leon's threats, the $200 for hush money. But where did the money go? Did I lose it? Was I robbed? Maybe it's in the car somewhere.* When she got home, she still felt sick. Smoking a cigarette had only made her feel worse. She would have to look for the money in the car later. All she wanted to do was lay down and go to sleep. She needed to confront Leon again, but it was too much to think about at that moment. She smiled to herself as she remembered the look on his face when she had mentioned the woman from the magazine. She got into bed with her clothes on, curled up, and went to sleep.

Leon was still awake at 1:40 a.m. He had been drinking beer and smoking all night as he pondered his next moves. He had managed to keep Carla quiet this one time. But his mind traveled from plan to plan as he tried to figure out how to silence her about his secret obsession with Lana. He couldn't predict how long she would stay silent with money, and even so, he was not inclined to give her any more money unless he was cornered, like in the bar. Although he had physically hurt people many times, he had never gone so far as to take them out altogether. But his psychotic obsession with Lana had taken him to extremes already, and he would let nothing or no one interfere with the goal to make Lana his own. He went into the kitchen and removed the photos of Lana from inside the cupboard door and put them in a cluttered drawer in his bedroom. Maybe he could convince Carla that she had never seen the photos to begin with at all. She was intoxicated so much and so often. So now he could either avoid her for as long as possible, or he could face her and see where that encounter would take them. He figured that she would try to get money again since the $200 was now missing from her pocket, and he couldn't avoid her for too long.

"Goddamn it. This whole deal is takin' my mind off that pretty, little darlin'. I don't want to think about fat, ugly, disgusting Carla. She's messin' with my head," he mumbled to himself as he lay back on the couch. He fell asleep until the cigarette in his hand burned down to his fingers and he woke with a jolt. He jumped up, ran his fingers under cold water for a minute or two, and went to bed.

Leon slept restlessly as his mind struggled with one plan after another that would keep Carla silent. But the morning light finally brought clarity to his thinking, and he settled on a couple of scenarios. He was not the least bit troubled by his thoughts. He would go to any extreme to keep Lana unaware of his twisted voyeurism. He picked up his phone to watch the monitor to see Lana dress for work. And there she was, walking around in a black bra and panties, tidying up the bedroom and bathroom, eventually settling on something to wear—a gray shirt, black jeans, and boots. "I'd sure like to wake up next to that purdy thing every day," he whispered to himself. He touched the back of his hand to his nose. The scent of Lana's perfume that he had brushed on his hand the day before was still lightly fragrant. As he walked through the house, he admitted to himself that Carla had made a little dent in the continuous mess that he lived in. The glass was cleaned up and one stack of dishes was washed. But those were the only charitable thoughts he would ever have of her. "Maybe I should be a little more charmin' to her." He laughed with great amusement as he pondered his ideas.

Lana was happy to begin a new day. The day before had been troubling for her as she'd struggled with the ugly feelings of misplaced jealously and distrust of Roadking. She was disappointed in herself. She hoped that the new day would bring redemption. Her workday was routine. The postholiday edition of the magazine was the focus now, and it included the first article in the series about travel in Colorado without a car. Her staff had written tremendously comprehensive articles on the assignment, and it appeared that the series would have to be split between the next two editions. The motorcycle article that had led Lana to her first meeting with Roadking would be the capstone feature of the series.

After meetings and consultations with the staff, Lana returned to her office and found that a phone message had been left by the president of the bank where she had deposited the $250,000 check from the proceeds of Lucas's life insurance policy. She dialed the phone to return his call and wondered if there was a problem with the check.

"Hello, this is Lana Ross, returning your phone call from earlier today."

"Yes, Ms. Ross. I'm Dierk Cowles, the president of First National, where you bank. I see that you recently deposited a large check to your account, and I was wondering if I could meet with you sometime to discuss some of the banking products that we offer that might benefit a large deposit like yours. Would you be available for coffee or for lunch one day this week?"

Lana should have expected that someone at the top in the bank would take notice of the large deposit. She grimaced as he made his pitch to her. She hated to be the subject of a sales pitch. She thought for a quick second, *I might as well see what he has to say, in the interest of good business and let him know that I'm not interested in doing anything with it for now. Maybe I can turn the conversation around to the possibility of the bank advertising with Boulder Essence.* "Well, I think I could swing a half hour for coffee one morning this week. How about tomorrow morning at nine o'clock at the Sunshine Café? It's located between both of our offices."

"That would work for me as well. I look forward to meeting you then, Ms. Ross."

Lana's mild annoyance was assuaged in a few short minutes when Roadking called to set up a dinner date for Wednesday night. "Hi, Lana. Are you up for seeing me tomorrow night for dinner? If you're not tired of seeing me," he teased her.

"Seriously, Vincent. I love to be with you. Of course I'm up for it. What's the plan?"

"There's a new, little Italian bistro in east Boulder that's hosting a wine pairing with pasta event tomorrow night at six thirty. I can make reservations for us, if you'd go with me. How about it?"

"Sounds like fun. Should I meet you there?"

"No, I'll swing by your office and pick you up at five thirty. That okay? I know you usually leave earlier."

"I always have plenty to do, and I'll see you then. Looking forward to it."

Carla left work at three thirty that afternoon and wondered if she should head to Red's Bar as was her custom. She was afraid to tell Leon that she had lost the money and didn't have the nerve to ask him for some again after he had threatened her. But those were just threats. He wouldn't ever really hurt her. Her need for a drink drove her to Red's Bar anyway and to the usual dingy, dark corner in the bar to drink the usual Long Island iced tea. The regulars were already seated at the bar to spend the rest of the night—evidently their only social life.

About five thirty, Leon walked into the bar and was welcomed with the usual obscenities. Out of the corner of his eye, he saw the hulking image of Carla, hunched over predictably in her corner booth. He didn't look her way.

"Hey, yer girlfriend is over there, Alvarez," said Toby Padilla.

"She ain't my girlfriend and that ain't none of yer business anyway, Padilla."

Padilla laughed and shook his head. "Buy me a beer, Alvarez? You make all that money unlocking cars fer the purdy, little mamas and their little kiddies." He continued to laugh at his own cleverness.

"Hey, Robinson. Hit me and this prick with a couple of beers." He turned to Padilla, "Don't know how ya convinced me to buy ya one, asshole."

The bartender brought a couple of draft beers. Leon sat at the bar with the guys for about an hour when he saw Carla slip outside for a smoke. He slid off the barstool and went outside to join her and smoke. A big puff of smoke drifted from the side of the building as Leon walked out the door. As he walked around the corner, he saw Carla.

"Hey, Leon. What do ya want?"

"Not to look at your fat face again." Leon laughed loudly.

But as he walked away from her, she said loudly, "Hey, Leon! It's gonna cost me more than I thought to fix that muffler on my car. How about another $200?"

Leon stopped in his tracks. He didn't think that she would have the nerve to ask him for blackmail money again after his last threats. He turned and walked quickly toward her.

"That pretty, little magazine lady would probably love to know about them pitchures, Leon."

Leon took out his wallet and gave her $200. "What did I tell ya the first time? Shut the fuck up or else!" He was furious, breathing hard, his red eyes bulging as he stared at her. "Have you got it, bitch?"

"Yeah, Leon. And thanks for the cash." Carla smiled as she waved the cash at him when he walked back into the building.

Leon sat at the bar with Padilla and drank beers. There was no exchanging of obscenities. Leon was quiet for a change. The evil wheels in his mind turned. He had some ideas about how to shut Carla up, but he couldn't decide which scheme he could pull off best. Carla sat silently in the dark, dingy corner of the bar and watched him. After an hour or so, Leon got up and walked outside for a smoke. Carla followed him and intended to taunt him some more. Leon saw her stagger out the door and walked toward her. He lit his cigarette and then hers.

"Well, Carla, I been sittin' at the bar there thinkin', and it seems I been kind of an asshole to ya, and I thought about how ya cleaned up the glass on my floor and tried to clean up that kitchen mess at my house, and I need to make it up to ya somehow. Got any ideas?"

Carla immediately started to walk to Leon's beat-up van.

"No, Carla, not that. I was thinkin' of spendin' some time with ya doin' somethin' other than that."

Carla stopped, turned around, and looked directly into Leon's face. He must be teasing her or leading her into some nasty trick. "Like what?" Her voice was lower and huskier than usual as she tried to sound sexy.

"Well, I think we should head up to the hills fer a little picnic or sightseein'. What do ya think of that? The weather ain't been too bad up there yet."

Carla studied his face and tried to detect if it was a joke or a sincere request. She took a couple of long drags on her cigarette while she watched him and blew smoke over his head.

"Well, can't ya talk? Do you wanna?" Leon tried to be patient.

"Okay. So what are the plans?"

Leon laughed to himself. "Well, I'll swing by the 7-Eleven and grab some of them sandwiches, some chips, and a six-pack and then pick ya up at yer house about eleven tomorrow and we'll head to the hills. Can ya get off work?"

"I'll just call in sick. Okay." Carla began to warm up to the idea. She had no friends or family. No one wanted to go anywhere with her. She forgot about blackmailing him. Forgot about the $200.

"Now here's the deal. You and I have to be a secret. Them guys in there will give us shit. So don't ya tell nobody about our picnic date. Got it? Let's go back in. You go first."

Carla's dense and foggy head tried to figure out if Leon was up to something. Maybe he was sincere, and he really wanted to be with her. Maybe it was a trick. No matter, she was so lonely. She wanted to be with someone even if it was Leon.

In a few minutes, Leon walked in the door, talking on his phone. He stopped near her table, and she heard him say to someone, "Yeah, I was planning to head up to the hills tomorrow anyway. Eight o'clock? Yeah, I can make that work."

Carla's heart sank. It sounded like their plans were scuttled by a service call.

"Hey, gal," Leon whispered, "I have a service call early tomorrow up Left Hand Canyon near Jamestown. Could ya drive up the canyon a ways and meet me there for the picnic or whatever? Then I won't have to waste time drivin' back down to pick ya up."

"I can, but how do I know where and what time to meet ya? Do you want me to get the picnic together?"

"Yeah. Get that picnic stuff. Let's see . . . why don't ya just head up Left Hand about ten and drive until you see me parked. Ya park and climb in my van. But remember this is a secret. We're a secret, right?"

"Yep, Leon," Carla hoarsely whispered and smiled at him. Carla ordered another Long Island iced tea. She would only drink one more of those potent drinks. She wanted to go home earlier than usual and get ready for her date with Leon, look through her pile of clothes and wash her hair. She finished her final Long Island and quietly slipped out of the darkness of the corner booth and went home. She called and left a message for her boss and told him that she wasn't feeling well and would miss work the next day.

Leon snickered to himself. "Dumb-ass Carla fell hook, line, and sinker fer my little plan. I'm a real charmin' guy when I wanna be."

"So which one of you pricks wanna play a round of pool?" he shouted to the guys parked at the bar.

When it got close to ten o'clock, Leon left the bar, went to his van, and opened the app on his phone with the monitor of Lana. She was a creature of habit, and in a matter of minutes, he saw her get up from the couch, turn off the TV, and head to her bedroom.

She stood for a long while looking at her clothes. Leon impatiently waited for her to undress. Eventually, the workout clothes she wore were stripped off, revealing a black sports bra and panties. The old, classic Police song popped into his head and in his raspy voice he sang softly to himself, "I'll be watching you." Leon smoked a joint while he drove home, smiling to himself at his cleverness for fooling Carla with his superior thinking and fooling Lana who had no idea about the hidden cameras.

Both Lana and Carla woke Wednesday morning and looked forward to their respective dates with Roadking and Leon. Lana remembered with some annoyance that she had agreed to have coffee with the bank president too. She put on a long-sleeved, tweedy, brown wool dress, black tights, pearls, and brown suede boots. Carla put on a yellow and green plaid men's shirt with pearl buttons over a lime-green tank top and tugged and pulled on her tightest jeans, which did nothing for her but enhance the muffin top that hung over her belt. Lana carefully applied her makeup, curled her hair, grabbed a brown suede jacket and her laptop, and headed to work. Carla pulled her hair into a high ponytail without brushing it, touched up the makeup that she had been wearing for days, grabbed a couple of packs of cigarettes and her lighter, and headed to the market to buy things for the picnic with Leon.

Lana left her office about nine o'clock for the short walk to the Sunshine Café to meet the bank president. She didn't know what he looked like and hoped it would be obvious when she walked in. She was right. A nicely dressed man in his early forties was sitting at a table for two, drinking coffee.

As she walked in, he stood up and said, "Lana Ross?"

Lana nodded as he reached out to shake her hand.

"Dierk Cowles. It's a pleasure to meet you." He pulled a chair out for her, and as she moved to sit down, he touched his hand to the small of her back. He motioned to a barista, who strolled over to take Lana's order.

"I'll have a hot chocolate this morning. Thank you."

"Anything else for you? A croissant? A muffin?"

Lana immediately observed that Dierk was trying a little too hard to win her approval. "No, I'm good. So I'd like to hear about your ideas for the money I deposited." Lana leaped right to the point.

Dierk Cowles was good-looking with dark blue eyes and dark, wavy, brown hair and chiseled features. But his zealous eagerness detracted from his good looks.

"Well, first tell me a little about yourself. I know the *Boulder Essence* magazine, but I don't know about the editor."

Lana thought that he sounded rehearsed and seemed a little nervous. She told him about being raised in the area, her college education, her job, and very little about her personal life. Out of politeness, Lana asked, "What about you?"

Dierk was more than willing to talk about himself. He first commented that he had twin daughters who were six years old and a ten-year-old son, and he then went on to say that he had gotten an MBA at Dartmouth and a BA at Tulane and that he had lived in Boulder for the past twelve years. He did not mention a wife. He stared at her face intensely. Occasionally, his eyes drifted to her chest.

"I knew Lucas Chisholm. A nice guy. Too bad what happened to him."

Lana did not respond. She picked up her phone to see what time it was. Fifteen minutes of their thirty-minute appointment had already passed, and he hadn't even begun his spiel. She decided not to say anything and let the silence carry him to the matter at hand. It worked. He began to talk to her about various investment products and types of bank accounts that would benefit her sizable deposit. There was so much information.

She finally asked him, "Do you have any written material or a website where I can review this information more thoroughly?"

"Yes, Lana—may I call you Lana?" He was stiff and polite with her.

"Yes, that's fine."

"Okay, here's my business card. Here are a couple of brochures and the website information. Please phone me or email me anytime with questions if you have any."

"Thank you for providing me with this information. I'm inclined to just leave the money in the savings account for the time being. I know that the yield is small, but I haven't made any plans for it yet. But I'm not moving it from your bank."

Then Dierk unexpectedly reached over and put his left hand on Lana's right hand, which rested on the table next to her cup of hot chocolate. "Now that I've met you in person, I'd like to spend a little more time getting to know you. You're a quite beautiful and interesting woman." He paused for a minute while he looked at her face, and then he added, "I mean, to discuss banking products."

Lana was stunned. The situation felt awkward. His intense gaze upon her face led her to believe that he was hitting on her. Or maybe he was just interested in her money. His demeanor had suddenly switched from pushy sales to flirtatious. She nonchalantly moved her hand to her lap and said, "Thank you for the compliment and for the hot chocolate. My schedule is quite full. Let me take a look at the information, and I'll get back to you." She stood and reached out her hand to shake his.

He took her hand and covered it with his other hand. "Good to meet you, Lana. I look forward to seeing you again."

Lana shook her head as she walked back to her office. That meeting had felt awkward and strange. She convinced herself that he was only interested in her money, since he had never indicated interest in meeting her before. But she wouldn't have been surprised if he had grabbed her little ass if he would have had the chance.

About nine o'clock, Carla went to the 7-Eleven and picked up a couple of ham sandwiches, some kettle chips, a six-pack of beer, and a package of Oreos and began her drive up the canyon. She looked forward to spending the day with Leon, and for the first time in a long while, she allowed herself to be cautiously happy. She continued to drive as the road climbed the canyon. After about thirty minutes, she spotted Leon's green van parked on a turnoff. She pulled behind him, parked, and walked over to the van.

Leon rolled down the window and a billow of smoke rolled out. He said, "Hello there, Carla. Ya made it. Go get the grub and climb in."

Carla obediently trotted over to the car and grabbed the lunch and her purse and climbed into the van. It was chilly in the canyon. After all, it was November. Leon drove a mile or so to a turnoff near the creek.

"How about here—let's picnic in the van and after we can take a stroll. I see ya brought yer puffy coat."

Carla and Leon climbed into the back of the van and sat cross-legged where they could find the room and ate their lunches. "Where were ya working today, Leon?" Carla attempted to make small talk.

"Over yonder." Leon pointed. "A guy needed a lock changed cuz this gal—his old girlfriend—was stalkin' him and just comin' in the house at all hours. She's some kind of psycho or somethin'. That was some coincidence that I'd get a call to come up here just after I asked ya fer a picnic in the hills."

"Sure was, Leon." Carla spoke softly as she attempted to muffle the huskiness of her voice.

"Hey—Oreos. Cool," Leon commented as he ripped the bag open and began to devour two cookies at once. Soon he lit up a cigarette and said, "Okay there, gal? Bundle up and let's take a little stroll out here in the fresh air."

Carla zipped up her puffy, red coat and pulled the hood with the fake fur up on her head and they slid out of the back of the van.

They walked along the bank of the river a little ways when Leon said, "Look over there. On the other side of the creek. There's a little trail that climbs up the mountainside a ways. We can get some good pitchures over there."

"How are we going to get over there, Leon? And it looks like a little trail for mountain goats. Are you sure?" Carla's voice quivered with apprehensiveness.

"Trust me, Carla. It'll be fine. I never heard of nobody fallin' off the mountain here before. If there's a trail there, then somebody must have been a walkin' on it."

"How are we gonna cross the river?"

"Jeez, Carla, the water in the creek is barely movin'. There's hardly any water in it. Just follow me and step on the rocks that I step on. Here, I'll even hold yer hand."

Leon stepped on one rock protruding from the riverbed and then took a long step to the next. Carla teetered as she stepped between the rocks.

"Jeez, Carla, with them size ten feet of yers, you should be able to balance on them rocks better than that."

After about eight rocky steps, they reached the creek bank on the other side. A narrow trail began on the shore. It was visible ahead as it gradually wound its way up the side of the mountain.

"I don't know, Leon. I don't like the looks of that trail. Can't we just walk alongside the creek down there? It's pretty enough." Carla was clearly anxious and held Leon's hand tightly.

"Ah, come on now there, Carla. Where's yer sense of adventure? Yer bummin' me out."

Carla didn't want to annoy Leon and remained quiet.

Leon continued to hold Carla's hand as they made their way along the narrow trail. It narrowed in some places, and Carla walked behind Leon. He heard her grunt and groan as they hiked. They both were winded from the exertion and needed to stop several times to catch their breaths. In a few spots, they were forced to climb over boulders that blocked the path. It was a scenic trail above the creek and the nearby road. A few cabins were in the distance. Wood smoke floated up from the chimneys. But Leon barely acknowledged the view. He seemed to be headed to a particular destination and dragged Carla behind. When they arrived at a wide spot in the trail, Leon stopped.

"Looky here, Carla. We done some climbin'." The wide spot in the trail was on a ledge above a sheer drop to the canyon floor below. "How about let's catch our breath right here for a spell?"

"Yes, please, Leon. I haven't done nothin' like this since I was a kid. I need a smoke, but I left my cigarettes in my purse down below." Carla was relieved that they had stopped walking but was visibly tense.

"Ya shouldn't be smokin' up here on the mountain. Wanna cause a forest fire or something? What are ya thinkin' anyway?" Leon was clearly annoyed.

They stood side by side looking down at the canyon below. Carla didn't like it. Looking down at the steep bank made her feel top-heavy and dizzy. Soon Leon pulled her over to stand in front of him and wrapped his arms around her waist from behind as they both looked at the view. It felt romantic to Carla to share such an experience with Leon. Maybe he did care.

But Leon took his arms away from her waist, and suddenly Carla felt a firm, hard shove from behind and heard Leon groan loudly as he pushed her. It felt like slow-motion to Carla. She was instantly airborne for a few feet and then hit the ground hard and began to tumble over and over like she would never stop, carried by her weight. She hit her shoulder and her thigh and her head on rocks and was poked by sticks from bushes in her path. The sky whirled and twirled above her, and her senses were jarred with each thud. Her broken body came to rest several feet above the canyon floor with her legs in unnatural positions, her head turned to one side. Carla looked around her. She was still alive somehow, but everything hurt, and she couldn't move. She was able to see Leon above her. He stood on the edge of the cliff above and watched her. Not moving. Not attempting to help. Doing nothing.

"Leon," Carla whimpered. "Leon, help me. What did you do?" Her voice was barely audible as she struggled to take a breath.

"Shit, she's still alive!" Leon growled to himself. His heart leaped in his chest. His hands were sweaty, and he rubbed them on the thighs of his jeans. He shuffled from one foot to the other.

"Leon, help me—please. "Carla's voice was muffled. Each word was an effort.

Leon continued to watch her as she struggled to move,

struggled to talk, struggled to breathe. "I can't leave her alive like that. If someone finds her, she's gonna talk. Fuck! What do I do? Why didn't ya die on the way down there?" he spoke out loud to himself. He began to pace a few feet from side to side on the narrow path, and his eyes twitched as he thought. "She'll eventually die of exposure, unless somebody finds her right away. I don't want to do this. Pushing her was one thing, but this . . ." Her body was in his clear view. He picked up a couple of stones about the size of baseballs and began to hurl them at her, hoping to hit his mark.

"Leon . . . Leon . . . Leon . . ."

He could hear her quiet, desperate voice. Then—thud! She was quiet. One of the rocks had hit her head. She was either unconscious or dead at this point. Leon wasn't going to stick around any longer. He made his way down the narrow trail as quickly as he could. When he reached the creek where the two had crossed just a short time before, his stomach wretched and he vomited. The lyrics of the song "Look What You Made Me Do" began to vibrate through his head. "Damn it, Carla. Look what ya made me do."

When he got to the van, he took the front of his jacket and wiped her handprints from the door handles and anywhere he thought that she might have touched. She had left her purse. He grabbed it, got out of the van, and hurled it to the other side of the creek. But he kept her phone. He had no idea what might be on it that could incriminate him. It was about noon when he drove away. He could still hear Carla's weak voice saying his name over and over. He began playing some heavy metal music, hoping it would drown out the sound of *Leon . . . Leon . . . Leon . . .* echoing through his mind. His most drastic plan had worked. Carla was out of the picture. His secret obsession with Lana was safe. It came at the price of his soul—but he thought, *My soul ain't never been worth nothin' nohow.*

CHAPTER 35

Leon was shaken by what he had just done. It was too easy. Just two small movements—one step forward and a shove. It had taken no effort at all. But now he was aware that he needed to be careful that he wouldn't be linked in any way to the scene and to Carla. He went over each moment in his head. *What did she touch? What did I touch? Her death has to be seen as an accident or a suicide.* After he drove a short distance, he saw Carla's car parked near the road. He felt sick again and threw up in a plastic bag. "Get it together, Alvarez. Be cool," he kept telling himself. But his head throbbed and his heart thumped loudly in his chest.

He jolted when his phone rang as he entered the mouth of the canyon. It was a service call that requested an unlock of a car door in Columbine Point. He declined and recommended another locksmith. He had to take care of a few things first. As he drove home, Carla's husky voice, soft and quiet, saying his name, *Leon . . . Leon . . . Leon . . .* continued to buzz in his head. He turned up the volume of his music. George Thorogood's song "Bad to the Bone" reverberated through the van. He lit up a joint to calm himself.

When he reached his house, he threw the plastic bag of vomit into his trash can. He removed the battery from Carla's phone and took a hammer and smashed the phone to pieces. He put all the pieces into a plastic bag and hid it in the cabinet under his kitchen sink. He took a cloth and wiped the inside and outside of the van, every inch, every dent, every scratch. He vacuumed the inside. He washed his own hands over and over. He changed his clothes and threw them into the washing machine. It wasn't likely that there was evidence on them, but something microscopic could be viewed as significant.

About five thirty, Leon made the decision to go to Red's Bar to keep the same routine. He walked into the bar and looked straight ahead, but in his peripheral vision, he could see that the dark corner where Carla usually loomed with her Long Island iced tea was empty.

"Hey, Robinson, hit me with a draft." Leon took a stool at the bar and began his routine exchange of obscenities with the bar regulars. The beer soothed him somewhat. He looked over at Carla's corner of the room and said, "Hey, where's the barfly today?"

"What's the matter—missin' yer girlfriend?" a guy next to him teased.

"Fuck no. She ain't no girlfriend of mine. She's just always over there starin' our way, lookin' fer some action."

"I ain't seen her today. Mebbe she found herself a sugar daddy."

"Goddamn, I hope so, but who would that dumb son of a bitch be?" Leon laughed loudly. But her voice was still playing through his head. *Leon . . . Leon . . . Leon . . .* and that gurgling, unearthly sound that was unlike anything he had ever heard before.

Suddenly, there was a light tap on his shoulder and a woman's voice said, "Hey." He was startled and jumped as he turned around. A woman stood behind him, holding a pair of sunglasses. "These were on the floor by your barstool. I thought they might be yours."

Leon's heart was in his throat. All the blood drained from his face and he was light-headed for a second. "Uh, thanks. I probably dropped them out of my pocket." Leon drank a couple more beers and decided to call it a night. "I think I'm gonna head home. Got paperwork. See ya jerkoffs next time."

The staff of *Boulder Essence* had already poured out of the office by the time Roadking came to pick Lana up for their dinner date. As she worked on her laptop, she detected a light spice scent in the air. She looked up and there he stood in the doorway with the beautiful smile and crinkly, smiling eyes. "Are you ready to go, sunshine?"

"Give me a minute to pack up my stuff. You can sit down if you want."

Roadking walked over to one of the oak side chairs, sat down, crossed his legs, and watched her. He wore a brown leather blazer, a light blue, collared oxford shirt, jeans, and brown boots. He looked like a star.

"How was your day, Vincent?"

"Good—getting better now."

Lana grabbed her purse, laptop, and brown leather jacket. She turned out the lights and they headed down to the parking garage.

"I hope you're hungry. These four-course Italian meals can be filling."

"I'll do my best and let you finish the rest."

Roadking had driven the black SS 396 to pick her up. He had not taken it out since the windows were shot out while it was parked at his parents' house a few weeks before. Lana smiled at Roadking and he could see that she was pleasantly surprised. She held on to his arm as they walked, and he turned and lightly kissed her lips.

"I knew you'd like that. And we can take a drive after the wine pairing."

Lana loved the sound of the SS 396 as it idled, as it accelerated. The beautiful, black car always attracted the attention of the other drivers.

They arrived at Lucca di Domenici's Ristorante around six o'clock and walked into the small adjoining bar that was in an alcove near the front door to wait to be seated at six thirty. Lana ordered a house red wine, not wanting to mix liquor with the wine they would be sampling. Roadking ordered a draft beer. As they walked to a high-top table, Roadking saw someone he knew. "Hey, Dierk, how are you doing?"

It was the banker that Lana had met for the first time earlier in the day. "I'm good there, Roadking. Are you here for dinner?"

"Yeah, the wine pairing. This is Lana Ross." Roadking introduced her to him.

"We've met. Good to see you again, Lana." Dierk reached out to shake her hand and looked directly into her eyes and continued with his intense gaze while he said, "This is my wife, Stephanie."

"Pleased to meet you." Lana and Roadking both shook her hand. Stephanie Cowles was plain-looking, wore no makeup, carried extra weight in her midsection, had short, dark red hair with some blonde highlights, dressed in a navy-blue pantsuit, and held a black purse as big as a diaper bag on her lap.

"Well, enjoy your dinner." Roadking put his hand on Lana's back to guide her past the Cowles' table.

"Vincent, I just met that guy for the first time today and he came on to me and asked me to go out to dinner with him sometime."

"Jeez, sounds like something he would do. Can't blame him, though, for trying," Roadking chuckled. "I play a round of golf with him from time to time, and he always talks about the ladies that want him."

"Well, not this lady. One minute he was promoting the bank and the next he tried to hold my hand and ask me out. I hope we don't get seated near them. He makes me uncomfortable."

"He saw you with me. He'll leave you alone now."

At six thirty, the maître d' announced that the wine pairing would begin. He seated Roadking and Lana at an intimate table for two in a corner. The restaurant was small with the possible capacity of fifty people. The owner of the restaurant, Lucca Di Domenici, was born in Tuscany. The restaurant was in a rare, stand-alone, frame building that was probably a residence decades before. There were a couple of open rooms that flowed together that appeared to have been a living room and dining room at one time. The floors were covered with light brown, travertine tile. A couple of the walls were exposed, traditional, redbrick. Two walls were a goldenrod stucco adorned with colorful oil murals of Italian landscapes. Light emanated from suspended, caramel-colored, basin-shaped, opalescent, glass fixtures. The intimate charm of the restaurant was enhanced by the placement of three ornate, walnut, china hutches in various locations in the dining area. Each table was covered with white linens, and instead of flowers in a vase, the centerpieces were small flowerpots of herb plants. The little terracotta clay pot on their table contained curly-leaf parsley. An earthy, rustic scent emanated from the fragrant herb pots and flowed through the restaurant. The place settings were simple but delicate white china so that the focus of each plate would be the food.

Prior to the serving of each course, a wine sommelier from Boulder Broadway Spirits talked about the wine selected, the vineyard that had produced it, and why it paired well with the corresponding course. The first course was bruschetta topped with applewood-smoked bacon, mushrooms, fresh tomato, Parmigiano-Reggiano cheese, and fresh basil leaves and paired with Montepulciano d'Abruzzo Pinot Noir. Lana was hungry since she had not eaten all day in anticipation of the big, Italian meal. She told herself to go easy on the first courses so that she could get through them all. But it tasted so good, she ate all of it. Fortunately, the sommelier took a little time between courses and highlighted the wines and the vineyards.

The second course was a sweet potato risotto with pancetta, roasted asparagus, and Romano cheese topped with toasted pine nuts. The wine selected was Le Bruniche Toscana Chardonnay.

Roadking lifted his glass and toasted Lana. "To a memorable Tuscan evening with my girl."

Lana touched her glass to his and smiled. Each moment with him was always memorable. "You were in Tuscany, Vincent. Does this little place and the food and wine remind you of it?"

"Yes, in many ways. They're doing a good job here. But there's no substitution for standing in Tuscany on a beautiful spring day and feeling the ambience of the place."

The third course was a *filetto di manzo Toscano*—a beef tenderloin fillet grilled, sliced thinly, topped with a Marsala butter glaze, and served with a butternut squash puree and a small serving of rigatoni with a light marinara sauce. The wine paired with the steak was a Fèlsina Fontalloro Toscana Sangiovese. Lana was beginning to get full but sampled a portion of the steak, squash, and rigatoni. Roadking helped her eat it. But for each course, she drank the wine.

As she scanned the room, she noticed that Dierk Cowles and his wife were seated on the opposite side of the room at a table for two facing them. Each time she looked in that direction, he was staring at them. After seeing his wife, Lana figured that her red hair must have been why he was attracted to her and, of course, the money.

Lana didn't know if she could eat another bite. Roadking managed to finish each course. When the fourth course was served, it was a small, individual fruit tart of baked plums and peaches with an apricot glaze paired with Folonari Moscato. In the alternative, there was a fruit and cheese platter served with cordial glasses of limoncello. Lana drank the wine but could not eat the tart.

Roadking and Lana remained at the little restaurant and talked to the owner after the meal. Lana was interested in his Italian heritage and his background as a chef and restaurateur. But eventually, the conversation turned to motorcycles. Roadking and Lucca hit it off. She knew they would return for dinner on another day.

It was nearly nine o'clock by the time they left the restaurant. A chilly wind began to blow out of the north as they walked to the SS 396. Lana wore a light leather jacket and was wearing the brown wool dress. Roadking held her hand as they walked to the car. When he opened the door for her, Dierk Cowles and his wife walked by.

"Beautiful wheels there, Roadking." Then he nodded his head at Lana.

Give it up, Dierk Cowles, Lana thought.

Roadking had planned their next destination. They headed west on Baseline Road and turned north on Flagstaff Mountain Road and drove about a half mile up the mountain. At Panorama Point, there was an unparalleled view of the city of Boulder, the CU campus, and much of the Boulder Valley. A light mist began to fall as they parked in the small parking lot.

"I haven't been up here since I was a student at CU. My friends and I came up here once with a case of beer. But we saw that the trip down might be tough, so we only drank one six-pack among all of us and then took the rest of the case to Olivia's house and drank it there. What about you? Did you bring all of your dates up here?"

"Well, to be honest, yeah. Not all of them though. But none of them were as pretty as you."

"Good answer." Lana laughed. He had had a life before her, but she tried not to visualize him with someone else. That made her uneasy.

As they looked down on the university campus, Roadking asked, "So Lana, what did you think your life would be like after college?"

"Well, I thought I'd have a career that I loved and that was compatible with my BA in English Literature. I thought that I would marry, maybe have a family, and I hoped I'd make good choices that would lead to a productive and happy life. It hasn't turned out entirely like that, but all in all, it's good. What about you?" Lana looked straight ahead through the windshield at the view below as she spoke.

"I knew I'd want a family eventually. Family is a big focus of the Romanos. But I was never in any hurry to do that. That changed when Ava was born. I wanted to ride my Harley as much as I could. I still do. I loved playing football, but I knew I wasn't cut out for the pros. But the Harley dealership was meant to be. Sharing my life with someone is important, but it has to be the right person." He paused for a moment. "Cameron was a colossal mistake." He looked out the side window for a minute after he mentioned her name and breathed a long sigh. A heavier rain began to fall. The lights below became a blur on the windshield. He turned to Lana and said, "Do you ever think about having children someday?"

"I do. I thought that Lucas and I would have had a couple of kids by now. We didn't, and in hindsight, that was a good thing. There's still time, but I'm thirty-three and should think about it some. I grew up all alone with no brother or sister and always envied my friends with siblings to bicker with, hang out with, to have my back. My parents never talked and rarely talked to me, so I became absorbed in music and books—clearly the reason why my degree is in English Lit. I would love to have a little boy or a little girl to love, to play with, to talk with, to teach, and to give them all I've got. Maybe two or three kids. I know I'd be a good mom."

Roadking liked her answer and smiled to himself. He leaned over to her in the bucket seat and kissed her on the lips. The console between them pressed into their sides and prevented them from getting close. "Let's get in the back seat."

"Really?"

"Yes."

"I don't think that . . ."

Before she could finish her thought, Roadking touched an index finger to her lips and said, "Don't think."

He got out of the car and climbed into the back seat. Lana did the same. He pushed the driver's seat forward. She got in on the passenger side and quickly scanned the parking lot. They were alone. Roadking pulled her over onto his lap. She took off the leather jacket. She straddled his waist with her legs and put her arms around his neck, and they began to kiss and kiss. Each one stronger and more passionate than the last. Roadking moved all her long hair over her shoulder to the front and unzipped her dress and unhooked her pink bra. All of it fell to her elbows. She pulled her arms out of the clothes and let them fall to her waist. Lana swiftly unbuttoned Roadking's light blue shirt, opened it, and pressed her bare chest to his. He put his hands on her rear and pulled her close into him.

"Take that stuff off." She slid off of him and pulled off the tights and the pink panties while Roadking unbuttoned his pants. She climbed back on his lap for a moment, then he said, "Lay down."

She lay on her back on the seat while they both moved to get comfortable. In a few seconds, his body weight was on top of her. The confinement of the back seat of the car prevented Lana from sliding on her back with each of Roadking's motions and he was deeper than ever before.

Lana was in ecstasy as she whispered softly in his ear, "More, more."

Roadking whispered in her ear, *"Te quiero."*

Neither of them wanted it to end. They lay locked together as one for a long while. Roadking sat up and stretched, pulled his pants up, and began to button his shirt. Lana buttoned the rest of it for him. She pulled her bra straps over her shoulders and asked him to hook it for her and pulled her dress up from her waist for him to zip. She sat for a moment before she put on her panties and tights. She looked at Roadking and they both began to laugh.

"Who would think that the two of us would end up doing it in an SS 396 on Flagstaff Mountain?" Lana smiled.

"Hey, I think that's what this car was made for." Roadking smiled. "And we should do it again." He kissed her cheek.

Lana continued to dress. They both moved to the front seat of the car. The rain became heavy, white flakes of sleet. Roadking adjusted his seat and then started the car.

"So much for the panoramic view." The windshield was covered with heavy, wet snow. "We better head down before it gets slick. This car doesn't handle snowy mountain roads very well."

They began the short but winding journey down Flagstaff Mountain Road. They were quiet as they listened to the music and the sound of the SS 396. The glow of the green lights from the dash illuminated their very satisfied faces. Within minutes, they were within a block or two of Lana's office where Lana would pick up her car and go home.

Roadking finally spoke. "Don't go home tonight. Come home with me. I'm not ready to say goodbye tonight."

"I don't want to go either, but I have work tomorrow. I don't have clothes to wear."

"You need to leave some things at my house for times like these. Stay with me tonight. We can get up early in the morning and I'll take you to your car and you can head home to get dressed."

Lana wanted nothing more than to stay with him. She said, "Take me home with you."

Oddly, when they began to drive east out of Boulder to Louisville, "Take Me Home Tonight" on Roadking's playlist began to play. The lyrics fit perfectly for that moment. Roadking rubbed his right hand on her left thigh as they drove.

Leon went to bed about ten thirty. He tried to sleep. He smoked three or four joints, hoping to get sleepy. When he continued to lay awake, he brought out a pint of Seagram's and took swigs from the bottle. He saw that Lana wasn't at home from the monitor on his phone. "I done killed a woman fer my darlin' and she ain't even around tonight." He knew that her car was still parked in Boulder from the GPS tracking device he had attached to it. He knew that she must be with him and did not know where that would be. He smoldered inside with jealousy and anger toward Roadking and the guilt that plagued his mind about Carla's demise, which he played over and over in his mind. *Leon . . . Leon . . . Leon . . . help me.* He could not shake her voice from his head. He finally dozed off.

About midnight, he woke with a jolt. He heard a light tap, tap, tap on his front door, like Carla's knock. He threw back the covers, adrenaline surging through his veins and his hands shaking as he jumped from the bed and bolted toward the door and thrust it open. There was no one and nothing there but snowfall. Maybe it was just the wind, maybe it was a dream. Until she was found, either dead or alive, he would be haunted by the unknown and tormented with questions. *What if she's found alive and then talks? What if I left a trace of myself behind? What if? What if?*

Leon threw on a coat, grabbed the pint bottle of Seagram's, jumped into his dented van, and began the drive to Boulder. He would wait in the parking garage until he could see Lana again. He didn't want to stay in his haunted house. The snow began to build into a slush on the roads. His van, which had nearly bald tires, struggled through the deep slush. He managed to make it to the parking garage and parked in a corner lot behind some service vehicles but with a line of sight to Lana's Mercedes.

"Lana, darlin'. What I done to keep ya my secret! But I know that yer gonna be mine. Yer gonna be mine." He drank the whiskey and watched the snow fall outside of the parking garage. A few cars passed by on the street. Some young couples trudged by from the local bars at two in the morning, and finally he passed out.

CHAPTER 36

The sound of water running in the shower was the first sound Lana heard as she awoke. The sky was still dark. It was six o'clock. Roadking was in the shower early so he could drive Lana back to Boulder to pick up her car and go home to get ready for work. She felt badly that it would be an inconvenience for him. She threw on a T-shirt that she had found in one of his drawers and went downstairs and started coffee for him. When she came back into the bedroom, Roadking was standing there with a fluffy, white towel wrapped around his waist, his black hair wet and shiny, smiling with those white teeth framed by the black mustache.

"Hello, sunshine. How did you sleep?" He walked over, put his arms around her waist, pulled her close, and kissed her on the forehead.

She patted him on his butt. "So well. But the night was gone so quickly. It's so early for you. I started the coffee. I'm sorry you have to get up so early." She always slept well with him so close to her. She felt like she belonged with him there in his bed.

"Don't be sorry. I wanted you to stay. I'm happy to spend a little time with you this morning driving you to Boulder. Please bring some clothes over here, though, so we can spend more morning time together when you stay here again on a weeknight."

"I did want to stay with you and I'm happy that I did. I just don't want to be a burden. You have to drive me over there now in the snow."

"It'll be fine. You'll be safe with me. I think it's just a pile of slush out there anyway. It wasn't cold enough to be icy. Do you want to shower here before you go home? It might save you some time at home."

"That's a good idea." She gathered her clothes and put them in a neat pile on the bed and went into the bathroom to take a shower. She liked using his soap and shampoo. His scent would be with her all day.

When she emerged from the shower, Roadking was already downstairs drinking coffee. She dressed quickly, towel-dried her hair as much as she could, put on a little makeup from her purse, and went downstairs to meet him. He had made some wheat toast for each of them, buttered it, and spread strawberry jam on it.

"I wish there was enough time to make you a Roadking breakfast."

"I know, but I'm good. I appreciate the toast though. Thank you. Are you ready to go?" Lana wanted him to have plenty of time to get back to Louisville after he dropped her off.

When Roadking backed the Road Ranger out of the garage, the snow was several inches deep, but it was wet near the pavement. As they entered a main road, the sun was just a sliver of light near the horizon. Lana could see that the snow was slushy. The Range Rover could handle it, but it would be a slow drive.

"I hope this snowy mess moves out before Sunday. Remember we have a date on the Harley this weekend."

"Yes. Me too."

"So how are those plans for Thanksgiving coming?"

"I invited my staff. A few have said they're coming. I need to call Olivia and see if she has plans or not and invite her. I was just thinking about it. It'll be different from before."

"What do you mean? Lucas?"

"Yeah, I'm beginning a new tradition without him. And it's good. What about you? I suppose your mom will prepare a big meal for everybody."

"Yes, she will. I'd love for you to meet my parents but in a quiet setting. I want them to meet you for the first time without the distraction of the family. I would invite you to dinner there, but I know my large, noisy family would be initially overwhelming to you. What do you think? Maybe in a week or two you could meet my mom and dad for dinner somewhere? I want them to know you."

"I'd love to meet the two people that raised you. After Thanksgiving would be good."

The sun began to rise, but the sky was covered with a thin layer of clouds, and the sunlight was dim. Roadking pulled into the parking garage and gave Lana a long kiss goodbye. "Be careful driving home, sweetness. Don't be in a big hurry and you'll be fine."

"I will. Hey, thank you for the great night. Talk to you soon." Lana blew a kiss to him as she got into the Mercedes and started the engine. At least she wasn't going to have to scrape snow from her windshield.

Roadking waved to her. It was a quarter to seven.

On the other side of the parking garage, Leon was passed out in his van from his alcohol and pot binge when someone knocked on his window. Tap, tap, tap! A man who might have been the building custodian or security said, "Sir, sir, are you okay in there?"

Leon jumped and then shook himself awake while he tried to figure out where he was. Adrenaline was pumping through his veins from being startled. Then he remembered where he was and why. *Waiting for my little gal.* "I'm okay. I musta fell asleep waitin' for a guy that I'm workin' with today. Thanks."

The man waved and walked away.

Leon glanced over to the corner of the lot where Lana's car had been parked. It was gone. He had missed seeing her when she'd picked up her car. He turned on the GPS tracking app on his phone and could see that she was driving north out of Boulder. She must have been going home. He could not figure out why she would be leaving Boulder at that time of day. He pulled out of the parking garage onto the snow-covered street and parked. He would just wait until she was home to watch.

He thought about Carla and decided to turn the radio on for the local news at seven o'clock. He needed to know if she had been found and if she was dead or alive. There was probably deep snow where her body was. She was wearing that big, puffy, red coat, though, and he knew that someone would eventually spot her there on the steep embankment. He turned and looked into the back of his van where he and Carla had spent maybe her last hours alive. He got a chill and turned away.

Her husky, raspy voice began to play in his head again. *Leon . . . Leon . . . Leon . . . What did you do?* He turned his attention to the radio. There was nothing on the local news about a body being found. *Maybe that means she's still alive and in a hospital somewhere, spilling her guts to anyone who'll listen?* He started the van and drove to the nearest convenience store to get some coffee while he waited for Lana to show up on his monitor.

The going was slow as Lana drove home. She would definitely bring clothes to Roadking's house or at least keep an outfit in her car or office. Last night with Roadking had been perfect, heavenly. She smiled to herself as she replayed the moments in the back seat of the SS 396 in her mind as she drove. She didn't want to spend even one night away from him. But it was too soon. They each had their own houses and lives. He gave no indication that he wanted her with him every night or even more often.

Roadking drove away from Boulder, happy to have seen Lana's pretty face and hear her sweet voice first thing in the morning. He began to realize that he wanted her to be with him night and day. But it was too soon. She had been through so much in the few short months since he had met her. She had given him no indication that she wanted to stay with him. She had her own beautiful house in the country. But he knew that there was no one else like her. He wanted her to belong to him.

Leon watched the monitor on his phone as Lana arrived at her house. He could see that she was in a hurry. She threw off all the clothes she was wearing, tossed them on her bed, and stood there nude for a few minutes while she pulled undies out of her drawer. Leon's eyes danced as he followed her nakedness move around in her bedroom. She eventually put on a white cashmere turtleneck, tan and white pinstripe pants, and brown leather boots. It looked like she was dressed for work and would leave again. He returned to the *Boulder Essence* parking garage to watch her arrive in person.

After Lana left, there was nothing left for Leon to look at, so he sat in the parking lot of the convenience store and drank his coffee, eventually going back in for a refill and a package of cinnamon rolls. He drove back to the *Boulder Essence* parking garage and parked in a different spot but still somewhat hidden. The snow was still slushy but melting fast. Carla was still bouncing through his head, calling his name, gurgling, lying there in a heap wearing the puffy, red coat. "I done it fer you, Lana, darlin'. Fer us." His demented mind was torn between guilt and his justification for what he'd done. His thoughts volleyed from Lana to Carla and back again. His hands shook.

In about a half hour, Lana's Mercedes pulled into the parking garage. Lana grabbed her laptop and purse and quickly walked toward the entrance of the building.

Leon jumped out of his van and ran up behind her and eventually walked beside her as she hurried. "Hey there, Lana, darlin'. How ya been?" He was out of breath and breathing heavily as he spoke.

Lana was startled by Leon's sudden appearance next to her. "Oh, jeez, Leon. You startled me. What are you doing here in Boulder on a morning like this?"

Leon thought for a quick second. He had no ready explanation for his appearance there. "Oh yeah, there was this guy that couldn't get into his delivery business because the lock was broken on the door and his key wouldn't work. His business is a block or two away and I remembered this parking garage and pulled in fer a spell."

"Where are you heading now?"

"I'm all finished with it now. Just headin' back. Saw ya and wanted to say hey."

"Oh, well hello, Leon. The security system at the house seems to be functioning well. You did a good job. I'll give you a call if it needs any adjustments anytime soon. Have a nice day." Lana opened the main door to *Boulder Essence* and rushed in and up the stairs to her office.

It was 8:10 a.m. She was a few minutes late, but the weather conditions had caused a few of her staff to trickle in after her too. She could still smell the whiskey and smokiness of Leon in her nose. In the short minute or two that she had been near him, his malodorous scent had permeated her nasal passages.

Seeing Lana had altered Leon's mood from frantic to mildly content. She was a breath of fresh air in more ways than one. She smelled so good and was so classy and beautiful. *Will she ever look at me the way she looks at that Harley bastard? I have to have her, and I'll make that happen. I have to make her realize that she belongs with me. I'll make her want me the way I want her.*

As Leon drove back to Columbine Point, he listened to the local news station on his radio for some word about Carla. His thoughts continued to hop from Lana to Carla. His stomach was churning from a whiskey hangover and the cinnamon rolls that he had just eaten. When he got home, he looked at his house. There was trash inside, trash outside, and a mess and filth everywhere he looked. *I shoulda let Carla clean up this dump first. Lana ain't gonna wanna stay in a mess like this*. His deranged mind believed that Lana would willingly stay with him there.

For the first time in weeks, he decided to take a shower and wash his hair in his filthy bathroom. The warm water felt good running on his hair and skin. When he emerged, he surveyed his dripping wet image in the bathroom mirror. "Yer lookin' good there, Alvarez. And ya smell better too." He chuckled to himself. He immediately lit up a cigarette and began to smoke. As he slid his jeans back on, he noticed the jagged "LANA" scar on his leg. *Jeez, I shoulda just got a tattoo.* He remembered the look on Carla's face when she had seen it. His phone rang. A woman was locked out of her car. "I'll think about this mess later."

The postholiday *Boulder Essence* issue was fully edited and ready for publication. Lana, satisfied with its content, began the outline for the January issue, which would contain part two of the travel in Colorado by various means series. She took time to work on her menu for Thanksgiving and make a grocery list. She called Olivia and left a message to invite her to come to dinner on Thanksgiving at two o'clock. Olivia knew many of her coworkers and had hung out with them before. She was always great entertainment with her animated conversation. In previous years if Lana and Lucas did not have dinner at the Chisholm's, Lana would invite Cate to dinner as well. This year that would not happen. The coming holidays would be a stark contrast to the past with Lucas gone, his family out of her life, and Cate hating her.

Lana's office phone rang. She could see on the caller ID that it was Dierk Cowles from the bank calling. Lana couldn't decide whether to answer or not. He made her uncomfortable. She picked up the phone.

"Hello, Lana. Dierk Cowles here. I just wanted to mention to you, in case you had misunderstood, that when I asked you to go out to dinner, it wasn't like it would be a date or something. You saw that I have a wife and everything. I just like to get to know my best banking customers in a more casual setting. And I wanted to clear that up and not have a misunderstanding interfere with our banking relationship."

"No worries. I didn't give it a thought." She was mildly amused and smiled to herself as she spoke.

"Great. Well, it was good seeing you last night with my golf buddy Romano. The dinner was really awesome too. Are you two serious?"

"Yes, we enjoyed it quite a bit."

He noted that she had chosen not to respond to his question. "Well, thanks, Lana. Stay in touch. Don't ever hesitate to call me—about anything."

Dierk was so transparent. He couldn't just let it go. He reached out again in what appeared to be an innocent call so that she wouldn't forget him, plus he wanted to cover his ass. Maybe another woman would fall for his line. But Lana was not able to divide her feelings that way. She could only open her heart to one man. If there were others interested, it wouldn't matter for as long as that one man was in her life.

Olivia called Lana to meet for lunch at the Sunshine Café. It was a short walk for each of them from their offices. Lana plowed through the slushy sidewalks. Olivia was already seated at a table when Lana arrived.

"How have you been?" Olivia stood and hugged Lana lightly.

"I'm good. How about you? What's been happening with Alex?"

"Well, that's going okay, but he leaves so often to return home to Wisconsin. I miss him so I think that must mean he's growing on me. I met his son. He's six. He was shy with me at first, but one day we took him to the zoo, and he seemed to warm up to me and was a real chatterbox. Alex is quite proud of him, and seeing him with his son is amazing. I'm trying to just go with the flow and let things happen as they may. What about you and the Harley guy? Things getting serious between you two yet?"

A waiter brought water to the table. Olivia and Lana each ordered chicken tortilla soup and a salad.

"His name is Vincent. It may be getting serious between us."

Olivia knew the private Lana well enough to know that the cautious, careful answer was a cover for something more serious.

Lana spoke next. "I wanted to ask if you made plans for Thanksgiving. I invited my staff, and some of them are coming for dinner. You know all of them and I'd love to have you."

"I would love to, Lana, but Alex is coming back to Columbine Point for Thanksgiving break and has invited me to dinner at his parents' house with him. I guess I would have thought you'd have dinner with your new boyfriend."

"I haven't met his parents yet, and he has a very large extended family in this area that gets together at his parents' house quite often. He wants me to meet them without the rest of the family around the first time. I'm good with that. Maybe next year."

"Oh shit." Olivia quietly exclaimed as she looked wide-eyed toward the door of the café and then quickly looked away. "Cate just walked in the door. I can't believe it. I haven't talked to her for a couple of weeks. She's walking with a cane right now. Maybe she won't see us."

Lana and Olivia sat very still and hoped that would keep them from being detected. Cate was always so quiet and proper. But she had already made a scene when Lana had run into her at the pharmacy before the accident.

The waiter brought their soup and salads to the table. When he set Lana's bowl of soup down, he dropped their spoons on the floor, and when he bent over to pick them up, he dropped his tray too. Cate, hearing the commotion, looked in their direction.

Olivia said again, "Oh shit. She sees us!"

Cate picked up her carryout order and began to walk slowly to the door, dragging her right leg slightly, but then she paused and turned and walked over to the table.

"Hi, Cate. How about that snow out there?" Olivia immediately began to talk.

Lana looked at Cate and tried to the mask the shock she felt when she saw her face. There was a long, deep scar on her right cheek that extended from her cheekbone to her jaw.

"Yeah, it's a wet mess." When she spoke, her mouth drooped on the right side. She turned to Lana and said quietly yet viciously, "Get a good look! Look at my face!"

Lana's mouth fell open. Then she closed it. "Cate, I didn't know what had happened to you. I'm so sorry."

"Are you? Are you really? You're the reason that Lucas is dead!" Fortunately, her hateful voice was still soft.

The waiter brought spoons to the table. Cate paused.

"Cate, it was an accident. They determined it was an accident." Lana looked directly into her eyes.

"Believe what you want. You ruined him. He thought he had nothing left. He had me, but he still wanted you! Every day when I look at this face, I hate you more."

Lana's eyes began to fill with tears. She quickly blinked them away and said, "I hope that in time you see the truth."

Cate turned to walk to the door and looked back and said, "Watch your back, Lana."

Olivia and Lana looked at each other. Both were in shock and couldn't say a word for a minute or two. "Jeez, Lana. The last time I saw Cate she still had a bandage on her cheek. I didn't know how bad it was. But to blame you—that's a stretch."

"I guess she has to blame someone for what happened. Lucas did it. He hurt so many people—Cate, me, his family, and himself. I guess I shouldn't be shocked. I feel sorry for her, too, but I'm so upset."

Neither of them could touch a bite of their lunch, and they asked the waiter to give them to-go containers. Both had to get back to work. Lana hugged Olivia, wished her a happy Thanksgiving, and tried to let the recent moments with Cate pass.

As Lana trudged through the snow on the way back to her office, she thought about how the events of the day had begun so beautifully with Roadking, but she had then run into Leon, received a call from Dierk, and encountered a hateful, angry Cate. It was uncanny. *There's still an entire afternoon left. What could happen next?*

Leon continued to be anxious about Carla. Still nothing was on the news about a body found in Left Hand Canyon. He believed that until the snow melted, she wouldn't be detected. Late in the afternoon, he decided to head to Red's Bar. On the way to the bar, he drove past Carla's house just to make sure that she had not made her way to her car and driven home, even though realistically he knew that was not possible. Not with that gurgling sound that she had made as blood ran from her mouth. He was relieved to see that her car was not there. But he got a chill as he drove by. Her husky, deep voice called to him, *Leon . . . Leon . . . Leon. Help me.*

"Shut up, Carla! Shut up, Carla!" Leon yelled at his windshield as he repeatedly pounded on the dashboard of the van with his fist. He turned the music volume louder to "Look What You Made Me Do" and played it over and over.

He walked into the bar, and once again he saw out of his peripheral vision that Carla's table was empty. "Hey," he said to no one in particular sitting at the bar. "A draft, Robinson."

"Hey, Alvarez, how's it hanging?" Jerry, the drywaller, mumbled, not really expecting an answer.

"Hangin' good."

The local news was on the TV. Leon was trying to nonchalantly listen to it while Jerry continued to talk. When the weather segment came on, he quit watching.

"I'm gonna hit the head." He had to walk past Carla's table on the way to the restroom. That corner was still dark and empty.

He walked out of the restroom and turned the corner to return to his barstool when he saw the back of a woman sitting at Carla's table in the dark corner. He could see that she was a big woman with broad shoulders and messy, coal black hair piled on top of her head, sipping on what looked like a Long Island iced tea. Leon's heart began to race, his hands began to shake, his palms got sweaty, and he thought he might pass out.

He took a deep breath, approached the table, and spoke to the woman's back, "Carla?"

The woman didn't respond. She didn't even turn her head.

Leon took a few steps forward and tilted his head to see her face. It wasn't Carla. "Excuse me there, ma'am. I thought you was somebody else."

The woman was expressionless and simply nodded at him.

Leon returned to his seat at the bar. His heart was still racing and his hands were shaking. He hollered, "Hey, Robinson, bring me a shot of Jack and keep 'em comin'."

"Hey, dumb-ass. Did ya think that was yer girlfriend over there?" Jerry chuckled.

"Man, I didn't think that there could be two gals that ugly." Leon laughed loudly. But the same questions continued to swirl in his mind. *Is she dead or alive? Who will find her? How much longer will it be?* His pounding heart had slowed down and his hands were no longer shaking. In relief, Leon chugged the shot of Jack Daniel's and hollered at the bartender, "Hey, Robinson, I said keep 'em comin'! Another shot of Jack! Now!"

CHAPTER 37

Lana finished the rest of the workday on autopilot. She was disturbed by Cate's final words to her—"Watch your back, Lana." She could not let it go. The Sunshine Café was not the place and time to say what she needed to Cate. She drove home with no music, in silence, thinking of what to say to Cate. When she arrived at home, she took out her laptop and sat down at the kitchen table to write.

Cate,

You know that I am not to blame for Lucas's behavior, the accident, and your injuries. I realize that you need somebody to blame, because there's no explanation for what happened. But not only have you lost Lucas, you have lost the trust and respect of a good friend. I cannot let your last words to me to be a threat without responding. Nothing you can do to me will bring Lucas back or heal your scars. You may or may not read this email from me, but either way I will have said what I needed to say. My last words to you are: "May you find peace."

Lana

Lana felt better. The words were out of her head and off into cyberspace for delivery. Although she could have said so much more and with scathing words, she chose to take the high road. Maybe the last words of her email would resonate with Cate. Maybe not. Lana had done nothing for which she should feel apologetic or guilty. In fact, she was hurt badly by Lucas, too, but she blamed only him.

She suddenly felt the need to connect with Roadking.

Hey, baby. Remembering last night on Flagstaff. Hugs.

He responded immediately.

Kisses.

Lana smiled as she reflected on their conversation about having children. *Was his question hypothetical or meant to be significant?* As she thought about it, a warm feeling came over her. Having a baby with Roadking would forever connect them in the form of a little human being. It would be a beautiful child born from love. Tears welled in her eyes as she suddenly realized how much she wanted that to happen. Not sad tears. Tears of hope and happiness.

She sat for a few minutes and looked out the window. The sun began to set and there was a band of white light outlining the foot-hills as it continued to sink. She looked at her reflection in the glass. The tears subsided. She rarely cried and had surprised herself that she had reacted so unexpectedly from her thoughts. She breathed a deep sigh and then ran upstairs to change into workout clothes. She jumped on the treadmill for forty minutes but began to feel a little light-headed. She had not really eaten any lunch after the en-counter with Cate. She went into the kitchen, poured herself a glass of red wine, and began to sauté some vegetables, but she craved protein. She sifted through her freezer and found salmon to grill. When she finished eating, she walked on the treadmill for another twenty minutes and worked out with the five-pound weights. The four-course Italian meal from the night before needed to be burned off.

Leon continued to down shots of Jack Daniel's at Red's Bar. He was so wrapped up in his fears about Carla's fate that he forgot to watch Lana for the night. "Jeez, Carla's gonna shit when she sees that big gal sittin' at her booth," he said out loud to no one sitting near him. "Maybe we'll get a catfight out of it."

The guys at the bar snickered. "Some hair-pullin' anyway," one of them said.

"Yeah, and maybe some torn shirts," chuckled another one.

Even with the Jack buzz, he knew that his comments in retrospect would allude to his expectation that she would walk in the door, and they would act as a cover for him. His eyes darted periodically toward the TV screen above the bar in case there was breaking news about a body found in Left Hand Canyon. It had been two days since he'd pushed her down the embankment, and there was still no news about Carla, dead or alive. Carla's voice continued to speak to Leon's psyche, but the alcohol silenced it for a few hours.

About ten o'clock, Leon stopped drinking shots. "Hey, one of you pricks wanna hit the pool table with me?" Leon walked over to the pool table and began to knock the balls around with the cue stick.

No one offered to play a game with him. He continued at the pool table until he decided he needed a smoke. As he walked outside, the chilly November night air sobered him somewhat, and he decided to go home and go to bed. He took a deep breath of air. He suddenly realized as he walked to his van that he hadn't looked at the monitor on his phone even once to see Lana. He pulled out his phone. Each monitored room was dark. He could see the outline of Lana's little shape in her bed. He quietly mumbled, "Good night there, little darlin'. Ya can't believe what I done fer ya to be mine." Leon's usual sullen, unfazed demeanor had been shaken by two women—Lana, whom he loved in his twisted way, and Carla, whom he had killed because of his perverted need to cover his lust for Lana. Still, Carla invaded every thought.

Leon decided to drive past Carla's apartment to see if her car was there, if lights were on, or if there was any sign of her. When he arrived, he drove by slowly and looked for any sign of life. The car was not there and the little garage apartment was dark. She must be dead—he saw the blood and heard that awful gurgling, choking sound and saw her in his mind's eye, unable to move. When he got home, he smoked a joint in the dark, reliving those last moments with Carla, and then he tried to shake it off. He smoked a second joint. He needed sleep. He threw off his work boots, walked into his bedroom, and jumped into his bed fully dressed in the dirty, dusty sheets and pillowcases. He lay on his back and looked at the ceiling until his eyes finally closed and he fell asleep. But sleep was not peaceful. He tossed and turned, his stomach churned from the alcohol, he was hot, then he was cold. His head ached.

Around two o'clock, he woke in a sweat, his heart pounded, and his hands shook from a nightmare. It took him a few minutes to shake himself awake. He had dreamed that he was at Red's Bar and he had approached the big, dark-haired woman who sat in Carla's booth from behind. But this time when he looked at her face, it was Carla's face—decomposed with hunks of yellowish-gray skin hanging from her jaws. Her lifeless eyes were black, there were holes where her cheeks had once been, and bugs crawled in and out of and between her teeth. She groaned as she turned her head toward him. "Leon . . . Leon . . . What did you do?" Followed by the unearthly gurgling sound in her throat as blood trickled from the side of her mouth. He was relieved that it was a nightmare, but he could not calm his racing heart. He decided right there and then that he would drive up the canyon at dawn to see if her car was still there. He would not go any farther—nowhere near the embankment where he had left her body.

Leon couldn't wait for the sun to come up to begin his drive up Left Hand Canyon. He jumped into his van about six o'clock. He stopped at a convenience store and bought a pack of cigarettes and a large, black coffee. The closer he got to the mouth of the canyon, the more apprehensive he became. He stopped on the side of the road for a minute before he began the drive up the canyon. His hands were sweaty and shaking. He gripped the steering wheel. He took a deep breath and drove up the road. In a matter of minutes, he arrived at the side road where Carla had parked her car. It was still there with a red tag from the state patrol hanging from the door handle, warning that it would be towed if not removed. He still had questions. *Is she dead or alive? Has she been found? If she was found, why is the car still there? She wouldn't have been able to drive it herself with the injuries she'd suffered. Did I leave any evidence? Did anyone see me with her?* He hurriedly turned around and made his way out of the canyon. He could go no further. He had seen enough. He watched the sun rise in the eastern sky through his cracked windshield as he drove back to Columbine Point. Some service calls were already scheduled. He felt lousy, hungover, and exhausted. He breathed hard and his hands continued to shake. He just wanted to go home and flop down on his bed. "I gotta make that money to take care of my little darlin' someday."

On the way back to Columbine Point, Leon drove past Lana's house. The pastoral scene in which she lived gave him a little sense of peace. In Leon's demented head, Lana was the reason that Carla had to be taken out of the picture in the first place, and she was so worth the torment that he experienced. He just had to make her realize that he was the man for her. He would make her see. He inhaled deeply and exhaled with a wicked cough.

Lana awoke with the usual positive energy with which she began each day. The weekend was coming, and she had a Harley date with Roadking on Sunday. The snow had melted from earlier in the week and the weather was supposed to be good. As she stood and stretched her arms over head, she looked out the window. As the sun lifted itself above the horizon, she saw what looked like Leon's van drive by on Hill View Road. *Hmm . . . he sure gets around. There must be some ambition there.* Lana was clueless about Leon's intentions; she did not have even a scintilla of suspicion of him. But her thoughts were of Roadking—increasingly so. She wanted to see him before Sunday, but she didn't want to interrupt his plans, whatever they were. She took the leathers that he had given her out of the closet and found the gloves in a dresser drawer. The helmet was perched under a writing desk in her bedroom. She laid them out on her bed to make sure that all the components were there. As she dressed for work in a light blue cashmere turtleneck sweater and a midcalf, gray pencil skirt, she thought about surprising him with an invitation to do something before the Harley ride on Sunday, but she didn't want to appear to be pushing herself on him. Even so, they were getting very close. They loved each other, but there was no permanent commitment from either of them.

She continued to think as she drove to work with music, not really listening. She decided to stop by the dealership after work and invite him to happy hour somewhere in Louisville for a drink. She hoped he wouldn't mind. He had made a couple of surprise visits to her work in recent weeks.

When she arrived at her office, she called the advertising manager in. "Andrew, can you think of an intimate, little place in Louisville for drinks? You know that area pretty well, right?"

Andrew was about thirty years old, single, blond, good-looking, and in the habit of dating several women at once. He would know. "Sure. Yeah. There's a little place called the Weeping Willow Bistro. It's in Old Town Louisville in the eight hundred block of Front Street. It's tiny but has kind of a romantic feel to it. Are you doing research or will your visit be a personal one?" He winked at her.

"Well, now that I think of it, maybe a little of both." Lana's mind was like a searchlight, always seeking a new angle for the magazine. An article or a series about romantic hideaways in Boulder County would be great for the Valentine's Day issue of the magazine. "I'm glad we talked. I think I'll check it out. Thanks, Andrew."

Even though it was Friday, the anticipation of seeing Roadking later in the day kept her energized and productive. She met with the staff to brainstorm some ideas for upcoming issues of the magazine. She suggested an article about romantic places to take a date for Valentine's Day. The writing staff loved the idea. Lana asked them to provide her with a list of suggested places on Monday morning, and she would make assignments. "Some of you might even want to begin to do a little preliminary research this weekend."

By five o'clock, the staff had all left the office except for Lana and Miranda, the receptionist. Lana made some notes on a yellow legal pad and listed other ideas for discussion with her staff on Monday, then grabbed her laptop and locked her desk. She looked at herself in the oval, oak-framed mirror on the wall and touched up her mascara.

"Come on, Miranda. Let's close. Let the weekend begin." She waited for Miranda to get her things, and they walked down to the parking garage together. Miranda was one of the staff who planned to come for Thanksgiving dinner at Lana's house.

Lana felt some butterflies with the expectation of seeing Roadking. But for a few seconds, she felt apprehensive about surprising him. *He might be too busy for me. What if he's annoyed? I wouldn't feel right about interrupting him.* But she soothed her doubt by telling herself that he would let her know if he was busy and she would wait.

She pulled into the parking lot of All Roads about five thirty. She looked at herself in the rearview mirror, brushed her hair from her face, and touched up her lipstick. When she looked up from the mirror and through her windshield, she saw a white Porsche Boxster drive up to the front door of the dealership. In a few seconds, the passenger, Roadking, got out of the car. When the Porsche pulled away and in front of Lana's car, she saw that the driver was a blonde woman. The sun had already slipped behind the foothills and Lana could only see the woman with the lights that emanated from the building. The image of her was dim, but she had seen enough. Her heart sank. *I knew it. I knew I shouldn't have come. I knew it.* For a few seconds, she couldn't decide whether she should go in anyway and surprise him. It would be awkward and unfair to spring herself on him, especially when she was not in a good place. She started the Mercedes and pulled away without headlights so as not to draw attention to her car by anyone inside the building.

Lana felt like someone had punched her in the stomach, and her throat ached. Even though she knew that there could be a reasonable explanation for Roadking and the woman, the sight of him with her had highlighted the reality of their relationship, such as it was. No expectations, no commitment. Lana saw the truth in bold, black letters flash in her mind. *FOOL.* She drove home in silence as that word thundered through her head. It reminded her of the Tom Petty song, "Fooled Again." But she didn't want to hear a note of music. She needed to sort it all out.

After Leon completed the service calls, he went home and tried to sleep. He never slept well when it was daylight. So he lay on his bed until he felt like he wanted to get up and move around. This situation with Carla was out of his control. He didn't have any idea of what to expect. Two days had passed since he'd pushed her. He paced back and forth and back and forth, from his living room to his kitchen, smoking, ranting and raving, and running his hands through his hair, heavy metal music blasting, and Carla's voice straining to be heard. Finally, when the sun went down, he jumped in his van and went to Red's Bar. He couldn't stand to be alone.

When Leon walked into the bar, he glanced toward Carla's booth out of the corner of his eye. It was still empty. He found a seat at the bar with the usual patrons.

"A tall draft, Robinson." He looked up and noticed that the local news was on TV. He began to talk to Jerry, the drywaller, next to him. "How's it hangin' there?"

Jerry responded, "Good. How 'bout yerself, Alvarez?"

"Can't complain." His eyes darted up to the TV every minute or so.

"Hey, Robinson, bring some of them pretzels on over here," Leon hollered.

Just as Robinson delivered the little bowl of pretzels, Leon heard a voice on the television. "A woman's body was found in the Left Hand Canyon area earlier this afternoon. A passerby spotted the body on a hillside around noon today. The woman's identity is unknown at this time. The body has been released to the Boulder County Coroner's Office. There is speculation that it could be a woman from Columbine Point who was reported missing earlier this morning by her employer when she failed to show up for work for two days. An abandoned car believed to belong to the woman has been found in the vicinity. Details at ten."

Leon could literally hear the blood rush from his head and through his ears as he heard those words. His hands began to sweat and his heart thumped loudly. His face felt hot. *It's her. It's Carla. She was found.* He sat perfectly still and didn't move. He was immediately consumed with paranoia. He was afraid that if he moved a muscle, everyone in the room would notice him and look at him and know it was Carla and that he had killed her. He felt like a spotlight was on him. He continued to sit perfectly still and looked up at the TV as if he were watching. He heard and saw nothing.

After about five minutes, he looked slowly to his left and then to his right. Some guys were playing pool and arguing. The regulars sitting around the bar were talking about football. No one commented on the news story. He stepped down from the barstool. "Goin' out for a smoke," he said to no one and no one responded.

He stepped out into the November night air and took a deep breath to calm himself, but the chilly air in his lungs made him cough. His hands still shook as he lit a cigarette. He could have sat in his van, but he wanted to be out in the open where he didn't feel confined. He stretched both of his arms over his head. He began to cough again and threw the cigarette down on the ground and walked back into the bar.

Still feeling paranoid, he expected everyone in the room to turn and look at him when he walked through the door. There were about fifteen people in the bar and no one noticed him. Even though he knew that Carla wasn't coming back, he still glanced toward her empty booth as he walked in the door.

When he returned to his stool at the bar, he hollered, "Robinson, a shot of Jack. Keep 'em coming." He had to wait for the next newscast. He had smashed his own television at home and had not replaced it yet. He must know what they knew.

"Bring some more of them pretzels on over here too," he yelled at Robinson again.

"Jeez, Alvarez, this ain't a diner." Robinson caught a glimpse of

Leon's pale face and red eyes in the soft glow of the dingy bar lights. "Man, you don't look so good."

"Neither do you, ya ugly bastard," Leon barked back as he waited for the news. "My face ain't none of yer business."

He sat quietly at the bar, tried to act like he usually did, and waited and waited until ten o'clock. Thoughts of Lana ran through his mind. He glanced at the monitor of her house on his phone. He saw her sitting still in a T shirt on a couch with her hand up to her face. "Lana, darlin', that thing ya made me do—it's a monster and it's comin' fer me," he mumbled to himself.

CHAPTER 38

The broadcast of the ten o'clock news carried no additional information about the body found in Left Hand Canyon. In his tormented mind, Leon believed that he couldn't sit at the bar and watch news about Carla without everyone knowing that he'd killed her. He quietly stepped down from the barstool and walked to his van to head home. He would get a new TV in the morning. Maybe a police scanner too. He smoked a couple of joints and fell into bed, wearing clothes and boots. The pot did not calm his racing heart or his tortured mind. *How long would it take 'em to identify her? What would the coroner say had happened to her? What if I left a shred of evidence behind somehow? What if someone saw them together? What if she told someone about their plans to meet in the canyon? What if? What if?* Then his thoughts turned to Lana. *What if I'd never known her? What if she hadn't called him for a lock change?* He had forgotten about her until then. *What is it about her that would make me kill someone to make her mine? Maybe my little darlin' is partly to blame for this? Look what she made me do.*

Lana sat motionless on the soft, brown leather couch in her living room, holding a celery-green toss pillow to her chest and pressing her right hand up to her right cheek. The room was mostly dark; one lamp was on. There was no music. She heard the ice maker in the refrigerator as it rattled new cubes into the ice bin. Otherwise, there was silence. She thought about Roadking, about how she loved him, about how quickly their relationship had developed, about what she wanted to know about him, about how she had mistakenly let herself be vulnerable, and how that vulnerability had left her without protection from the glare of the truth, whatever that was or would be. Those heavy thoughts weighed on Lana as she ended the day that had begun with promise. For a few moments, she let thoughts of an innocent explanation for the blonde in the Boxster flow through her mind, but she was only kidding herself. "Look at him. He's so good-looking and successful. He could have anyone he wanted. And it might not be me," she whispered to herself. A single tear rolled down her cheek, but she refused to let herself cry. Her imagination had done enough to shake her up. It was time for bed.

Around midnight, Leon finally dozed off into an unsettled sleep. He was driving Lana's new, black Mercedes. It was a sunny spring day. The windows were rolled down in the car. Lana sat next to him with her left elbow resting on the console. The smell of her light perfume drifted to his nose from the breeze through the window. They were driving up Left Hand Canyon. He could see Lana sitting next to him out of the corner of his right eye as he drove. He put his right hand on her leg. It felt mushy and bony at the same time. Something wasn't right. He was driving his van now. Lana's fragrant scent was replaced by an odor that was so putrid and rotten that it stung his nose. He turned to look at Lana. It wasn't Lana. It was Carla, decomposing and becoming skeletal before his eyes—yellowish skin falling away from her face, dried blood on her neck where it had puddled, maggots crawling in and out of the empty spaces where her face had once been, with a misshapen head from her injuries, looking at him with blinking eyes that were lifeless and black. Suddenly, she grabbed his arm with bony fingers that had the strength of Vise-Grips. He tried to pull away but then the hold became tighter. "Leon . . . Leon . . ." she gurgled in a low, demonic voice as blood gushed and dripped out of the corner of her mouth. "Leon . . . What did you do? Leon . . ." He tried to pull his arm away and still steer the van as he drove. The grip was getting even tighter. Leon heard his own voice yelling, "Let me go! Let me go! You monster! Get away from me!" and jarred himself awake. It was three thirty. He lay there cold with fear, still shaken from the dream.

"Carla's hauntin' me like a ghost. I'll be good when she's in the ground. I'll be okay. They won't know I did it," he spoke out loud, trying to convince himself that his words were the truth. His stomach was upset and churned. He touched his right arm where Carla had held on to him with a death grip in the dream. He got up, drank an Alka-Seltzer, and went into the kitchen to find something to eat. Maybe that's what he needed. He found some salami and a chunk of moldy cheddar cheese. He cut the mold off the cheese, laid the cheese on a slice of bread with the salami and some mustard, and ate. He pulled out his phone and checked the monitor of Lana's house. There she was—sound asleep. As he watched, she turned over, curled up in a ball, and pulled the covers over her head. "Peaceful little darlin'," he whispered to himself.

But Lana was restless throughout the night as she replayed the sight of Roadking and the Porsche and the blonde in between bouts of sleep. But in the morning light, there was clarity. She had sorted it out. Roadking was free to do as he pleased and so was she. There were no expectations of a relationship or a commitment. He owed her no explanation and she wouldn't ask. She could only hope that time with him would bring him closer to her. A Harley date was planned with him for the next day. But the truth was that her own happiness was up to her and she needed to make herself a priority. No one else would. She was on her own. She pushed aside thoughts of the blonde and the Porsche and began to work on a grocery list for the Thanksgiving dinner. She made another list of tasks that needed to be completed in the house. There would be seven guests on Thanksgiving. She was going to be busy.

As she drove to the market to buy food for the big dinner, she thought about the magazine. She thought of some innovative ideas for a slight trajectory for the magazine. *Sure, the magazine encompasses the essence of Boulder with fitness, art, entertainment, dining, and fashion articles, but what if there was some more substantive content added to the format? Not necessarily political content, which could polarize readers. But perhaps an article or two in each issue that would cover previously controversial topics from a historical perspective.* She decided to bring it up at the staff meeting on Monday and request a brainstorming session. As she drove home from the market, she decided she would call Olivia to discuss the trip to the Pink Sands Beach in the Bahamas that they had talked about several weeks before. She had been hesitant to go when Olivia had first suggested it. She hadn't wanted to be away from Roadking for a week or two. But today it seemed like it wouldn't matter anyway.

As soon as the retail stores opened, Leon went to an electronics store and bought himself a new flat-screen TV. He just couldn't sit at Red's Bar every night with his paranoia and wait for news about Carla. It was Saturday, and perhaps because of the weekend, there would be no additional information from the coroner or the Sheriff's Office. He brought the TV home and worked to program and set it up. He selected one the of the local TV stations and endured hour after hour of cartoon shows and paid advertising shows just in case a news anchor interrupted the broadcast with breaking news.

"Hey, Olivia. How have you been? We haven't talked for a few days. Is Alex in town yet for Thanksgiving or does he arrive next week?"

"Hey, Lana. He gets in tomorrow and will be here a week. Sorry we can't make it to your house for dinner Thursday. Maybe we can stop by later for your fabulous and famous Hershey Bar pie."

"Of course you're welcome. After the dinner is done, we'll just be hanging out. Going with the flow. Remember a few months back, we were talking about going to the pink beach in the Bahamas? You know, that was just before those things with Lucas happened and everything else, and we haven't talked about it since. Are you still up for taking a trip to the Bahamas together?"

There was a quiet moment before Olivia responded. "Um, Lana, you know, I didn't think that you'd still be interested in going, at least not in the next few months after everything with Lucas and you seeing Roadking now, so Alex and I have planned a trip together there in February. I'm sorry. I probably should've made sure you weren't in for it before I booked it with him."

Lana paused before she spoke. The truth was that she hadn't really been interested in the trip to the Bahamas until a few hours before. "Oh, okay. That' s okay. That's good. The pink beach isn't going anywhere. Maybe another time. Things must be getting serious with you and Alex if you're planning a vacation like that."

"I don't know if we're serious. We have fun together. I just take one day at a time. You can't force these things, you know. And I'm not sure if he's the one for me or not. And he probably feels the same way. How are things going with you and Roadking?"

"I guess I'd have to say the same as you. I have an exciting time with him. But I guess I'm not sure if this is headed anywhere either. I kind of hope it does." Lana surprised herself by revealing that much, even to her best friend. "Well, have a great Thanksgiving dinner and we'll talk soon. But please stop by if you can on Thursday for pie at least."

"Will do. See ya, Lana."

Lana was disappointed about the Bahamas, but it had been an impulsive thought that she might have regretted later. She continued with her lists and tasks for the rest of the day, went to the liquor store and bought six bottles of wine, listened to music, cleaned the house, worked out twice on the treadmill, and opened one of the new bottles of wine.

About five o'clock, Roadking called her. "Hey, Boulder Girl. What's up?"

"Hi, Vincent. I'm just doing some things to get ready for Thanksgiving. I think there will be seven or eight of us for dinner. And then I worked out some, just keeping busy. How was your day?"

"Good. Sold a couple of bikes, took in a couple of trade-ins. Started talking with some of the women in the office about the Christmas open house that we do each year with a Santa Claus and presents. But I wanted to let you know that I made reservations for us at the Greenbriar tomorrow at noon for the champagne brunch. I'm bringing the Harley, remember? The weather is supposed to be great. You still have the leathers and the helmet and gloves?"

"Yes, I do. I'll be ready when you come. I love the brunch there. That was a great idea. Thanks."

"Have a good evening. See you tomorrow, bella. About eleven thirty."

"You too. Bye, Vincent." It didn't seem like a sufficient goodbye, and it felt like she had cut him off somehow, but there had been nothing left to say. At least there was a plan to see him soon.

Leon made a couple of service calls for lockouts during the day, but made it a point to get home and watch the news at five o'clock. He popped the top of a beer can, plopped down on his droopy sofa, and waited. And finally, there was the story he had been waiting for. An unflattering photo of Carla flashed on the TV screen. Probably from her driver's license.

"The Boulder County Coroner's Office has released the name of the woman whose body was found in Left Hand Canyon yesterday. She was Carla Bennett, forty-four years old, from Columbine Point. Her body was spotted by a passerby on an embankment in the Left Hand Canyon area of Boulder County. The coroner has determined that her death occurred on Wednesday. She had been reported missing by her employer at Carousel Dry Cleaners on Friday morning when she failed to report to work. Sources in the Coroner's Office indicate that she died from blunt force trauma sustained in the fall. Ms. Bennett's car was found parked on a residential road about two miles from the area where her body was found. The Sheriff's Office is still investigating the incident. Ms. Bennett is survived by an eight-year-old son who lives in Rawlins, Wyoming, with his father. Funeral arrangements in Rawlins are underway. Stay tuned for updates on this story and more at ten."

Although he had waited for this news since Wednesday, Leon was stunned. He sat with his elbows on his knees and buried his face in his hands. Even though his eyes were closed, he could still see the image of Carla's face from the television screen burned on the inside of his eyelids—staring blankly with that coal black hair piled on top of her head. He felt anxious and his stomach churned. The words were so final, so harsh, so cold. There had been no mention of foul play, but on the other hand, there had been no mention of an accident either. But the mention of a little boy rattled Leon the most. Carla had never talked about a son. But they never talked anyway. And he was young—like Leon had been when he'd lost his own mother. Leon's mind flashed to that time in his life when his mother was alive and protected and loved him. He thought of her gentle voice and the way she had smelled and how it had felt when she was gone. And now he was responsible for taking a mother from her young son. He tried to convince himself that she couldn't have been like his mother. Carla's son hadn't even lived with her. She had never talked about him. She hadn't cared. But maybe she had cared and it hadn't been easy for her to talk about it. Leon wished he would have known about the little boy. *But would it have changed what I needed to do to protect my love and lust for my little darlin'?* His mind snapped back to those big looming questions in his mind—*Will this be called an accident or suspicious, and if so, are they gonna suspect me? And how long will it take fer the coroner and Sheriff's Office to investigate?* And then he thought of Lana. He became cognizant of the still tender "LANA" scar on his right thigh while his elbow rested there. *Look what she made me do. And she still don't know that she's gonna belong to me—and soon.*

He rubbed his face with both hands as if to wipe away the scattered thoughts that had been provoked by the news story. He decided to go to Red's Bar like normal and pretend not to know about Carla and see what the regulars would say about the discovery of her body. He smoked a joint and guzzled the beer, which upset his stomach even more. He hurried to the bathroom and threw up and then felt good enough to leave the house for the bar and told himself, "Be cool. Be cool."

The second he walked in the door, Jerry, the drywaller, shouted out to him, "Hey, Alvarez. Did ya hear about yer girlfriend?"

Leon scowled at him. "What the fuck are you talkin' about? What girlfriend?"

"Yeah, I seen it on the news. They found Carla dead up in the hills. Like she fell or somethin'. She's dead, man."

"Where'd ya hear that? And she ain't my girlfriend." Leon appeared to be annoyed.

"It was on the news, man, about an hour ago. I was sittin' right here, and they flashed a pitchur of her up on the TV news. And said her body was found in one of them canyons by Boulder."

"What'd they say happened to her? Christ, that's crazy. Robinson, hit me up with a draft."

"She fell down an embankment or mountainside or something. I wasn't none too clear on it. Don't know if they know either. They found her yesterday. I noticed that she ain't been here for a couple of days."

While Jerry talked, Leon tried not to look at the other guys sitting at the bar. He was paranoid that they would look at him and know that he had killed her. But they were drinking and talking among themselves like they always did. One of them looked up and turned to him and said, "Hey, Alvarez. Did ya hear about—"

But before he could finish the sentence, Leon cut him off, "Yes, asshole. I heard about her."

Leon was careful not to say anything else. He just took it all in, sat quietly, and looked straight ahead, sipped on the beer, and glanced at the television. But he felt a little bit relieved as well. *Nothing said so far seems to point to me. Now I just gotta wait for them to say it was an accident. Then I'll know if I'm in the clear.* He looked at the monitor of Lana's house on his phone. He had forgotten about watching Lana again with the news of Carla. She was busily moving around from room to room, which wasn't too interesting to Leon since she was fully dressed. But she was still the prettiest thing he had ever known. He watched her for a minute or two and smiled to himself until someone came up behind him and slapped him on the back.

"Leon, did you hear about ole Carla—ya know, the old barfly that was sweet on you?"

Leon was startled and jolted in his seat. His heart stopped. "What the fuck, Padilla? Don't come poundin' on me like that. Yeah, I heard about it from Jerry. Jeez, what are you bastards bustin' my balls about it for anyway?"

Padilla laughed when Leon jumped. "Well, ya lost yer girlfriend, that's why."

"Ya ain't funny and she ain't never been my girlfriend. Jeez, let her rest in peace, jerkoff."

Padilla laughed again, shook his head, and took a seat on one of the barstools. "Robinson, pass them peanuts down here and hit me with another draft."

Somehow, the jostling and banter with the guys in the bar felt normal and calmed Leon. "How about a game of pool? Any of ya bastards wanna take me on?"

"Yeah, I'll take yer money, Alvarez. Ya got plenty of it," shouted Padilla.

For the next few hours, Leon tried to put Carla out of his mind. Around midnight, Leon went out to his van to smoke a joint. But after he took a few hits, he decided to go home and not head back into the bar.

In the van, though, he began to wonder if he'd bought some bad weed, maybe laced with something. When he came to a darkened intersection near his house, he saw a dark figure float in front of his van. The apparition stopped in front of him, and in the headlights, he saw Carla looking back at him. He whispered as if someone was listening, "She's dead. That can't be her. This weed is tainted, man." But his usually narrowed, red eyes were open wide, and he shook his head in disbelief. He could hear the blood coursing through his veins. He hit the gas and drove through the apparition and continued to drive, still bewildered by the sight of Carla.

When he parked in front of his house, he saw her again. This time, a dark figure that looked like Carla was standing by his front door in the red, puffy coat, knocking—tap, tap, tap. He heard it.

He sat in his van, shut his eyes tight, and waited for three or four minutes for her to disappear. When he opened his eyes again, the hallucination had disappeared. He ran into the house and locked the door behind him. He sat on his saggy couch in the dark and chain-smoked until he believed that she was gone. When he went to bed, he lay there with his eyes open and continuously scanned the room as he watched for her to appear again.

"I ain't never gonna feel safe till that bitch is in the ground," he said aloud to himself. When the hallucinogenic high and paranoia wore off, he finally closed his burning eyes to sleep.

Roadking arrived to pick up Lana at eleven thirty on the Harley like he'd promised. Lana had dressed in tight, faded blue jeans, a bulky, maroon, turtleneck sweater, and black, knee-high boots, and then had proceeded to dress in the leather chaps and jacket and wrap a rose-colored scarf around her neck. She loved the smell of the leather clothes.

"Did I dress warmly enough, Vincent? It's chilly this morning."

"You're good and you look good too." He kissed her lightly on the lips. "Good to see you this morning."

Lana smiled. She was so in love with him, but after she had seen him with the blonde in the Porsche, she was afraid that she had revealed her feelings too soon. She put her arms around him and hugged him tightly. He put the full-face helmet on her head and helped her fasten it.

"Let's go drink some champagne." He held her hand as they walked to the motorcycle.

The ride to the Greenbriar Inn at the mouth of the Left Hand Canyon was only five or six miles away from Lana's house. The restaurant buzzed with Sunday brunch patrons. Roadking and Lana were seated at a cozy table away from most of the noise. The waitstaff arrived at their table immediately and poured the sparkling wine.

Roadking held up his glass and said, "To a great ride today. Cheers."

Lana tapped her glass to his and they each took a sip. The brunch selection was extensive with oysters on the half shell, shrimp cocktail, omelets, quiche, scones, waffles, carved prime rib, turkey, ham, poached salmon, fruit, cheese, roasted potatoes, tiny pastry selections of crème brûlée, truffles, tortes, and mousse parfaits. So much to choose from. Lana took tiny spoonfuls of many selections to sample as much as she could. Roadking's plate was heaping with oysters, a Spanish omelet, salmon, and fruit.

When they sat down, Lana mentioned to Roadking, "Did you hear that a woman's body was found up the canyon from here the other day? She was from Columbine Point. No one I knew or recognized."

"Yeah, I saw something on the news about it yesterday. I noticed some of the yellow crime-scene tape dangling from a fence post when we turned into the parking lot."

They sat quietly for a minute or two while they took bites of their food, and then Lana spoke. "Have you ever heard of a place called Weeping Willow Bistro on Front Street?"

"Yeah, I have heard of it, but I haven't been there yet."

"Well, one of my reporters told me that it's a quiet place to get a drink after work. I was going to surprise you Friday after work and take you there for a drink."

"Why didn't you?"

"Oh, there was just a change of plans." Lana didn't look at him and moved food around on her plate as she spoke.

"I might not have been there about the time you got off work now that I think of it. My neighbor Donna Torres bought her husband, Eric, a Harley for his birthday. He's an airline pilot, and she planned to surprise him for his fiftieth birthday with the new bike when he got home later that night. So I drove it to her house and parked it in their garage, and she gave me a ride back to the office. I talked to them yesterday when they stopped by All Roads to buy leathers and helmets. He was so happy about it. Maybe we could ride along with them sometime."

Lana was relieved of suspicion and doubt when she heard the

innocent explanation for the blonde in the Porsche. She literally breathed a sigh of relief. She was pleased with herself that she had chosen not to confront him with something that would have sounded accusatory when she really had no right to behave that way with him.

"They've been married for thirty years and they seem to be happy. They raised a couple of kids in the neighborhood. They're a good match," Roadking commented between bites.

"It's lucky when two people find their soulmate. Some never do. I'd like to meet them sometime."

Roadking didn't respond. After a minute or two he said, "Lana, do you ever think about getting married again?" Roadking took a sip of the wine and set his glass down.

A waiter came by and refilled it immediately.

Roadking looked directly at Lana.

Lana was taken aback by the question. She had just taken a bite of quiche and used the time chewing to think about how to answer him. She hadn't really thought about it in a meaningful way. Maybe fantasized about what married life with the right man would be like. With him. On the other hand, she was hesitant that she would make a mistake again. Or answer too eagerly. She looked in his crinkly, smiling, hazel eyes as she spoke. "Yes, I have thought about it recently. With Lucas gone, it feels like closure from the divorce came sooner than I thought it would, and I'm finished tying up loose ends from the past. I'd like to be married to someone someday whom I love and respect and who feels the same about me. You know—a partner to share each day and night with in good times and bad. Someone who places a lot of importance on me. Jeez, I sound like a Valentine's Day card, don't I?"

"No, not really. It's just you being honest. I like your answer. It sounds like what I would say if I expressed things as well as you." He reached across the table and held her hand for a few minutes. "Well, how about it? Got room for any more? I'm going to sample one of the crème brûlées."

"I think I'll try one of the tiny fruit tarts. And more champagne, of course. And that's it. I'll flatten the back tires of the Harley if I eat any more."

"Well, when we finish here, I think we'll take a little drive up the canyon to Buckingham Park and then turn around and head up US 36 to Lyons this afternoon and visit some of the antique shops up there. What do you think of that plan?"

"I like it." She thought, with anticipation, about putting her arms around Roadking while they rode. She had been wrong about him and the blonde, and she let go of any negative thoughts about their relationship. She would just hold on tight to him, today and every day.

Leon woke early on Sunday, but he was not rested. He looked worse than usual. His eyes were somehow redder and puffier than usual. His hair, which hadn't been combed in weeks, was in a stringy, dark mess hanging over his eyes. His long black beard and mustache hung stiffly. He still wore his work clothes from days before—a dirty, white T-shirt and rumpled jeans, which were torn where he'd cut through them to carve Lana's name on his leg. He looked in the mirror and then turned away.

"I gotta get rid of that weed I smoked last night. Man, that stuff was a bad trip." He walked out to his van to grab the baggie of weed to throw away when his heart stopped. A Boulder County sheriff's car pulled into the driveway behind his van. "Fuck! Be cool, Alvarez," he told himself.

The deputy sheriff got out of his car and walked toward Leon. "Are you Leon Alvarez?"

"Yes, I am. What do ya need, Officer?"

"I just have a couple of questions for you about an acquaintance of yours named Carla Bennett."

Leon folded his arms in front of him so the officer wouldn't notice his shaking hands.

CHAPTER 39

The sheriff's deputy approached Leon in the driveway and handed him his business card. The reflection from his badge caught Leon's eye, and the darkness of his uniform made him loom larger than he was. In a deep monotone voice, he said, "We're investigating the death of Carla Bennett. And we're just trying to find out a little about her. We have reason to believe that you knew her. What can you tell me about her?"

"Well, I seen her at this bar I go to sometimes. Red's Bar. She sometimes would be outside smokin' when I went out to have a smoke. I don't know much about her. Never even knew her last name."

"When was the last time you saw her?"

"Well, probably about a week ago. Not exactly sure. She was sittin' in a booth in the bar havin' a drink." Leon's heart was racing as he spoke. He tried not to let his voice quiver as he talked.

"Did she say anything to you about plans to go hiking in the Left Hand Canyon?"

"No. We didn't talk much. She never said much. Didn't really know her." Leon unfolded his arms and put his hands in the front pockets of his ripped jeans.

"Do you know if she had friends or family in this area? We've been talking to the few people who knew her. Mainly at the bar. We're trying to gather information to figure out why she was in the canyon. Trying to retrace her steps. From what little we know, hiking isn't an activity that she seemed to partake in. Did she seem depressed?"

Leon paused for a moment before he answered, as if he were

truly pondering the question. "Yeah, she might have been depressed. She kept to herself. What do ya think happened to her?"

The deputy was wearing reflective sunglasses. Leon couldn't see his eyes, and it bothered him that he couldn't discern the officer's expression or see his intense stare. "There's been no official determination of the circumstances surrounding her death. We're looking at the possibility of an accident or suicide or if a criminal act has been committed. We're looking for any leads. So if you can think of anything about her, even if you think it wouldn't be important, let me know. You have my card."

Leon looked at the business card. "Thank you, Officer, uh, Bryant. Keep up the good work." Leon's heart beat began to slow down as the officer walked away. He was afraid that the officer could hear it beating. He took a deep breath. He stood by his van, opened the door, and pretended to be looking for something, but instead he watched the officer through the side window as he drove away slowly.

"Now why would he be drivin' away so slow? Was he lookin' at somethin'? There ain't nothin' fer him to look at over here. Who told him to come around here talkin' to me anyway? One of them son of a bitches at Red's," he spoke softly to himself. Paranoia returned. He frantically fished around on the floor of the back seat of the van, trying to find the baggie of weed that he had smoked the night before. As he pushed aside tools, paper bags, food wrappers, and cans, he came across a woman's lavender, knit glove wedged under the pile. He had never seen it before, but he knew who it belonged to. Carla might have lost it during one of their romps in the back of the van. He found the baggie of weed, opened it, and scattered it to the wind. That was some heavy toxic stuff. Then he took the glove, threw it on the ground, and lit it on fire. When it dissolved to ash, he kicked the remnants of it and spread them all over the driveway and into the gravel.

It was Sunday morning. Leon went into the house and turned on the TV. It was too late in the morning for local news. He pulled his phone out of his back pocket and tapped on the app for the monitor of Lana's house. "Damn that Carla. She's takin' my time from my little darlin'," he said to himself when he realized how little he had watched Lana since the murder. And then he saw her with Roadking, standing by the front door of her house wearing motorcycle gear. She must be going somewhere with that "Harley pretty boy." "Lana, darlin', save some fer me," Leon whined out loud as he looked longingly at the scene. He was exhausted from the night before and went into the house, plopped down on his couch, laid his forearm over his face, and fell asleep.

Lana and Roadking finished up their meal at the Greenbriar, put on their helmets, and got on the Harley. The drive to Buckingham Park was only a few miles up Left Hand Canyon, but Lana was happy to squeeze him again. The park was isolated as they pulled into the lot. It was a little chilly, but the sun felt warm. Roadking pulled a small flask out of the breast pocket of his leather jacket. It was a Harley-Davidson flask encased with black leather etched with a design of the first Harley-Davidson.

"Have a little taste of the good stuff. It'll warm you."

Lana took her helmet off and sipped a little of the scotch. It was smooth and warm going down, and she felt its warmth slowly radiate to her extremities.

Roadking took a couple of sips. "Want a little more?"

Lana drank a little more. It gave her a little buzz. As she stood there face-to-face with Roadking, she couldn't resist putting her arms around his waist, and she laid her head on his chest. The black leather from his jacket was warm from the sun and it felt good on her cheek. They stood quietly for few minutes, lost in the moment. She wanted to hold on to him and feel his strength and draw it into her memory for the days when they were apart.

"Let's go, little lady." In a minute, Roadking started the Harley and stayed put for a few minutes just to listen to its distinctive sound.

Lana was solidly perched on the seat with her arms around him. The sun was high in the western sky, but the November days were getting shorter. It would only take about twenty minutes to get to Lyons. There would still be plenty of time to walk around. When they arrived in the tiny town surrounded by red stone hills, they parked and began their sojourn up and down the main street from one antique shop to the next, looking at vintage, silver jewelry, hand-painted china, darkened oak and walnut furnishings in various conditions, Indian rugs, carnival glass, and jars full of glass marbles. They found a little table outside of the Bull Canyon Antique Mart and sat in the late autumn sun. Roadking reached into the pocket of his jacket and pulled out the Harley flask again. They each took a swig.

"I'll be back in a minute." Roadking stood and walked into the antique mart. He came back momentarily with a little, white bag containing a small, carved, Austrian crystal bowl. "I saw you pick this up in there and thought you should have it to use on Thanksgiving, if you want to. It'll remind you of me." He winked at her as he spoke.

"Thank you so much. You didn't have to—I don't need a reminder when it comes to you. It's lovely and I can use it for cranberries or jam." She stood up and kissed him on the cheek. "You're so generous."

"Well, the sun is hanging lower in the sky. It'll begin to get chilly. Are you ready to go?" Roadking squinted as he looked toward the sun.

"Yes, that sounds good. One more sip?" Lana liked the warm feeling of the scotch as she swallowed it. The little buzz relaxed her and made her feel affectionate. She handed the flask back to Roadking and then leaned over and kissed him on the lips—a little more intensely than Roadking had anticipated.

He liked that she wasn't shy about it. Roadking leaned in for another deep kiss. Lana began to get that liquid feeling in her body. She put the crystal bowl in the saddlebag and kicked her right leg over the seat and situated herself behind Roadking.

In a brief time, they arrived at Lana's gate. Roadking put the security code in and drove up to the house. She retrieved the crystal bowl from the saddlebag. They walked to the front door.

"Come in for a few minutes, baby." Lana gave him a long, pleading look but didn't whine.

"I'd love to, but I told the family that I'd swing by at some point today. I'm sure my mom has whipped up an Italian or Mexican concoction that she'll want me to sample."

Lana was disappointed. She wanted him to spend the night. But she wouldn't push the idea on him. She never wanted to appear to be demanding. There would be other nights she guessed.

"Okay, I guess they're expecting you. Thank you for the awesome brunch and ride on a beautiful day. I wish you could stay tonight."

Roadking could hear a little tightness in her voice and sensed that she was disappointed that he would not stay, but he appreciated that she didn't pout about it. He loved that about her—she didn't create drama or make demands. She wanted to ask him to come back later but didn't want him to change his plans for her.

"Let's hook up one night this week before Thanksgiving, bella. Okay?"

"Okay, can we talk later?" Lana took her helmet off.

"Yeah, I'll call you. We'll do something." He raised his helmet off his face and leaned in for a long kiss and hugged her tightly. "You know I love you."

Lana had not heard him say those words for a while. The disappointment she felt began to wane and was replaced with reassurance. He meant so much to her. "I love you, too, baby. Be safe."

Roadking slipped his helmet back on. The sun was low in the sky and would fall behind the foothills soon. He turned and waved to her as he mounted the Harley. She watched him drive away until he was no longer visible.

"I wanted you to stay," she quietly said aloud to the night and went into the house. She took off the chaps, jacket, gloves, and scarf and carried them along with the helmet to her bedroom and placed them on a shelf in her closet. She stood for a moment, looking at the neat pile and thought about their day together. She looked toward the window and said it again, "I wanted you to stay."

Leon woke from his long nap about four o'clock. He lay there and looked at the ceiling for a few minutes and tried to piece together recent events—the deputy's visit, finding the glove, the sight of Lana with that Roadking bastard. Most of the day had slipped away while he'd slept off the effects of the pot and booze from the night before. He had somehow made it through the initial questions from the deputy and felt some relief from his paranoia and some renewed energy and was in the mood for some mischief. His mind hopped from one act of vandalism to another. He tapped on the phone app for the monitor of Lana's house. She did not appear to be there. She must be away with that "pretty boy." Without truly deciding about what to do, he jumped in his van as the sun began to set and started to drive. When he reached Louisville, he turned right on Pine Street and pulled over to the curb and parked. He let his mind wander as he surveyed the layout of the approaching intersections. His eyes darted from side to side as he thought. After several minutes he said, "Hmm . . . at least I should make the trip over here worthwhile." He immediately drove to All Roads Harley-Davidson and circled it a couple of times as he pondered a new act of vandalism to get the attention of that "Harley son of a bitch."

"He just ain't getting' it. His trouble would be far over if he'd just let that little darlin' alone and let her be mine like she's s'posed to be," he whispered to himself as he twirled the end of his mustache.

Roadking had left his Range Rover in the parking lot at the dealership to be detailed on Monday morning. Leon surveyed the site for surveillance cameras. The camera that he saw was on a light pole aimed at the entrance. The Range Rover was parked near the side of the building, by the service entrance. He believed that the view of the Range Rover was on the periphery of the camera's vision, if it was visible at all. The sun set and the lights of the dealership came on.

Leon parked on a residential side street about a half block away. He reached into the back seat, found a gray, hooded sweatshirt, pulled it on over his head, and covered his face with a dark handkerchief. He looked in the back of the van and found his switchblade knife and stuffed it in the pocket of his jacket. He walked toward the parking lot of the dealership and approached it from the dark perimeter. He pulled the switchblade out of his pocket and thrust it into each tire of the Range Rover. *Hisssssss*—the tires hissed in unison as the air escaped. That wasn't enough for Leon. It took so little time and effort that it didn't even begin to mitigate the jealously and anger that he carried with him. He took the knife and began to scratch the paint in zig zags on the front driver's side door and then continued with a serpentine line that circled around the entire car. Still not enough, he scratched the words "Harley SOB" on the hood. His eyes lit up as he stepped back a few feet to survey the damage.

"I shoulda burned the son of a bitch's car. Aw, but this'll get his attention fer now. What's comin' is gonna be so much worse." Leon chuckled diabolically to himself.

When he was ready, Leon walked quickly back to his van, staying on the unlit sidewalk as much as possible. But just before he reached the van, he encountered a middle-aged couple walking their beagle. The man looked directly at him and said, "Good evenin'," as he passed. Leon didn't respond but kept walking at a quick pace and decided to walk past the van in case the couple became curious about him and turned to watch him go. He walked in a straight line ahead and returned and got into his van when the couple was no longer in sight.

"Shit. Where the fuck did they come from?" He took off the sweatshirt and bandana and chucked them into the back of the van and pulled away slowly without headlights for a block or two. He returned to the intersection of Pine and Front Street once again as he left town. The satanic wheels turned in his head. As he waited to make a left turn at the stop light on Courtesy Road to head back to Columbine Point, Leon was stunned when Roadking appeared on his Harley and waited to make a left turn onto Empire Road as Leon crossed in front of him when the light turned green.

"That bastard is gonna be pissed when he seen what I done," he snickered to himself as he lit a cigarette. "Wish I could see that," he said as the smoke billowed from his nose.

CHAPTER 40

He had wanted to stay with Lana. Roadking thought about her as he rode the Harley fifteen miles to his parents' house in Louisville. The sun had sunk lower and the blue of the sky had become a darker shade with each mile. She had walked into All Roads just a few months before and, without any effort, won his heart just by being herself—pretty, smart, sexy, confident, fun, resilient, kind, gentle, and occasionally vulnerable. And now she loved him. Although it seemed soon, asking her to marry him had recently crossed his mind. There was still so much to learn about each other, but he trusted that she was genuine—the real deal. Shortly after he had met her, he had taken a moment for some rare self-reflection, and it had occurred to him that perhaps she had been his fate. Maybe it was a blessing that the others before her hadn't worked out. If she said yes, the engagement could be long or maybe there was no reason to wait. They would have a lifetime to learn all the intricacies of each other. *Yes,* he decided, *when the moment is right, I'll ask her. She's the one and yes, I want to stay with her.*

In a short while, he arrived at his parents' house with the usual crowd of assorted relatives and friends. Eva had prepared a big batch of pork green chili, homemade tortillas, pinto beans, and chile rellenos.

"I think I made enough to last us until Thanksgiving. Have some, *mijo*. There's plenty," his mom said as she handed him a white, china dinner plate. There was always plenty. For Eva, despite her career as an interior designer, taking care of the family came first, and they were the fortunate beneficiaries of her love of cooking.

Roadking loaded his plate and found a spot at the dining room table next to Tia Luisa, his mom's sister. "Vincent, by God, you get better looking every time I see ya. When is some lucky gal gonna snatch you up?"

Roadking laughed. "I don't know if she'd be lucky or not."

"You kiddin'? Handsome blend of Italian and Spanish. Yeah, that would be one lucky gal." Luisa continued to talk to him about his many cousins while he ate.

He nodded occasionally as she chattered on about their health and marital problems. When he was nearly finished, one of the toddlers climbed in his lap. Roadking balanced him on his leg. "Hey, little guy. Want some, Jacob?" he said to the little boy with dark, curly hair and hazel eyes as he offered him a bite of beans.

"No, no. Don't want it. Olives. Want olives."

Roadking laughed and reached for the green glass bowl of pitted, ripe black olives in the middle of the table and held it while the little boy took some.

"I eat some. I eat olives," he said as he shoved a few in his mouth. "More please."

Roadking laughed to himself when he heard him say "please." He knew that Eva had had a hand in teaching the little guy manners. Jacob took the olives and inserted an olive onto the tip of each of the fingers of his left hand.

"Look at this," he said as he held his little hand up and wiggled his fingers to show Roadking. Then he ate each of them, one at a time. Jacob continued to sit on Roadking's lap and leaned his head back on Roadking's chest, completely content, until he saw a battery-operated, yellow, dune buggy scurry across the room, and he jumped down to join the numerous children chasing it. "Down, down," he said.

But before Roadking set him down, he hugged his little body as he squirmed and kissed him on top of his head. He looked across the room at the children of all assorted ages as they played, and it reminded him that Lana had said that she wanted children. Perhaps she would know one day how important that was to him.

Roadking carried his plate into the kitchen when he was finished. "Need some help in here?" he asked when he saw the pile of dishes that his mother and the female guests were working on.

"No, you get on out of here. Go watch the football with the men. We can handle it," Eva said as she shooed him away.

"Okay, if you insist." He knew that as they cleaned up the mess, they enjoyed gossiping among themselves. It was a Sunday ritual that they would not let him infiltrate. He went into the living room and found an empty spot on the black-and-white couch. The men were watching a Broncos-Vikings game. Luisa's husband, Alberto, was from Minnesota, which led to light bickering among all of them. Roadking looked at each of them—each of them with families and the problems that come with families—but each of them secure in their place in the world and content with the choices that they had made for themselves. It made him feel a little lonely.

"I think I'll take off and call it a night," he said to his dad. "It's getting chilly and I'm on the bike."

"Okay, son. Be careful. See ya Thursday, right?" Angelo turned away from the TV and looked at Roadking as he spoke.

"Sure, Pop. I'll be here. Wouldn't miss it." Roadking walked into the kitchen and kissed his mom on the cheek. "See ya Thursday. I'm headin' out."

When he walked out of the room, Eva said quietly, as if he were still in the room,

"I think Vincent has a new woman. He's been gone quite a bit on the weekends. I know he went to Walsenburg one weekend with a lady. He's going to be forty next week. Maybe he's found the one."

The assorted aunts, nieces, and cousins nodded in agreement.

Roadking got on the Harley. It was chilly and dark. His house was a few miles away. When he got home, he pulled the bike into the garage and jumped in the SS 396. He was going back to Columbine Point. He wanted to stay with Lana for the night.

Lana worked out on the treadmill for an hour after Roadking had brought her home. She found some new music by Ariana

Grande to work out to—"Into You" and "No Tears Left to Cry." The new tunes energized her. When the workout was over, she decided against the usual glass of wine and opted for a margarita and some chips and salsa. She turned on the TV and watched the end of the Broncos game and then switched to the Food Network to watch a Thanksgiving special.

Soon her phone rang. It was Roadking. "Hey, baby. I want to let you know that I'm coming over. I didn't want to alarm you when I came through the gate."

"What a nice surprise! Where are you? When will you be here?"

"I'm about ten minutes away. At Hover and Nelson Road."

"Okay, see you soon." Lana jumped up from the couch, ran to the powder room, and looked in the mirror. She touched up her makeup and brushed her hair. *Oh shit, that salsa did a number on my breath.* She ran upstairs to the master bathroom and brushed her teeth and gargled with mouthwash twice. She dabbed on a little bit of musk oil perfume. Roadking liked that scent. She didn't change out of her workout clothes. She was so surprised that Roadking was coming over, she got butterflies in her stomach while she waited for him to arrive. She had been with him earlier in the day, but the anticipation of seeing him again generated an adrenaline rush.

She pressed both of her hands to her face as she stood by the window to wait for him to pull through the gate. It seemed to take a long time for him to get there. Soon she saw the headlights as he stopped at the gate and entered the code. Lana disarmed the security system. She didn't wait for him to knock, and she opened the front door as he approached. When he walked in, he put his arms around her waist and lifted her up and kissed her. When he set her down, he rested his hand on her little rear end.

"I didn't feel right when I left today. I had to come back. I know you wanted me to stay. So here I am." He smiled with those crinkly eyes and beautiful white teeth.

"I did. I really wanted you to stay. Come with me." She took his hand and led him upstairs to her bedroom. She wanted to make love to him and didn't care if she seemed aggressive or not. But he liked it. The bedroom was dark. She lay on the bed and pulled him down next to her. She kissed him passionately, took her T-shirt off over her head, slipped out of her yoga pants, and straddled him, leaning forward to continue the kiss while both of his hands rested on her little behind. She slid off him momentarily while she unbuttoned his Harley shirt, gently kissed his chest, unbuckled his pants, kissed his belly, and slid her hand inside. He rolled her onto her back and lay on top of her, pressing his body onto hers.

"Take them off," Lana whispered.

Roadking sat up and removed his clothes, and while he undressed, Lana took her sports bra and panties off. Roadking lay on top of her and eagerly began the long, intense, impassioned connection between them that ended like it had started—with Lana on top—both drenched in sweat. Lana's usually long, straight hair was wavy from the wetness. She leaned forward and rested her head on his shoulder while he stroked her back with both of his hands. Lana rolled onto her side and slid close to him and rested her hand on his chest and kissed him lightly near his ear. He could smell the light scent of her perfume, which was enhanced by the heat between them. Every inch of her body was tingling from the intensity of those moments of passion. She felt the rapid beat of his heart. Roadking pulled her closer and held her with both arms.

They were silent in the afterglow for a few minutes until Roadking whispered, "That was amazing. You are amazing. You're my girl."

Lana smiled, "I truly am."

Roadking lay on his back and looked around the room. Lana could see that he was thinking hard about something. "You know that pretty dress that you wore to the art gallery opening? You know the black and copper one? I want to see you wear it again. My birthday is Sunday. How about it? Would you celebrate my birthday with me in that beautiful dress?"

"A present! I need to get a present for you! Of course I'd love to wear that dress again and celebrate with you, baby. But where would we go all dressed up like that?" Lana was ecstatic that she would see him again so soon.

"Leave it to me. Don't worry about a present. You're all that I need." He pulled her closer to him. When their bodies cooled off, Lana pulled the light green comforter up over them. They both dozed for several minutes as they continued to lay close together.

When Lana awoke, she sat up and put her bra and panties on. The motion of her movement woke Roadking. He sat up and leaned against the headboard. "Hey, baby."

"Are you hungry or thirsty for anything, sweetheart?"

"Definitely not hungry. But I could use something to drink. Ice water?"

"Okay, I'll be right back." Lana, wearing only her underthings, ran downstairs and brought Roadking a glass of water and poured herself some wine. "Do you want to stay up here? Should I turn the TV on?"

"We can stay here. I'm not leaving tonight. You know, I realized when I was at my mom and dad's today that it didn't feel right being there without someone—without you. I want you to meet them soon. Are you okay with that?"

"Sure. I'd love to meet the two people that raised such an awesome man." Lana turned the TV on. The light from it created a glow and shadows on their faces. Lana suddenly felt emotional and her eyes teared up for a moment. She set the glass of wine down on the nightstand and laid her head on his shoulder.

"Okay, then soon it will be. After my birthday." Roadking felt the wetness on his shoulder from the tears. He turned her face toward his and said, "Hey, what's that about?"

"Nothing. Nothing but happiness," Lana smiled at him and laid her head back on his shoulder.

Leon drove the van into his neighborhood slowly and kept an eye out for law enforcement vehicles as he returned from the vandalism at All Roads. He believed that he'd dodged a bullet so far with the investigation of Carla's death, but he was still uncertain if some tiny shred of evidence would eventually point to him. Even so, some of the pressure lifted and vandalizing Roadking's car had given him the boost he'd needed. The coast appeared to be clear. He bought some new weed and immediately lit up a joint when he got inside. *Aah, this stuff is good, clean stuff.* The pot seemed to mellow the raw emotions that he had felt since he'd shoved Carla over the embankment. He checked the monitor app on his phone and saw that Lana sat alone, drinking a margarita. He went to his kitchen and rustled up canned spaghetti and hot dogs. Dirty dishes dotted with crusty bits of food were piled high in his kitchen sink, but he found a paper plate to use for his grub in one of his drawers and turned on the TV to watch football.

When the football game was over, Leon glanced at the monitor of Lana's house. He couldn't see her as he checked each room, except there appeared to be movement on the bed in the dark bedroom. He immediately clicked on the driveway monitor. The SS 396 was in the driveway. "That dirty son of a bitch is nailin' her again," he ranted when he realized that Roadking was with Lana on her bed. "Yet gonna ruin that little gal fer me. You dumb fucker, wait til ya see what I done to yer other piece of shit car! I gotta get that pretty boy out of the pitchure! She's mine, mother fucker! She don't know it yet!" He continued to rave as he paced back and forth in his living room, stepped over trash, and kicked it out of the way. He picked up a lamp and hurled it across the room, narrowly missing a picture window. Heavy metal Megadeth songs vibrated through his head. "Wake Up Dead" and "The Skull Beneath the Skin." When his rage subsided, he looked at the monitor again and saw that they were sitting in bed together, watching TV. "Yer in my spot, prick! Ya look all cozy now, but you just wait. I got a plan."

Suddenly, there was a tap, tap, tap on the front door. Leon stood frozen with alarm. It was that familiar Carla knock. Then again—tap, tap, tap. Leon surmised that the knock was real and someone was really at the door. He looked out the front window and saw an unfamiliar, dark sedan. He opened the door.

"Leon Alvarez?"

Blood rushed to Leon's face when he realized who was at the door. "Yeah?"

"I'm Detective Desmond Lancey with the Boulder County Sheriff's Department. I'd like to ask you a few questions."

CHAPTER 41

Detective Lancey flashed his badge and handed Leon a business card. Leon tried to stay cool at the sight of the detective. Fortunately, the darkness of the doorway hid his red and sweaty face. He felt like he had been hit in the face with a hammer and took a step back.

"What I can do fer ya, Detective, uh, Lancey?" Leon nearly forgot the detective's name that he had just heard.

"You know we're investigating the death of Carla Bennett. I believe someone has been here to ask you a few questions about her because you were acquainted with her. We'd like for you to come to the Sheriff's Office and make a statement."

"Okay, I guess. Why me?"

"We're taking statements from anyone acquainted with her to piece together the last hours of her life. You may come in at any time, preferably tomorrow. Just go to the investigations desk and you'll be assisted."

"Well, I don't know nothin'. Don't know how I can help ya."

"Like I said, we just need a statement from you."

"Okay, Detective. I'll try to make it over there to the Sheriff's Office soon."

"We appreciate your cooperation. Have a good rest of the evening." He turned and as he walked to the sedan, he paused for a second and took a quick look around the yard.

"Jesus! Shit! What are them guys lookin' for? Why do they keep comin' around?" Leon was frantic and spoke loudly to himself. He pulled at his hair with both hands and walked around in small circles near the front door. "What'll they ask me? What if I say too much? What the fuck?" It was only nine o'clock and Red's Bar was still open. He decided to head over there to see if he could find out anything from the regulars there.

When he walked in the door, someone shouted out, "Hey, Alvarez."

Leon nodded but didn't respond. "Robinson, hit me with a tall draft and a shot of Jack," he hollered as he straddled a barstool.

"What's shakin' there, Alvarez?" said Padilla as he took a seat next to him.

"Not much, Padilla. How 'bout yerself?"

"Well, some cops been comin' around askin' us guys about that barfly Carla that they found dead up in the canyon. You seen 'em?"

"Yeah, they came by, asked me a couple of questions. I don't know nothin' and that's what I told 'em."

"They asked me, like, who'd she hang out with and stuff. One of them guys told 'em they saw you talkin' to her a couple of times."

Leon thought, *Those sons of bitches.* But he said, "That don't mean nothin'. I was just tellin' her I wasn't interested in a roll in the hay with her." Leon downed the shot of Jack and asked for another. When Robinson handed the shot to him, he tossed it down immediately. "Hit me with one more," he shouted.

"Hey, go easy there, Alvarez."

The television was on above the bar. Leon looked toward it from time to time. There had been no news about Carla since yesterday. The detectives didn't seem to have any answers yet anyway. At ten o'clock when the local news came on, Leon stared at the screen, not even blinking. The third or fourth news story was indeed about Carla. He strained to hear the broadcast. The volume was turned down and the conversation around him was loud.

"Circumstances surrounding the death of Carla Bennett of Columbine Point, whose body was found in Left Hand Canyon last week, have not yet been determined. Her body was found on a hillside above the Left Hand Creek. It is not apparent how she fell to her death. Ms. Bennett was buried in Wyoming on Saturday. If anyone has any information, please contact the Boulder County Sheriff's Office."

Leon took a sip of his beer. He continued to look at the television screen but did not really hear or see anything. He was fixated on the words "not yet been determined." He wanted them to shove the case file into a drawer and forget about it. He wanted to know for sure that he was not a suspect. He wanted it to go away. He wanted to forget about it. From a quiet place in the back of his mind, he thought he heard Carla's voice again. *Leon . . . Leon . . . help me. Leon . . . what did you do?* He jumped up from the barstool. "I'm headin' out fer a smoke. Don't take my beer there, Robinson. I'm comin' back."

The smoke he needed was marijuana smoke. He got into his van and lit one up. With each toke inhaled, he felt a little relief from the anxiety that had erupted with the officer's appearance, the newscast about Carla, and hearing her haunting voice. He sat in his van and lit up another. He tapped the monitoring app on his phone screen to check on Lana. The appearance of the detective at Leon's door had interrupted his surveillance of her. It was too dark in the bedroom for him to see clearly, but there were two figures in her bed. "That'll be my spot someday, little gal, yer gonna want me," he spoke venomously through clenched teeth to the screen on his phone. "And you, pretty boy prick, are gonna be a sorry bastard and gone."

Lana and Roadking pulled the covers up and turned the TV off. They lay face-to-face, their bodies touching from head to toe. Roadking spoke softly to her, "Lana, it's getting harder and harder to leave you when we're together."

Lana whispered, "Then don't."

"I'm here tonight," he said and kissed her on the forehead and pulled her close to him. The longer he held her body next to his, the more they wanted each other again. And again they made love as passionately, intensely, and deeply as before. Lana loved the feeling of Roadking's weight on her body, and that is where he stayed. She buried her face in his neck and with her hands pushed on his hard behind and with each stroke, he pushed her closer to the headboard until she touched it with her head. He slid her closer to him and after a few strokes more, they exploded to a satisfying finish.

Lana softly breathed the words, "I love you, baby."

Roadking rolled off, drenched in sweat, and pulled the covers off them to cool down. Beads of sweat rolled off Lana's torso and onto the bed.

"I love you too," Roadking whispered softly and took hold of her right hand. Both fell asleep in a matter of minutes.

When Roadking woke about an hour later, he pulled the comforter up to cover them. Lana didn't stir. He looked at her lying on her back with her head turned slightly toward him, and even in the dark, he could see how beautiful she was. He kissed her on the cheek and quietly said, "Good night."

At dawn, Lana awoke to the sound of the shower running. Roadking had awakened and quietly went into the master bathroom to take a shower. Lana, who had been nude all night, quickly walked over to her dresser and found a long T-shirt to wear. She sat cross-legged on the bed when Roadking emerged in a towel, carrying that great smile.

"Hello, sleeping beauty. I hope you don't mind, but I need to leave soon to stop by my house to change clothes and then head to All Roads."

"I guess you, too, need to leave a few things here to wear when we have another impromptu sleepover here again."

Roadking leaned over and kissed her lightly on the lips and said, "You can count on that."

Lana asked, "Can I make you some breakfast? Coffee, eggs, toast?"

"Yeah, I'll take a coffee to go. But you don't need to bother with breakfast. I'll grab a bagel or something on the way home."

Lana had hoped he would say yes to breakfast because she wanted him to stay longer. She slipped on a short, pink, satin robe over the T-shirt, pulled on some white socks, and went downstairs to make coffee.

When Roadking walked into the kitchen, he was looking at his phone. "It looks like Rick, my service guy—you met him here once—called me this morning. Seems early, but it can wait until I get to the office in a little while."

Lana poured black coffee into an insulated container for him and walked him to the front door. Roadking put his arms around her waist and kissed her goodbye and reached up under the T-shirt and patted her little bare behind as he left.

Lana whispered in his ear, "Love you. Have a wonderful day." And she slid her arms from around his neck.

As he walked out to the SS 396, he waved and smiled at her, and she blew him a kiss in response. As she watched him drive away in that awesome car, she thought, *I would be happy to wake up each day to that great smile and to go to sleep each night next to that great body.*

Lana needed to get ready for work herself. She remembered that the turkey that she would be preparing on Thanksgiving needed to be thawed for three days, so she pulled it out of the freezer and slid it into the refrigerator. She ran upstairs to shower and get dressed for work. She slipped on a brownish-mahogany knit dress with a turtleneck, brown Australian boots, black tights, and dangly, silver earrings shaped like a feather. She hummed to herself the lyrics to the song "I'm in Love" by Tom Petty until she got in her car and plugged in her playlist. The time she had just spent with Roadking surrounded her with love and happiness. Nothing had ever felt so right.

As Roadking drove away, "Beautiful" by Gordon Lightfoot played on the classic radio station. *A song about my girl*, ran through his mind. Roadking stopped by his house in Louisville, popped inside, and changed his clothes. He jumped back in the SS 396 and drove to All Roads. When he arrived, he saw Louisville Police, Rick, and a couple of the service guys standing in the parking lot near where the Range Rover was parked. He drove up next to them as he pulled into the parking lot and rolled down the window.

"What's going on? What happened?"

"Damn, Roadking. Somebody did a real number on your car parked here. Take a look."

Roadking immediately pulled the SS 396 into a parking spot a few feet away and walked over to the Range Rover. "Jesus Christ! What the hell happened here?" he blurted out loudly as he slowly walked around the car, looking at all of the damage.

"Roadking, look at the hood. This doesn't look like a random act of vandalism. It looks to be directed at you," Rick said.

Roadking was silent and walked around the car two or three more times. He stood and looked at the words "Harley SOB" scratched on the hood for a few minutes and then reached both arms up, resting his laced fingers on the top of his head.

"Jeez, I just don't know who would do something like this. But there have been a couple of other recent vandalism incidents involving my cars and the office here. It appears that this might be directed at me, but I don't think I've pissed anyone off that would do something like this," Roadking spoke to the police officer, who continued to take statements and photos.

Rick spoke, "I checked the surveillance cameras, and they show a shadowy figure entering the side of the parking lot and wearing a hooded sweatshirt and a handkerchief on his face, but for the most part he's out of range of the camera."

"Well, we're gonna fix that. We need to increase the number of security cameras and alarms on this place that nothing is left unguarded. I better call the insurance company and get the ball rolling to get this thing fixed. When the adjuster is finished, Rick, can you bring the tow truck around and we'll put the car in the shop for now before something else happens to it? I should've left it in the shop instead of out here."

"Sure thing, Roadking."

The magical beginning to the day was wiped out by serious reality. Roadking was troubled that he appeared to be a target and probably had been all along. His stomach churned, but he told himself that it was a car and that it could be fixed. But he wondered how far this unknown vandal would go next time. He began to wonder if Lana was in danger, too, and questioned whether he should tell her about it. It would just upset her, and he wanted to spare her that. But on the other hand, he didn't want to be dishonest with her. There were already some things about himself that he had chosen not to reveal to her yet.

He called the insurance company and they promised an adjuster would be there soon. Roadking wanted to move the car out of the parking lot. It would look bad to customers. "Rick, bring the All Roads pickup around and park it next to the Range Rover until the adjuster can take a look. That way it's not quite as visible to people coming here today."

Leon hadn't slept well the entire night following the visit by the sheriff's officer again. And as the sun rose, questions and more questions spun through his stoned mind. *What did they mean by "make a statement"? Am I just gonna say a few sentences? Are they gonna ask me questions? Am I a suspect? Do I need to get a lawyer?* Then there was a scintilla of realization that none of this would have happened if Lana had never walked back into his life. *If only she'd see that I'm the one fer her. That I love her and will protect her. And if only Carla hadn't snooped in my house and attempted to blackmail me. If only Carla had stayed in Wyoming.* But his thoughts turned back to Lana again. *Look what you made me do.* The song lyrics taunted him, and yet he played them over and over in his van and in his head. He didn't want to think it or believe it, but maybe it was his beloved Lana's fault.

Okay, he decided, *I'll go to the Sheriff's Office and make a statement, whatever that means.* He wanted to get it over with. He decided that it would make him look guilty if he avoided them. At eight o'clock, he got into the beat-up van, stopped at a convenience store for coffee and cigarettes, and made his way to the Boulder County Sheriff's Office.

While both Roadking and Leon were filled with apprehension that morning, Lana was in a bright mood. At the Monday morning staff meeting, she was less serious than usual. It was a short week anyway with Thanksgiving on Thursday. She asked her staff about their ideas for a historical article to be added to each of the up-coming magazine issues. They bounced around ideas, such as the impact on Boulder and the surrounding county of Prohibition in the 1930s, the vibrancy of the Hill and the student protests in the 1960s, gold mining and the settlers of the 1860s, the history of coal mining in the eastern part of the county, and the impact of immigrants to the state at the turn of the twentieth century. Lana thought they were good and would assign one to research for each issue beginning in February. January's issue was nearly complete. Lana, satisfied with its content, began the outline for the February issue, which would contain another in the series of the travel in Colorado by various means. The third series of travel in Colorado by means other than a car was planned for February, as well as an in-depth article about the Modigliani art exhibit on display at the new art museum in Boulder, which Lana intended to write herself. Lana was energized by the Sunday time with Roadking and promptly got to work.

Leon skulked into the Sheriff's Office and made his way to the investigations desk on the second floor. "I'm Leon Alvarez and Detective Lancey told me that I have to come over here and make a statement," Leon mumbled as he spoke.

"For which case?" the middle-aged, bespectacled receptionist asked in a monotone without looking up at him.

"I guess for Carla Bennett. You know, that gal they found in the canyon."

The receptionist didn't respond but continued to look at the computer screen and, in a monotone, nasal voice said, "I'll let Detective Lancey know you're here. You can have a seat."

Leon felt uneasy there. His paranoia resurfaced. He felt like everyone knew what he had done, and it was just a matter of time. And maybe it was. He felt edgy and wanted to walk around but didn't want to draw attention to himself.

"Mr. Alvarez." Leon was startled when Detective Lancey approached from behind. "Follow me." Detective Lancey was in his fifties, balding, and tall but muscular. He reeked of cologne but was clearly all business. "Would you like a water, coffee, or tea?"

"Yeah, maybe a water." His throat was dry from nervousness.

"Okay, Mr. Alvarez." He handed Leon a bottle of Aquafina. "Since you're giving a statement, you'll be on record. Do you understand?"

"I do. Do I need a lawyer or somethin'?" Leon gulped some water from the bottle.

"No, we want to gather as much information as we can in order to come to a disposition in this case."

"Okay. Well, what do ya wanna know?" Leon wanted him to get to it so he could leave.

"Well, you were acquainted with Carla Bennett, right?"

"Yeah, I seen her at this bar that I go to—Red's Bar downtown."

"How well did you know her?"

"Well, she didn't say much. Set by herself in the corner, drinkin' them Long Island iced teas. Alone all the time. Seemed lonesome. Maybe depressed." Leon hoped to steer the detective's thoughts to suicide. "I seen her outside a couple of times when we both went out to take a smoke."

"Did you ever have an occasion to visit her at her home?"

"No way."

"Did she ever visit you at your home?"

"No. Don't know why she would've."

"Did she ever enter any vehicle that you drive?"

"I just got my van. No. I hardly talked to her. Didn't even know her last name."

"What did you talk about?"

"Nothin' really. She didn't say much. She just stared a lot. And drank and smoked."

"Did she ever talk to you about hiking in the hills, specifically Left Hand Canyon last week?"

"No."

The detective continued to ask basic questions, and Leon

answered them all in the negative. But then the detective paused for a moment with the questions and said, "The coat that Ms. Bennett was wearing when she was found had unfastened Velcro tabs on it. Those tabs evidently picked up fibers and hair from places to which she wore it. So . . . I'll ask you again—did she ever visit you at your home or you at hers or did she ever enter your vehicle?"

Leon felt like his head would explode and his eyes widened. He gulped another drink of water. *Damn.* He remembered that she had worn that puffy, red coat when she'd showed up a couple of times at his house and one time while she'd slept on his couch. *And what about that last day in the canyon?*

His mouth was dry, and he had to clear his throat before he could answer. "No, Detective, that Velcro could pick up stuff anywhere." Leon thought that he'd covered his tracks in every way possible. *But who'd think that Velcro could be the evidence that might point to me?*

"Okay, Mr. Alvarez, if we have any further questions, we'll give you a call. Thank you for your time today." Detective Lancey looked straight into Leon's red eyes as he spoke, which unnerved him.

"Okay, er, okay, I guess." Leon couldn't leave the building fast enough. His hands were shaking. Adrenaline poured through his veins.

The detective stood at the window of the second-floor conference room and watched him as he made his way through the parking lot. When Leon got in his van, he sat and stared straight ahead through the windshield while he rested both hands on the steering wheel to steady them. Suddenly, he began to regret killing Carla.

"Mebbe it woulda been easier just to give her a little money and attention from time to time. Gettin' rid of her made a whole new set of troubles fer me. All I wanna do is have that little darlin' Lana fer me and that bitch was gonna fuck it up." From the dark corners in the back of the van, he heard it again. It was almost imperceptible—the low gurgling, growling voice, *Leon . . . Leon . . . why?* He turned his head quickly to look behind him and saw nothing.

"Shit—yer buried in the ground in Wyoming and ya still can't leave me alone, bitch."

His hands began to steady enough so that he could light a cigarette for the drive back to Columbine Point, but his thoughts were frenetic and scattered. *Hair and fibers!* He and Carla had exchanged DNA on his couch, and she'd slept there. *What if the sheriff gets a search warrant and they find matching fibers from my house or one of my hair strands on that Velcro tab? What if they find her DNA or one of her coarse, black hairs on my couch or on the floor?* Ping went his phone. It startled him. There was a voice message. A service call in Columbine Point. He listened to the message. The sound of his phone halted his manic thoughts somewhat as he shifted his thoughts to his work.

He returned the call. "Leon Alvarez here. Locksmith. What's the address? Okay, I'll be there in twenty minutes, ma'am."

CHAPTER 42

Lana knew what she would buy for Roadking as a birthday present. A Saint Christopher medal. She knew that he had owned one before and that Cameron had tossed it away. Now it was a matter of finding one before his birthday. She checked out the websites of Boulder jewelers to see if she could find a sterling silver medal without the stress of waiting for an express shipment from an online site. No luck. During her lunch hour, she called her dad, the jeweler, for some advice. He created custom pieces and did not carry medals of that type but advised her to check out a Catholic website.

"What do you need a Saint Christopher medal for anyway?" her dad inquired.

"It's a gift for someone I know."

"A man of faith, I take it."

"Yes, he is. Have a happy Thanksgiving, Dad. I'll talk to you soon."

She took his advice and went directly to the Vatican gift website. She found exactly what she wanted—a sterling silver medal about an inch in diameter and a sterling silver chain and purchased them with FedEx express priority shipping. She hoped it would arrive by Saturday so it could be engraved.

Roadking, on the other hand, spent his lunch hour talking to an insurance agent, Mike Brown, and an insurance adjuster about the damage to the Range Rover. "I don't have any idea who could have done this. Maybe it was just some dumb kids with nothing to do." Roadking strained to think of who might target him, if anyone. But it was clear that the person who had vandalized the Range Rover had been aware of the security cameras and had purposely avoided them. A kid might not have been that aware or careful.

"Yes, Mr. Romano, but I see that there has been some previous vandalism here in the past few months—broken glass at the business here and then those windows on your other vehicle, the 1966 Chevrolet, that were shot out. It is possible that all these incidents were random, but they may also be intentional. I really suggest that you step up the monitoring and security devices here. Your insurance premiums are going to increase on the property here and on the vehicles because of these recent incidents, and the company might be able to knock down some of the cost if you do."

"Yeah, I plan to add cameras with a wider surveillance area and I'll let you know when that's completed. I expect it'll be in a couple of weeks. Fortunately, they didn't mess with the Harleys inside. That could have amounted to tens of thousands of dollars in damage."

Roadking motioned to Rick, who was standing outside of the service entrance, smoking a cigarette. "Tow the Road Ranger inside the shop, Rick. It looks bad sitting out here."

Then he turned to the insurance agent. "In the meantime, I'll arrange to take it to an auto body shop here in Louisville for repairs."

Mike Brown nodded his head. "Yeah, we'll work directly with them. You have a $1,000 deductible to keep in mind."

"No problem." Roadking shook his hand. "I'll be in touch when the repairs are scheduled." He walked into All Roads, went into his office, closed the door, sat down in his big leather chair, turned toward the window, and looked at the clouds in the sky. He leaned his head back and swiveled slowly to the left and to the right as he thought. *If someone is targeting me, who could it be? And could that someone become increasingly violent or direct their animosity not just at my belongings, but at me? And could Lana be a target as well?* He didn't want to tell her about it, but it would be irresponsible of him not to give her a heads up to be more aware of her surroundings and pay attention to people near her.

He called her. "Hello, Boulder Girl."

"Vincent, what a nice surprise to hear your voice already."

"I know, but I had to call and let you know about something that happened this weekend. I had parked the Range Rover outside the dealership and left it there so it could be detailed by my service guys today. But sometime over the weekend, the tires were slashed and it was keyed in a major way. You know that someone slashed the SS 396 tires at your house, another time they broke windows at the dealership, once they shot the windows out of the SS 396, and now this. I don't know if I'm a target or just the victim of bad luck. I don't want to scare you or upset you, but I want you to be aware of this stuff and to pay attention to your surroundings. If this stuff is directed at me personally, whoever is doing this may be aware of my relationship with you and victimize you too."

"My God, Vincent. Why would anyone harass you that way? Do you know who it could be? You know, you could contact that guy I know—Leon Alvarez, who installed my security system. Remember the guy who shot Lucas when he attacked me? He could probably help you out with some increased surveillance."

"Naw, thanks. I'll just use the company I already used before. That way the upgrades will sync with the old ones. But did you hear what I said? I want you to be careful and be aware of people around you and what they're doing. I don't want anything to happen to my lady."

"Okay, I'll be fine. But you do the same. I don't want anything to happen to you."

"I'm talking about when you're in the parking garage and walking down the street. Anywhere. Be aware of anyone following you when you're driving." He paused for a few seconds and said, "So how's your day going?"

"Quite good for me, compared to you. The staff has startled to dwindle. Some are heading out of town to visit relatives for Thanksgiving. But those of us who are here are hard at it."

"Okay, baby. Talk soon. Love you."

"Love you. Bye."

After the visit to the Boulder County Sheriff's Department, Leon made the conscious decision to fly under the radar for a week or two. *If I stay away from Red's, mebbe the guys'll ferget about me if the police come back around askin' questions. And if I stay out of sight and quiet, maybe the sheriff's investigators'll turn their attention away from me.* On his way home, he stopped at a convenience store, bought a six-pack of beer, some turkey lunchmeat, potato chips, and bread to tie him over for a few days at home. When he got home, he went in and closed the curtains to each and every window to shut himself in. He lay on the couch, smoked, and watched game shows and crime shows on TV until the evening when he monitored Lana's house again. He watched as she purposefully moved about the house and arranged things. It looked like she was getting ready to have a dinner there on Thanksgiving. "Probably for that Harley pretty boy. It'll be yer last Thanksgiving, pretty boy prick," he snarled to himself. He surveyed the rooms of his house, wondering if there was some type of evidence there that would connect him to Carla. He got the vacuum cleaner out and began to vacuum the floors and the couch—anywhere she may have been. He wondered if they were going to come for him or let it go. *Carla was nothin' and nobody—why are they makin' such a big deal about her?* For a few seconds, he remembered that she had had a son. Maybe she had been important to him. But then his malevolent mind persuaded him that the kid was better off without a mother like that.

The next few days were busy for Lana while she prepared for Thanksgiving. She made the Hershey Bar pie on Monday and put it in the freezer for Thursday. She began to set the dining room table with white china and crystal goblets after covering it with a white tablecloth. On Tuesday, she made the pumpkin pie. She let the staff go home early on Wednesday. She bought flowers in fall colors of orange and yellow with some purple to arrange for the centerpieces of the tables and picked up some last-minute things that she had forgotten earlier. By the time she went to bed on Wednesday evening, all that was left to do was cook the turkey and make the jalapeño cornbread stuffing, sweet potatoes, and mashed potatoes and gravy. Some of the guests were bringing side dishes to help out.

On Thursday morning, she got up early and stuffed the turkey with apples sliced into quarters and brushed olive oil on the skin and put it in the oven. The entire time Roadking stayed on her mind. She fantasized that maybe in the future, he would be there to help her prepare a big Thanksgiving meal with his flair for food prep.

Guests began to arrive about one thirty, carrying whole wheat rolls, a relish tray, broccoli salad, mac and cheese, brussels sprouts topped with hazelnuts, green beans, and several bottles of wine. Lana asked them to pour themselves wine and beer. Football was on TV and light classic rock was also playing in the background. Miranda asked if she could help in the kitchen. Lana asked her to pour ice water into the water goblets, open additional bottles of wine, and help her set the dishes of food out buffet-style on the pinewood dining table that was covered with a mint-green linen tablecloth.

When everyone was finally seated, Phillip from the art department made a toast to everyone, "Here's to all of us and to a successful year. May the thankfulness that we feel today extend to each day of our lives. And to Lana—a big thanks to you for this fabulous meal and for being a terrific boss. Cheers!"

The guests sat at the dining room table and ate and drank for two hours, talking and laughing, reminiscing about previous Thanksgivings in each of their lives. When it became quiet for a moment, Lana said, "Well, I think it would be a good time for each of us to say something that we're thankful for, in the spirit of the day. I'll begin . . . let's see, I'm thankful for your friendship and the support each of you have given me in the past months during some tough times."

The staff in unison said, "Aw . . ." and lifted their glasses to her, but there was more.

"And I'm thankful for new friends, new love, and new horizons."

"Here, here!" And they lifted their glasses again.

When each of the guests finished proclaiming their individual blessings, the group dispersed to the living room while Lana and Miranda cleared the table. Phillip began to set up the karaoke machine on the far end of the living room. They lost track of the football game while they ate dinner and drank enough wine and beer that they didn't feel shy about making fools of themselves.

"Okay, who's first?" The guests each took turns, picked songs, and sang to the best of their buzzed abilities until eventually they slipped away one by one to a spot on one of the leather couches to lean back and chill. Pretty soon each one of them began to feel sleepy. Andrew, the advertising manager for the magazine, fell asleep and fell over onto John's shoulder, who promptly shoved him away.

Lana slipped into the kitchen and set out the Hershey Bar, pumpkin, and pecan pies that she had made on the pinewood table and sliced each of them into eight pieces and then announced, "Who would like pie and coffee? The pies are on the table. Help yourself. There's whipped cream too. Coffee is in the pot."

As Lana had hoped, each of them came into the kitchen and took some pie. Lana hoped that the coffee would liven them up and that there wouldn't be any leftover pie. The group quieted down when the sun began to set. Soon there was a knock at the front door. It was Olivia and Alex. Olivia knew the gate combination, so they had been able to drive in without Lana noticing. "Hey, Olivia! And you brought Alex! Come on in. This group needs to liven up. The tryptophan from the turkey and the wine seems to have taken effect," she laughed. "Can I get you some wine or pie or coffee?"

Most of Lana's coworkers knew Olivia from previous gatherings at Lana's house. "Hey, Olivia. How ya been?"

"I'm good. And this is my friend, Alex. He went to high school with Lana and me. Lana, you know I want a piece of the Hershey Bar pie and how about some red wine?" Olivia sat down next to Miranda and began to talk.

Alex followed Lana into the kitchen. He served himself some pecan pie and poured goblets of cabernet for himself and Olivia and set them on the table. Lana dished up the Hershey Bar pie for Olivia and sprayed some whipped cream on top. She walked to the far side of the kitchen to grab some forks. When she turned around, Alex was standing right behind her, and in an instant, he kissed her on the lips. Lana could hear Olivia chattering away in the other room.

She took a step back and whispered, "Jeez, Alex. What the hell? My friend and your date, Olivia, is just in the other room."

"I've just always wanted to kiss those lips. Olivia is great, but it's always been you that I'm interested in—since high school," he whispered.

In a few seconds, Olivia walked into the kitchen, smiling. "Hey, where's that pie?"

"I was coming. Grab your wine. Alex poured it—it's on the table."

"Looks great, Lana. You put the crushed Hershey almond bars on top." Olivia was thankfully oblivious to what had just happened between Alex and Lana.

Lana gave Alex an annoyed look and went back into the living room and joined the others.

In the early evening, the guests began to leave after Lana packed each of them a hearty plate of leftovers. It had been a fun afternoon with them, but Lana felt wistful and wished that Roadking had been with her. Soon only Olivia and Alex remained. While Lana and Olivia chatted together, Alex watched TV—another Thanksgiving broadcast of *National Lampoon's Christmas Vacation*. Lana caught him staring at her at one point and it made her uneasy.

Tap, tap, tap.

"Someone's at the door. Maybe somebody forgot their coat or something." When she opened the door, she saw Roadking standing there and smiling with those crinkly eyes and white teeth. Her heart began to race with the happy excitement at seeing him standing there.

"Oh my gosh! Vincent! I'm so happy to see you. Come in!" She hugged him around his neck and he kissed her on the cheek. "Let me have your coat. What do you have there?"

Roadking held a little container in his hand. "Well, it's something special that my mom whips up for special occasions in the Romano house. It's a cannoli filled with whipped cream and ricotta. I know you're probably stuffed, but I wanted you to try one."

Roadking walked into the living room and Lana introduced him. "This is Vincent Romano and this my friend Olivia and her date, Alex." Roadking walked over and shook each of their hands. Lana couldn't help but notice that Olivia's's mouth was hanging open when she saw him. Alex's eyes narrowed as he sized Roadking up.

"Come on, Alex, we should get on out of here and let these two enjoy the rest of the evening." Olivia hopped up and went to get their coats. "Lana, where did we put them?"

Lana followed her into the entryway to assist her.

Olivia whispered to her, "I knew where the coats were, but I just wanted to tell you—oh my God—that Vincent is so unbelievably good-looking. What a catch!"

Lana smiled, "He truly is. I'm very lucky."

"So is he. I can read your face, Lana. I know how you try to hide things, but I think that you are clearly in love with this guy."

"I think I am." As she said that, Alex walked into the entryway, picked up his coat, and walked toward the door.

Olivia hugged Lana and thanked her. "We'll talk soon, okay?"

Alex said a terse goodbye and they left. Lana was alone with Roadking.

"Okay, now let me taste some of that specialty that you brought here." Lana went into the kitchen and grabbed a spoon and took a bite of the cannoli. It was creamy, sweet, and rich. She took another bite and another. "I better stop. This is really good and it's so different."

"My grandmother always made it, and the secret recipe was passed down to my mom, who never misses an opportunity to make it. It reminds her of her mom and her childhood. It's a tradition in the Romano household."

"Thank you. It's so cool that you brought some to me. I like it. You'll have to pardon the mess around here. The dishes are stacked high and I'll take care of them tomorrow. Can I make you something to eat?"

"No, I'm stuffed. I didn't come to eat. I just wanted to see you."

Lana sat down next to him. He put his arm around her and began to play with her long hair. "How was your dinner?"

"It was good, and we had a lot of fun. I'm happy that so many were able to come here today. It would be dismal to be by yourself on Thanksgiving."

"Well, I just wanted to come by and tell you since it's Thanksgiving that what I'm thankful for is you. That I met you. That you're with me. And for all of the time I've spent with you these past months and for the time I hope we'll spend together in the future." He pulled her close and hugged her tightly.

Lana looked down and turned the silver bracelet on her wrist that he had given her around and around. Then she turned to him and said, "I'm thankful every day that I met you. You have given me so much. Saying thank you doesn't seem like enough. I'm so in love with you." Although Lana could have said more and said it very poetically, she kept her words simple and heartfelt. She knew that he would remember them. She snuggled in closer to him and lifted her leg across his lap. He put his hand on her thigh. She reached for the remote next to her and turned the TV off and left the music on that had been playing softly in the background all day.

"Well, ain't that sweet." Leon watched them on the monitoring app. He growled to himself under his breath. "Look at her all over him. I expect they'll be doin' it here any minute." He was one of those dismal souls who spent Thanksgiving alone. His brother in Denver had invited him to come to dinner, but Leon didn't feel safe out in the open. He was estranged from the other four brothers. He made himself a turkey sandwich, ate a Hostess cherry pie, and smoked a couple of joints. There was nothing for Leon to celebrate or be thankful for. As he watched them, the wheels in his filthy, sick mind turned with evil thoughts of revenge and hate for Roadking. "I'm gettin' tired of waitin' fer that little gal. Next Thankgivin' it'll be me snugglin' on that couch and lovin' her up." Leon gave himself a little thrill as he thought about that possibility.

To Leon's disappointment, Roadking and Lana continued to sit together on the couch, talking softly and occasionally kissing. "I think I better head out. I'm taking the Road Ranger to the body shop first thing tomorrow."

Lana looked up at him and almost said, "Please stay." But she didn't. She was tired and wanted to get up early herself to finish up the dishes and work out in a major way. "Okay, can I keep the container with the cannoli? I'll finish it for breakfast."

"Of course. I'm happy that you enjoyed it so much."

"I did. Thank you for sharing it with me. Maybe we can make it together someday." Lana immediately thought that maybe she shouldn't have said that. She didn't want to sound like she assumed anything permanent about their future.

Roadking thought nothing of it. He stood and headed to the entryway to grab the black leather Harley coat that he had worn. Lana followed. He gave her a long, deep kiss and picked her up off the ground as he hugged her.

She laid her head on his chest for a minute. "Goodbye, Vincent. Be safe."

"Don't forget—Sunday—the fancy date that I have planned for my birthday."

"I know. How could I forget? I can't wait."

He walked out and started the SS 396. Lana loved the sound of that car. She stood by the door and listened to it idle before he drove away. She reset the security system and went to the kitchen to begin to clear the tables and bring dishes to the sink. The tediousness of the task was lessened by her constant thoughts of Roadking. "This is what love feels like," she said to herself as she rinsed some china plates.

CHAPTER 43

Late Friday morning, FedEx delivered the Saint Christopher medal. It was exactly what she wanted, and it had been blessed by the Holy Father before it had been sent. Lana immediately took it to a jeweler in Columbine Point to have it engraved. As luck would have it, even though it was Black Friday, he was able to engrave it while she waited for about a half hour. Then, even though the office was closed, she headed to work anyway to catch up on email. When she returned home, she went upstairs to her closet to look at the black and copper dress and shoes for the Sunday date with Roadking. They looked great. She would be ready.

On Sunday morning, Roadking texted Lana early and told her to be ready at four o'clock and he would pick her up. She hadn't expected that he would come that early, but she was happy that the day wouldn't seem so long while she waited. She jumped on the treadmill for an hour and worked out with the light weights. She went to get a manicure and pedicure about eleven. She returned home in the early afternoon and began to get ready for their fancy date—showering, moisturizing, curling hair, and applying the perfect makeup as she listened to her playlist of love songs. Occasionally, she sang along and swayed to their gentle rhythms. She was finally dressed and ready. She believed that she looked pretty good. She stood by the window to wait for him. She didn't want to sit and crinkle the dress before he saw her.

Around four o'clock, Lana saw a white stretch limousine pause at her gate. Her heart skipped a beat. *Roadking brought a limo to pick me up for our special birthday date!* In a matter of minutes, Roadking was at the door, smiling. He was wearing a black leather blazer, a light blue, collared oxford shirt, and black dress pants with black cowboy boots. She took a deep breath when she saw him standing there. He was so handsome, and he smelled so good—so manly with a light spice scent. When Roadking looked at her, he saw her reddish hair reflected in the copper of her dress that hugged her little figure so nicely. He looked into her blueish-green eyes and could see the love for him emanating from somewhere deep inside. She had never looked more beautiful to him.

"You brought a limo? You really know how to celebrate your birthday."

"Well, it's not every day that a guy turns forty and gets to celebrate with a beautiful redhead."

She grabbed the small, black leather clutch purse, which contained his birthday present. Roadking helped her slip on a long, white wool coat. The limo driver, whom Roadking called Buck, emerged from the limousine and opened the door for them. There was a bottle of pink champagne in an ice bucket inside placed on a pull-down tray with crystal champagne flute glasses on either side. They slid into the back seat. Lana moved close to Roadking. He poured them each a glass of champagne.

Lana held up her glass and said, "Here's to forty years! May your next forty be happy! Happy birthday, Vincent. Cheers."

Roadking smiled, clicked his glass to hers, took a sip, and leaned over and kissed her.

"So where is this limo taking us?"

"Well, you'll see. It's a special place in the hills. Just enjoy the ride in this limo with me for now."

Roadking's phone contained a special playlist that he had created specifically for the ride, and it was plugged into the limo stereo system. Love ballads sung by Elvis Presley, Ed Sheeran, Michael Bublé, Keith Urban, John Legend, Adele, and a couple of Motown classics played in the background as they talked and drank champagne.

"So Vincent, what would you say is your most memorable birthday?"

Roadking looked out the window at the outline of the mountains in the Coal Creek Canyon as the sun sank behind them and thought about it for a moment before he answered. "I think it was my tenth birthday. Because my birthday is in November, most of the time it had to be an inside party. But that year, it snowed about two feet the day before my birthday. My mom had some games planned for us to play inside, but instead all of us boys went outside and built a snow fort. Then we had a snowball fight and drank hot chocolate and ate cake later. It was an awesome day—so spontaneous. But celebrating my birthday while I was in college was always a big blowout. Football season was over by the time my birthday rolled around and so I was always ready to party in a big way. And I did." And then he added, "But I hope this birthday will be my most memorable."

Lana leaned on his shoulder and rested her left hand on his hard, muscular right thigh. "Well, yes, forty is a milestone and you're with me."

After about forty-five minutes, the limo turned into the parking lot of the Northstar Inn. Lana knew of the place—a tiny but very popular and intimate restaurant with a world-renowned chef. Because of its size and local acclaim, reservations were made months in advance. And it was well known for its romantic ambience.

"This place is always so busy. How were you able to get a reservation so quickly? There are no cars in the parking lot. It doesn't look busy, though, but it is early, I guess."

"I know the owner, Tim Wolniewitz. He and I played football together. I called him and he made it happen for us. He owed me a favor or two from our college days." Roadking laughed to himself as he remembered why Tim owed him a favor.

Buck emerged from the limo and opened the passenger doors for them.

"Buck, it'll be a few hours."

"Yes, sir. I'll stand by."

When they went inside, they hung their coats in the foyer and were greeted by Tim. "How ya doin' there, Romano? Good to hear from you. And this must be your lady?"

"Yes, this is Lana Ross."

Tim reached out to shake her hand.

"Nice to meet you, Tim," she said as she looked around the inn. The dining room was around the corner to the right from the foyer. It was dark inside, but as they walked in, there was one table in the middle of the room, which was covered with a white tablecloth and illuminated by a trio of white candles. And in the corner of the dining room was a small stage illuminated by backlighting with a young man who began to play an acoustic guitar and sing softly "Timing Is Everything" by Garrett Hedlund.

Lana whispered to Roadking, "Where is everybody? It seems odd that it's so quiet here."

"The place is ours for the night. I reserved it only for us."

Lana was surprised and impressed that Roadking had gone to such lengths for the night. "What a beautiful idea! And the guitarist?"

"Yeah, he plays here regularly for special occasions for Tim. I was able to give him a list of songs to play. And he sings too."

Tim brought glasses of Montepulciano d'Abruzzo Pinot Noir for each of them and a silver appetizer tray containing bruschetta topped with sun dried tomatoes, a small bowl of Greek olives, and thin slices of smoked cheddar. Lana sampled each item but was reluctant to eat too much since she didn't know what would be served.

Roadking reached over and held her hand and watched her face in the flickering candle light as she turned toward the guitarist. Sometimes he softly sang the lyrics to the songs and other times, he simply played the acoustic guitar. At that moment, he sang "A Song for You" by Leon Russell, which was a favorite of Lana's.

Lana turned toward Roadking and smiled. "This is so perfect. I could stay here forever."

"Me too." His heart was warmed by seeing the glow of her happiness. He knew that the night was going to be a perfect one.

Tim brought salad plates with a small pile of arugula, baby spinach, diced figs, and shaved Parmesan with a light balsamic vinaigrette.

"The food is wonderful and the presentation is so lovely. But I don't know if I can finish everything."

"It's okay. Finish what you can. Tonight is about a celebration—the food isn't the sole reason we're here."

When Tim returned to remove the salad plates, Roadking wanted to give Lana a little time between courses and said, "Hey, Tim, there's no rush with the main course so take your time, if you need to."

"We're good here. The chef is preparing the main dish now and it should be out in about fifteen minutes."

The guitarist began to play and sing "If I Ain't Got You" by Alicia Keys.

Roadking looked at Lana and said, "Well, you heard Tim. It'll be awhile before dinner is served. Care to dance with me? This place belongs to us tonight."

Roadking took her hand and they walked over to a bare space in the room. He put his arms around her waist and she put her arms around his neck. They swayed slowly to the music, taking small steps, and looked at each other's faces occasionally. Lana leaned her cheek on his chest, and he held her tight. They remained and held each other closely as the song finished.

When the guitarist began to play and sing "Perfect" by Ed Sheeran, Roadking sang along quietly in her ear and said to her, "You look perfect tonight." Lana was lost in the moment with him and felt that she could spend the rest of her life just standing there with him as he held her so close.

Tim stood near the kitchen entrance when Roadking noticed him. "It looks like the main course is ready to be served."

They reluctantly uncoupled and went back to their table. Tim refilled the wine glasses and set plates of sliced roast duck brushed with a cherry glaze, a puree of butternut squash, and a few herb-roasted baby potatoes. The food was beautifully presented. Lana took her phone out of her purse and took a photo of it.

Then she handed her phone to Tim and said, "Please take a shot of us."

Tim took the phone and clicked three or four photos of them.

"Could you take a couple of us later too?"

Roadking and Lana began to eat the special meal. When Lana could not eat more, she sipped her wine and reached into her purse for Roadking's birthday gift and set it on her lap. "Baby, you've outdone yourself tonight. Just when I think that we've had the most perfect day, you surprise with me another. Thank you for letting me celebrate your birthday with you."

"You're welcome. But the night isn't over yet."

Lana had no idea what he was planning. *What he's already done has been outstanding. What else could there be?*

Tim removed the dinner plates from the table. The guitarist took a short break. Roadking got up to talk to him for a minute. Lana guessed that he made a song request. When he returned, Lana handed him the little birthday gift wrapped in white paper with red hearts on it.

"What's this? A present for me?"

"Of course. It's your birthday."

He unwrapped the jewelry case and opened it. "A Saint Christopher medal! How thoughtful of you. You knew that mine had been lost and you remembered. It's beautiful and so meaningful to me."

"I did remember. Read the back of it. It was engraved."

"'Vincent, Always My Love, Lana.' That's beautiful. I'm putting it on right now."

"Let me do it." Lana took the medal, stood, and slipped it over his head and kissed him lightly on his cheek.

"Thank you, baby." The guitarist returned and began to set up to perform again. Roadking gestured to him and he began to play and sing softly as she sat down. "Lana, it's my birthday. And I wanted to celebrate it with you. If I could have any gift in the world tonight, it would be you. And the best birthday present that I could ever receive is for you to say yes."

Roadking took a little, white box from his pocket. Her eyes glowed with anticipation as he carefully opened the jewelry case and handed it to her. Inside was a solitary, one-carat, round diamond mounted on a simple, thin, white gold band. Lana gasped and put her right hand over her mouth and at that moment she heard the song that the guitarist was singing—"Marry Me" by Train.

"Lana, I know it may seem soon, but I could think of no reason to wait. Will you marry me? I'm sure that you're the one I want to spend the rest of my life with."

Tears instantly welled up in Lana's eyes. She swallowed hard and took a deep breath and held it and tried to shut them off, but they streamed down her cheeks anyway. "Oh, Vincent. Yes! My answer is yes! Yes!"

Roadking, upon seeing her reaction, felt a lump in his throat and began to tear up as well. She took the ring from the box and handed it to him. He gently slid the ring on the ring finger of her left hand. She held it in front of her and admired it for a second, and they both stood and embraced as tears continued to flow down her face and he kissed her through the tears. Fate and love had found them both and put them together for the rest of their lives.

Tim and the chef, both of whom knew had known about the proposal, stood on the other side of the room and smiled and clapped. The guitarist grinned at them, so pleased to have been part of such a romantic moment in the lives of these two strangers, and he began to strum and sing "Happy Birthday."

CHAPTER 44

Tim brought a small chocolate mousse to the table with an unlit candle on it. As the guitarist sang the birthday song, Roadking looked at him and nodded, indicating to the guitarist to sing "True Companion" by Marc Cohn.

Roadking quickly turned his attention to Lana, who was still holding him tightly. They continued to be locked in an embrace while he performed the song. Lana laid her cheek on his chest. Roadking stroked her hair. Lana was consumed by that moment with Roadking as he held her close. She suddenly realized deep down in her soul that every step she had taken, every decision she had made, every direction she had chosen in her thirty-three years, right or wrong, had led to this very moment with Roadking. Those thoughts washed over her like rain, and she knew beyond a doubt that Roadking had been her destiny. Tears began to subside amid big smiles of happiness. Lana and Roadking returned to the table. Lana dabbed at her eyes.

"Congratulations to you both," Tim said as he reappeared to light the tiny candle on the mousse. "Make a wish, Romano."

"No need to. My wish already came true," he said and blew out the candle. "Thanks, Timbo. This place was perfect for me to propose to this beautiful lady and to convince her to say yes."

Lana beamed at Roadking. "No convincing was necessary." She held up her left hand and looked at the diamond ring again. It sparkled with little rays of brilliance in the candlelight.

"You're welcome, Romano. Happy to do it."

Lana tapped Tim on the arm and asked, "Could you take a couple more shots of us?"

"Of course."

Lana handed her phone to Tim and he took several photos of them. Lana looked at the photos when he handed the phone back to her. It was the most important night of her life. The stillness of the photos couldn't begin to radiate the blissfulness that they both felt. But they would remember.

"Does the ring fit? I guessed at the ring size. The jeweler will size it if you need it to be sized."

"It's perfect. It's so beautiful. I don't know how you did it. I'm not taking it off—ever. I love it so much." Lana was afraid she might cry the happy tears again.

Roadking could see that she was still overcome with emotion and took her hand and squeezed it lightly. "Want a bite?" He took a spoonful of the dark, creamy mousse and held it to her lips.

"It's so chocolatey. Everything about tonight was perfect, Vincent."

The guitarist continued to play softly in the background. She leaned over and kissed Roadking lightly on the lips.

He gestured to the guitarist. "One more dance with me, beautiful?" Roadking took her hand and led her back to the bare space in the candlelit dining room. The guitarist began to play and sing "Perfect" by Ed Sheeran once again. It was, indeed, a perfect night for the perfect couple.

Buck emerged from the limousine and opened the back door when he saw them step out of the inn and walk across the gravel parking lot toward the limousine.

"Buck, this lovely lady has agreed to be my wife."

"Congratulations, sir. You're a very lucky man."

"Don't I know it."

The couple slid into the back seat. Lana arranged her dress. The half-full bottle of champagne was still chilling in the ice bucket in front of them. But neither of them wanted any.

"Where to, Mr. Romano?"

"Louisville. To my house." And he turned to Lana and said, "You're staying with me tonight."

Normally, Lana would have commented about having to work the next day and the need to change clothes and not having her car, and more. None of that mattered. She wouldn't let those practical thoughts intrude on the exceptional night. "It's where I want to be tonight," she whispered.

Roadking turned his head and looked out the side window as they rode down the canyon. In it, he could see a dark reflection of the features of his face and of Lana sitting next to him in the beautiful copper and black dress, leaning her head on his shoulder. Moonlight shone down on Lana's red hair through the sunroof in the limo, giving her an angelic glow. He had decided to ask her to marry him just a few days before. His initial thought had been to whisk her away to a dazzling destination somewhere like Aspen, Jackson, San Francisco, Santa Fe, or New York City and propose to her there. As wonderful as those places would have been, the distraction of the sites and the lights and the sounds and the people would have overshadowed his true purpose and would have taken some time to arrange. He couldn't wait any longer. Something inside him told him that the time was right. He knew Lana well enough to realize that she treasured private moments that belonged only to them. The night in its unpretentious, quiet simplicity was theirs and would never be forgotten. He turned to look at her face and pulled her closer.

"What are you thinking?"

"I'm not thinking for a change. I'm committing every moment of this night to my memory. There will be plenty of time to think about the future, the wedding, details, and arrangements and to let my mind race through it all. Not tonight. I'm only thinking of you—of us. And how much I love you."

Roadking pulled her close, turned his head toward the window and looked up at the night sky, and said a silent prayer to God. "Thank you, God, for bringing this beautiful person into my life. Bless her and bless us as we begin our lives together." He remembered the Saint Christopher medal around his neck and held it in his hand as he prayed.

"Lana Romano. That will be my name. It rhymes. Lana Romano! I love it. It's perfect like it was meant to be my name."

"It was, sweetness."

"I believe that too."

The ride down the canyon in the limousine seemed to go too fast. Lana already missed the intimate, little world of the North Star Inn—the little bubble on the planet, the little space in time that belonged only to them. But the night wasn't over and there would be a lifetime of nights with him.

"Would you like a glass of wine, baby?" Roadking asked when they were delivered to his house.

Lana took her coat off, kicked her shoes off, wrapped the black and copper dress around her legs, and curled up on the soft leather couch in the big, open living room."Yes, one more for tonight."

Roadking poured a glass of pinot noir for each of them, turned on some music, and joined her on the couch. It was ten o'clock.

"I was just thinking that you should have the access codes to the entrances to my house just in case. So the front door code is 8-0-0-2-7, actually the zip code for Louisville. The access code for all the other entrances that have a key pad is the same one—2-0-6-7-5. Remind me to write them down before you leave again."

"Okay, I guess that would be a good idea. Thank you. I can't think of a reason that I'd be here without you, but sometimes things happen. I should give you access to my security app so you can have access to my house without triggering the security alarm. I'll figure out how to do that." But Lana didn't want to talk about those practical, everyday things, so she sat silently, sipped the wine, and listened to the music.

They both leaned their heads back on the couch. Roadking reached for Lana's left hand, held it up to admire the beautiful diamond, and then kissed the back of her hand. "Well, it's official. It's you and me. You have made me so happy. We're going to have a great life together."

"I didn't expect this would happen—that you'd ask me to marry you. I can't describe the happiness I feel."

"We don't have to rush. We have time to figure it out and have the perfect ceremony. There's a lot to talk about, but I wanted you to be mine and I wanted you to know that. The engagement seals the deal."

Lana set her wine glass down and wrapped her arms around Roadking's waist and held him tightly. She couldn't stop thinking about the events of the evening. Every song played, every word spoken, the proposal, the ring.

Roadking set his wine glass down and said, "Let's go to bed."

Lana stood and straightened her dress.

Roadking took her hand as they walked upstairs. They entered the dark bedroom and they stood and kissed. He unbuttoned his shirt, lifted her hair, and unzipped her dress. It fell to the floor as it had done the first time when he unzipped it at the Boulderado following the art gallery opening. She stepped out of it and unbuckled Roadking's pants. She lightly kissed his lips, then his chin, and then slowly moved to his neck, his chest, his belly, and then pulled his pants down a few inches and continued to kiss his lower body. Roadking closed his eyes and she heard him begin to breathe harder. Roadking gently pulled her up and laid her on the bed, then quickly removed his clothes and lay down next to her. She wrapped herself around him and they became one, joined together, as close as is humanly possible, physically and emotionally, wanting it to last. One last beautiful memory of the perfect night with each other.

They lay joined together for a few minutes after the lovemaking. No words were spoken. They huddled close together and fell asleep. Lana woke during the night and looked at her left hand to make sure she hadn't been dreaming. And reached over and lightly touched the arm of that great man who would someday be her husband.

When morning arrived, all the logistical issues that they had ignored the night before were staring them in the face. After they both showered, Lana met Roadking in the kitchen, where he made coffee and breakfast burritos for them. He thought she looked just as beautiful as the night before wearing the black and copper evening dress. Roadking beamed as she walked into the room.

"Why don't I just call an Uber and they can take me to my house so I can change and grab my car?"

"No, I'll drive you to your office. You can uber home later in the day to change and pick up your car. If I drive you, I can spend a little more time with you. Besides, no one's going to notice that you're wearing a beautiful gown from last night after you show them the diamond ring." Roadking winked at her.

"You're right. I think that's what I'll do. And I need to call my parents and Olivia and let them know the wonderful news. They should know right away." She held her left hand up and looked at the ring again and looked up at Roadking's very handsome face as he stood over her and poured her coffee.

Lana had a Facebook account and used it to check out her friends and acquaintances, but she rarely posted to it. Her private nature would not allow her to post every moment of her life as many of her friends did. Photos of the two of them and the beautiful ring and the good news about her engagement to Roadking would be the kind of thing she might consider posting. But her preference for privacy outweighed any desire to blare her good news on social media—at least for now.

"I'll let my parents know about us today when I see them. They'll want to meet you soon. Are you ready?" Roadking asked as he scooped up the plates and cups from the table and set them in the kitchen sink. "Mrs. Sullivan will clean this up today."

"Yes, I guess I'm ready to go. Back to the real world but dressed like a fairy-tale princess."

Roadking helped her with her long, white wool coat, and then they walked to the SS 396 parked in the garage.

"My Range Rover should be finished later this week. But I know you like to ride in the SS anyway."

"Yes, I'm good with that." The drive from Louisville to Boulder took about fifteen minutes. They were each quiet as they drove, both thinking about the upcoming workday.

"Bye, baby. I mean, Mrs. Romano." Roadking smiled and then kissed her as she hugged his neck. One kiss wasn't enough. He kissed her again, this one a little longer, a little deeper, a little stronger.

"Mrs. Romano. I'll be so proud of that new name. I love you, Vincent. Have a good day."

"I will. I love you too."

Lana hustled to the building, holding up the beautiful dress as she stepped in the front door. Roadking waited and watched her, wanting one more glimpse of her. As he drove away, he thought about her, how much she meant to him, how much he wanted to be with her, how much he wanted to have children with her, and how much fun it would be to make those babies. He smiled to himself. There were many plans to be made.

Andrew noticed Lana as she approached the office door. "Jeez, Lana. You didn't mention that we have a new formal dress code around here."

The rest of the coworkers turned and looked at her.

"Okay, okay, you guys. I was out last night for a formal event and I haven't been home yet. So there you have it."

They continued to stare at her and some of them smiled and jabbed each other.

"Your dress is beautiful, Lana," Miranda said. "What kind of an event did you attend?"

"Well, it was a private event. Attended by me and Vincent Romano, my fiancée." And she held up her left hand to show them the beautiful, one-carat diamond ring. "I'm engaged to him!"

"Congratulations!" "Wow!" "Lucky man!" "When can we meet him?" "What's he like?" the coworkers gushed as they gathered around her to see the ring and hug her.

"Thanks. Now all of you need to ignore the fancy dress. I'll be ready for a full staff meeting in an hour. But just this once, Miranda, go out and get some prosecco and orange juice. Mimosas for everybody this morning!"

Leon had been alone in the house for a few days, holed up,

hidden from the police. His paranoia and frustration increased each day as he waited for the other shoe to drop, fearing that the police would make a connection to him somehow from the "fucking Velcro" on Carla's coat. But his frustration with the criminal investigation had evolved into fury at Roadking. He had seen them leave the night before on the monitoring app. "All dolled up, like they're royalty or something,"

It was morning now. She had not returned home. "That son of a bitch can't keep it zipped up. I just gotta see her. Or she's gonna ferget about me." He lit a joint and sat and thought about it. He needed a plan, a way to get close to her. With a sudden burst of twisted intuition, he hatched a plan. The television had been on continuously since he'd shut himself in the house before Thanksgiving. The morning news had just begun. He halfway listened to it from his kitchen as he made himself a salami sandwich for breakfast. Then he heard the words "Left Hand Canyon" and scurried out of the kitchen to watch.

"The Boulder County Sheriff's Office continues to investigate the death of a woman found in Left Hand Canyon several days ago. They have not yet determined the official circumstances surrounding her death, although they have received many tips in the last few days that may lead them to conclusive results. We will keep you posted if there are new developments. Investigators are following any lead, so if you have information that may help with the case, please call the Boulder County Sheriff's Office."

Leon's eyes bulged, his head throbbed, and his heart rose to his throat when he heard the word "tips." "Jesus, tips! What kind of tips? Who has tips? There was nobody around when she fell down the mountain! Nobody seen us!" He began to pace and pull at his hair and yank at his beard. He sat down on the dumpy couch and rocked quickly back and forth. He began to second-guess himself and go over everything in his mind. "Did I fuck up somehow? Damn it, Carla. Why did ya have to go around snoopin' and askin' fer money?" And then that awful gurgling voice began to play in his head, *Leon . . . Leon . . . Leon . . .* He shouted, "Go back to hell where ya came from, bitch!"

Nothing he did could settle him down. He was forced to admit to himself that he was scared. And he didn't like it. This thing was out of his control. And he couldn't change its course. He could only hope that the investigation led nowhere. He unconsciously stroked both sides of the long Fu Manchu mustache as the ends came together at the bottom of his beard. "I want to hear her voice. I can't wait much longer to see her." He took out his phone and searched his contacts for Lana's number. His heart ached as he dialed.

Lana saw that it was Leon and answered, "Hi, Leon. What's up?"

Leon had a rush of adrenaline when he heard her voice. "Well, I got some info that there may be a recall on one of them there parts on that there alarm system in yer house. I need to check the part number to see if yers is one of them. When can I swing by and take a look?"

"Oh, well, let's see, I'm kinda tied up today after work with stuff to do. How about Wednesday about five? Will that work for you?" Lana dreaded the thought of seeing him, but if there was a security problem, it must be fixed.

"Okay there, Lana, darlin'. I'll swing by then. See ya."

Leon walked into his bathroom and looked at himself in the mirror. He smoothed the strands of his greasy hair and tried to comb it. "I ain't bad lookin'." He imagined how they would look standing together. *Like husband and wife.* Her delicate beauty and his self-described "rugged good looks."

"That there pretty boy ain't got a chance with me in the pitchure." As much as he wanted to destroy Roadking, his need to stay hidden persuaded him to stay home and not pursue any mischief—at least not yet. The thought of seeing Lana in a few days calmed him and put his mind at ease temporarily. He turned the TV off. He didn't want to hear about Carla anymore. He turned on the music of Megadeth, Metallica, and Black Sabbath and let it roar through the house. With nothing to do, he picked up his laptop and entered a google search for engagement rings. "Man, them things are pretty high priced." He narrowed the search to Walmart. "Now that's more like it. A pretty ring for my pretty, little gal."

CHAPTER 45

"Hi, Mom. Yeah, I'm good. I have good news. I'm engaged! Last night!" As soon as Lana's Monday morning status meeting had been completed with her staff, Lana had gone into her office and called her mom.

"Oh? Who is he?" her mother said with her usual lack of exuberance.

"Vincent Romano. He's from Louisville, owns a Harley-Davidson dealership. He's so handsome and smart and treats me so well. I'll send you a photo of the beautiful diamond ring and of us."

"Well, I didn't date for almost a year after your father and I divorced." Still no sign of excitement from her mother.

"I wasn't looking to date anyone. I met him on assignment and it was like I'd always known him. He makes me happy and we really love each other."

"So . . . what are your plans for the wedding? Has he been married before?"

"We haven't talked about that yet. It was a surprise when he asked me on his fortieth birthday. We aren't necessarily in a hurry. No, he hasn't been married before, but he has a daughter, Ava, who's about nineteen or twenty and goes to CSU."

"Well, I guess I should congratulate you." Her mother was always emotionally unavailable, and this was no exception.

"Yes, please do. Mom, I've never been happier or more in love. He's the perfect man for me." Lana began to feel a little sad and disappointed as she continued to press her mom for some kind of acknowledgement of the happy event in her life.

"There is no perfect man," her mother responded in a monotone.

"Yes, there is. You'll see when you meet him. I hope you had a great Thanksgiving. Maybe we'll see each other before Christmas?" Lana asked, still trying to sound cheerful.

"We'll see. Have a good day." Lana's mother was still bitter about her unhappy marriage to Lana's dad and her inability to connect with a new man. She had dated a little following the divorce, but had seemingly given up on finding a companion, even though she was attractive.

Lana surmised that her unyielding, cold demeanor turned men away. She sat for a minute and thought about the conversation with her mom, who had a way of casting a negative light on everything. Lana began to dread calling her dad.

"Hi, Dad. How are you?"

"I'm good, honey. How are you?"

"Well, I have some wonderful news. I'm engaged. To Vincent Romano."

"You mean that Harley-Davidson guy that I made a ring for once? Him? What kind of ring?" Lana realized when he asked about it that her mother hadn't even asked about the ring. She felt a little pang of disappointment. But she knew that the ring would interest her dad more anyway.

"Yes, it's Vincent Romano. He's a wonderful man and I love him very much. The ring is a round, one-carat diamond on a slim, white gold band. Very beautiful. I'll send a photo of us and the ring."

"I would have designed one for him, if I'd known."

"This ring is perfect. He picked it out for me. It's simple and elegant. I love it."

"Well, if you're happy, then that's what I want for you. Congratulations, honey. Did he marry that other little gal that I made the ring for? So what are the wedding plans?" Her dad sounded genuinely happy for her, and she breathed a sigh of relief. But she wished that he wouldn't have mentioned Cameron.

"Thanks, Dad. I'm very lucky to have found someone like him after all the bad that was attached to Lucas. No, he wasn't married before. Well, we have no plans yet for the wedding. We haven't talked about it at all. I think he was waiting for me to say yes first. It just happened last night."

"Don't make it during March or June or, I think, August next year. I have plans with my gal to do some travelin' for a couple of weeks here and there. I wouldn't want to miss the wedding."

"I'd hate for you to miss it too." Lana felt that little pang of disappointment again. She should have known that he would put his plans above hers, whatever they turned out to be. If Vincent wanted to be married in March or June or August, then that's when it would happen whether her dad was there or not. "Bye, Dad. We'll talk before Christmas."

"Bye, honey. You need to meet my new gal, too, sometime."

When Lana hung up, she took a photo of her left hand and sent it in a text along with one of the shots of them from the North Star Inn to both of her parents. Then she sent the same set of photos to Olivia along with a text letting her know she would call her later. There was no response to the photos from either of her parents, but Olivia, with her usual vitality, texted, "OMG! You and that handsome hunk! He asked you to marry him? You make a beautiful couple! Call me soon! I want to know everything!"

A little before noon, Lana called Uber to arrange for a ride to Columbine Point to get changed and pick up her car. While she rode home, Roadking called her. "I told my mom and dad just now about the engagement. They're very excited to meet you. Can you make it tomorrow night? I was thinking about the Weeping Willow Bistro here on Front Street—the one you mentioned to me once. We can meet them there."

"Of course. I'm looking forward to meeting them too. Should I just drive on over to Louisville after work?"

"Yes, that would be good. Come to All Roads. They're going to love you. Hey, bring extra clothes in case it turns into another sleepover."

"Okay, I'll get there about five thirty. How's your day?"

"It's good. Especially after last night."

"Yes, that was very special. All of it."

"Have a good day, baby. I'll call you tonight to say good night. Love you, Lana Romano."

"I like the sound of that. I love you too. I'm on my way home in an Uber right now to get changed and head back to Boulder."

"Be safe, Lana. Talk soon."

After Lana entered the gate code and disabled the alarm, the Uber delivered her to her house. She ran inside and quickly changed into a black turtleneck dress and hopped in her car to return to work in Boulder. As she drove, she called Olivia.

"Oh my God, Lana! I'm so happy for you. I saw the strong connection between you two on Thanksgiving. What are the plans? When? Where? How soon?"

"Jeez, Olivia. That's a lot of questions. We haven't talked about the wedding or arrangements or anything. It just happened last night on his fortieth birthday. I don't think it'll be really soon. I'm so happy that he chose me to be his wife. You saw him—anyone would love to be with him. But you, of course, will be involved in the wedding."

"The ring is beautiful and you both look so happy in the photos that you sent. Congratulations, Lana. You deserve a fine man like that."

"Thanks. I'm so lucky to have met him. Talk soon." Lana felt so good to talk to someone who was truly excited for her.

Leon continued to surf the web for an engagement ring to give to Lana. *I need a real diamond, no cubic zirconia for my little darlin'.* In his tortured and demented mind, he believed that all he needed to do was give her a ring and she would belong to him—no courtship or connection required. After all, he had saved her life and she was indebted to him. She could pay him back by marrying him. He finally settled on a quarter-carat diamond ring on a rose and gold colored band. Walmart's website indicated that the ring was in stock in the local store. For the past several days, he had referred all of his service calls to another lock shop to stay under the radar of the sheriff's investigators. But he finally decided to chance being out in the open to go to the store and purchase the ring for Lana. He would keep it with him until the time was right. Just the thought of becoming engaged to Lana and making her his in every way brightened his sullen mood. His twisted imagination let him believe in the possibility that they would have babies together someday. His red eyes gleamed as he twisted the end of his mustache, and he smiled at the thought of making babies with her. The ring would be the first step.

His phone rang as he drove to Walmart. It was a service call. As long as he was already out of the house, he would take it. Besides, he was going to buy a diamond ring and could use some extra bucks. "Yeah, I'll be there in a half hour," he said to the caller. "I know, that's as soon as I can get there."

Leon went to the jewelry counter and immediately saw the ring that he wanted to buy.

"Do you know the young lady's ring size?" the sales associate asked.

"Jeez, no. It's a surprise fer her. She's kind of a small gal. I guess I ain't never looked at her fingers before. Can she bring it back here and you can fix it to make it fit her finger?"

"Yes, sir, we can size it if necessary."

"Let me see yer hand," Leon clumsily grabbed the left hand of the sales clerk, much to her astonishment. "Hmm, would this ring fit on yer finger?"

The sales clerk pulled her hand away from him and took the ring out of the display counter and tried it on. "Yes, it would fit, but it's a little bit big. What do you think?"

"I'll take it," he said as he pulled cash out of his pocket.

The sales clerk explained the warranty information that surrounded the purchase of the diamond ring, to which Leon half-heartedly listened. He was wrapped up in his deranged thoughts of Lana.

"You've purchased a beautiful ring for your lady," the sales clerk remarked as she wondered who the woman might be who would agree to marry the likes of him. She put the ring box in a small bag and handed it to Leon. "Congratulations, sir."

He hurried out of the store to take care of the service call. He put the bag with the ring in the console of his van for safekeeping.

For Lana, it was Tuesday and the clock was ticking slower than usual. She was excited to meet Roadking's parents, but on the other hand, she was also nervous. Even though he was forty years old and clearly made his own decisions, he was close with his mom and dad, and she knew they would have an opinion about her—hopefully a positive one. They clearly loved him very much, as did she. She wore an emerald-green, long-sleeved, fitted wool dress that extended to the top of her knees with black tights and boots. She had chosen green because it enhanced her hair color. To project a little classic elegance, she wore a strand of pearls and pearl earrings.As the end of the workday finally approached, she checked her makeup, brushed her hair, and slipped on a hip-length, black leather coat. As she drove closer to Louisville, a little apprehension began to take hold. *What if they don't like me for some reason? That would be hard on Vincent to choose between us. What if I just don't click with them or if I say something that accidentally offends them? What if? What if?* But those worrisome thoughts left her psyche when she pulled up to All Roads. Roadking emerged and they got into the SS 396. His calm presence and warmth assuaged her momentary insecurity.

"Hi, baby. I think we're a little early, but let's go in and get a table and order drinks."

"Okay. I have to say that I'm a little nervous about meeting them."

"Why? They'll love you. I love you. That's all it takes."

The hostess for the little café seated them in a corner booth near a window. Roadking and Lana sat side by side and ordered drinks. Lana ordered a sangria and Roadking decided to try a tall house draft beer.

"They're here," he said a few minutes later as he looked out the window and saw them drive up. Lana grabbed his right arm with both of her hands and leaned her head on his shoulder for a minute. "Hey, it's okay. You're great."

Mr. and Mrs. Romano walked in the door and the hostess directed them to the table where Lana and Roadking sat. Eva Romano was about five feet, four inches tall with a small frame and dark, curly hair with a little bit of gray weaving through it, much like Vincent's. She had flashing, deep brown eyes and looked younger than her true age would reveal. She was wearing a blue dress with black flats. Angelo Romano was the same height as Vincent, heavier, balding some with salt-and-pepper hair, wearing gold-rimmed glasses and a dark gray overcoat, and had a white mustache. Roadking stood up and hugged Eva and then patted Angelo on his left shoulder.

"Well, Mom, Dad, this is Lana Ross, my fiancée now."

His mother smiled at her with the same crinkly eyes as Roadking. Lana stood and reached out her hand to greet them. Angelo took her hand with his right hand and then placed his left hand on top of hers. It felt warm and genuine. He was a charmer like Roadking.

"We're pleased to meet the little lady who's been keeping our son so occupied lately," Angelo said as he slid into his seat in the booth.

"Thank you. I'm pleased to finally meet you both. I've heard so much about you," Lana quietly said. She smiled at them, admiring them as parents for the son they had raised. She could clearly see their affection for each other and it left her with the hope that it would be the same for Roadking and her.

"Angelo, this place reminds me of the Blue Parrot," Eva remarked. "Look at the red leather seats in the booths and the old cast-iron cash register and the mirrors behind the bar. And the barstools turn. I wonder if those came from the Blue Parrot." The Blue Parrot had been an Italian restaurant that was a destination for many for nearly a hundred years and had recently closed. Eva, as an interior designer, honed in on the decor.

"I don't know, hun, I guess so. Maybe it's the ambience of it or the smell of the food. Well, son, tell us how you met this lady."

The waitress brought glasses of water and menus.

Roadking turned and smiled at Lana and put his arm around

her. "Well, she just kind of found me, you know. She's the editor in chief of the *Boulder Essence* magazine, and she wanted to interview me about travel on a Harley for the magazine. When I saw her, I knew that I wanted to get to know her better. And I have." He hugged Lana a little closer.

Lana looked at his parents while he spoke, and she could see that his mom studied his face as she listened to each word that he spoke. "The interview with Vincent went so well. You'll have to read what he said and what I wrote about him in the issue, which is about travel in Colorado by means other than a car. It was a very worthwhile interview." Lana smiled at Roadking and then turned and smiled at his parents. "Mrs. Romano, Vincent brought a little container with cannoli to me that you made for me to try on Thanksgiving evening. I have to say it was so good. It was like elegant comfort food."

Eva smiled at Lana. "Thank you. I'm happy you liked it. It's a tradition in our family for any special occasions and sometimes just because. My mother taught me how to make it. The recipe isn't even written down. Not yet anyway. Now I know what happened to one of my Tupperware containers." She winked at Roadking. "So did you spend Thanksgiving with your family, Lana?"

"No, my dad lives in Steamboat Springs and my mother lives in Durango. They both had other plans. I have no brothers or sisters. So I invited several of my coworkers to my house and made a Thanksgiving dinner for all of us."

Although Eva had a professional life as well, it was important to her to know that Roadking's future wife had a strong domestic streak like she did. She looked at Roadking and he could read in her eyes that Lana had begun to win her over. Eva had never been too fond of Cameron because she thought that she was too self-absorbed.

"Growing up as an only child. What must that have been like?"

"It was a quiet existence. I read books, listened to music, and valued the time with my friends and their siblings. I have to say that I hope to have a family of my own someday. Two or three children.

I hope that I'll be blessed with more than one." For an instant, she thought that she may have said too much, but Eva and Angelo were both smiling at her. Lana leaned her head on Roadking's shoulder for a few seconds.

He pulled her close again and kissed the top of her head lightly. *I did it! I won them over!*

The waitress returned to the table and took their drink and meal orders. Angelo ordered a bottle of cabernet sauvignon for the table. When the wine bottle arrived and the waitress poured each glass, Angelo raised his glass and said, "Here's to my son and his beautiful bride-to-be. Cheers."

They each clinked their glasses together.

"Thanks, Dad."

"Excuse me, I need to visit the ladies' room."

Roadking stood and Lana slid out of the booth. When she was out of ear shot, Eva said, "Vincent, what a lovely woman! Smart and pretty. So down-to-earth."

"I know—she's perfect. I knew it early on. I hoped you'd see why I love her."

"Well, I have to agree with your mother. You know, she needs to meet the rest of the family."

"I know. We'll do that. It'll be fine."

When Eva spoke again, Roadking knew what she was about to say. "So what are your plans for the wedding? In the church?"

"Mom, we haven't talked about the wedding yet. I knew that you'd want a Catholic wedding. She isn't Catholic, but she's very receptive to what she knows of my faith. We'll work it out. I'll have to let her know about Pre-Cana at the very least. Don't worry about it. Lana wants what's best for us."

Lana returned as the dinners arrived. Angelo and Roadking had ordered veal Parmesan and sides of spaghetti with handmade marinara sauce. Eva's dinner was a petite sirloin, and Lana had ordered a short order of spaghetti.

"So Lana, what do you do when you aren't managing a big magazine?" Eva was still interviewing her.

"I work out a lot—treadmill and light weights. I have a little window herb garden. I'd like a bigger garden someday. I dabble in poetry writing, read books, spend time with my friends, and manage to take care of my house. I keep myself busy. I'm often researching or developing ideas for the magazine, like the story that has developed from the Modigliani exhibit at the new art museum in Boulder. But I have to say that Vincent has kept me quite busy lately."

Eva and Lana continued to talk while Angelo and Roadking talked about a house that Angelo was building in Boulder Canyon for an investment banker from Massachusetts. When the waitress brought the dinner tab, both Roadking and Angelo reached for it.

"Dad, I'll get it. It was my invitation for you to meet Lana."

Lana loved hearing him say her name. She hoped that his parents would accept her easily if they could only see how happy she and Roadking were with each other.

As the foursome departed, Eva and Angelo hugged both Roadking and Lana and said, "Welcome to our family."

Lana smiled and said, "I'm honored. It was so good to meet you."

As they exited the restaurant, the couples walked in opposite directions. When Roadking and Lana got into the SS 396, he said, "They really like you. They told me. See, I told you they would. But I love you."

Lana was relieved and happy. She had passed the initial test. It was only eight o'clock, and Roadking and Lana drove to his house to spend the rest of the evening there together.

"Can I get you anything, Lana? Wine, water, beer, tequila?"

"A glass of wine if you have an open bottle. Otherwise, ice water."

"I have an open bottle of Shiraz." He returned with the glass of wine and the bottle and sat down beside her on the leather couch. "So have you thought any about a wedding since Sunday night?"

"Well, yes, but my thoughts aren't really focused yet. I guess the date and the venue need to be figured out first and then everything else can be planned based on that. I spent a lot of time just thinking about the fact that I'm engaged to you."

Roadking took her left hand as he spoke. "I know my mom is hoping for a Catholic wedding. And I think I'd like that too. How do you feel about that?"

"It feels right to me. But I'm not Catholic. Can that be done?"

"Yes, but there is something called Pre-Cana, which I guess I can describe as counseling with the priest. I think it would be best to meet with the priest and talk about what we need to do. Are you sure that's something you want to do?"

"Yes, I'm certain. I was baptized but had a very minimal Christian education and I feel ready to embrace faith. It's important to you, and so I know it'll be important to us as a married couple and parents someday. I think I've been missing that spirituality all along."

Roadking hugged her tightly. Her belief in him was so genuine and intense. It had been another momentous evening—her meeting his parents and their religious discussion.

"Oh, I just remembered. I left a bag of clothes in my car to wear in the morning. Should we go pick up my car?"

"No, you just relax. Give me the keys to your car and I'll grab the bag and drop you at your car tomorrow morning when I go to work."

"Are you sure? Can I come along now?"

"Sit tight. I'll be back in a few minutes."

She dug into her purse and found the keys. He patted her behind before he left. While he was gone, she turned on some music. She was in the mood for Motown music. It always made her feel like dancing. And dance is what she did, getting into the rhythm of Al Green singing "Let's Stay Together." When Roadking arrived with her clothes less than five minutes later, he walked in on a dancing Lana grooving to Marvin Gaye's "Let's Get It On." He set her bag down and began to dance with her. Gyrating, turning, spinning, smiling first, then laughing at the spontaneous dance party that continued through "What's Going On" and then "My Girl" to which Roadking sang along to his girl. He took Lana's hand, pulled her into his chest, laughed, and said, "Let's get it on!" They made their way upstairs to bed. It had been another perfect night for them together. As they drifted off to sleep, the same thought ran through both of their minds: *Let it always be like this.*

Leon was simultaneously excited and frustrated. He was stoked by the idea that he would see Lana the next day. He had bought the engagement ring for her. He just needed the opportunity to ask her before it was too late. *Probably not tomorrow, but soon—when she realizes that she'll only be safe with me.* He was getting increasingly impatient. She was always with Roadking. And now the cops were breathing down his neck too.

"Damn that GPS. I ain't never shoulda got one. She never takes that car where I want her to. I wanna know where that son of a bitch lives. I know she's with him. And I ain't seen that little gal in her birthday suit doin' much paradin' around that house lately." He stroked his tangled black beard, thinking about the last time he had seen her naked.

Late Wednesday afternoon, Lana arrived at home. Leon was waiting in the driveway. He knew the gate code and could drive in, but she hoped he had not impolitely gone in the house without her. He had not. She drove up and he bounded out the door of the beat-up green van.

"Hey there, Lana, darlin'. How ya been?"

"I've been good, Leon. Let's go on in and you can check for the recall part on the system." And to make small talk as they walked, Lana asked, "Did you have a good Thanksgiving, Leon?"

"Naw, just stayed home. My family's all spread out. But it was okay."

Lana disabled the system and reached for the doorknob to open the door when Leon saw a sparkle on her left hand. They walked in the front door to the entryway and Lana turned on the foyer light. Then he saw it. She was wearing a big diamond ring on her left hand. *It can't be!* He stood in front of her and, without even thinking, he grabbed her left hand and held it up and looked at the ring.

"What is this? You done got yerself engaged?" His voice shook as he spoke. The blood rushed to his head with such fury that he heard it roar in his ears. The left side of his face began to twitch slightly. To him, it felt like the bottom had fallen out of his stomach.

Lana was alarmed when he suddenly grabbed her left hand. She pulled her hand away, clenched it, and held it close to her chest. She wasn't certain that she read him correctly, but he seemed upset. "Yes, I got engaged this past weekend to Vincent Romano. I think you met him once."

"Oh yeah, that guy." He said no more, but the fury he held inside was overwhelming. The twitching continued and his hands shook.

Lana spoke in order to move him along to check the alarm system. She wanted him to leave. There was a subtle, scary vibe about him. "So did you need to check the control panel?"

Leon didn't answer for a few seconds as her words seemed indecipherable. "Uh, yeah. Uh, right here. Uh. Okay."

Lana left the room and went into the kitchen and set her purse and laptop down on the granite kitchen counter. She stood there for a few minutes, not wanting to enter the room with Leon again. She heard some sounds as he opened the control panel and closed it.

"Uh, Lana?" Leon called for her.

"Yes, Leon?" She came back into the room with him.

"It's all good." Leon wouldn't look at her. His eyes were trained on the floor.

"Okay, thanks for checking it out for me." Lana walked to the front door and opened it, hoping that it would be a subtle hint for him to leave.

Leon looked at her face, and then his eyes traveled up and down her body once and then twice. "Okay, see ya soon. Bye."

Lana noticed the twitch in his face and the sullen darkness in his reddened eyes, which made her feel like something wasn't right. He finally stepped outside the door. Lana closed it and enabled the alarm system. Leon sat in his van in her driveway for several minutes and looked through the windshield. Lana thought that he must be talking on his cell phone. But instead, he banged his fists on his steering wheel and on the dashboard.

"Son of a bitch! Son of a bitch! He's tryin' to take her from me fer good. I have no choice now. I gotta do it! I gotta do it! I gotta do it again!"

CHAPTER 46

"Hey, Boulder Girl. I just scored two tickets for the Eagles New Year's Eve concert at the Pepsi Center. It's been sold out for months. How about it?" It was Friday morning and Lana had just arrived at work

"Sounds fantastic! How'd you get tickets?"

"A guy I know, Marcus Jackson, got some tickets and can't go to the concert after all, and I knew you'd want to see them. I think I'll make reservations at the Oxford Hotel right now for New Year's Eve, and then we can just stay down in Denver and celebrate the New Year after the concert."

"That'll be a lot of fun. Thanks for picking those tickets up. I'm looking forward to that. You know how I love the Eagles. I wonder if it'll be the same without Glenn Frey."

"We shall see. It's the same music. It'll be great. So what do you want to do this weekend? Got any ideas?"

"Well, it would be hard to top last weekend at the North Star Inn. How about you come over Saturday late afternoon and I'll cook for us? I haven't had that opportunity too often. And if the weather looks to be good on Sunday, we could take the Road King out for a short drive. What do you think about that?"

"Sounds great. If the weather's good. What are you doing tonight?"

"I don't really have any plans. How about you?"

"There's a family thing I have to go to. My eight-year-old niece has a piano recital in Louisville. Do you want to go with me?"

Lana thought for a second. She would love to go just to be with him, but maybe she would be a distraction. There would be plenty of opportunities for her to be involved with family activities. She hadn't met any of them yet and would feel like a third wheel. "You go ahead. I'd feel like an intruder, not having met any of them yet. It's okay—this one time."

"You sure? I'd love to show you off."

"Yes. I'll just hang at home and take care of things there."

"Okay, baby. You know I love to be with you. I guess I'll see you tomorrow afternoon. Love you."

"Love you enormously. See you tomorrow." Lana sat and swiveled back and forth in the chair at her desk and thought about what to make him for dinner. *How can I compete with his or his mother's cooking?* Although she knew that she was a good cook, she also knew that Roadking was used to a different style of cooking. *I better keep it simple and not try anything new that could be a disaster.*

She shook the thought away for the time being to prepare for a meeting with the advertising director of the magazine. As she walked through the magazine lobby, she grabbed a copy of the most recent issue of *Boulder Essence* and slipped it into her laptop bag to give to Roadking for his parents to read about him.

Leon was still beside himself as he reeled from the realization that Lana had gotten engaged to Roadking before he'd gotten his chance to convince her to marry him. He thought for a minute about returning the ring to Walmart. But that thought was displaced by the diabolical plan in his head to replace Roadking with himself. Timing would be everything, and when the opportunity arose, he would have to act on it quickly. In the early afternoon while Leon was smoking a joint and listening to heavy metal music, there was a solid tap, tap, tap on the door. He had kept his house closed tight, trying to stay out of the sight of the sheriff's investigators. It wasn't the light tap of that ghost Carla. Leon walked to the front door and opened it. He took a step back and gulped air when he saw that it was the sheriff's investigator plus three other officers standing there.

"Leon Alvarez? We have a search warrant signed by a Boulder

County Judge to search your vehicle and the premises here." He held it up for Leon to see.

Leon roared at them. "What for? You bastards can't just come into my house and look for stuff! What's this about anyway?"

"This warrant says there's probable cause that you were involved in the death of Carla Bennett. The search of the premises and your vehicle has been authorized by the warrant. Here's a copy for you to read. Now step aside."

Leon was in utter shock. He hadn't anticipated that this would happen. His heart was in his throat and beating so hard that he was afraid that the investigators could hear it. He told himself over and over like a mantra, *Be cool. Be cool. Be cool.* Leon went out on his front porch and sat on a ragged lawn chair and chain-smoked as he watched them carry bags of things from his house and van and place them into the police vehicles. But the adrenaline continued to surge through his body. Fear enveloped him and he couldn't shake it, though he tried to hold it together. *Just a little longer. They'll leave. Just a little longer. Be cool,* he chanted in his head.

After what seemed like hours, the chief investigator said, "We're finished here, Mr. Alvarez."

"So what did ya take from here? What's in them there bags?"

There was no answer. The investigators each carried a plastic bag as they entered their vehicles to leave.

Leon opened the door to his house and it suddenly felt like it was not his home anymore. The place where he had felt safe from the outside world had been invaded and violated. He walked through each room slowly and looked around to see what was missing. It looked as messy as it always did, so it was hard for him to see what they might have put in the bags. *The iPad's gone! Shit! They might see that I monitored Lana's house, but that won't implicate me in Carla's death.* He had cleaned everything the best he could as soon as he had begun to feel like they'd suspected him. *But what about those fibers and hair that the sheriff's deputy had suggested were significant on the Velcro tab on Carla's coat? From his couch, his van, from the floor? Did they find something there?* When he walked into the kitchen, he reacted with horror and held his hands over his face. The cabinet door under the kitchen sink was open where he had hidden the bag containing Carla's phone that he'd smashed to pieces. He had forgotten all about it. *I shoulda gotten rid of that, but I fergot to take care of it. Maybe it was broken up too badly fer it to be connected to her.* He continued to stand in the same place, unable to move. He felt that if he moved from the spot he was standing on, he would fall through the floor into a dark hole that he could never escape.

Finally, he took a step back, turned slowly, walked back into his living room, sat on the couch, and thought long and hard. "I'm gonna have to hurry. I gotta do it soon, before I lose my chance at that little darlin' Lana. All of it is fer her cuz I love her, and she'll love me, but she don't know it yet," he reassured himself. His frenzied thoughts turned to his evil plan, which was fueled by the fear that had just been generated by the search of his house in connection to Carla. He lay on his back on his couch as sick and twisted thoughts ran through his mind. He could not sleep. His red and watery eyes were trained on the ceiling the entire night as his hatred for Roadking grew stronger with each hour that passed. He felt it surge through his body.

Lana left early Saturday morning for the market to buy special items for the dinner that she was going to make for Roadking in the evening. She had decided to make a shrimp alfredo with mini penne pasta in a Parmesan and mushroom sauce, a green salad with her special vinaigrette dressing on it, and steamed carrot slices in a honey-butter sauce topped with toasted, sliced almonds. She bought a couple of bottles of white and red wine and a baguette. At fifty-five degrees, the weather was especially warm for December, so she hoped that Roadking would bring the Harley. She went home and set the dining room table with white china and crystal. She bought purple irises and white calla lilies for a flower arrangement for the table. She created a new playlist of romantic ballads for dinner. She prepared as much of the food ahead of time as she could.

She worked out early in the afternoon, showered, and changed into jeans and a long, heavy, navy blue turtleneck.

About four o'clock, before the sun set early as it does in December, Roadking texted Lana to let her know that he was on his way. He arrived about four thirty. Lana greeted him at the door with a kiss and a hug, took his leathers and laid them in the entryway on a deacon's bench, took his hand, and led him into the living room where a glass of chardonnay had been poured for him. Romantic music floated through the house.

"Well, that's a special kind of greeting." He smiled as he took a sip of the wine. Then he took off his boots and stretched out next to Lana. Lana lifted her legs over his and sat close to him.

"How was your day?"

"It was good. It's getting close to Christmas, so people are coming in to look at the Harleys and accessories for gifts. It's surprising how many bikes we sell in the winter. We'll have a Christmas open house with Santa in a couple of weeks. Of course I want you to be there so I can introduce them to the future Mrs. Romano."

Lana leaned over and kissed him on his cheek. "I'll be there. It sounds like a fun time."

For a second, thoughts of the last open house at All Roads ran through her mind as she remembered when she had received the call about Lucas's accident and death. The nightmares about him had recently stopped. Thoughts about him occurred less and less often. And she wouldn't let them intrude on her precious moments with Roadking. She shook them off.

"More wine, baby? I'm about to start the shrimp alfredo. Do you want to join me in the kitchen or just chill here?"

"I'll come in the kitchen while you cook. I like to watch you in action. And yes, I'll take some wine." He sat and watched her toss shrimp in the Parmesan sauce she'd made and then drain the pasta, toss the salad, season the carrots, and glaze the almonds while they talked.

"You know, now that I think of it, it was risky to make pasta tonight. You've been eating pasta made by an expert your whole life. Oh well."

"It'll be great," he reassured her.

Lana brought the food to the dining room table and poured more wine.

When they finished dinner, Roadking helped her clear the table and rinse the dishes. Lana selected a movie to watch—*Up in the Air*, a romantic drama with George Clooney. She sat close to him, alternating between leaning her head on his shoulder and holding his hand. He was so comfortable, affectionate, kind, playful and funny, smart and respected, and loving and understanding of her. At the same time, he thought about how lucky he was to have met her, and what a passionate, loving, partner she was going to be—and already was.

"I spoke to the priest at St. Louis Catholic Church yesterday about our plans to be married. He said we should make an appointment with him and begin to take the steps to prepare to get married."

"That's great. Let's make an appointment next week. I'm ready."

Roadking hugged her tightly when he saw her enthusiasm and then leaned against the arm of the couch and pulled her on top of him.

"Dinner was great tonight. You're an excellent chef."

"I really want to learn from your mom about all the special things she makes for you and your family."

"She'll love it that you're interested. Cameron . . ." he didn't finish the sentence.

Lana knew what he was going to say. She already knew that she was nothing like Cameron. No comparison possible. She laid her head on his shoulder while she was on top of him. He held her tightly. She kissed him on his neck. She was safe with him and he would always love her. It felt so perfect. "Are you staying tonight?"

"Absolutely. It's getting harder and harder not to be with you every night."

"Let's go upstairs." Lana rolled off him, stood up, and took his hand.

Leon watched them the entire night. He was excited. Everything was in place for his ungodly plan. Roadking had brought the Harley-Davidson to Lana's house. Leon was able to watch their movements. Soon his excitement turned to anger as he watched them once again undressed, making love. Even in the darkness of the room, he could see Lana's euphoric face. "That's how she's gonna look when she's with me real soon," he muttered to himself. "I seen enough. It's gonna happen tonight. Kiss yer pretty boy goodbye, Lana, darlin'." He put his fingers to his lips and blew a kiss into the air and laughed loudly.

Leon got in the battered green van and drove to Louisville. It was about eleven o'clock. He would wait a couple of hours after the town had gone to sleep before he made his move.

Lana and Roadking slept peacefully until Roadking's phone rang about one in the morning."Jesus, Rick. What is it?" he answered sleepily. "When? Son of a bitch. I'm coming over."

Lana listened to the annoyance in his voice until he tossed his phone on the bed.

"Somebody's busted out the windows at All Roads. I have to go. I gotta see if the bastard is still roaming around." He threw his clothes on.

Lana got up and slipped on a T-shirt and a short robe.

"Do you have to go? Can it wait until morning? You can't do anything until then. It'll be cold riding on the Harley so late. Please stay. Or take my car."

"Lana, somebody has been jackin' with me for a couple of months now and it has to stop. I told Rick that I'd meet him there. I'll only be gone a couple of hours. We still have plans for tomorrow." He found his boots and pulled them on and hurriedly slid the leathers on. He kissed Lana and then threw his full-face helmet on but didn't fasten it. "Bye, baby. I'll be back in a while. Promise. Love you."

Lana hugged him tightly around his neck until he pulled away. She could smell the leather jacket while her face was buried in it for a moment. "I love you too. Be safe. I'll be waiting for you." Lana watched the taillight of the Harley for as long as she could as he drove up the road. She saw that the moon was hanging low, ready to set, in the southwestern sky above the Flatirons. She returned to bed and held the pillow that he had slept on close to her. She could smell his scent. She fell into a restless sleep.

Leon's eyes glowed with anticipation. His heart raced with excitement as he watched the scene unfold on his phone as if he had scripted it himself. He parked on Front Street south of the intersection of Pine Street and waited. He estimated that Roadking would turn off Courtesy Road onto Pine Street in about twenty-five minutes. He sat motionless and watched for the sign of a motorcycle. Then there it was. The motorcycle approached the turn quickly. Leon started the van and gave it some gas so it wouldn't falter when the time was right. Roadking gunned the engine and quickly accelerated after he had slowed for a second to cross the railroad tracks on Pine Street. The Harley came closer and closer and closer in a matter of milliseconds. Leon floored the gas pedal on the van and jolted out just as the motorcycle approached the Front Street intersection. Then—*thud!* The van jolted with the impact as he hit the motorcycle broadside with the front bumper of the van. *Bull's-eye!* Roadking was thrown from the motorcycle, went airborne, and landed in a heap in the road. His helmet flew off as he hit the pavement. His leathers tore, blood oozed from his head and face, and his left leg and arm were twisted in contorted positions. The motorcycle skidded to a rest in a mangled heap of metal and parts scattered across the road and onto the nearby sidewalk. A broken mirror and shards of glass from the shattered headlight sprinkled the scene like snowflakes illuminated by a nearby streetlight. Gasoline spewed across the ghastly site from a ruptured fuel line; the smell of it hung in the frosty winter night. Then silence.

Leon peered through his windshield for a minute to survey the wreckage that he had just created. Roadking did not move, just as Leon hoped. As much as he wanted to continue to watch,

Leon knew he must leave. He knew that the sounds from the crash were going to generate phone calls to the police. *Shit—one of my headlights came loose and is dangling.* He slowly pulled away from the scene and began the drive back to Columbine Point, taking the backroads. He had such a rush of adrenaline that his hands were shaking. "I did it! Die, you bastard! She's gonna be mine now!" he yelled to himself. "Mine! My little darlin'!"

CHAPTER 47

Lana dozed off a few times while she waited for the sounds of Roadking to return. She reached across the bed to touch him several times. He wasn't there. At five o'clock, she sat bolt upright in bed. It had been four hours since he'd left. Lana felt uneasy about him being gone so long. *Maybe he went home instead of returning to my bed. But he would have let me know, wouldn't he?* She didn't want to be one of those women who always questioned his whereabouts, but she needed to know where he was.

She texted him, "Where are you? Are you coming back?"

She sat cross-legged on the bed and waited ten minutes for a response. Nothing. Her mind began to jump from one scenario to another until she decided that it was a waste of time and emotion to do that. She called him. His phone immediately went to voice mail. *Perhaps he turned his phone off or the battery's dead.* Her thoughts began to leap back to random speculation. The only thing left to do was call All Roads and hope that he or someone there would answer at five in the morning. She found the number and dialed. The phone rang five or six times.

She was ready to disconnect when she heard, "Hello. Uh, All Roads Harleys."

"Uh, hi, this is Lana Ross and is Vincent Romano there? He left here a few hours ago and I thought he would be back. Could I speak to him?"

"Oh . . . Lana, uh, this is Rick, you know, we've met before. Uh, I guess I have to be the one to tell you this . . . uh, Roadking was in an accident on his way here. A hit-and-run. He's at Boulder Community right now in surgery I think. He was hurt pretty bad. None of us knew your telephone number to call you."

Lana gulped. All the blood rushed from her head. Her lips were numb and she could barely speak. In an almost inaudible voice, she spoke to Rick, "What do you mean 'pretty bad'?"

"Lana, I can't tell ya, but he was unconscious when they found him, and he has a broken leg and arm from what I know."

Lana could no longer speak. She felt like she had been punched in the stomach. She began to shiver as if she were cold. Her mouth was dry and her throat ached.

"Lana, are you there?"

After a long pause, Lana spoke. "I'm here. I have to go, Rick. I have to go there. I have to see him. Bye, and uh, thanks, I guess. Yeah, thank you, Rick."

She sat on the bed with her face buried in her hands for a minute while she pulled her thoughts together. But she couldn't think. She got up and threw on the clothes that she had worn the night before. She washed her pale, white face, brushed her teeth, grabbed her purse, and left the house. She wasn't consciously aware that she was driving, but her body was able to maneuver the car to the hospital. She felt numb. She talked out loud to herself, "You're just afraid. He'll be okay. You don't have the facts yet. You're just afraid. He'll be alright."

It wasn't daylight yet and the bright, fluorescent lights inside the hospital glared and cast a harsh reality on Lana. She approached the emergency room desk and spoke in a whisper.

"My fiancée, Vincent Romano, was brought here several hours ago. He was in a motorcycle accident. Can you tell me where is? Can I see him? Do you know anything about his condition?" Tears welled in her eyes.

A nurse spoke gently to her as she saw how distraught Lana was.

"Let me take a look. Yes, they're taking him to recovery right now and he'll be admitted to a room thereafter. I can tell you that there are some people, I believe his family, waiting in the recovery area. Go down that long hallway and take a left and then a short right. Just follow the signs."

Lana turned and walked quickly down the long maze of tunnel like hallways to the waiting area. Angelo was sitting on a chair and Eva was sitting on a couch with an occasional table piled with magazines between them. Angelo looked up at the TV mounted on the wall and Eva looked down at her hands.

Angelo jumped up when Lana walked into the room and he saw her pale face in the doorway. "Lana, honey. How did you find out? We didn't have a number for you."

Lana blurted out her words. "I called All Roads. He didn't answer his phone or texts from me. He was with me and said he'd come back and he didn't, and I got worried. How is he? What do you know? What happened?"

Eva reached up and took Lana's hand. Lana held her hand momentarily and then sat down next to her.

Angelo then moved over and sat on the other side of her and put his arm around her as he spoke. In a calm and soothing voice, he said, "This is what we know. He was hit by a hit-and-run driver at Front and Pine as he drove into Louisville about one thirty this morning. Someone on Front Street heard the noise of the crash and called police. So I don't think he was lying there in the street for too long. His left leg and arm are broken, and he's in surgery now. He hasn't regained consciousness since the accident. His helmet flew off at some point. His bike is a mangled mess."

Lana remembered that she had seen the helmet unfastened when he'd left her house.

"He's strong, Lana, and I have no doubt that he'll recover from his injuries to his body. I have to be honest. I'm most concerned about his lack of consciousness. Do you have any idea why he was out on that Harley in the middle of the night?"

Although Angelo had the information that she needed, the words that he'd spoken about Roadking's injuries made her hurt all over. To think of him in pain was overwhelming. Her chest ached. Her eyes burned. Lana spoke softly, "Someone, I think Rick, called him about one o'clock and told him that someone had broken windows at All Roads again. Vincent was mad that the place had been vandalized again, and he wanted to go there. I begged him to stay. But he wouldn't. He said he'd come back."

"Oh, I see." Angelo shook his head and placed both hands on his knees. "Yeah, there's been vandalism at All Roads lately and once at our house."

Lana thought about it but didn't mention that the tires on the SS 396 had been slashed at her house too.

Eva did not say a word until she turned to Lana and said, "Honey, he'll be okay. Our son is strong. Send positive thoughts his way. And pray for him."

Lana rarely prayed. She believed that God had kind of left her on her own. But Roadking appeared to have a strong faith. God would listen if she prayed on his behalf. "Do you know where the chapel is here in the hospital?"

"Yes, dear, it's actually close by and on this floor. Down the hall a little way and to your left. There's a sign."

Lana made her way down the hall to the little chapel and sat down on a wooden oak bench. There was no cross at an altar like she had expected. It was clearly meant as a place for which those of any faith could pray. She sat still and quiet and looked around the room for several minutes as she organized her thoughts. Then she folded her hands, and in a whisper, she said, "God, I know I don't turn to you very often. And I should. I'm not praying for myself, but for Vincent. Please bless him and heal him. Help the doctors give him the care he needs to bring him back to me. I'm afraid. Please, God. Please. Amen." Tears rolled down her cheeks and there was a quiver in her voice as she whispered. She felt some relief as she said those words. But as much as she wanted to hold a positive thought for Roadking, there was a nagging feeling in her gut that she couldn't dispel. She wiped away the tears and folded her hands in prayer, looked up to heaven, and returned to the waiting room.

Angelo and Eva were as she had left them. The sun was beginning to rise, and daylight was streaming through the skylight in the room when Roadking's orthopedic surgeon stepped into the room in his blue scrubs. "Mr. and Mrs. Romano?"

"Yes, is it all done?" Angelo spoke. "This is our son's fiancée, Lana."

The surgeon nodded at Lana.

"Yes, his leg was badly broken—the femur and the tibia. We have successfully pinned it in five places. He won't be able to put weight on it for several weeks. His broken arm was set but didn't need surgery according to the x-rays. It was a clean break just below the elbow. We stitched a wound on his cheek and on his forehead. We, of course, sedated him. It remains to be seen if he regains consciousness any time soon. And he'll be in a lot of pain. We're administering pain medication with fluids in the IV. I believe his primary physician has ordered a CAT scan to make sure that nothing has been overlooked."

"How long will he be in recovery?" Lana asked.

"It depends, but I believe he'll be there for a couple of hours. And then he'll be placed in intensive care. You'll have to speak to his primary physician about that."

Lana was relieved that the surgery was over. Now it was just a matter of time before she could see him. She gathered her wits sufficiently to call Miranda, the receptionist at *Boulder Essence*, to tell her about the accident and to say that she might not be in the office on Monday. "Please have one of the assistant editors call me when they come in tomorrow so I can have a word with them. Thanks, Miranda. Yes, I'll take care."

"Let's go get some coffee. Eva? Lana? How about it?"

Lana didn't want to leave the waiting room. She needed to be there as soon as he was moved to a room. But she agreed and the threesome went downstairs to the cafeteria.

"Anyone want any breakfast?" Angelo asked.

Both Eva and Lana replied, "No. Not now."

They each poured themselves some coffee. Angelo bought himself a blueberry muffin. They sat silently. But it wasn't an awkward silence. Each was lost in their own thoughts about Roadking. Angelo and Eva thought about Roadking as a child. Lana thought about her future with him and how much this accident could change things for a while.

Around eight o'clock, Eva said, "It's probably not too early to call Ava and tell her about her dad's accident. Dana and Bianca already know. Dana's at the house taking care of things. Who else should we let know? I can't think."

"I guess we'll figure that out. Well, at some point this morning, we should call the dealership and let them know what's happening with him. Someone will need to keep the place running while he's on the mend. Want me to do that, Eva?" Angelo asked.

"Yes, Ange." Eva left the cafeteria and stepped outside to call Ava. When she returned she said, "It's cold out there. Ava will be here later today. It's finals week at CSU. She's been cramming for exams. I don't know if she'll stay or not. It's bad timing for her. She's upset and maybe seeing her dad will put her mind at rest and she can take the exams. I don't know."

They returned to the waiting room on the second floor for what seemed like days. But a few hours later, a nurse entered to tell them that he had been moved to intensive care and that he was breathing on his own but had not regained consciousness.

"How soon can we see him?" Lana asked.

"Now. Intensive care is on the north side on this floor. Room 210."

"Okay, can we all go in at once?" Angelo asked.

"Yes, but it might be best if there isn't a crowd in the room. The ICU nurses watch the patients very closely."

Lana said, "You two can go in first. Then I'd like to spend a little time with him alone. Is that okay?"

"Sure, Lana. That's okay. Let's all walk over there and find the room."

The threesome found the room and Angelo and Eva went in. Lana peeked into the room as they opened the door and saw Roadking as he lay in bed. His leg and arm were in traction. An oxygen tube was in his nose and an IV had been inserted in his right hand. Just hours before, that great man had been making love to her, talking about tickets to an Eagles concert, and talking about the wedding. She looked away. She needed to get close to him. She sat on a chair near the room and waited. Angelo and Eva emerged from the room after about twenty minutes. Eva made the sign of the cross as she came through the door. Both looked grim, but neither looked devastated. It was a hopeful sign for Lana.

"Your turn, little lady," Angelo said as held the door for Lana.

Lana stepped quietly as she slowly tiptoed into the room as if she would wake him. "Vincent?" she whispered in a voice barely audible as she got closer to the bed. "Vincent? Baby?"

She stood next to him. There was a bandage on his cheek and another on his forehead from wounds that had been stitched. His face was swollen. An oxygen tube ran into his nose and a cardiac monitor was attached to his chest. His left leg was suspended in traction as well as his left arm. An IV was inserted into his right hand to provide him fluids and medication for pain. In her eyes, he was still as handsome as he had been just hours before.

"Baby? I'm here. You need to sleep. I don't want you to feel the pain in your leg and arm. I'm going to stay here with you until you wake up." She leaned over and kissed him on a bare spot on his cheek and laid her hand on top of his head for a moment. She pulled a chair up to the side of the bed and took his right hand in hers and leaned her right cheek against his chest. She could feel him breathe and feel his heart beat. She loved him so much.

She picked up her phone and picked out one of the playlists that they listened to, turned the volume down softly, and laid it on the pillow next to his head. If he could hear it, he would like it. Some of the songs were light rock and others were more raucous. Bob Seger, Eagles, Jason Derulo, Bruno Mars, Elvis. She laid her head back down. *Maybe he'll dream he's dancing with me. I hope he knows I'm here.* She was pleasantly surprised that Angelo and Eva had not come back into the room and had let her have so much time with him.

"Vincent," she whispered. "I've been thinking some about the wedding. I think I'll have purple and white calla lilies in my bouquet. And a few lilies of the valley too." She continued to talk, hoping he could listen even though he couldn't respond. She rested her head once again near his chest and squeezed his hand tenderly—the hand that had been touching her just hours before. "Feel the love," she whispered. She would not let a negative thought enter her head while she was in that room.

An hour went by. Nurses came in and out and checked his vital signs. But they didn't ask her to leave. Soon she heard the door open, and Angelo and Eva walked back into the room, carrying a little boy with curly, dark brown hair and dark green eyes.

"Oh, Lana! We didn't see that you were still here." Eva looked at Angelo. They seemed uncomfortable.

"I was resting my head against Vincent. I guess you couldn't see me. Nothing has changed since I've been here." She turned the music off, picked up her phone, and held it in her hand.

Then the little boy said in a toddler voice, "Hi, Daddy . . . Wake up, Daddy . . . Daddy? It's me. It's Jacob."

Lana looked at Eva and Angelo. Her eyes bulged with surprise, and with a quiver in her voice, she said, "Does Vincent have a little boy?" Her heart sank to her stomach.

"Yes, he does," Eva said quietly.

Lana felt her face flush and she sat back in her chair.

"Why won't he wake up?" Jacob looked at Eva, who was still holding him.

"Daddy got hurt and he needs to sleep to get better. He knows that you're there."

"Excuse me, I'll let you have some time with Vincent." Lana opened the door and stood outside of the room.

As the door closed, she heard Jacob say, "He has Band-Aids."

In her head, over and over, the words repeated, *Why didn't he tell me? Why didn't he trust me enough to tell me?* She turned in a circle, not knowing where to go or what to do. She stepped back into the chapel and sat in the far corner, not wanting to be seen or noticed by anyone. There she could be alone and deal with the emotions she felt until she could sort it out, if she could. So many questions—*Who's his mother, where has he been, why, why, why didn't he tell me?*

"God, please give me strength and understanding right now. I'm confused and hurt. Amen." She suddenly realized that she was in the chapel and prayer would be the right thing at that moment. She couldn't choke back the tears any longer and let them flow where no one would see her.

In a moment, she felt a tap on her shoulder. Angelo stood behind her. She looked up at his kind face.

"Lana, I think it's time that you should know about Jacob. You need to understand. He wants you to know." His voice was gentle.

Lana wiped her eyes and nodded yes as Angelo sat down beside her and took her hand in his and began.

"Vincent was engaged to a woman named Cameron a few years ago."

Lana responded weakly, "Vincent and I ran into her once in Boulder. I saw her. He was uncomfortable when he saw her."

"Well, she became pregnant. She didn't want anything to do with a baby and made arrangements for an abortion. Vincent found out and was devastated. He begged her not to do it. He believed that like with Ava, the child was meant to be theirs. That it came from love. Cameron spouted off the usual stuff like, 'It's my body. It's my right. It's my choice.' Vincent's faith just couldn't allow it to happen. So he devised a plan that he figured she would agree to. Clearly the engagement was over. So he offered to pay her $50,000 if she would have the child, give up her parental rights, and never contact him or the child again. Cameron saw that there was a good thing with this baby and asked for $75,000. Vincent agreed. Cameron gave birth to Jacob and still had no motherly feelings for him. She handed him to Vincent and left with the money and never looked back. So Jacob has been living with Eva and me. He's two and a half now. Vincent couldn't care for an infant and manage the dealership at the same time. But the understanding is that when Jacob is three or four, he'll live with Vincent permanently. Vincent visits him every day. Sometimes he tucks him in bed at night, sometimes he comes by and makes him chocolate chip pancakes for breakfast or eats mac and cheese with him at lunchtime. Eva doesn't know this, but Vincent came to me shortly before he proposed to you and asked me what to do about you and Jacob. His main concern was that he didn't want you to think that he wanted to marry you just so Jacob would have a mother. He wanted to wait until he was certain that you would be okay with the idea of Jacob and what that might entail. He was going to tell you of course. He wanted it to be right. You see, he loves both of you."

Lana listened to every word he said without speaking. Tears continued to flow, but they were tears of love for Vincent and compassion for his son. Angelo put his arm around her and hugged her.

Finally, she softly spoke, "Angelo, that little boy is so precious. I understand now. Of course I'm willing to help Vincent raise him. He is Vincent's son. He's part of Vincent. That's all I need to know."

Angelo reached over and hugged her tightly. "Vincent is right about you. He told me that he found the perfect woman. I believe he has."

Lana dabbed at her eyes. She was embarrassed by so many tears. She didn't want to be one of those weepy-eyed women who had no self-control. But the day was wrought with emotion. "I'm going to stay here in this chapel for a while, Angelo. Thank you for telling me. Can I meet Jacob soon?"

"Of course you will. Eva is probably ready to go. The ICU nurses don't like to allow little children into the ICU rooms. We convinced them somehow to let us bring Jacob in for a minute. We thought that Vincent might respond to him. You should get something to eat."

"I'll think about it." She had forgotten to eat all day. It didn't seem to be important.

Angelo left the chapel.

Lana returned to the ICU room to be with Vincent and began to talk to him again. "Vincent, I know about Jacob now. I'm okay with it. You could have told me. We can talk about it when you wake up. But know that I'll take good care of both of you."

Soon nurses asked Lana to leave so that they could tend to Vincent. Lana could not stay in the hospital any longer. She decided to go to Vincent's house to spend a little time. She knew that he wouldn't mind. He had given her the access codes to the doors. She was wobbly but was able to drive to Louisville. She stepped in the front door of the house. It seemed so big and quiet without Vincent. She sat on the long leather couch where they had spent so much time. She turned the TV on and pulled up the alpaca throw that they sometimes covered themselves with. The scent of Vincent was on the blanket and she held it to her nose. The local news was on.

"In other local news, prominent Louisville businessman Vincent Romano was severely injured in a hit-and-run accident in Louisville early this morning. Romano is the owner of All Roads Harley-Davidson. He was apparently riding a Harley-Davidson in the early morning hours when he was hit by an unknown driver at the intersection of Front and Pine Streets. He was transported to Boulder Community Hospital. No word on his condition at this time. Louisville Police are investigating the accident scene. Apparently, Romano's Harley-Davidson dealership was vandalized just hours before the accident. Surveillance tapes show a lone perpetrator throwing objects through the windows of the dealership. Police are investigating whether there is a connection between the two incidents. More details later on our five o'clock broadcast."

Lana felt numb. The words were so cold and harsh. She turned the TV off and buried her face in the alpaca blanket.

Lana wasn't the only one who had seen the local news. Leon had seen the broadcast too. Since he'd hit Roadking with his van, he had been euphoric, believing that he'd killed him and gotten him out of the way so he could have Lana for himself. He danced around his house singing, "Look What You Made Me Do." When he got home from the hit-and-run, he smoked several joints, poured himself a shot of Jack Daniel's and drank a toast to himself. "Here's to me and my gal!" He couldn't sleep. He was wired with adrenaline. He was certain he had gotten away with it.

"There ain't no evidence. No nothin'." He fixed the headlight on his van, which was not broken but just loosened during the impact with Roadking. The van was not noticeably damaged by the impact. It was already dented and scratched. He was no longer concerned that he would be arrested for Carla's death. It had been several days, and they hadn't come back. "Them bastards are takin' so long cuz they ain't found nothin' in my house. There ain't nothin'."

Now his mood was dampened with the news that Roadking was still alive. "Son of a bitch! He ain't dead yet? I should've run over him too. Damn!" He immediately turned to the monitor app of Lana's house on his phone. She wasn't home. "She's probably by that pretty boy's side. Mebbe he ain't too pretty no more," he snickered and snarled out loud. He noticed, though, that the GPS tracking device on Lana's car showed that she wasn't at the hospital in Boulder but at a location in Louisville. Maybe she had finally given away Roadking's home address. He saved it on his phone. "Hell, I don't need that now. He ain't gonna be there fer a while, if he lives. I'll make her mine now. She ain't gonna want him after she's with me." His laugh was maniacal.

Lana returned to the hospital. And every day thereafter, she spent every moment that she could with Roadking, talking to him, playing music for him, stroking his head, kissing his face, holding his hand. When she wasn't with him, she prayed in the chapel or answered email and messages from the staff at *Boulder Essence*. The assistant editors were so competent, and Lana mapped out the future issues of the magazine so far in advance that she didn't need to be onsite each day to manage assignments. The magazine would publish on schedule, unaffected by her absence.

Sometimes she talked with Roadking's parents about him. They both enjoyed telling her stories about him as he had grown up. Lana wasn't eating, she was losing weight, and she had dark circles under her eyes. His condition drained her. But her only focus was to get Roadking through this so that he could heal and they could begin their lives together.

About a week had gone by and Roadking was still unconscious. A CAT scan and an EEG were performed. Doctors told Lana that there was no brain damage or any other apparent injuries and that there was an eighty percent chance that he would regain full consciousness.

"When will he wake up?" Lana asked.

"We can't know the answer. He'll wake up when he's ready to. His body is healing while he's unconscious. He's not feeling any pain while he's asleep."

Lana brought an issue of *American Iron* to read out loud to Roadking. The music continued to play softly. She hoped that he knew she was there and could hear her. She laid her head on his chest again to feel his breathing. He was still with her. He would come back.

Suddenly, Roadking's body stiffened. Lana lifted her head to look at him. He began to shake violently and then he stopped. No movement. The high pitch of the heart monitor pierced the silence in the room. Lana ran to the door to scream for help just as nurses threw the door open and rushed into the room. Lana backed into the corner of the room and watched in horror as the chaotic scene unfolded. She heard the medical staff running down the hall with the crash cart. They burst into the room. One nurse started CPR. Another nurse placed an oxygen mask on his face. Another ripped open Roadking's hospital gown and applied lubricant to his chest, grabbed the defibrillator and yelled, "Clear!" Everyone stood back while a jolt of electrical current ran through his body, lifting it from the bed. All eyes fell on the heart monitor. It was still a flatline—no heartbeat. The skin on his chest began to turn red from the electrical current that was administered. The nurse tried again. "Clear!" No heartbeat. The attempt was made twice more with no results.

One of the nurses looked at her watch and said, "The patient, Vincent Romano, is pronounced dead at 1:40 p.m."

Lana ran out of the room with her hands over her mouth as she shouted over and over, "Oh my God. Oh my God! Vincent! Oh my

God! Bring him back! Bring him back!" She stood by the door and sobbed uncontrollably.

A nurse came out of the room. "Hon, I'm sorry for your loss. We'll contact his parents. Why don't you sit down over here? The doctor will come by shortly to talk to you." She pointed to a red, upholstered armchair near the door.

Lana sat down and buried her face in her hands. "No, no, no, no! Please—no!" Her stomach lurched like she would be sick, but she had not eaten for days.

Leon was impatient. As each day passed, Leon became more certain that Roadking would survive. He could see on the monitor when Lana was at home that she was sad and suffering and not taking care of herself. Day after day, night after night, he saw her cry or sit quietly alone and stare at the TV when she wasn't at the hospital with Roadking. She quit working out. She isolated herself and would not talk to anyone. Leon didn't like seeing her like that.

"If that bastard died like he was s'posed to, she'd move on to me. She ain't gonna come my way and be my little darlin' as long as he lives." That thought provoked evil ideas in Leon's head. "Mebbe I should pay a visit to that sorry bastard in the hospital. Mebbe he'll just stop breathin'." Leon's demented brain began to cycle through a series of evil scenarios. He began to snicker and realized that murder was getting easy for him. "I'm gonna take care of him now."

Leon got in his dented, green van and drove to Boulder Community Hospital and chain-smoked the entire way. He was determined to put an end to Roadking's life and Lana's pain. He checked the directory as he walked in the door and saw that the intensive care unit was on the second floor. He took the stairs up and then began to walk down the long hallway and followed the signs. He cautiously watched ahead of him for any sign of Lana. He didn't want to run into her there. He steered clear of nurses and hospital personnel. He didn't want to be noticed by any of them.

When Leon turned the corner in the corridor leading to the ICU, he saw Lana standing in the hallway with a doctor and sobbing. She looked small and fragile and alone. She was looking down at her hands. Her shoulders shook.

The doctor spoke quietly to her, looking at her face as he spoke with his hand on her shoulder. "I'm sorry. We did everything we could. His heart stopped. An autopsy will tell us what happened. There was no indication that he would go into cardiac arrest."

Lana's voice was soft and muffled by grief. "Can I . . ." She paused for a few seconds as she sobbed and tried to catch her breath. "Can I go in there and be with him? Please? Can I stay with him?"

"Yes, you can, Lana."

She opened the door as slowly and quietly as she had the first time she'd entered the ICU room. She laid her head on his chest and held his right hand. "Vincent? I'm here again. I'm going to stay with you. I'll stay."

CHAPTER 48

Leon quietly took two steps backward and turned to leave the ICU after he had witnessed the sad scene with Lana and the doctor. He headed for the elevator, pushed the button, and waited for its arrival. When the elevator doors opened, a handsome older man and a small woman stepped out; their faces were grim and pale. Leon surmised that they were Roadking's parents. His state of mind was a tangle of moods—happy that Roadking had died, frustrated that he hadn't been the one to end his life, sympathetic for Lana's pain, and excited and confident that she would want him now. He walked to his van, lit a joint, and laughed out loud to himself. "That pretty boy bastard is gone! He's dead! He's dead!" he shouted while he pounded his fist on his thigh. His mood settled on ecstatic. He knew that he needed to give Lana some space, but in his mind, his pursuit of her had already begun. He restrained himself from any further outburst after passersby in the parking lot of the hospital looked at him with alarm when they witnessed his manic behavior.

Lana continued to rest her head on Roadking's chest, silently waiting and hoping that he would take a breath. She touched his hand. It was still warm. She was shattered and felt pain in her body like nothing she had ever felt before. There were no words in her head to accompany what had just happened. She quietly whispered, "I love you, Vincent. How will I go on without you?" Tears streamed down her face in torrents as she sobbed. "Not yet . . . Not yet . . . It's too soon."

The door to the room opened quietly. Lana lifted her head and turned to see Angelo and Eva there and laid her head down again and continued to sob.

Eva cried out when she saw him lying there. "Angelo—our son! Our beautiful boy! He's gone! Why?"

Lana stood and stepped back to let them come nearer to him. Angelo, with tears streaming down his stoic face, put his arms around her and hugged her. She buried her face in his shoulder and cried. After a few minutes, Lana struggled to catch her breath and whimpered, "I'll let you two be alone with him."

Eva leaned over her son's body and wept loudly. Lana touched her on her shoulder and walked out of the room. Angelo joined his wife to comfort her.

Lana returned to the red, upholstered chair in the hall on which she had sat earlier, leaned forward and rested her elbows on her knees, clasped her hands to her face, and rocked back and forth. Tears continued to fall. "God, how could you let this happen?" She couldn't fathom how she would ever regain control of her emotions. The grief was too much to bear.

After several minutes, Angelo and Eva emerged from the room. Angelo's arm was around Eva as he held her up with each step that they took. His face was wet with tears. Lana managed to stand up.

"They told us that there will be an autopsy and then the mortuary will pick him up and we can make funeral arrangements."

Lana looked at them and weakly said, "Okay. I want to know what to do because I don't know." She tried to pull herself together, but she burst into tears again. "I'll stay here until they take him."

"Okay, honey. We can talk later."

Lana sat on the red, upholstered chair. She was so alone. No one could help her. She couldn't bear to call anyone and say the words "he's dead." She had to be alone for now. She stared at the floor. Tears began to subside as if there were none left. Her insides were empty. Her mind was numb. Her heart was shattered. Her body ached with grief. Soon orderlies entered the room, covered Roadking with a white sheet, and wheeled his body out of the room and down a long hallway away from Lana. She quietly whispered to them, "Take care of him."

An ICU nurse approached her with a bag and a manila envelope containing Roadking's personal effects. "Here, hon, these are Mr. Romano's things. Can I give them to you?"

"Yes," Lana weakly nodded and took them from the nurse. She clutched the bag to her chest for a moment and stood and steadied herself and began the long walk to the parking lot. She got inside her car but didn't know where to go or what to do.

Roadking had been alive when she'd arrived earlier. Now as she drove out of the parking lot, she felt compelled to drive to Roadking's house. She was barely conscious of driving the car as thoughts of Roadking's last moments circulated over and over in her head. She held her breath each time she visualized the heart attack.

Lana somehow remembered the access code to the front door and entered. She brought the bag of Roadking's things in with her and set it on the couch. She stood in the great marble entryway for a long moment and looked around at the empty house that he would never set foot in again. She smelled his subtle scent as she walked through the living room. She was suddenly light-headed and braced herself on the back of one of the leather sofas so she wouldn't faint. She knew that she needed some food. She entered the kitchen, opened the refrigerator, and took out some orange juice to drink. She opened a cabinet and found some whole wheat crackers to eat. She sat down at the dining room table in the silent house and forced herself to eat and drink. She felt slightly better.

She went upstairs to Roadking's bedroom. She immediately noticed that there was a new silver-framed photo on his dresser—one that had been taken the night they were engaged—that joined the framed photos taken in Trinidad in front of the SS 396 at the bed-and-breakfast and at the art gallery opening. Tears began to lightly fall as she relived those precious moments with him. They must have been special to him too. She walked into the bathroom and wet a washcloth with cold water to lay on her swollen eyes.

Roadking had tossed a black Harley-Davidson polo shirt on the bed that he had probably worn before their last day together. She picked it up and held it to her nose. His scent was still alive. She clutched it to her chest and rocked back and forth. Tears dripped down her face and onto the shirt. She lay down on the bed, still clutching the shirt and embraced one of the pillows that he slept on. She curled up on her side, held the shirt and the pillow, laid the cold washcloth on her face, and closed her eyes. She couldn't sleep and didn't intend to. Since she was away from the stark, glaring reality of the hospital, she was able to think. She thought about their time together, how quickly it was over, how much she loved him, how much she would miss him, how her life was forever changed, and about Jacob. She thought about God and how he didn't listen to her when she had prayed for Roadking. She was right; God had left her on her own. It had always been that way.

Lana continued to lay curled up on Roadking's bed for the rest of the afternoon. The room grew dark as the sun set. She closed her eyes again and hoped for a little sleep. The shock of Roadking's death would not allow her to sleep. For a moment, she felt the subtle warmth of a gentle hand rest lightly on the top of her head. *Am I dreaming?* The warm sensation emanated from the top of her head through her body to her toes. She turned her head ever so slightly to look around the darkened room. No one was there. Then in her mind, she heard unspoken words. *It'll be alright. You'll be alright.* The hand that rested on her head lifted. *Who spoke to me? Vincent? Jesus? Was it a hallucination?* Whoever or whatever it was, it provided her with some comfort and a little strength. Her body relaxed, and she fell asleep for a few hours.

Leon was still in a high mood as he left the hospital. He headed to Red's Bar to celebrate Roadking's death and Lana's unattachment. It was early afternoon and some of the regulars were already propped on their barstools.

"Hey, you assholes! Don't any of ya do nothin' but sit here?" he shouted as he walked in the door.

"Hey, Alvarez! Done fer the day. Hey, we ain't seen ya fer a while. Where ya been hangin'? Got a new lay out there keepin' ya busy?" one of them hollered back.

"Naw, been hangin' low. Not like you jerkoffs, I have to work. Robinson, a shot of Jack and a draft over here!" Leon plopped down on one of the barstools. "Send some of them pretzels down this way! So what's new in this dump?"

"Them cops keep comin' around here askin' about Carla. We don't know nothin'. Ain't seen them for a week. Must of give up. Dumb broad just fell off a mountain. Why the hell would any of us know about that shit?" said Padilla, who was sitting next to Leon at the bar.

Leon said nothing about the search of his house. But he agreed with Padilla. They didn't find anything or they would have come back. "Hey, ya know what, Robinson? I'm in a generous mood. A round of drinks for all these dumb bastards?"

"Did ya hit the lottery or somethin'?" one of them yelled.

"Naw—well, kinda." Leon smirked to himself. He spent the rest of the afternoon drinking beer, smoking joints and cigarettes in his van, and playing pool. Once again, he caught the local evening news.

"Prominent local businessman Vincent Romano passed away early this afternoon at Boulder Community Hospital. As of our broadcast, an autopsy had not yet been performed, but a spokesman at the hospital indicated that Romano succumbed to injuries he'd received in a hit-and-run accident eight days ago in Louisville when he was responding to an early morning vandalism incident at his business, All Roads Harley-Davidson. Police continue to investigate the accident and have not yet identified a hit-and-run suspect. Funeral arrangements are pending. Romano is survived by his parents, two sisters, a daughter, and a son—all from Louisville, and a fiancée from Columbine Point. We'll continue to update this story as it develops."

Leon grinned. He knew all about it. *Dumb-ass police. They won't never figger it out cuz I'm good.* Killing Roadking had been so much easier than it had been to kill Carla. There was no battle with his conscience. His reward for killing Roadking was Lana. He would give her a little time before he asked her to marry him. He checked the monitor of her house several times. She still wasn't home. The GPS tracker showed that her car was in Louisville. "That's okay. She ain't with him." His saggy, red eyes flickered as he sneered to himself.

"Did ya say somethin', Alvarez?" one of the barstool residents asked.

"Naw, dumb-ass, yer hearin' things."

Lana awoke before sunrise. She had slept restlessly throughout the night with fragmented dreams of Roadking. He was still alive in her dreams. When she woke up, reality jolted her once again. Somewhere deep inside her chest was pain. She lay on her back and held her left hand up above her face. The diamond ring sparkled slightly from light that filtered in the window from the neighbor's yard light. "I won't ever take this ring off, Vincent. I belong to you." The silver bracelet that he had given her slid up her arm. She touched it with her right hand and turned over and pulled Roadking's black Harley shirt up to her face and then closed her eyes and waited for daylight.

When the sun rose, she took her phone out of her purse. There were missed calls from Olivia, coworkers, and from Angelo Romano. She wasn't ready to call her mom and dad yet and doubted that they would have heard about Roadking's death on the local news where they lived. She would wait until eight or nine to return Angelo's call. She decided to take a shower. As she undressed in the recessed light of the master bathroom, she caught a glimpse of herself in the mirror. Her eyes were puffy with dark circles beneath them. Her body had shrunken and was bordering on emaciated—little breasts and bony shoulders and arms. She showered and washed her hair with Roadking's shampoo. She found the clothes that she had brought to Roadking's house in case of an impromptu sleepover and dressed. She didn't bother with makeup. Her hair was hanging in wet strands. She decided to eat something to gain the strength she needed to make some phone calls. She went downstairs. The house was still and solemn without Roadking. Tears began to fall again. She swallowed hard and clenched her jaw to practice controlling them. She poured orange juice, took some bread from the freezer, and made toast. She drizzled honey on the toast and sprinkled chia seeds on it. She forced herself to eat one piece. Roadking would want her to take care of herself and she should try.

"Hi, Angelo. It's me, Lana. I see you called yesterday. I'm sorry I missed your call." Lana voice was quiet.

"Yes, honey, I did." His voice was gentle. "We wanted to let you know about the autopsy results. A blood clot evidently traveled to Vincent's heart, possibly from his leg, and caused the heart attack." Lana was silent. "Are you still there, Lana?"

"Yes," she whispered quietly.

"Eva and I met with the priest at our church, St. Louis Catholic, and the funeral is tentatively scheduled for Friday, which means there will be Rosary on Wednesday and a vigil on Thursday at the church. We've been working with the mortuary. The Romanos have a family plot at Louisville Cemetery. Vincent will be buried there." Angelo's voice cracked when he mentioned the burial.

"Okay. But I'm not Catholic. Can I be a part of all of it?"

"Yes, we want you there. You were going to be his wife."

Her throat ached. She gritted her teeth and tried not to cry. "Thank you. I don't know if I can be of any help, but please ask if you need anything."

"Yes, honey, we'll talk soon."

She gathered all her strength and dialed her dad. "Dad, I have some sad news. I just have to say it, I guess. Vincent, my fiancée, died yesterday. He was in a hit-and-run motorcycle accident a week ago. He had a heart attack from a blood clot, possibly from his broken leg. He never regained consciousness, but the doctors were hopeful and then this happened." She tried to not to cry, but saying the words that she had to say were so painful.

"Oh no, baby. I'm so sorry. Are you okay? You were so happy. Do they know anything about the accident?"

"No, I'm not okay. It's so unfair. I have to get through this. No, there's no news about the hit-and-run. The funeral is Friday. He'll be buried in the Louisville cemetery."

"I'm just so sorry. Do you need me to come? I don't know if I can make it for a funeral. I don't really know that family."

"The funeral—it's up to you. I don't expect it. But I would like to see you, Dad, sometime soon. Love you."

"Love you, too, honey. I'm so sorry. I'm here if you need to talk."

Lana dialed her mom—the call she dreaded. She repeated the exact words to her that she had said to her dad. "Oh, well, that's a tragedy," her mom said.

"Yes, it is and I'm really hurting now, Mom. I really loved him and he's gone."

Lana's mother heard Lana's voice shake with emotion and she responded, "I'm so sorry. Time will take care of it."

"I don't expect you to come up here from Durango, but I'd like to see you soon—"

Her mom interrupted her. "We'll see. You know the holidays are coming up and I've made some plans already."

"Okay, well, I wanted to tell you about Vincent. And I won't be getting married to him now." Tears rolled down her cheeks as she heard herself say those words. "Bye, Mom. Talk soon."

"Yes, you take care now. Be strong."

Lana's grief became intertwined with her lifelong disappointment at her mother's emotional unavailability and chronic disinterest of her. Her heart ached. *Well, I should have expected that*, she thought.

When she looked up, she saw the bag from the hospital that contained Vincent's belongings that she had left on the couch. She walked over and peeked inside and saw his torn and bloodstained clothes. She couldn't bear to take them out of the bag. But she opened the small manila envelope that contained his wallet and belt and the Saint Christopher medal. She took the medal out, read the words inscribed to him, clutched it in her hand, and held it up to her chest. "Oh, baby, Saint Christopher didn't protect you this time. But I want you to have it and take it with you," she whispered to him.

In a moment, Angelo called. She was still clutching the medal as they spoke. "The funeral services have been arranged for Vincent." His voice cracked as he spoke and there was a brief silence as he regained his composure. "There will be Rosary for him at seven o'clock on Wednesday, a vigil at seven o'clock on Thursday, and the funeral will be at two o'clock on Friday. All the services will be at the St. Louis Catholic Church here in Louisville. Do you know where that is?"

"Yes, I can find it. I'll be there."

"Eva and I know that Vincent would want you to be a part of all of it. You'll sit with the family and ride with the family to the cemetery for burial. We have a family plot at the Louisville cemetery. After the burial, there will be a reception in Vincent's honor at the church."

"Angelo, when you pick out his clothes, could you choose a light blue shirt for him? He looked so good in that color."

"Yes, I think that would be perfect. Eva is kind of in charge of picking his clothes and will be stopping by his house later today to get his black suit. I'll mention it to her."

"Okay, so is there anything I can help with or need to do? Please let me. I feel like I need to do something."

"We'll let you know. Otherwise, we plan on seeing you at the church tomorrow evening before seven."

"Thank you, Angelo." Lana sighed a deep breath. She was all cried out.

She decided that it was time to go home, especially since Vincent's parents would be coming to get clothes for him. She just didn't want to be there. She slipped the Saint Christopher medal into a pocket in her purse. She grabbed the black Harley shirt and one of his bed pillows to take home with her and slipped out the front door.

As she drove home, she called Olivia. She had heard the news about Vincent and had been calling and texting Lana. Now that Lana had composed herself, she could call.

"My God, Lana. How are you holding up?"

"I'm not. I don't know. I'm crushed. And I'm numb."

"Do you need me to come over? I didn't know Vincent, but should I come to the funeral? I don't know what to do for you. This is so sad. I feel so sad for you, Lana."

"I know. If you come to the funeral, it would be for me. My parents aren't coming. Vincent comes from a large, extended family and had so many friends, so there will be a crowd. You decide what would be best for you."

She rolled into her driveway and into the garage. She walked into the quiet, empty house where she had last seen Vincent alive and where she had slept with him for the last time. For a moment, she hated her house and hated being there. *Why didn't I do more to stop him from leaving? Why didn't I make him fasten the strap on his helmet? Maybe if I could have kept him there another minute or two, the collision in Louisville wouldn't have happened.*

She sat down on the couch, clutched the Harley shirt, and called her office. She needed to touch base with her staff. She was assured that everything was running smoothly in her absence.

"Miranda, I'm coming by the office tomorrow for a couple of hours. I'll be there about ten o'clock in case anyone wants to meet with me. I need to get back on track somehow."

She called the florist and ordered a large bouquet of purple and white calla lilies from her for the funeral. *The flowers I'd planned to carry in my wedding bouquet.*

"We'll have to have the calla lilies flown in. They're not in season right now. There will be an extra charge. And how would you like the card to read, Ms. Ross?"

"Fly them in. The arrangement needs to be delivered to the St. Louis Catholic Church tomorrow for the Rosary at seven o'clock. Just write, 'With love, Lana'." There was a litany of things that she thought of to include on the card, but she kept it simple.

She went upstairs to her closet and began to pick out clothing for each of the three services—a navy blue dress for the Rosary, a gray wool dress for the vigil, and a plain, black dress with a black leather collar for the funeral. She sat on the edge of the bed for a moment and then lay on her back with her arm resting across her forehead to think. She remembered the last night that they had been together in the very bed she now lay on. She remembered how and where he had touched her, how and where she had kissed him, the way he'd felt, the way he'd looked at her, and the way he had loved her. She had lost so much. She realized that she would never have a child with him—a baby that would have been conceived out of that great love they had shared, a baby that would have been blessed with their devotion all its life. Tears started to fall again. Unanswered questions swirled through her mind. *Why did this have to happen? Who hit him? Why didn't God protect him? How will I ever get through this? What do I do next? What is left for me?*

Leon watched the scene unfold. Lana, with her great grief and pain, gave him a little pang of guilt. He was, after all, responsible for Vincent's death. He whispered to the monitor as he watched her, "Little gal, I'm gonna make ya feel all better," he smirked as he thought of what he would do to her. "It's my turn now and nothin' will stop me this time."

CHAPTER 49

It had snowed during the night, but the roads were clear as Lana drove to Louisville for the Rosary service. She had gone to the *Boulder Essence* office that morning; at least she had made an appearance and tried to be present during short meetings with her staff. She felt confident that everything was as it should be and planned to return to work the following Monday. There was a dull ache in her chest that would not go away. It felt like a hollow emptiness that could implode and suffocate her.

She arrived at St. Louis Catholic Church in Louisville at a quarter to seven and quietly stepped inside. Family and friends began to assemble in the church for the rosary prayers. Roadking's casket was displayed in a separate room from the chapel. Some people were gathered near it, talking quietly among themselves. Lana slipped inside the room to catch a glimpse. She wasn't sure if she wanted to get close yet or not. She would try to be brave, but she didn't know if she could. But as she approached the casket, people stepped away. And there he was—as handsome as he ever was, with a cut on his cheek and one on his forehead from the accident. His beautiful eyes with the long, dark eyelashes were closed. He was wearing a light blue shirt like she had requested of Angelo, a black suit, and a royal blue silk tie. His hands were clasped across his chest, holding a set of blue rosary beads. She longed to touch him. She longed for him to sit up. She longed for it to be a bad dream. She reached into the side pocket of her purse and pulled out the Saint Christopher medal and held it in her hand for a minute. Then she kissed it and slipped it into the pocket of his suit jacket. "Take this with you as you go, baby," she whispered. She laid her right hand on his clasped hand that held the rosary beads and kissed him on his cheek as tears rolled down hers. The warmth and energy she knew from his touch were gone.

She stayed with him until she regained her composure. At a few minutes before seven, she entered the chapel. There were several colorful funeral sprays and large bouquets of flowers at the front near the altar. She saw Eva and Angelo seated in the front row, talking to an elderly couple. Lana realized that she had not met any of his family and only a few of his friends and did not want to interrupt. When the older couple stepped away to find a seat, Lana approached them. Both Eva and Angelo stood and hugged her.

"The flowers you sent are quite beautiful, Lana. Calla lilies in December? How did you find them?" Eva asked.

"I asked the florist to special order them. Those were to be the flowers in my wedding bouquet."

Eva's eyes filled with tears and she sat down. She took Lana's hand and gently said, "Here, be seated next to me."

The church began to fill with family and friends. Lana turned to look behind them and recognized Rick from All Roads and Tim from the restaurant where Roadking had proposed to her. Ava sat next to Angelo and leaned on his arm. Roadking's sisters sat in the row behind them with several children of all ages. At precisely seven o'clock, the pallbearers brought the casket into the church and placed it in front of the altar.

The priest began the series of rosary prayers. "Hail, Mary, full of grace . . ." Since Lana was not Catholic, she did not know the rosary prayers, but she sat with her hands in her lap and prayed silently with them. She prayed that God would bless him and that she would see him again in heaven. His faith was strong and it would have become a part of their lives together. She wanted that too. The rosary service was finished after about forty-five minutes.

As Angelo and Eva stood, friends of Vincent and the family approached them to express their sympathy. Angelo and Eva became involved in conversation with them. Lana knew no one. She backed out of the pew and slipped toward the back of the church. There was a pew in the entryway and she sat down and watched mourners as they filtered out of the church, quietly chatting among themselves. She knew that there would be opportunities to meet them at the vigil or the reception following the funeral. She was also afraid that she would cry if anyone spoke to her about Roadking.

Lana felt someone sit down next to her on the bench. It was Angelo and he held little Jacob. "Lana, here's the little guy that you wanted to meet. Jacob, say hi to Lana."

"Hi, Lala."

Lana smiled. "I'm Lana."

"Nala," Jacob said.

Lana laughed, "I guess that will do. You know, Nala is a Disney lioness."

Jacob's eyes were crinkly like Vincent's when he smiled, and his dark, wavy hair was like his dad's, too, absent the silver strands. He wore a button-down, white shirt with a little, blue bow tie and gray pants with blue suspenders. Angelo set Jacob down. He stood in front of Lana. She reached slowly and tenderly and took his little right hand in hers.

"I'm happy to know you, Jacob."

He let her hold his little hand and looked steadily into her face and said, "When Daddy wakes up, he's going to live at heaven."

Lana felt a lump in her throat as big as an orange and began to tear up, as did Angelo. "Yes, he will." She wouldn't say any more than he could understand. She held her breath for a few seconds and didn't cry.

A man approached and Angelo began to talk to him, leaving Jacob with Lana.

"I have cars." Jacob was holding a little, red Hot Wheels car in his left hand. He held it up to show her.

"That's a good one," Lana said. "Can I see it?"

Jacob handed it to her. Lana held it in the palm of her hand and said, "I can see it's a fast one too."

"Yeah, it is," Jacob squealed. He took the car from Lana's hand. He continued to gaze at her face.

Eva made her way out of the chapel and approached Lana and Jacob. "I see you met Vincent's little boy."

"Yes, he is precious. He resembles Vincent so much."

Eva looked at Jacob for several seconds before she spoke quietly. "Yes, he does. In many ways. He's a blessing. Jacob, we need to go home and get you to bed."

"Bye, Jacob. I liked your red car."

"Okay. Bye-bye," he said as Eva took his hand.

Eva hugged Lana. "I'm happy you were here with us."

"I'm honored." The lump in Lana's throat returned and she strained to speak. "I'll see you at the vigil tomorrow night."

Eva nodded and picked up Jacob and walked toward the coatrack to gather her and Jacob's coats. Jacob watched Lana over Eva's shoulder as Eva carried him. Lana waved to him and he waved back. Lana stood to leave. Angelo was still standing near her, talking to an older couple.

She walked over and touched his sleeve and quietly said, "I'll be going now. I'll be here for the vigil tomorrow night. Goodbye, Angelo."

He turned and hugged her lightly.

While Lana drove out of the church parking lot, she thought about the intense devotion for Roadking and the strong faith she had witnessed at the Rosary service and how it had been such an important part of Vincent's life. He had only touched on it with her. She thought about Jacob, the beacon of light in the dark tragedy of his daddy's death. She would have loved to be a mom to him and any other little ones who may have blessed their lives. They would have been happy. She let the tears flow. They were private tears from a heart so badly broken.

On Thursday morning, Lana looked at the *Daily Camera* obituaries to see if an obituary had been published about Roadking yet.

Vincent Angelo Romano, 40, passed away on December 14 as a result of injuries incurred in a motorcycle accident on December 8. He was born to Angelo and Eva Romano on November 29, in Louisville, Colorado. Vincent attended parochial schools in his elementary and middle school years. He was a graduate of Boulder High School, where he played as a quarterback. He was selected to All State in his senior year. He continued his successful football career as a quarterback for the CU Buffs at the University of Colorado, where he earned a BS in Business Management. Shortly after graduation, he opened a Harley-Davidson dealership, All Roads Harley-Davidson, in Louisville. He enjoyed the Harley business and loved riding his classic Road King. He was fond of classic cars, classic rock and roll, and playing golf. Vincent was a man with a generous heart, often hosting fund-raisers for various local causes, especially those for military veterans. For the past 15 years, he sponsored an annual charity golf tournament to raise funds for the Wounded Warriors Project. He was a member of the Catholic faith. He is survived by his parents, Angelo and Eva Romano, two sisters, Dana and Bianca, and their families, a daughter, Ava, and a son, Jacob, all of Louisville, and his fiancée, Lana Ross, of Columbine Point. A Rosary service was held last night. A vigil will be held tonight, December 17 at 7:00 p.m. at St. Louis Catholic Church, 902 Grant Avenue in Louisville. The funeral will be Friday, December 18 at 2:00 p.m. at St. Louis Catholic Church. Burial will take place at the Louisville Cemetery. A reception will be held at the St. Louis Catholic church immediately following the burial. Memorial contributions may be made in his memory to the St. Louis Catholic Church, the Wounded Warriors Project, or a charity of your choice.

The words written seemed so detached and indifferent. They didn't even begin to convey the personality of the man she knew. But in truth, there were no words that could adequately describe him, and perhaps the obituary said just what needed to be said about him.

Lana did not plan to return to work at her office until the next week. She was maintaining contact with her staff and directing them the best that she could under the circumstances. She was fortunate that they were competent enough to see that the magazine maintained the schedule she had set forth before the accident.

Leon watched Lana through the monitor app after she returned home from Roadking's house. There wasn't very much to see. She seemed lifeless. Most of the time, she sat wrapped in the alpaca blanket with the TV on, staring straight ahead—sometimes crying, other times no expression at all. She spent more time than usual curled up in a ball in her bed, clutching a pillow. There was no dancing around the house, no working out, no movement from room to room, no prancing around in undies or less.

"I guess I gotta give her a couple of days to get over that bastard." He thought about the engagement ring that he had bought for her. "I wonder how long I gotta wait to give it to her," he mused out loud with no question in his mind that she would say anything other than yes. "I don't want no other pretty boy to come swoopin' in and grab her up again."

Lana began to get dressed for the vigil service. The gray wool dress that usually hugged her little figure hung on her and made her look gaunt. She decided to wear a black wool blazer over it. At a little after six o'clock, she drove to the church. The parking lot was even fuller than it had been for the Rosary. She had googled the vigil service, not knowing for sure what it was. She had learned that it was a wake that consisted of a short service directed by the priest and was the opportunity for family members and friends to visit the family of the deceased and to express their sympathy and share remembrances.

When she entered the church, a large group of people were standing in the entryway. Since she knew only Angelo and Eva, who were surrounded by people, she waited a minute or two before she approached them.

"Hello, Lana," Eva said when she saw her. "Please join us again for the service. There are many people I want to introduce you to after the service. You haven't met this big family yet."

Lana nodded and stood by Eva until they filed into the church.

Roadking's casket was once again at the front of the church. She had not noticed before that the satin lining of the casket was light blue like the shirt he wore.

There he is. There's the man I was to marry. The man I love so much. Oh, Vincent, I'm having a tough time. Give me some strength tonight, she silently appealed to him.

The vigil service began. Roadking's sixteen-year-old nephew—Dana's son Ben—delivered the scripture reading. Ecclesiastes 3:1-8. "To every thing there is a season, and a time to every purpose under the heaven. A time to be born, and a time to die . . ." His voice cracked once or twice as he read it. There were prayers for mercy and strength, for faith and hope, for comfort and support. Lana listened to them and wanted to believe that prayer would work for her. But the pain was still so acute.

When the service was over, mourners passed by Roadking's body to pay their respects and then filed into the visitation room to meet with the family. The procession of people was a blur in Lana's mind. There were so many—a testament to the number of people his life had touched.

"Go ahead of me," Lana told Angelo and Eva. Lana wanted to be last. She wanted to spend time with him and not feel rushed by a line of people waiting for their turn.

Lana heard Eva tell someone that the rosary beads that Roadking held in his hands were from the Grotto of Lourdes in France and depicted Saint Bernadette and the Virgin Mary. Eva had given them to him when he had been confirmed. Lana didn't know what the significance of all of that was, but she made a mental note of it to google it someday.

She entered the Visitation Room last. She saw Ava.

"Hello, Ava. Do you remember me?" Lana hugged her.

"Of course, Lana. Dad was so happy when he told me about your engagement. I'm so sorry, Lana."

"Oh, Ava. I'm so sorry about your dad. I was so happy about the engagement too. I miss him so much." Lana struggled to remain stoic and to find words.

"Let me see the ring." Lana held out her left hand with the beautiful, solitary diamond ring.

"Dad picked a beautiful ring for you." Ava held her hand while she looked at it. Her chin began to quiver and tears welled in her eyes.

"Yes, he did. He surprised me with it." Lana tried to smile.

"I know. He told me all about it. He was so excited."

Eva approached them with her two daughters. "Lana, I don't believe you've met Vincent's sisters. This is Dana. She's married to Will; he's over there I think. Yes, that's him. Ben, who did the scripture reading, is her son. She also has twin boys—Gabriel and Dominic, who are ten—and a little girl, Nina, who's three. She and Jacob are good buddies."

"I'm pleased to meet you, Dana."

Dana hugged her. Dana was tall and thin with long, very dark, wavy hair and deep brown eyes. There was a smattering of freckles on her nose and cheeks that gave her a youthful appearance. "Lana, I wish you had met this large family under different circumstances."

Eva continued. "And this is Bianca. Her husband is Jason—standing over there with my brother. They have four children as well. Two boys—Dante, who's twelve, and Davis, who's nine—and two girls—Mara, who's six, and Cristina, who's four."

"Hello, Bianca. Oh my gosh. You both have your hands full."

Bianca was short like Eva with blonde, chin-length hair and green eyes. She had a very definite dimple in the middle of her chin. Bianca smiled for a second. "It's nice to meet you. Yes, we do. Having the kids right now is helping us deal with Vincent's death. Taking care of them keeps us occupied. We have no choice but to keep going." She became serious and looked at the floor.

Lana hugged her and struggled not to cry. "I don't see Jacob here," Lana said and turned to Eva.

"No, it's a bit too much for the little guy. It disrupts his routine. But he'll be at the funeral tomorrow. I don't want him to be over-tired for it."

Soon Lana was introduced to brothers and sisters of Eva and

Angelo, a myriad of nieces and nephews and cousins, most all of them with beautiful Italian and Spanish names. Lana would never remember them all. She wished that she had met them before the accident. She was a stranger to them. But they welcomed her with open arms. They asked her about the magazine, about her family, about her childhood, and about how she met Roadking, and they intertwined their own recollections of him. She saw the stark contrast to her own family—a mom and dad with no desire for a real connection to her.

Before Lana left, she slipped back into the chapel by herself and approached the casket and whispered to Roadking, "I met them. Maybe all of them. You were right. That's a big and overwhelming family. You were lucky to have them. I'm leaving now, but I wanted to say, 'Good night'. I love you, Vincent." She kissed him on his forehead and touched her hand to his mouth. She felt the tickle of his mustache on her fingers. As hard as she tried, she could not stop the tears from falling and dripping on the interior satin of the coffin. She slipped out of the church unnoticed and drove home.

On Friday morning, Miranda from *Boulder Essence* called Lana to tell her that several bouquets of flowers of condolences had been delivered to her office. Lana told her to display some throughout the office and put the rest on her desk. She planned to return to work on Monday and would have a look at them then.

"Some of us are coming to the funeral tomorrow to be with you. How are you doing?"

"I appreciate that. I'm in a fog. I'm trying hard."

As the morning progressed, Lana forced herself to drink some orange juice and eat two pieces of toast with peanut butter on them. She began to dress in the black dress with the black leather collar, black tights, black flats, and a pearl necklace and earrings. But as she drove through Columbine Point on the way to the funeral, she stopped at a Target store and quickly purchased a couple of Hot Wheels cars for Jacob, in case she got to spend some time with him.

She arrived at St. Louis Catholic Church about one thirty. The parking lot was not only full of cars already, but there were at least a hundred motorcycles parked there and more continued to pull in. She squeezed into the church and signed the guest book and picked up a memory pamphlet.

Rick from All Roads stood near the door. "Hi, Lana. How are you handling everything?" He hugged her and looked directly into her face for the answer.

"I'm numb. Not good. How are things going at All Roads?"

"Oh, it's going on for the moment without him. Angelo has kind of stepped in to manage the place. People have been showing up daily with condolences and their own recollections about him. Somebody organized Harley riders that were customers and friends and those from his riding groups to honor him. They'll be in the procession to the cemetery. Roadking will be amused looking down from heaven at the whole scene."

"I saw all the bikes outside. That's a beautiful tribute to him. He deserves so much."

"Yes, he was the best." Rick looked down at his feet.

Family members took their seats in the front pews. Lana was seated next to Ava and Eva.

Jacob was sitting on Eva's lap. "Nala," he said when he saw her.

She touched his little nose with her finger. Lana turned to look behind her. The church was full of mourners. The front of the church was covered with flowers of every color in sympathy. Lana's flowers remained toward the front of the display.

The priest began his walk up the center aisle of the church and sprinkled holy water as he walked. When he arrived at the altar, Roadking's cousin Gina, who was a student at the Juilliard School of Music, sang "Amazing Grace." Her soprano voice was polished and serene. The priest began with opening prayers of mercy and prayers that Roadking's soul would rise to heaven. Lana believed that he was already there. There were scripture readings from the Bible. Lana's mind wandered. The scripture readings were listed in the pamphlet. She would read them again to herself later. The priest began a sermon about life and the end of life, entrance into heaven, and how this was Roadking's journey.

At this point, Gina returned to sing "Ave Maria" so beautifully and with such clarity that many of the mourners cried. The procession began for Holy Communion.

Eva whispered quickly to Lana, "Cross your arms over your chest and bow your head. The priest will bless you."

The family proceeded to the front of the church. Lana followed the instructions that Eva had given her and was blessed. The communion procession was long with so many mourners.

When Communion was finished, the Elvis Presley version of "How Great Thou Art" was played. The priest sprinkled holy water on the casket and blessed Roadking. He lit some incense and placed it in a gold incense burner hooked to a chain. As he prayed, he waved the incense burner over the casket. The distinct smell of the incense wafted over the pews.

When the Mass ended, each aisle of mourners was escorted past the family to express their condolences. Many wanted to look at Lana's ring. Jacob began to get impatient. Lana pulled one of the Hot Wheels cars out of her purse and showed it to him. Eva put him down and let him stand by Lana, who held his hand. She managed to keep him occupied until the family was escorted to the limousines for the drive to the cemetery. The pallbearers—who were Vincent's cousins and uncles—closed the casket, covered it with a blanket of red and white roses, pushed it to the hearse, and loaded it for the funeral procession to the cemetery site. Lana suddenly realized that she had just seen Vincent for the very last time here on earth. She sobbed quietly as she slid into the limousine.

The hearse and the limousines made a wide loop to the Louisville cemetery to allow for the long motorcycle procession. The hearse, followed by the limousines, then the motorcycles, and then the cars, drove through Louisville to South Boulder Road, made a right turn on Courtesy Road and proceeded to Highway 42 and the south entrance to the cemetery. It was an impressive sight to see the parade of motorcycles carrying riders who cared so much about Roadking. Lana could hear the vibrating rumble of the many motorcycles behind them. There were police escorts and traffic was stopped for the procession. The hearse and limos pulled into the cemetery driveway. A tent had been set up over the grave with folding chairs for the family to sit on. Motorcycles and cars continued to pour into the little cemetery; many of them parked along the roads on each side.

The priest began the rite of committal. "The body that lies before us is but the earthly tabernacle, the house in which Vincent Romano lived among us for a time. Tenderly and reverently, we commit that house to the grave and to God, who gave it, waiting for the day when both the spirit and the body shall again be united at the coming of the Lord. In Jesus's name, amen."

After the final prayer, the priest sprinkled holy water on the casket. He announced that a reception would be held at the church upon the return from the burial. Mourners began to slowly move out of the cemetery.

Lana walked over to the casket and touched the lid with both of her hands. "I won't say goodbye. I know I won't see you, but I believe you'll stay with me and watch over me. I will always love you, Vincent. Rest in peace." She bent over and kissed the casket and looked to the sky.

Angelo, who stood near her, walked over to her. Tears ran down his cheeks. He held out his arms and hugged her while she sobbed. He could see that she was alone—no family there with her—and she needed somebody to hold her up at that moment. She regained her composure, and in a moment, Lana's coworkers and Olivia walked up to Lana and hugged her.

"Are you returning to the church for the reception?" Lana asked them. Her coworkers said no, but Olivia said that she would be there. "Thank you so much."

"Of course, Lana, you have been through so much."

Lana turned to walk back to the limousine, and as she looked at the crowd, she thought that she saw Leon Alvarez mixed in among the mourners a short distance away. The crowd moved and she could no longer see him. When she looked a second time, she thought that she saw his head with the greasy, stringy hair and the long grizzled beard and mustache. There would be no reason for him to be here. Maybe someone resembled him. It didn't matter anyway.

Leon was indeed there. He had come to the funeral unnoticed. There were so many people. He had sneaked out of the funeral service early to find an ideal spot in the cemetery to watch the burial without being spotted. The cemetery plot had been dug and was ready for the casket. The plot was in the old part of the cemetery where there were well-established, broad trees and bushes—places to hide. He had parked on the side of the road and walked in and waited. When the funeral procession had begun to proceed into the cemetery, he could see the direction in which the people would face and found a spot near a peony bush behind all of them. He had seen his darlin' Lana get out of the limousine. She had looked so sad and small.

"Just get that jerk in the ground and I'll fix that little gal up." He was so deranged that he believed he could step into Roadking's shoes, that she would want him, and that she would be happy with him. He had already killed for her. That was real love in his eyes. The song "Look What You Made Me Do" was stuck in his head. Even the music of the funeral couldn't wipe it out. It had become his anthem for his darlin' Lana. He waited impatiently for all the people to leave the cemetery. When it looked like the last car and motorcycle were gone, he walked over to the cemetery plot. The casket was still suspended over the grave and rested on straps. He was going to spit on the grave, but just as he stood right in front of it, a cemetery caretaker walked up and said, "Can I help you? I'm going to lower the casket now."

"Naw, just paying my respects." Not wanting to make a big thing of it, Leon turned and began to walk to his van. "Damn jerk. I was gonna pay my respects alright." And he spit on the ground.

It took an hour for the people to return to the church for the reception. Police had escorted them back. Church women had prepared and purchased food for the big crowd of people. There was fried chicken, cold cuts, pasta salad, green salad, fruit salad, potato salad, chips, several lasagnas, enchiladas, and crackers and cheese, plus dozens of cakes and pies. People lined up to fill their plates. Lana sat at a table by herself to wait while the people filed through the food line. Olivia found her and sat with her.

"Lana, how can I help?"

"Well, I think I just have to get through it each day. I don't know if the pain will ever go away. It hurts so bad. Olivia, I really loved him."

Olivia took hold of her left hand to get a glimpse of the diamond engagement ring. "Oh, Lana, it's really beautiful in its simplicity."

"I'll never take it off." Teardrops fell from her eyes.

"I know." Olivia said and hugged her. "Can I get you some food? You're too thin and you need to eat something. You know I'm always hungry."

"Well, I guess you could get me a little of something over there. You pick it out."

When Olivia left, Ava sat down next to her with a plate. Along came some of the young cousins who sat down at the table with her. The table was full. Lana pulled a chair up from nearby for Olivia to sit on next to her. Olivia brought the plate of food and set it down in front of Lana. Lana had no appetite but forced herself to take little bites of the enchiladas and the fruit on the plate that Olivia had brought for her. The reception hall was abuzz with animated chatter. There was the motorcycle crowd—some of them with their helmets on their laps or under their chairs—Roadking's friends, his parents, his friends from high school and college, church members, and that extensive family.

After everyone appeared to be seated and eating, someone clicked a spoon on a water glass. It was Dana's husband, Will. "Welcome to all of you who are here to honor my brother-in-law Vincent Romano. My son Ben sat down and wrote a eulogy to Vincent shortly after he learned of his death. He'd like to share it with you. When he's finished, if anyone else cares to speak, you're welcome to do so. Ben?"

Ben, who had read the scripture during the funeral, walked up to the front of the room with a piece of paper in his hand and began to speak. "My earliest memory of my Uncle Vince is when I was just a little guy and he tossed me a blue, rubber football. And he continued to toss me footballs all the time up until the accident. I know he tossed the football to my cousins, even the girls. And Ava, I'm sure you have the same memory of him."

Ava nodded and smiled as the mourners turned to look at her.

Ben continued. "Another early memory of Uncle Vince was sitting on his Harley with him. I was too young to actually ride. Helmets were too big for me. I couldn't really hold on. But I sat there in front of him, holding on to the handlebars pretending to drive while Uncle Vince would start it and rev it up a little. Like the footballs he tossed, I'm sure that all of you have the same memory of the motorcycle and Uncle Vince. Football and motorcycles were a common theme in Uncle Vince's life. But what they represented were passion and commitment, which were both present in his life. He was passionate about his family, his faith, and his business, and he made them part of his daily life, and they remained constant commitments to him. Vincent never missed any of my football games or my cousins' recitals or basketball games. He was always there for us. I had the great privilege of working at All Roads for him last summer. Uncle Vince made me dust the showroom bikes, clean the glass windows, sweep the floor, and do odd jobs. But I got to witness Uncle Vince in action firsthand as he conducted his business with his customers and interacted with his employees and his friends. The same as with his family. So honest, so genuine, so pleasant, and so passionate and committed. Uncle Vince was a giant of a man who showed us all what life's about. He was a mentor and a role model to me and to many of you. And with God's help, I hope to fill the same role for his son, Jacob. Enjoy your ride to heaven, Uncle Vince, while you listen to your favorite biker tunes. May God bless you as He blessed us with you. Love ya, Uncle Vince."

Ben's voice cracked as he read the last sentences of his eulogy. He looked down, took a deep breath, looked around the room, and forced a smile. Lana looked at Ben's mother, Dana, and smiled broadly as tears rolled down her face. There wasn't a dry eye in the room. Ben had said it all with his simple words that no one would forget. The room was silent. Then someone started to clap. Ben's face got red and he sat down.

Will once again spoke. "Anyone else care to speak?"

Someone in the large group hollered, "How could we top that?" And there was a murmur of agreement among the audience.

"My wife, Dana, and her sister, Bianca, looked through the family photos and have prepared a slideshow of special moments in Vincent's life. Continue to eat up. There's a ton of food over there. Enjoy. Thank you to the ladies of the church for this generous meal."

The slideshow began and was accompanied by Bob Seger tunes that Roadking had liked so much. The photos began with an elementary-school-aged Vincent camping with his friends and were followed by high school and college football photos of him in uniform and in action. There was a series of photos from a fishing trip as a teenager, his high school proms, homecoming dances, playing with a dog, and then a series of motorcycle photos—his first Harley and his favorite Harley, the Road King. Photos of the dealership that he loved, the charity golf tournaments, Halloween and Christmas parties, and photos of his trip to Tuscany continued to project on the screen. He smiled in every one.

The Seger song was over and soft piano music began to play "Jealous of the Angels" by Donna Taggart. Photos of Roadking as a newborn, as a toddler—smiling with those crinkly eyes—portraits of him with his sisters, a photo of him holding a snake with a terrified Bianca. Photographs of him sitting on Angelo's lap reading a book, his high school senior portrait, him wearing cap and gown at his CU graduation, him cradling Ava as a baby, Ava holding his hand on the first day of kindergarten, photos of Christmas mornings with her, handing her keys to her first car, kissing her goodbye as she left for college. Photos of him holding the newborn Jacob, one of him asleep with a sleeping Jacob on his chest, another of him reaching out to Jacob as he took his first steps, Jacob sitting on the Road King with him. Then the last of the series—the three photos that Vincent had framed on his dresser of Lana and him at Trinidad, at the art gala, and their engagement night. Lana used all her self-control to prevent herself from gasping. She put her fingers over her lips and watched. People in the crowded room turned and looked at her with sympathetic eyes. Nothing would ever be the same, but she had had the privilege of loving a great man.

"Olivia, come with me. I want to look at the flowers in the chapel." Lana wanted to see who had sent flowers and read the messages that accompanied them. But what she really wanted to do was to leave that room for a few minutes to compose herself.

The flowers emitted a soft perfume. She took photos of them with her phone. Even though it was early evening, it had been a long and difficult day. Lana was emotionally and physically drained and just wanted to go home.

She approached Eva and Angelo. "I hope you don't mind. I really need to go home soon."

Angelo and Eva both stood. "Of course, honey. It's been an exhausting few days. Will you be alright?"

"I hope so. I don't know." She attempted a feeble smile. In her mind, the answer to the question was no.

Angelo and Eva hugged her and said goodbye. As she walked away, Eva said, "Honey, do you have plans for Christmas? Would you like to join us?"

Lana lied. "I think I do have plans. Thank you anyway. Both of you have been so generous to include me in so much."

"You were going to be our daughter-in-law. You're part of the Romano family now," Angelo said as he patted her softly on the back.

Once again, Lana drove home somehow unaware that she was driving at all. So much had happened. She thought about the service, the people, the music, the prayers, the slides, and mostly about seeing Roadking for the last time. She walked into the house in a daze, slowly went upstairs, threw her clothes off, jumped into bed holding Roadking's Harley shirt, and laid her head on Roadking's pillow.

"Lord, if you're here with me tonight, help me to sleep and to be strong. Amen." There would be many more nights like this for Lana.

CHAPTER 50

Lana was indeed alone on Christmas Day. Her mom and dad did not come to visit her. Her mom had other plans. Her dad had intended to visit her for a few days, but a snowstorm that dumped three feet of snow in Steamboat Springs had kept him there. Lana had bought Jacob a Christmas present—a Hot Wheels racetrack. For Angelo and Eva, she bought some Tuscan wine. About three in the afternoon, Lana drove to the Romano house. She had never been there, but it had been pointed out to her on the drive back from the cemetery on Friday. Lana tapped on the door lightly.

"Lana! Come in. We didn't expect you. Merry Christmas!" Eva answered the door.

"Yes, Merry Christmas! I don't plan to stay. I just wanted to bring Jacob a little present and this is for you." Lana handed her the bottle of Tuscan wine with a red bow tied around it.

"Thank you so much for the lovely wine. Jacob, look who's here!" Eva beckoned Jacob.

"Nala!" Jacob ran over to her and hugged her legs.

"I brought you a present. And I found this in my pocket too." Lana handed him a little Hot Wheels police car. He held it in the air and made siren noises.

"Can I open it now?" His little eyes were wide.

"Of course. It's for you." Jacob ripped the package open. "Look, Grandma, it's a racetrack! Put it together! Please!"

Eva laughed. "He's got cars in his blood like his dad. Tell Lana thank you, Jacob."

"Thank you, Nala." Jacob looked up at her for a second and was immediately distracted by the toy.

"I have a present for you, too, Lana. I was hoping to see you at some point during Christmas." Eva handed Lana a small rectangular package. "Go ahead, open it."

Lana carefully unwrapped the package. It was a photograph of Roadking sitting on his Harley in a silver frame inlaid with mother of pearl. He was so handsome and full of life. She missed him more than words could say. Lana felt a lump in her throat and her eyes welled with tears. "That's how I want to remember him. Thank you, Eva. I must be going."

"Oh no, you must stay and eat," Eva implored her.

"No, I plan to eat Christmas dinner later with some friends. Thank you anyway," she lied again. She wanted to be alone. She had no appetite. She needed time to sort things out without distraction or noise. She would never accept Roadking's death. But she needed to be able to function again.

When she got home, once again she curled up on the couch wrapped in the alpaca blanket and stared at the TV. She remembered the warm hand that she had felt on her head that had told her, "It will be okay." *Can I believe that?* She asked herself, *What would Vincent want me to do?* And she knew the answer was, *He would want you to always remember him and love him but to enjoy your life.* For the first time in weeks, Lana got up from the couch and stepped on the treadmill—just for ten minutes. She had no energy. *Maybe I'll find my way back someday. Not yet.*

Leon watched her on the monitor every day. He saw her mourn. He saw her pain. He watched her sleep. He watched her do nothing. He decided that he needed to begin moving in on her. He went to his cluttered dresser and took out the little, white box with the engagement ring in it that he had bought for Lana. He slipped it into the pocket of his dingy, white T-shirt, threw on his smelly, black ski coat, and started to walk to his van when he noticed a dark sedan parked behind it, blocking his driveway. Then he noticed a Boulder County sheriff's SUV parked at the end of the street, blocking access. Two more sheriff's vehicles were parked a block away.

"Leon Alvarez?" A sheriff's deputy approached him with a piece of paper. His hand rested on the handle of the gun in his holster. He was followed by two uniformed deputies, who walked slowly and cautiously behind him. One held a pair of handcuffs.

"What the fuck do you want? Jesus, it's Christmas, for Christ's sake."

"Leon Alvarez, I have here a warrant for your arrest for the first-degree murder of Carla Bennett. You have the right to remain silent. Anything you say can and will be used against you in a court of law . . ."

CHAPTER 51

"Ms. Ross, Mr. Cowles is available now." Two months had passed since Roadking's death. Lana had come to the bank to transact some business. The teller told her that she would need to see the bank president to complete the transactions. Dierk emerged from his office and reached out his hand to greet Lana. She followed him into his office and seated herself on a dark blue leather side chair in front of his desk.

"Well, Lana, it's good to see you. I want to express my sympathy to you at the loss of Vincent. I didn't know that you were engaged to him. I was sorry to hear of his passing. He was a good guy. Great golfer too."

"Thank you. We were only engaged a couple of weeks before . . ." Her words drifted off and she looked down at her hands in her lap as she spoke. Dierk made her uncomfortable and she didn't want to deal with him coming on to her.

Dierk watched her for a few seconds. "Well, I also want to apologize for our last meeting here. I'm afraid I got off to a bad start with you. I don't quite know what came over me, but it was unprofessional and uncharacteristic of me to be so forward with you. My wife and I recently separated, and I think our issues at that time clouded my judgement. So I apologize."

"I accept your apology. No worries." None of that mattered to her now.

"So what can I do for you today?"

"Remember the $250,000 deposit that I made a few months ago—insurance proceeds from my ex-husband's death?"

"Yes, I do remember."

"I want to set up a trust fund with $100,000 for Jacob Romano, Vincent's son. And I also want a cashier's check for $50,000 to be made out to St. Louis Catholic Church as a donation in memory of Vincent."

"I can take care of those things for you. Would you like to wait, or would you like to stop by tomorrow and pick up the check and sign the trust account documents?"

"I'll stop by tomorrow. Right now I have a date with a two-year-old." She managed a smile. She shook Dierk's hand again.

He looked directly into her eyes as he held her hand for a few extra seconds.

Lana took the afternoon off from the magazine to spend time with Jacob. Since she had returned to work, the magazine had been her sole focus, but in her spare time, she tried to spend some time with Jacob. He was the bright spot that remained from the agony of the loss of Roadking. Eva and Angelo were very fond of her and had been very generous to allow her to visit with him. She and the little toddler had bonded. Roadking would have been happy to see them together.

The pain of Roadking's loss would not diminish. Lana had some very bad days and a few good ones. She was too thin and often felt nauseous. There was a dull ache in her throat that would not go away. The hollows under eyes were little reservoirs of tears that she was afraid would spill over spontaneously.

Sometimes she dreamed that he called her on the phone. "Hi, baby," he would say. Other times, for a millisecond out of the corner of her eye, she saw him standing in the doorway of her office, wearing leathers, lying beside her in her bed, or sitting on her couch with his legs stretched out, drinking a beer. She was empty. She felt that her insides had spilled out onto the floor of the hospital room the day Roadking had died. She asked herself what, if anything, she had learned from that intense love and loss of Roadking. She concluded that she learned that if love is true, it runs deep and that there is strength in faith, which she knew Roadking would want her to turn to. But she would never know the answer to the question why. *Why did I have to lose him?*

Eva and Angelo needed to attend a funeral in Boulder at two o'clock. They planned to drop Jacob by her office around one o'clock. It was a beautiful, unusually warm February day. She planned to take him for ice cream at Ben and Jerry's on the Pearl Street Mall and then to a park to play.

When Jacob arrived, Lana's coworkers surrounded him and talked to him with baby talk. He enjoyed all the attention but wanted to go when he heard Lana mention ice cream. She grabbed his little hand and they took the elevator down to the ground floor. To Jacob, riding on an elevator was like being on an amusement park ride. They walked a couple of blocks to the Ben and Jerry's, and Lana carried him partway when he got tired of walking.

"What kind, Jacob?"

"Strawberry! It's my favorite."

"Okay, a kiddie-size strawberry for him with some sprinkles and a kiddie-size vanilla bean for me."

They sat near a window and ate their ice cream and talked about his birthday that was coming up on April 10. He would be three years old. His daddy was gone, his mommy was nonexistent, and yet so many loved him—Lana included.

"For my birthday, Grandma is giving me chocolate cake and it'll have candles on it—for me! And chocolate frosting and a motorcycle on it too. Are you gonna come? To my party?"

"Yes, I will."

Jacob slowly ate his ice cream until most of it melted.

Lana wet a napkin and cleaned his little face and hands. "Let's go to the park now, Jake. Okay?"

They slipped on their jackets and walked back to the parking garage at *Boulder Essence* and got into Lana's car. She had purchased a car seat and kept it in her car for Jacob. There was a park in North Boulder that usually wasn't too crowded, so there was less competition for the toddler swings.

As she drove, a news story interrupted the music from KBCO. "An inmate from the Boulder County Jail escaped sometime overnight and is thought to be in the Boulder area at this time. He is Leon Alvarez, who was being held without bond at the Boulder County Jail, awaiting trial for the murder of Carla Bennett of Columbine Point. Authorities are not sure how the prisoner managed to escape. Be on the lookout for him. He is about five feet, ten inches tall with long, dark brown hair and a long, dark black beard and Fu Manchu mustache. He was last seen about ten o'clock last night during a routine inmate check. He may be driving an older model, black Subaru. A car of that make and model was stolen early this morning in the area near the jail. If you see anyone matching this description, do not approach him but notify authorities."

Lana had been alarmed when she had heard about his arrest on Christmas Day. He had been so helpful to her setting up her security system. But shortly after the arrest, police had informed her that they had discovered an elaborate system of cameras put in place in her house to watch her and that the security system he'd installed had been completely fake. She had been clueless about his intentions and felt foolish, shocked and violated. He had been arrested and was no longer a threat. And now he was on the run. *He couldn't be dumb enough to try and come near me,* she thought. She put thoughts of Leon out of her mind. She was with Jacob. He deserved her full attention.

Lana pulled into the parking lot at the park. She took Jacob out of his car seat and set him down on the grass. He began to run ahead of her a little ways.

"Wait for me, Jake."

There was no one in the park. The swings and slides and sand belonged to him. "Put me on the swing!"

Lana lifted him into the toddler swing.

"I want to go high."

Lana began to push him a little higher each time until Jacob got a look of apprehension on his face. "Too high, Jake?"

"Yeah, Nala. Too high."

She continued to push him lightly.

"Get me down now. I want to go on the big slide."

"Okay, buddy." She took him out of the toddler swing and helped him climb up the toddler slide. He slid quickly and landed on his bottom at the end of the slide. He stood and Lana wiped the sand off his pants.

"Do it again!"

Lana continued to play with Jacob. He made her smile. They sat at a picnic table a couple of times while Jacob ate fruit snacks and drank juice from his sippy cup. Lana ate a few of his animal crackers to calm her stomach. She looked at his little face. She saw Roadking there. Her heart ached for Jacob and for herself.

Sometime later, a black, older model Subaru pulled into the parking lot of the park a short distance from the Mercedes. The driver looked through the windshield at Lana and Jacob and smoked while he stared and stroked his bare face, where just hours before a long, tangled, and matted beard and mustache had existed.

"There ya are, Lana, darlin'. Are ya ready for me yet? I'm comin' soon. Yer gonna be mine. I ain't a gonna wait no longer. And nothin' and nobody's gonna stop me this time."

LIST OF SONGS

Chapter 2

- "I'm No Stranger to the Rain" by Keith Whitley. RCA, 1988.
- "One of These Nights" by Eagles. Asylum, 1975.
- "Goodbye Time" by Blake Shelton. Warner Bros., 2005.
- "Freebird" by Lynyrd Skynyrd. MCA, 1973.

Chapter 3

- "Either Way" by Chris Stapleton. Mercury Nashville, 2017.

Chapter 5

- "Cinnamon Girl" by Neil Young. Reprise, 1970.
- "Uptown Funk" by Mark Ronson, featuring Bruno Mars. RCA, 2014.
- "Simply Irresistible" by Robert Palmer. EMI Manhattan, 1988.

Chapter 6

- "Tears in Heaven" by Eric Clapton. Warner Bros., 1992.
- "Maria, Maria" by Santana, featuring The Product G & B. Arista, 1999.

Chapter 8

- "Roll Me Away" by Bob Seger. Capitol, 1983.

Chapter 9

- "Can't Get It Out of My Head" by Electric Light Orchestra. Warner Bros., 1974.

Chapter 10

- "Try and Love Again" by Eagles. Asylum, 1976.

Chapter 12

- "We've Got Tonight" by Bob Seger. Capitol, 1978.

Chapter 13

- "Beautiful Blue" by Mudcrutch. Reprise, 2016.
- "Landslide" by Fleetwood Mac. Reprise, 1975.
- "Tequila Sunrise" by Eagles. Asylum, 1973.
- "Someone Like You" by Van Morrison. Mercury, 1987.

Chapter 15

- "Wicked Games" by Chris Isaak. Reprise, 1991.

Chapter 16

- "Open Arms" by Journey. Columbia, 1982.

Chapter 17

- "Someday Soon" by Firefall. Atlantic, 1977.
- "Can't Stop the Feeling" by Justin Timberlake. RCA, 2016.

Chapter 18

- "Taking You Home" by Don Henley. Warner Bros., 2000.

Chapter 20

- "Dancing in the Dark" by Bruce Springsteen. Columbia, 1984.
- "I Can't Tell You Why" by Eagles. Asylum, 1980.

Chapter 22

- "La Bamba" by Ritchie Valens. Del-Fi, 1958.
- "In Case You Didn't Know" by Brett Young. Republic Nashville, 2017.
- "Born to Be Wild" by Steppenwolf. Dunhill RCA, 1968.
- "Always on My Mind" by Willie Nelson. Columbia, 1982.
- "Can't Help Falling in Love" by Elvis Presley. RCA Victor, 1961.

Chapter 25

- "Silver Blue" by Linda Ronstadt. Asylum Rhino, 1985.
- "Faithless Love" by Linda Ronstadt. Capitol, 1974.
- "Long, Long Time" by Linda Ronstadt. Capitol, 1970.

Chapter 26

- "Born in the U.S.A." by Bruce Springsteen. Columbia, 1984.

Chapter 27

- "Break on Me" by Keith Urban. Hit Red, Capitol Nashville, 2015.

Chapter 28

- "Want to Want Me" by Jason Derulo. Warner Bros., 2015.

Chapter 29

- "I Was Wrong" by Chris Stapleton. Mercury Nashville, 2017.

Chapter 33

- "I'm in Love" by Tom Petty. Reprise, 2009.
- "Take Me Home Tonight" by Eddie Money. Columbia, 1986.

Chapter 34

- "Every Breath You Take" by The Police. A & M, 1983.

Chapter 36

- "Fooled Again (I Don't Like It)" by Tom Petty and the Heartbreakers. Shelter, 1976.

Chapter 39

- "Into You" by Ariana Grande. Republic, 2016.
- "No Tears Left to Cry" by Ariana Grande. Republic, 2018.
- "Wake Up Dead" by Megadeth. Capitol, 1986.
- "Skulls Beneath My Skin" by Megadeth. Combat, 1985.

Chapter 40

- "Beautiful" by Gordon Lightfoot. Reprise, 1972.

Chapter 42

- "A Song for You" by Leon Russell. Shelter Records, 1970.
- "If I Ain't Got You" by Alicia Keys. J, 2004.
- "Marry Me" by Train. Columbia, 2010.

Chapter 43

- "True Companion" by Marc Cohn. Atlantic, 1991.
- "Perfect" by Ed Sheeran. Asylum Atlantic, 2017.

Chapter 44

- "Let's Stay Together" by Al Green. Hi, 1971.
- "Let's Get It On" by Marvin Gaye. Tamla, 1973.
- "My Girl" by The Temptations. Hitsville USA, 1964.

Chapter 49

- "Amazing Grace" by Alan Jackson. EMI Nashville, 2013.
- "How Great Thou Art" by Elvis Presley. RCA Victor, 1967.
- "Jealous of the Angels" by Donna Taggart. Donna Taggart, 2013.
- "Schubert: Ave Maria, D. 839" by Barbara Bonney. Warner Classics International, 2012.

ACKNOWLEDGEMENTS

I would like to thank Amber Byers of Tadpole Press for the brilliant suggestions and copy editing that were provided to this novice author. Deep gratitude goes to #33 for collaborative and editorial assistance so generously given. I thank my family and friends who have endured my very active imagination for decades. And a thank you goes to my grandfather who instilled in me the love of literature and perhaps, the genes to create literature of my own.

CPSIA information can be obtained
at www.ICGtesting.com
Printed in the USA
LVHW112140160120
643949LV00001B/11